False Confidence

By Sophie Snow

TOUCH AND GO SERIES

The Rule of Three

• • •

SPICY IN SEATTLE SERIES

Legally Binding

False Confidence

Dearly Unbeloved

• • •

WINTERMORE SERIES

Naughty or Nice

False Confidence

SOPHIE SNOW

To Claire—

For every inappropriate conversation in a coffee shop, the late night car cries, twenty-minute voice notes, screaming over Taylor Swift together, and the video chats where it got so late we almost fell asleep.

But mostly for teaching me I could open up and let people in and the world wouldn't end. My world got a whole lot brighter when you came into it. Thank you.

Content Warnings

False Confidence is an adult novel that features explicit content and some topics that may be triggering for some readers. The following is a list of topics featured in False Confidence:

Alcohol, anxiety, arrest/detainment, blood/injury, body modification (genital piercings, tattoos), cheating (past, not between MCs), clowns, death, discussions of kids/pregnancy/infertility, drug use (edibles), explicit language, explicit sexual content (anal, biting, bondage, bratting, cum play, degradation, dirty talk, face sitting, fingering, gagging, hair pulling, impact play, masturbation, oral sex, orgasm denial, pain for pleasure, porn, sex toys, slapping, spanking, squirting, swaddling, vaginal sex), family pressure, fire, homophobia (off page), job loss, panic attacks, severe period pain, vomiting.

You can read about these content warnings in more detail at www.sophiesnowbooks.com.

PROLOGUE

Jazz

I t had been ten long years since Jasmine Cannon last had an orgasm, and it didn't look like that was changing anytime soon. Not that it was Liam's fault —the man was trying his best. And his best felt fucking good.

Her head fell back against the pillows, a gasp falling from her lips as Liam's fingers skated over her skin, his mustache tickling her neck where his lips had set up shop. *That damn mustache*. It had lived up to her intrigue, even if she hadn't been able to come with his tongue on her pussy. Again, not his fault. It was a Jazz problem.

She could sense the orgasm locked away somewhere deep inside her, but she just couldn't quite reach it. So much time had passed that she'd forgotten how it felt to truly let go. She'd tried—god, she'd tried—but Jazz couldn't take that last step off the ledge. That hadn't stopped her from having sex—she just tried to focus more on the journey than the destination. Some journeys felt better than others, and

Liam... Well, she wasn't surprised he knew what he was doing.

Like father, like son, and all that. She'd heard all about how good Liam's dad, Cal, was in bed, because, as of that afternoon, Cal was married to her best friend. Jazz knew enough from Maggie to know that *Daddy Michaelson* specialized in multiple orgasms, and she'd hoped it ran in the family. It probably did, given how good Liam was at this, but alas, she wasn't the right person to test the theory.

Maggie likely wouldn't approve of Jazz falling into bed with her new stepson, but she was used to Jazz's poor decision making. And it was hard to worry about it with so much liquor running through her veins, making everything feel a little hazy, like she was three layers deep inside a dream.

Liam nipped at her jaw with his teeth. "Fuck, you feel incredible, Jasmine."

Jasmine. It was almost enough to tip her over the edge. Jazz squeezed her eyes closed and tried to focus every scrap of her attention on Liam. She breathed in the sweet, spicy scent of him, felt the tingle of his finger as he brushed the tip over her clit, drawing perfect circles. She forced her breathing to match the pace of his cock sliding in and out of her, the perfect mix of soft and rough, slow and desperate. Even as wasted as they both were, he had this down. His cock was big enough that she felt beautifully full, but not so big that she was uncomfortable.

Everything was perfect. The finish line was right. Fucking. There. She just had to reach it. Liam slid his hands under her ass, angling her hips. His next thrust hit her G-spot, and sparkles edged into Jazz's vision. *So close.*

"Oh my fucking god," she fisted the blankets, writhing below him. *Holy shit, it was going to happen.* Liam pressed his lips to hers with a rough moan, slipping his tongue between them. He tasted warm, like whiskey and orange, and she drank him in greedily.

"Jasmine," he groaned against her lips, her name even sweeter than the taste of the Old Fashioned he'd had to drink before they came upstairs.

She was a hairsbreadth from the edge, reaching into a long forgotten part of her, and then… nothing. Like a wave crashing over a fire, every flame, every ember was doused in something icy cold. Her body slammed the door closed on the finish line with a firm *no*, and Jazz turned her head into the pillow to hide the tears of frustration prickling her eyes.

She took a deep breath that caught in her throat, grabbed Liam's back with a white-knuckled grip, and forced herself to do the one thing in the world that she was best at: faking it.

Liam

If you'd told Liam Michaelson three years ago that he'd be single, jobless, and spending more time with his father's twenty-nine-year-old wife than anyone else, he might have tried a little harder to stop the devastatingly fast downfall of his life.

Maggie, his dad's wife, sat across from him, weighing the ivory envelope in her hands and wrinkling her nose. "It's definitely something important."

"They wouldn't do that, though. Right?"

She lifted a shoulder in a halfhearted shrug. "You'd hope not, but once upon a time you probably would've said they wouldn't sleep together and they did that."

They'd definitely done that. Liam had been so sure India was the one—sure enough to have a ring tucked away in his desk. A ring he'd excitedly shown his best friend of twenty years, who had pretended to be happy for him, even though he was already sleeping with India behind his back.

In one night, he'd lost his girlfriend, best friend, and the entire friend group they'd shared. He'd been so sure *that* was his rock bottom, until he'd gotten too drunk at the VIP party for the Seattle Art Museum's Spring Exhibit, spotted India's dad, and lost it. It turned out telling one of the museum's biggest donors that he should've spent more time at home and less with his many mistresses so his daughter wouldn't grow up to be a cheater was a one-way ticket to losing his job as Head Curator. And there it was: rock bottom.

"I'm just not going to open it. If I don't open it, I'll never know." Liam sat back in his chair, as if he daren't get too close to the envelope.

"True," Maggie agreed, but she didn't put the envelope down.

They shared a weighted look before Liam added, "Of course, *you* could open it. You wouldn't have to tell me what it said."

Maggie raised a brow, but slipped her thumb into the envelope seal anyway and pulled out a matching card. She scanned it, her face betraying nothing.

"Well?" Liam asked, leaning forward on his elbows. So much for never knowing.

Maggie met his eye and her expression said it all. His heart twisted uncomfortably in his chest as she said, "You are invited to celebrate the wedding of Bartholomew Charles Heasman the third and India Beatrice Avery on June twentieth."

"Christ." Liam's head fell into his hands and he rubbed his face. "What kind of people do that?"

"The kind of people named Bartholomew Charles Heasman the third and India Beatrice Avery. What the fuck kind of names are those?" Maggie asked, staring at the invitation with disdain and dropping it on the table between them.

Liam snorted and slid it closer. It was exactly the gauche invitation he'd expect India and Bart's parents to pick out, because fuck knows they would have no say in their *special day*.

"Honestly, as far as names went at my school, those are pretty tame." Liam would never blame his parents for sending him to a fancy prep school—they were just trying to do what was best for him—but he'd never quite blended in with the other kids. His moms were both well respected in their fields, owning a successful optometrists practice and teaching criminal psychology at the University of Washington, and his dad was the top business lawyer in the region, but there was a big difference between old money and new money, and Liam had been in the minority among his classmates.

"We had very different upbringings," Maggie replied with a shake of her head. That was an understatement. Maggie's family had used her as free labor for most of her life until she'd put her foot down; Liam was pretty sure no one in the world had parents as great as his. They'd taught him the value of hard work, but they'd also given him unconditional love and support every step of the way.

Liam had been a surprise, born when his parents were still in college. Neither of them had known the first thing about raising a kid. He couldn't remember the early years, when they'd fought and eventually divorced, but it had been the best thing for them. His dad had introduced his mom to

Danisha when he was seven, and she'd fit into their little family like she was always meant to be there. Liam had grown up with two moms and a dad who loved him more than anything in the world, and he would never take it for granted. And now he had a stepmom, even if she was seven years younger than him, and glared whenever he jokingly called her *mom*.

"Are you going to go?" she asked, nodding at the invitation.

Liam snorted. "Sure. And while I'm at it, I'll just book myself in for a colonoscopy, do my taxes, and stick needles in my eyes."

Maggie ignored him, reading over the invitation again. "People usually send wedding invitations months in advance. This is in three and a half weeks."

"Great. Not only are they trying to rub my face in it, but they're doing it as an afterthought. That makes me feel much better, thanks."

"Maybe. Or maybe they're trying to feel like the bigger person by inviting you. You should go," Maggie said, and he blinked at her.

"What? Are you kidding?"

"Nope. Show up and show off. Show them exactly what they're missing."

"Maggie, I'm a lonely, jobless man in my mid-thirties. They're missing nothing. I have nothing to show off. You're basically my only friend and you're technically my stepmom."

As expected, she narrowed her brows in a glare. "First

of all, fuck you. Second, fake it." She shrugged. "Take a hot date that's going to make them crazy jealous."

"And should I just conjure said date out of thin air?"

Maggie mulled it over, and he was sure she was flicking through a mental list of everyone she knew. "You should take Jazz," she said, finally, and Liam's heart dropped into his stomach. "She's used to faking it at fancy events because of her parents, and she's never met anyone she couldn't charm."

"I'm not sure that's a good idea," he replied quickly. Probably too quickly.

"Why not?"

"Because she's your best friend. And she works for my dad." And because he'd been head over heels obsessed with her since the second he'd laid eyes on her.

Jasmine had taken over as his dad's assistant when Maggie quit, and she'd been permanently on Liam's mind since the day he'd walked into his dad's office expecting to see Maggie, and instead seen a smiling redhead with hazel eyes that now had a starring role in his dreams.

"I'm not suggesting you actually date," Maggie said, rolling her eyes. "Just pretend. A little dancing, maybe a kiss on the cheek for show. You don't have to make out at the reception or drag her back to your hotel room."

She wrinkled her nose like she couldn't imagine anything worse, and Liam was struck with the realization that she didn't know. Maggie had no idea that they'd done just that after *her* wedding. A onetime drunken hook up that he'd been certain Jasmine would tell her about. He'd assumed Maggie was choosing to ignore it, just like the two of them were.

"I'll think about it," he said, not wanting to make promises. He'd seen Jasmine plenty since the wedding, but they'd never spoken about what happened. When the morning after had dawned, they'd sat next to each other at breakfast like nothing had happened.

That didn't mean he hadn't thought about it. He had. Constantly. Jasmine's energy was electric—bright and sparkly, and really fucking weird—and he couldn't get enough.

He'd considered asking her out when they'd first met, but after finding out how close she and Maggie were—and taking the fact that she worked for his dad into consideration—he'd let it go. Falling into bed together hadn't been part of the plan, but the only part Liam regretted was doing it so drunk he could barely remember it. But the flashes he *could* remember were better than anything his imagination could have dreamed up.

"You okay?"

He started at Maggie's question, clearing his throat. "Yeah. Just, you know." He gestured to the wedding invitation. Better for Maggie to think he was thinking about that and not her best friend naked.

Sympathy shone in her blue eyes. "It's been a rough couple of months—years, I guess—but it can only be uphill from here."

That wasn't as comforting as she probably intended it to be. "True."

"I didn't actually invite you over for this."

"You mean you didn't guess that my asshole ex-best friend and girlfriend's wedding invitation would arrive today and I'd be too chickenshit to open it?"

"I'm good, but not that good," Maggie replied, tucking the invitation back into the envelope and sliding it across the table toward him. "I wanted to talk to you about something."

"Shoot."

"I want to be clear that I'm just floating the idea out there. You're not obligated to agree, and I'm not suggesting it just because we're family."

Liam frowned. What the hell was she talking about? "Noted."

"Okay, so you know Grace that works on sourcing and staging for me?" Liam nodded. He'd spent a lot of time hanging around Maggie and her team at work since losing his job. Maggie owned a home renovation and interior design company and had a big social media platform. Mostly, he sat around, tearing through romance books on his Kindle and wondering how he'd fallen so far from grace, but she liked to pick his brain about designs, and he liked having an excuse to get out the house. "Well, she and her family are moving back to Taiwan. She found out yesterday. Her husband got a promotion and his company wants them over there next week."

"Shit. That soon?"

"Yeah." Maggie sighed. She only had six people on her team—losing even one would be a headache. "I'm happy for them. It's what he's been working toward, but giving a family of five a week's notice to relocate almost five thousand miles isn't ideal. Anyway, I'm obviously going to have to replace her and I know it's not exactly what you're used to, but I was wondering if you might be interested? You have experience and you've been a ton of help over the past few weeks. The team all love having you around."

Surprise flitted through him. As much as he enjoyed being with Maggie and her team, he'd assumed he was annoying them. Though he'd worked at the Seattle Art Museum for over a decade before *the incident*, he'd only been the Head Curator for a few years. And as much as he'd loved running the curatorial department and overseeing everything, he had missed being in a more hands-on role. He had plenty of experience staging exhibits and sourcing pieces for the museum, and for the smaller galleries he'd worked at when he was in college. But he'd never worked in any kind of home design capacity.

"What does sourcing and staging look like for you?" he asked, and Maggie, ever-prepared, opened her tablet to a job description he knew she would have written up as soon as she found out Grace was leaving.

"Sourcing would be specific pieces, if me or one of the other designers has something in mind, or sourcing a selection based on a brief so we can pick the best thing for the space. Staging would basically be the final touches in a space, making sure everything looks intentional," she explained. "The staging is more about the video side of things than the design side."

It was all stuff he was familiar with, just with a different medium. But even though she'd told him otherwise, he couldn't shake the feeling that she was only asking him because of who they were to each other.

Maggie must have taken his silence as hesitation because of the job itself, not the fact she was offering it, because her face fell a little and she said, "I know it's not art in the traditional sense but—"

"Of course what you do is art," Liam interrupted. "I love your work." That wasn't the problem. He knew he would enjoy working for her, and he loved the Maggie Makes Home team. Maybe he needed to just get over himself. Maggie put a hundred and ten percent into every area of her business; she wouldn't be suggesting this if she hadn't thought it through.

"You're only saying that because you're my stepson," she replied with a wry smile and he laughed.

"Of course I'm not. Can I call you *Mom* at work?"

"Try it and see what happens," she warned. "Does this mean you're in?"

"Are you sure you want me?" he asked, and her face softened. She swiped on her tablet and slid it across the table. It was an employment contract with his name, probably written by an attorney from his dad's firm. Liam scanned it, raising his brows when he spied the date. "This was written two weeks ago." Before Grace gave her notice.

Maggie nodded. "I was planning on offering you a job anyway, but I wasn't sure how you'd take it, so I've been procrastinating. It's just become a little more urgent with Grace leaving. I really think you'd be a perfect fit."

Liam took a deep breath, his eyes roaming the contract

and job description. It was something new, and definitely more exciting day-to-day than his work at the gallery. And he'd been working with Maggie.

"Yeah," he said, finally. "I'm in."

CHAPTER TWO

Jazz

Jazz must have been a bad girl in a past life. There was no other reason the universe would punish her with an almost two-hour phone call with her mom on a Sunday night. Every time she tried to lead the conversation toward *goodbye*, her mom suddenly remembered some other family friend Jazz didn't care about that she *had* to update her on. They'd been on the phone so long that Instagram had run out of posts to show her and she'd been forced to move her scrolling to Facebook. She supposed that's what she got for avoiding the past three monthly Cannon family dinners.

"Are you even listening to me, Jazz?"

Shit. She took the phone off loudspeaker and held the phone up to her ear. "Sorry. It's been a long week. What was that?"

Her mom sighed, as if Jazz's shitty attention span was the world's biggest inconvenience for her. "I *said* I ran into Denise Hamilton at brunch this morning. Do you remember her?"

"Vaguely."

"Her son is engaged now. And her oldest daughter has a newborn."

Jazz rolled her eyes. She knew where this was going. "That's nice for them."

"It *is* nice. Denise has a wedding to plan and grandchildren. And not one of my three children is even in a long-term relationship."

It was the same conversation every time one of her mom's friends' kids settled down. "Take it up with Xan. He's the oldest."

Her mom tutted. "You know he's so busy working for your dad and getting ready to take over the company when he retires. And Rose has med school. They're focusing on their careers."

"I'm not allowed to focus on my career?"

"Maggie's husband offers a good maternity policy."

He did, but that didn't mean Jazz was planning to take him up on it anytime soon. "How do you know that?"

"There was an article about him on Facebook. Maggie settled down and got married. Why can't you find yourself a nice rich man like she has?"

Jesus. "I don't think Maggie would appreciate the implication that she married Cal because he's rich," she pointed out, dodging the question.

Her mom ignored her completely. "I'd appreciate grandchildren before I'm too old to show them off, that's all I'm saying. And you're thirty now, Jazz. You don't have forever."

"As fun as this was, I have to go if I'm going to make it

out in time to meet my friends." Jazz said goodbye and hung up before her mom dragged the conversation on even longer.

By *meeting her friends*, she meant flicking through movies, trying to find something new to watch before getting bored and turning on reruns of her favorite TV shows for the five hundredth time just so she wasn't sitting in silence. She knew if she called Maggie, she'd invite her over in a heartbeat, but Jazz had third-wheeled Maggie and Cal last weekend and the weekend before that.

Jazz had other friends—ex-colleagues, old college friends—but most of them were married with kids and Jazz never had anything to add to the conversation when they went out. Those friendships were fizzling out, which was fine by her. Her life was how she liked it. Sure, she wanted a partner and babies someday, but she was only thirty, for fuck's sake. She was perfectly happy as she was.

And it didn't matter what she did, her parents would still ask for more. Her brother and sister excelled in everything they did, constantly trying to outdo themselves. But unlike her siblings, Jazz was no longer competing.

Alexander and Lilia Cannon had exactly zero interest in who their children were as people, just what they achieved. In their eyes, Jazz had achieved nothing in her thirty years. Her college degree didn't count—that was the bare minimum expected of the Cannon children. Her parents *did* approve of her job, at least. Michaelson and Hicks was the best business law firm in the region, and that was something they could brag to their friends about. Jazz was sure they never specified her role within the firm, but it was something. And she didn't care what her parents, or their friends, thought of how she lived her life.

She settled on a crime show she hadn't re-watched in a few weeks. Now to find something to do while she watched… Jazz was well prepared for weekends in the house. Her apartment was her own personal activity center, with piles upon piles of stuff she'd picked up to try and never gotten around to.

Paper bags crinkled as she rummaged through them, picking out the first thing she found: a rock painting kit. Okay, maybe not that. Jazz dug a little further, her fingers closing around another box, and smiled when she withdrew a cat embroidery kit. It was perfect. The cat looked exactly like Maggie and Cal's cat, Peach, and Cal's birthday was in a couple of months. She could definitely finish it on time.

She tipped out the box onto the couch and only just managed to stop the tiny packet of needles from slipping between the cushions. There were instructions, but where was the fun in that? And how hard could it be anyway? Jazz clamped the fabric in the hoop, struggling with the bolt to tighten it, before realizing she'd put it in upside down. She righted it and grabbed a needle, threading it with dark brown embroidery floss and kicking her feet up on the couch.

With her tongue between her teeth, she made the first stitch around the cat's right ear. It was uneven, but it was only the first stitch. She continued, cursing when she pricked her finger on the needle. A tiny bead of blood formed on the end of her finger, staining the cat's pink nose. "Shit."

She dropped the hoop and headed to the kitchen, running her finger under the faucet. This wasn't her first embroidery rodeo, and she'd forgotten how bad she was with needles. She rummaged around below her sink for a band-aid, before suddenly remembering that she'd stashed her first aid kit in her pantry for safekeeping after the last time she'd burned herself on her toaster.

Her kitchen wasn't tiny, but the sheer amount of clutter she'd brought with her—and everything she'd added since—made it hard to navigate. She found the first aid kit and slapped a band-aid on her finger before knocking a bag of butterscotch candies to the floor. Where had they come from? She scrambled to pick them up, remembering the craving for butterscotch cupcakes she'd had a few weeks ago.

"No time like the present," Jazz said to herself, grabbing flour and sugar from the shelves. It had been a while since Jazz baked anything, and she liked playing around in the kitchen, so she grabbed one of the recipe books from the pile on the floor by the air fryer she'd bought six months ago and hadn't taken out of the box yet. She'd get to it. The page with her favorite cupcake recipe was sticky, and a portion of the ingredients list ripped away as she peeled the pages apart. It wasn't like the measurements had to be exact—she'd figure it out.

Something resembling a batter eventually came together, and she scooped it into a tray filled with mismatched cupcake liners. Batter splattered across the tray, but it was easier just to pick those pieces off when they were baked—and they always tasted the best.

She shoved the baking tray in the oven and turned it on, remembering too late that she was supposed to pre-heat the damn thing. The part of the recipe that told her how long to bake them for was covered in some kind of chocolate, so she set a timer for twenty minutes and hoped for the best. The dining chair wobbled as she dropped into it, the crochet chair cover scratchy on her thighs. Another project she hadn't finished—she'd made two and a half chair covers, and then accidentally spilled pasta sauce on one.

It was the polar opposite of the home she'd grown up in. Her parents never visited her in Seattle and it was just as well, because her mom would freak out at how messy and chaotic everything was. She'd hated how much stuff Jazz had accrued over the years growing up, hated how cluttered her spaces were. But Jazz had always felt at home in chaos.

"What the hell did you click?" Jazz sighed, dropping into Cal's desk chair and flinching at the blaring alert sounding from his computer. The screen was covered in flashing windows, promising Cal he'd won a car, a new phone, an all expenses trip to Belize.

"A link in an email from my bank," Cal replied with a sigh. "Though I realize now it probably wasn't actually my bank."

"Probably not."

"I'm a fucking idiot," Cal groaned, rubbing his forehead. Stress always seemed to make Cal's Irish accent a little thicker, and Jazz couldn't always grasp what he was saying, but even she understood that.

"No comment," Jazz replied as she tried in vain to close the windows.

Whatever malware had been attached to the link had already sunk its claws into Cal's computer. She sighed and crawled under the desk, pulling out the plug. "I'll call tech, but I think we should leave it off until then."

"Christ. Thanks for checking. Any chance you're not going to tell Maggie about this?"

"Zero chance."

"Wonderful."

Jazz laughed, offering his chair back to him and grabbing her phone from the desk. "You could download a virus on every one of her devices and she'd still think you're the best person in the whole world. Other than me, obviously," she amended, and Cal flushed, his eyes lighting up.

"Maybe since I don't have a computer, I should just call it a day and go see her," Cal mused and Jazz shook her head. Maggie really had hit the partner jackpot.

"You might not have a computer, but you do still have a day of meetings. Including one in five minutes. Sierra is waiting for you," Jazz pointed out. Sierra was Jazz's assistant, and much better at taking meeting notes than Jazz was. She got less distracted by… everything.

Cal's face fell, and Jazz sighed. "You're scheduled to read through case notes for next week after lunch. Take them with you and go see Maggie."

"That works. Thanks."

"Anytime. Actually, no—don't click any more links. But other than that."

They both turned as a knock sounded and Liam peeked his head around the door. "Hey," he said, stepping into the room with a blinding smile that was a carbon copy of his dad's, dimples and all. Liam mostly took after his mom, with wavy dark hair, olive-toned skin and thick black lashes, but he had his dad's bright green eyes and charm. Though he hadn't inherited Cal's Irish accent, Liam Michaelson was just as devastating. And then, of course, there was the mustache. That fucking mustache she hadn't been able to get out of her head since the very first time she'd seen it. It was worse now that she knew how soft it was.

Jazz forced herself not to think about that night. She'd become very good at pretending it never happened.

"Everything okay? Sierra said something happened to your computer," Liam asked his dad and Cal muttered something under his breath that sounded suspiciously like *fucking computers*.

"He opened a link in an email from *the bank*," Jazz explained, raising her eyebrows. Liam laughed, the rich sound washing over her like an autumn breeze.

"Of course he did."

"Moving on," Cal said with a pointed look. "What brings you here?"

"I was hoping to speak to Jazz, actually. If you have time," Liam replied.

Surprise fluttered in Jazz's belly. What could he want with her that involved him coming by in person? "Sure."

"I have to head down to a meeting," Cal said, and they said their goodbyes, Jazz, and Liam following him into the lobby and watching as he stepped into the elevator and the doors slid closed.

"How are you doing?" Liam leaned in the doorway, almost too casually. Tension lined his shoulders and jaw.

"I'm good. Are you okay?" Jazz sank onto the plush couch in Cal's lobby.

"I'm fine," he said quickly and Jazz stared him down until he took a seat beside her. "I'm going to be working for Maggie starting next week. Did she tell you?"

"She mentioned she was going to ask you. You're perfect for the job, and her spreadsheets don't scare you."

"They scare me a little, but I can handle it," Liam snorted. "Speaking of Maggie—"

"What a natural segue. What's up? Is something wrong with Maggie?"

"Shit, no." Liam winced. "Sorry, I didn't mean to worry you. Maggie said something when I saw her on Saturday that made me think you hadn't told her. About us. At the wedding."

His cheeks blazed more and more red as he spoke, and knots twisted in Jazz's stomach at the reminder of their night. "I meant to—you know I tell her everything—but I..." Jazz trailed off. She didn't have a good reason not to have told her best friend. Every other hook up had been a topic of conversation and, while Maggie probably wouldn't have thanked her for details of a night with her husband's son, Jazz didn't think she'd judge her too harshly.

She could make excuses for not saying anything: Maggie and Cal had left for their honeymoon the next day and she'd forgotten. But that would have been a lie. She hadn't forgotten—there was just something about that night that made her want to keep it to herself. She was used to exaggerating when it came to talking about sex. If Maggie asked how it was, Jazz wouldn't be lying if she said she'd enjoyed herself, but she still hadn't fucking come. And she wasn't sure she could hide that disappointment from Maggie.

"I just never got around to it," she finished lamely. "Why?"

Liam toyed with the edge of his mustache. *Why was that so hot?* "She suggested something that I don't think she would have suggested if she'd known."

"Go on."

Liam cleared his throat and scratched the back of his neck. "You know my ex-girlfriend and best friend are getting married?" She nodded. "They invited me to the wedding."

Jazz sucked in a breath. "You're kidding me. Cunts. Sorry," she offered at the last second, not that she expected her language would faze Liam.

"No need to be sorry. You're not wrong. Anyway, I got the invitation on Saturday and Maggie thinks I should go but—"

"You have to. They had the fucking audacity to break your heart and then rub it in your face. The least you can do is make them uncomfortable on their wedding day, and show them what they're missing."

"That's what Maggie said. But she also suggested I take a fake date to, I quote, *show off.*" He hesitated. "She suggested I ask you."

Jazz sat back in her chair, surprised and impressed with Maggie's scheming. She loved her best friend, but she was more of a strongly worded letter person than an in-person revenge scheme kind of girl. In fact, Maggie had refused to let Jazz do anything to her ex-boyfriend. That hadn't stopped her from putting his number on a marketplace ad offering a free computer. Twice. But what Maggie didn't know, she couldn't be mad about.

"And you think she wouldn't have suggested that if she knew we'd slept together at the last wedding we attended," she surmised, and Liam nodded. "I'm not sure she'd care, but I'll tell her if that makes you more comfortable."

"I don't exactly love the idea of my dad's wife hearing about the ins and outs of my sex life, but I feel guilty asking you to do this when she doesn't know what happened last time. Not that it would happen this time, obviously," he added quickly.

Obviously. "I'll tell her this week, I promise."

"Thanks. I…" Liam's voice was soft, hesitant. "And, uh, are we okay? We never really talked about things after the wedding and I don't want to make things weird by asking—"

"We're good," she interrupted. It had been her choice not to talk about it. Liam had tried to check in on her the morning after, but she'd just thrown his sweatshirt on over her bridesmaid dress, kissed him on the cheek, and told him she'd see him at breakfast before heading to her own room.

It was easier not to talk about it. It was impossible not to think about it.

Liam was the closest she'd come to, well, *coming* in a decade and, as drunk as she was, the memory of how good it felt was crystal clear. She couldn't help but wonder *what if.* What if they hadn't been so drunk? What if she'd been *more* drunk, so she could get out of her head? What if she'd just told him instead of faking it? That was the one that plagued her most. She knew he would have taken a step back and done everything he could to get her there.

But she'd never told anyone about her inability to finish, not even Maggie. Bringing it up mid-sex for the first time probably wasn't ideal, even with Liam.

"Jasmine?"

She started at Liam's voice, her cheeks flushing as she realized she'd zoned out again.

"Sorry. We're good, I swear. I get why you want me to talk to Maggie, and I will, but I'm happy to come to the wedding with you. I can't promise to be civil, though," she replied with a wry smile and Liam chuckled.

"I'd never expect you to. Thank you, seriously. I owe you."

They both stood and Jazz spied a purple smudge on Liam's *Mucha* t-shirt. She reached for him. "You have some —" she paused as her finger brushed the sticky purple spot. "This is frosting."

Liam looked down, the tips of his ears turning pink. "Yeah. Sierra gave me one of your cupcakes downstairs. It was delicious," he offered, with a smile sweeter than the pound of powdered sugar she'd dumped in the rainbow frosting the night before.

And Jazz would be damned if it didn't make her stomach flutter.

CHAPTER THREE

Jazz

"So theoretically, on a scale of one to ten, how weird would it be if I hooked up with your stepson?"

Maggie paused, her coffee an inch from her lips. She took a deep breath and put the cup down. "First, please don't call him my stepson."

"But technically—"

"Zip it," Maggie interrupted, pinching her brow. "Second, because I know you, *did* you hook up with him?"

Jazz squinted, trying to read Maggie's tone. They'd been best friends since middle school, and, even though Maggie was happily married, Cal would never know her as well as Jazz did—something she'd made clear to him a couple of weeks before their wedding, while crying and drunkenly telling Cal, her fifty-seven-year-old millionaire boss, that *she knew people* if he ever hurt Maggie. She didn't know people. But Cal had patted her on the head, offered her a cup of coffee, then waited until she was sober to reassure her he knew she would always be Maggie's person and promise that he'd never hurt her. At that point, Jazz had zero recollection of her drunken conversation, and no doubts that Cal would never hurt Maggie. He was a great guy, and exactly what her best friend deserved.

"Jazz. Did you sleep with Liam?"

Right. They were talking. "Um, possibly?"

Maggie groaned. "Ugh. When did you even… Oh my god, Jazz, did you seriously have sex with Cal's kid at our wedding?"

Jazz screwed up her face. "Don't call him Cal's kid. That makes him sound like a child."

"He *is* Cal's child."

"Need I remind you that you once agreed to go on a date with him," Jazz pointed out. "*After* sleeping with his dad."

Maggie glared at her. Her almost-date with Liam, when Cal had been trying to push her away because he thought she deserved better, was something Maggie liked to forget.

"I didn't go on that date, so it doesn't count." Maggie shook her head, pushing her dark hair back. "Okay. You had sex with Liam."

"We were drunk, if it helps," Jazz offered.

"It doesn't. Why didn't you tell me? That was months ago."

"I was worried you'd be mad," Jazz said. It wasn't a complete lie, at least. "And I was right, clearly."

"I'm not mad," Maggie said with a groan. "I just… Gross. Liam's like a brother to me."

"That's weirder than me sleeping with him, for the record, considering you're married to his dad."

Maggie waved her away. "We've never claimed to be traditional. Why are you telling me now?"

"Liam asked me to. He felt weird about taking you up on your suggestion to ask me as a date to the wedding without you knowing everything."

Maggie grabbed her coffee cup again and took a long draw, mulling it over before speaking. "I don't really know what to do here. Am I supposed to ask you about it? I know we always talk about this kind of stuff, so I can pretend it's not weird if you want to talk about it."

Jazz shrugged. "There's not much to say. We were drunk. Neither of us remember much of it."

Maggie narrowed her eyes suspiciously. "Since when do you not remember a million details, even when you're drunk?"

Shit. Maggie had her there. Thanks to her inability to come, Jazz had gotten good at embellishing when talking about sex. "I mean..." she searched around, trying to find an excuse and coming up blank. Peach, Maggie and Cal's cat, jumped up on the table and nestled into her, and Jazz bought a little extra time kissing her face and sneezing when her orange and black fur tickled her nose.

"We were both wasted and tired after such a long day, but what I remember was good," she said, finally. Adding, "I was sore the next day, if that tells you anything," just as Cal walked into the kitchen. Let the ground swallow her the fuck up.

"Hi, love," Cal said, stooping to kiss Maggie. Jazz ignored the tightness in her chest the sight of her best friend and her husband. They looked at each other like nothing else in the world existed and she couldn't be happier for them. She couldn't explain the little twinges of anxiety seeing them together gave her, and she didn't need to explain them if she pretended they weren't there. When they broke apart, Cal plucked Peach from the table and kissed her nose. "Hey, Jazz."

"Hey." She exchanged an awkward look with Maggie as they both sat in silence.

"Don't stop on my account," Cal said, grabbing a cup from the cabinet. "I'm just getting coffee, then I'm heading upstairs to catch up on my YouTube."

Maggie's lip twitched, fighting a smile. Her TikTok had been a gateway to Cal, and he now not only scrolled the app mindlessly for hours, but watched YouTube religiously, sending any video he found mildly interesting to Maggie. She watched every single one. They were disgusting.

Cal turned around and frowned while he waited for his coffee. "Why are you being weird?"

"We're not being weird."

"You never stop talking because I'm here. What am I missing?"

"You don't want to know. Trust me," Maggie said, and Cal shrugged, but took her at face value.

"Cool, I'm going to head out so you can stop being weird." He lifted his cup in goodbye before leaving the room.

"Are you going to tell him?" Jazz asked Maggie when the coast was clear. She didn't know why, but the thought of Cal knowing was infinitely worse than Maggie. It was just sex—it wasn't a big deal. So why was she making it one?

"We generally don't go out of our way to talk about Liam's sex life," Maggie replied with a snort. "But if he asks… I mean, shit, you're my best friend and obviously I'm not going to tell him if you don't want me to, but he's my husband and—"

"It's okay." Jazz cut her off before she could spiral. It was one of Maggie's greatest skills. "I'd never ask you to lie to him. But also, it was *one time*. That doesn't make it Liam's sex life. He's a single man in his thirties who looks like that. I bet I was barely a blip on his radar."

Maggie said nothing, narrowing her eyes as she sipped her coffee.

"What?"

"You're going to do it again, aren't you?" Maggie asked.

"Of course not. I'm not interested in him like that."

Would she like to do it again? Of course she would. She was only human, after all, and Liam had gotten her closer to finishing than anyone else had. But that didn't mean she was going to. Besides, there was nothing to imply that Liam was even interested in her. She was tagging along to the wedding to support him as a friend, that was all.

"Sure," Maggie replied sarcastically and, for a moment, Jazz hated how well Maggie knew her.

"It was one night. It's not going to happen again." There was more bite to Jazz's words than she intended, and Maggie held her hands up in surrender.

"Okay, okay. It's not going to happen again. But you're going to the wedding with him, right?"

Jazz leaned back in her chair with a sigh, running her hands through her unruly hair. She knew she'd regret letting it air dry the night before, but she'd done it anyway. A trip to the salon would be essential before the wedding—she wasn't going to make Liam's ex jealous with three inches of root growth and uneven bangs that she'd cut herself, because she couldn't see anymore but didn't want to deal with a salon appointment.

"Yeah. As long as you're okay with it."

"Why wouldn't I be okay with it?"

"You know. Because of the last wedding." Jazz gestured unintelligibly, because that somehow felt better than repeating it.

"You're both adults and you can do what you want. Not that it matters, since you apparently aren't interested in him like that."

Jazz glared at her best friend. "I'm not."

"Good."

"Good." Jazz pushed back from the table, needing to move her body. She stopped by Maggie's fridge, running a finger over the god-awful pencil drawing of what she suspected was supposed to be Peach.

"Nadia's kids drew that for us," Maggie said, noticing her focus. "I forgot to mention, actually. We're going to brunch at that new Tiffany's themed place this weekend. Do you want to come?"

"With you and Nadia?"

Nadia was Maggie's realtor turned friend—a mom of twins, businesswoman, and all around badass. It wasn't that Nadia had done anything in particular to piss Jazz off, it was just *her*. She was charming, funny, drop dead gorgeous, always perfectly put together, and she had the kind of life you imagined the happy families in department store catalogs had. And Jazz hated her, no matter how much Maggie loved her.

"Cal and Nadia's partner are coming too, and—"

"I'm not going to fifth wheel your double date," Jazz interrupted. She turned back to the fridge, so Maggie wouldn't see her rolling her eyes. "It's bad enough that I'm always bugging you and Cal. I don't need to do it to anyone else."

"What are you talking about? Since when do Cal and I not like having you around?"

"That's not what I… Never mind. I'm still not going to fifth wheel your double date."

Their empty cups clinked as Maggie gathered them up and rinsed them in the sink. She opened and closed her mouth twice, before finally saying, "It's not really a double date, it's just brunch."

"I'll pass," Jazz said, schooling her face and tone into something that sounded semi-neutral. Maggie could hang out with people without her. Maybe it had been just the two of them for a long time, but it wasn't anymore. Maggie was married now. She had new friends. Friends who were also married, and had babies, and businesses, and didn't forget to pay their electric bill every other month, even though they had a reminder on their phone.

And Jazz was happy for her. Even if she didn't want any of those things yet, there was nothing wrong with Maggie having them. She and Maggie had always moved at different paces, and she had plenty of time to catch up.

"Is everything okay?" Maggie asked gently.

Jazz turned to her, pasting a smile on her face. "Of

course it is. But I could use your help to pick out a dress for the wedding, if you have time."

The concern didn't entirely leave Maggie's eyes, but she took the subject change and ran with it anyway. "I always have time for you, you know that. And I need a dress for one of Cal's old colleague's retirement parties too, so that's perfect."

"Great!" Jazz replied, sounding cheerier than she felt. "Let's order lunch and do some damage to our credit cards."

CHAPTER FOUR

Jazz

"Bride or groom?"

Jazz glanced between the usher and Liam, Liam's almost imperceptible flinch giving her the urge to wrap her arms around him and get him out of here. Why did they think this was a good idea? No petty revenge was worth him putting himself through this.

But as quickly as his face had fallen, a steely, determined glint flooded Liam's eyes, and he met her gaze with a small *I'm okay* nod.

"Both," Jazz told the usher with a saccharine smile, before tugging Liam toward the seats on the left-side of the aisle, ignoring the usher's self-important splutter.

The thirteen hour drive down the coast to Northern California had been surprisingly calm. They'd taken turns driving Liam's beat up old Volvo that he refused to let Cal replace, trading the aux cord and alternating between music and podcasts. Jazz treated Liam to some of her favorite conspiracy theories, and he returned in kind with a podcast that covered niche internet drama. Who knew

Jazz could become so invested in the online puzzle community?

By the time they arrived at The Bowery Estate, an hour outside of San Francisco, it was after ten and they'd both fallen into bed, too exhausted to bat an eye at the fact they were sharing a bed. At least they'd been clothed this time.

Jazz dropped into a gaudy gilded chair with a white satin bow slung across the back. Liam followed, eyeing the decor with as much distaste as she felt. Why the hell anyone would book out an entire estate full of beautiful, lush gardens and choose to get married inside a ballroom that had the vibe of a less impressive, significantly tackier, Italian chapel was beyond her. It wasn't even a religious ceremony.

"I guess it's true that money can't buy taste," Jazz said under her breath. "For what it's worth, I bet it would've been less tacky if it was you she was marrying."

Liam snorted, his smile working wonders to relax the tension Jazz hadn't realized she was holding in her spine. "That sounded suspiciously like a compliment, Jasmine."

"Feel free to let it go to your head. You could use an over-inflated ego to make you a little less perfect," Jazz replied, gesturing to him. God, the man could really wear a tux. It was ridiculous.

Liam just rolled his eyes, neither bashful nor boastful. *Michaelsons.* "This style was definitely India's parents' idea," he told her. "And they'd probably have taken over just as much if I were marrying her."

"You dodged a bullet."

"Yep. What do you want your wedding to look like if

you get married?" he asked, and Jazz gave him an exaggerated frown.

"What do you mean *if*? I'm forcing you to marry me so I can be a Michaelson, remember?" They'd joked about it, drunk, at Maggie and Cal's wedding, and Liam's eyes lit up as she reminded him, as if she was actually managing to distract him from the fact his ex-best friend was about to marry the woman he, himself, had been planning to propose to.

"Alright, well, what will *our* wedding look like then?"

Jazz took a deep breath, humming as she stared around the venue. There had to be hundreds of thousands of dollars' worth of white roses covering the room, but all they did was make the place feel cluttered. The aisle was white marble with gold veining, not unlike a serving board she'd picked up a couple of years ago on clearance from T.J. Maxx. It looked expensive, sure, but that didn't mean it looked good.

"Not like this, that's for sure. Let's see... Halloween," she said, finally, and Liam quirked an amused brow.

"Oh?"

"Yeah, we'd make it seem like it was just a Halloween party and everyone would show up in their best costumes, and we would throw everything into chaos by announcing we were getting married. I would wear—"

"It's bad luck for the groom to know what the bride is wearing," Liam interrupted and Jazz gasped, holding a hand to her chest in mock outrage.

"You're right. I don't know what I was thinking. I'll guess you'll have to wait and see."

"That sounds like a perfect wedding to me. Think of the Halloween cocktail menu op—"

"Liam?"

The light instantly drained from Liam's face, the end of his sentence catching in his throat. He swallowed it down and Jazz didn't think twice before grabbing his hand and pulling it to her lap, squeezing.

She looked up at the couple hovering beside Liam.

"Hey," Liam said, a forced smile on his face that soured her stomach. "Um, Jazz, this is Thomas and Veronica. We went to school together. Guys, this is Jazz. My partner."

He didn't hesitate before calling her his partner, but his voice softened, his lips lifting in a hint of a smile. If the job with Maggie didn't work out, he should give acting a shot.

She'd never been called a *partner* before. Girlfriend, yes, but more often than not, she was just a *friend*.

"This is my friend Jazz, everyone." The guy she'd been dating for five months who had asked her to be exclusive— but only her. He continued to see other people.

"Everyone, meet Jazz. She's a friend from work." The woman who'd told her she loved her every morning and night, a few days after they'd discussed moving in together.

It stung, sure, but it was what it was and Jazz never let it bother her. She didn't need a label to be happy. Nor was she particularly interested in being in any kind of relationship. She just wanted to have fun. But *partner*… fake or not, it felt nice to be spoken about like she mattered.

Which was stupid. Of course she mattered. It was just a word, and Jazz didn't care about it one bit.

Thomas and Veronica took the two seats on Liam's other side and leaned in closer.

"How have you been? It's been a while since we last spoke," Veronica said, and Jazz wanted to wipe her look of faux-sympathy from her face. If they hadn't spoken in a while, they'd clearly taken Liam's ex's side and, by default, Jazz hated them.

She felt rather than saw Liam stiffen, and ran her thumb across the back of his hand, reminding him she was there. His body relaxed into hers a little.

"Yeah, it's been a while. I've been good, thanks. How have you been?"

"All good here," Thomas answered with a dismissive wave of his hand. "We were sorry to hear you're not at the museum anymore. I know that was your dream job."

Jesus, had these people never heard of *not the time or place*?

Liam's jaw ticked, but he was putting on a perfect show of being fine. Jazz was sure neither Thomas nor Veronica could see anything wrong with him.

"Oh, it's fine. I was ready for a new challenge anyway, and my new job is perfect."

The couple raised their brows. "We hadn't heard that you had a new job. What are you doing now?"

It was like a carefully crafted dance, back and forth with forced politeness as if they weren't just trying to collect gossip to spread around their fucked up little social circle. Jazz felt more than one person staring at them, likely just as surprised to see Liam here as Veronica and Thomas were.

But, as Liam answered, explaining his new role with

Maggie, Jazz realized he knew what he was doing: he was deliberately giving them a story he wanted them to spread around. By the end of the night, everyone who had been talking about the shit show of his past couple of years would be talking about how he was thriving now. It was the perfect plan.

Veronica clapped her hands together. "We love Maggie Makes Home! I've been begging Thomas to renovate the townhouse so we can hire her to design it. And how did you two meet?" she asked, gesturing between Liam and Jazz.

He glanced over at Jazz. His smile was like warm sugar, but she could see the exhaustion in his eyes.

"Maggie's my best friend," she answered, giving him a reprieve. "And I work for Cal, so we've known each other for years. Just took us a while to see what was always there."

"That's… lovely," Veronica answered, and Jazz fought a laugh at the obvious lie. "And how long have—"

She trailed off as the soft classical music that had been playing in the background faded out, and a classic rock song Jazz vaguely recognized faded in. The floor to ceiling door behind the altar opened wide and a man in a perfectly tailored tuxedo walked in with a grin on his face, flanked by an older couple who looked like the epitome of wealth.

Bart and his parents, she assumed. Liam's ex-best friend was tall, with perfectly slicked back blond hair that she suspected always looked like that. He looked like he'd just stepped off the pages of an Abercrombie catalogue, ready to harass a customer service associate, or accost a woman at a bar, acting like *no* didn't apply to him.

Flames swarmed Liam's eyes as he glared at the front of the room. Jazz leaned into him, resting her head on his shoulder, and murmured in his ear, "He's no Michaelson, that's for sure."

They both shook as Liam chuckled. "You know I look more like my mom than my dad."

"Yeah, well, your mom's hot, too. Actually, both of your moms are hot. There's definitely something in the water in your family." She neglected to mention how unbelievably gorgeous *he* was. But she was sure it was written all over her face. There had to be some kind of rule against being so nice *and* so gorgeous.

Liam wrinkled his nose. "Please don't call my moms hot. I already have to deal with the fact that Maggie and my dad…" He shook his head, as if he couldn't bear to finish the sentence.

Jazz gave him a wicked grin. "Oh, the things I could tell you about your dad."

"I'm begging you to shut up," Liam groaned, but his eyes were lighter. Distraction successful.

For a moment, anyway, until a hush fell over the crowd and the familiar chords of Pachabel's Canon sounded across the room.

Liam

What the fuck had he been thinking showing up here?

Liam held Jasmine's hand in a death grip, every note of the music clanging through him like a knife in the chest. He sucked in a breath, willing his heart to keep pumping blood around his body. Was the world tilting, or was that just his body rebelling against his stupid brain for RSVPing *yes*?

He heard the doors open, but stared straight ahead, unable to look back. The bridesmaids passed, a blur of pink in his peripheral. He knew exactly who India would have picked, just as he knew who Bart would have picked as groomsmen. Of course, once upon a time, Liam would have been standing up there as his best man, not Bart's cousin. And once upon a time, all those people were his friends too, just like Thomas and Veronica.

A collective gasp sounded across the room just as the music reached its crescendo, and Liam steeled himself, ready for the pain that was going to blind him the second he saw India in a wedding dress. *It should've been him. It was supposed to be him.*

Every muscle in his body was drawn tight, pain lancing down his spine with how tense he was holding himself. A small hand moved across his back in comforting circles.

"You're okay. I've got you," Jasmine whispered in his ear.

Fuck, he was glad she was there. He couldn't imagine anyone else distracting him so much and keeping him calm.

Liam breathed in Jasmine's sweet vanilla scent, letting it wash over him, and finally turned his head to look at India. And he felt... nothing.

No searing agony, no painful regret, no longing. Nothing. In fact, when Liam wracked his brains, he couldn't remember the last time he *had* felt the agony, the regret, the longing. Truthfully, he couldn't remember the last time he'd thought about India or Bart—other than when someone else brought them up.

India looked beautiful, exactly like he'd always imagined when he pictured their wedding, but her perfectly practiced smile as she kissed her dad and took her place beside Bart did nothing for him. He didn't know how he'd missed it for so long. Bart and India existed in a bubble that had felt like home when he was in it, but now that he was on the outside, he saw it for what it was: cold, controlled, lavish.

Never in decades of friendship had he and India sat on a dirty, glitter covered floor and played cards, like he and Jazz had at his dad and Maggie's wedding. Never had Bart joined him for lunch with his dad, or danced around the kitchen making pancakes with him like Maggie did. His parents had tolerated India and Bart, and Liam had ignored every red flag because he'd been too caught up in them to know any different.

Part of him wanted answers from them. Why had they done it? How had they been able to look him in the eye for months, knowing that they were doing something so wrong? But as Liam watched them together, he had to wonder: what is really so wrong? The cheating was, obviously, but they really did seem perfect for each other.

And looking back, his relationship with India had been fucking boring. Where was the spontaneity? Where was the excitement? His dad and Maggie arranged surprises for each other all the time, and his moms were always trying new things together. He and India had been picture perfect, if the picture was one of those generic stock photos used to show off frames. There had been nothing exciting to their relationship, nor to his friendship with Bart.

And Liam was much happier, much more excited, without them in his life. In fact, he could pinpoint the exact moment he'd stopped thinking of them, stopping missing them. A Thursday afternoon in mid-April, a little over two years ago, when he'd walked into his dad's office and a chaotic redhead had greeted him with a smile and a, *"Can I help you?"*

Liam tuned out of the ceremony entirely, turning to take Jasmine in. She was gorgeous, as always, wearing a floor length black gown with mesh panels in the skirt, embroidered with wildflowers. A simple gold chain with a single teardrop topaz hung around her neck, and she'd swapped her usual plain gold nose ring for a tiny topaz stud.

Since he'd last seen her, she'd had her hair done, the copper bright and fiery. Her choppy bob was curled in loose waves, her bangs just tickling the top of her brows. Her hazel eyes were lined with smokey shadow, her heart-shaped lips painted cherry red. As drunk as he'd been the night of his dad and Maggie's wedding, he still remembered how those lips tasted—hazelnut and chocolate and—

"Are you okay?" Her whisper was barely audible, but Liam jumped. Shit. He'd been so busy staring at her he hadn't even noticed her staring back. He slung an arm around Jasmine's shoulders and tugged her closer in to him.

"Yeah. I am, actually. I'm glad we did this." She searched his face, the worry in her hazel eyes softening as she realized he meant it. "Thank you for being here."

She hesitated before leaning in and leaving a light kiss on his cheek, wiping her lipstick mark away with a smile. "Red looks good on you."

The burn of her lips lingered long after they turned back to watch the ceremony, long after the groom kissed the bride. With one brush of her lips against his cheek, Jasmine had obliterated every wall Liam had spent the past two years building, every lie he'd told himself and anyone who asked. But he couldn't lie to himself any longer: he'd been falling hard for Jasmine since the moment he laid eyes on her, and maybe, just maybe, it was time to do something about it.

CHAPTER FIVE

Jazz

If ever there was an argument *against* expensive prep schools, it was the man standing beside her. Sure, Liam was a well adjusted, well educated, person with a soul, but it seemed like every single person he'd gone to school with was fucking insufferable. Jazz knew he was insecure about the fact that he'd lost all of his friends in the breakup, but if these were the friends he'd lost? Good riddance.

Liam navigated them all like a pro, the anxious, heartbroken man she'd been expecting nowhere to be seen. It was… troublingly attractive to watch him surprise his ex-friends, who'd clearly been expecting the same. He was charming and friendly, cool as a damn cucumber, and Jazz liked it. A lot. Somehow, she had to make it through the rest of the night without throwing herself at him. She could do that. It was no big deal.

She smiled politely at yet *another* man named Chuck who worked for his dad's company and drove a fancy ass car (which, it seemed, everyone here did). She turned to

Liam with an expression that she hoped portrayed *help me*, and his lips quirked up, his arm around her waist tightening.

"If you don't mind, Jazz and I love this song. Shall we dance, darling?"

Darling. Why the fuck was that so hot?

It wasn't real, but that didn't stop her from wanting to rip his tux off and tackle him in the middle of the dance floor. She just had to make it through the night…

Liam spun her around and pulled her in close to him, holding her tightly and ignoring the nosy eyes of the other dancers. "What are you thinking about?" He brushed a cool finger over her burning cheek, the glint in his eyes making it clear he knew *exactly* what she was thinking about.

Jazz took a deep breath, willing her heart to stop racing. But Liam's fingers trailing over her bare back made it impossible. Why had she chosen a backless dress again?

"I'm thinking," she began, pretending she couldn't hear how badly she wanted him in her low, breathy voice, "that you're doing amazing. Seriously. You wanted to show them you're thriving? Consider it done. You're *actually* thriving here, Liam."

His smile softened into something almost shy. "Thanks. I realized, when India was walking down the aisle, that I don't miss any of this. I thought I did, but… I guess distance has made me see it all more clearly for what it is."

"Awful?" Jazz suggested, and he laughed, spinning and dipping her like he'd been dancing since he could walk. They probably taught shit like this at the school he'd gone to.

"Exactly. I still couldn't have done it without you, though. Thank you, Jasmine. I mean it."

Her skin warmed under his smile, her stomach doing something akin to somersaults. It was the dimples. No wonder Maggie hadn't been able to resist Cal.

"It's no problem. Happy to be here. With you." Those last two words weren't supposed to slip out. Shit. Jazz cleared her throat. "Actually, I've been wanting to ask you something."

Liam swerved them out of the way just in time to stop her from colliding with a couple who glared like it was Jazz's fault they couldn't dance in a straight line. "Shoot."

"You call me Jasmine when you're talking to me, but when you're talking to anyone else or introducing me, it's Jazz. Why do you change it?"

Liam's cheeks turned rosy—and Jazz didn't think that had anything to do with the one glass of champagne he'd allowed himself. She'd followed suit, not wanting to drunkenly accost his ex, however tempted she was.

Liam spun her in time with the music, her dress twirling around her legs. She was so focused on him, she could hardly hear the music. "I like that it's just our thing. Just for me and you," he said finally. *Oh.*

Jazz swallowed, her fingers itching to sink under the soft fabric of his jacket.

"I like that too," she said as the music drew to a close. Applause sounded for the band before they began their next song, but Jazz and Liam stood still, green eyes and hazel glued together. Jazz stepped away, looking down. "I have to run to the restroom. Back in a sec."

She pulled herself out of his grip and turned on her heel, dodging dancers as she rushed across the dance floor toward the gilded hallway. Rainbow light streamed through the stained glass windows flanking the giant entrance, but Jazz turned right, scurrying down a smaller hallway and holding her breath until she was tucked safely behind the restroom door.

The restrooms were as luxurious as the rest of the place —the private room had marble flooring, gold hardware, and a giant mirror on the wall above the sink, with a mother-of-pearl frame. A vase of yet more white roses sat on the vanity, perfuming the room with a sickly sweet floral scent that made Jazz suspect they'd been sprayed with something.

She didn't even have to pee, she just needed a little breathing room. Her breath rushed from her in a sigh. "When in Rome," she grumbled, pulling up her dress and pushing down her underwear before sitting on the toilet.

Jazz let her head fall in her hands, trying not to smudge her makeup. What was wrong with her? Perhaps one glass of Champagne had been too many. Or maybe it was just the tux. Or the dimples. Or Liam's dancing skills. Or that godforsaken fucking mustache.

Whatever it was, she just had to wait it out. In a few hours, they'd be in their PJs, lying several feet apart in the massive hotel bed, and she wouldn't be so tempted to stick her tongue down his throat. Liam would be reading on his Kindle, and his cheeks would turn red when she asked him what he was reading, just to fuck with him because she already knew it was a steamy romance. She would open TikTok and pretend she was just going to scroll for five minutes, then an hour would pass and they'd go to sleep and wake up fully dressed. They would tuck their drunken hookup at Maggie and Cal's wedding away as ancient history, and Jazz would move on with her life, making do with another decade of orgasmless sex.

She finished up in the restroom, washed and dried her hands, wrinkled her nose at the cloying rose-scented soap, and headed back into the reception room with a newfound resolve. Determination fueling her steps, she didn't see the server carrying a tray of canapés until someone grabbed her arm and tugged her to the side.

"Thank—" She looked up at her savior, the words dying in her mouth as she found herself face to face with the bride and groom. She swallowed down the anger that fought to rise in her throat. "Thank you."

"No problem. They just seem to appear out of nowhere, don't they?" India said with a practiced smile.

On principle alone, Jazz hated her, but she couldn't help but admit that Liam had good taste. India was gorgeous. Her long blonde hair fell to her waist in perfect finger waves, though Jazz was sure most of it was extensions. Her makeup was natural but flawless, and her ballgown fit her like a glove. Even her soft, high-pitched voice gave princess vibes. She'd never seen a picture of Liam and India together, but she could imagine how perfect they must have looked.

And Bart was… there.

She cleared her throat. "Congratulations. It was a beautiful ceremony, and you look incredible."

India's smile widened. "Thank you. You're Jazz, right?

Liam's… girlfriend?" Her facade slipped, her lips curling slightly around the word. And just like that, any insecurities Jazz had around this gorgeous woman were gone. India had hurt Liam, they both had. How dare they invite him here to rub it in his face?

"I'm Liam's partner, yeah," she said, forcing a cheery smile onto her face. *Partner* felt more serious than *girlfriend.*

"We've been hearing a lot about you tonight," Bart said, his face more stoney than his bride's.

"I've heard a lot about you guys, too." Satisfaction coiled in her belly at the minor flare of panic in Bart's eyes. Did they think she was going to bring up how they'd broken his heart? Hell, wasn't that why they'd invited him in the first place? There was no reason for them to have done so, other than to tell themselves he was miserable, lonely, and missing them. It was an ego trip, pure and simple, and Jazz hated them.

"Liam talks about you both all the time," she continued. "It sounds like the three of you had a blast growing up!" Let them think Liam only talked about the good times. Let them think they hadn't crushed him. "Actually, he was just telling me the other day about that summer resort trip you all took when you were seventeen? The one where you played spin the bottle and crashed your dad's boat? The pictures were hilarious."

Liam hadn't told her a single thing about that trip, but Jazz was nosy and had found the pictures when looking through old photo albums at Eliza and Danisha's place, trying to find pictures of young-Cal for his and Maggie's wedding. Danisha had told her all about that summer—how Liam had begged to go with Bart's family, and how he'd been glowing when he'd come home, because he'd had a crush on India forever and finally gotten to kiss her during spin the bottle.

India and Bart, it seemed, remembered too. Their cheeks flamed, and they shifted awkwardly.

A warm hand settled on Jazz's lower back. "I was wondering where you'd disappeared to. I thought I was going to have to send out a search party."

Oh god. She'd hoped to get Liam out of here without him having to talk to India and Bart. Well, if she couldn't do that, she would at least play the part of the doting girlfriend perfectly. She looped her arm around his waist and snuggled into him, looking up at him with a mock-affronted expression.

"My sense of direction isn't *that* bad."

Liam's answering, slightly exasperated smile was a work of art. Where had he picked up these acting skills? And why was it such a turn on?

"Of course not, *darling*," he said, layering so much affection on the word that even Jazz almost believed it. He turned his attention to India and Bart, not a trace of anxiety or heartbreak on his face. "Congratulations, you two. What a beautiful wedding."

"Thank you," Bart replied, somewhat stiffly.

"We were just talking about that summer trip you told me about, baby. In the Maldives?"

Liam's eyes flared when she called him *baby*, emerald green disappearing as his pupils swallowed it. Interesting.

"Oh yeah, when we crashed your dad's boat, Bart. That was a fun trip."

If Jazz hadn't been watching for India's reaction, she would have missed her minute flinch, as if she couldn't quite bear that Liam's first thought was of the boat, and not their kiss. Or what had happened after the kiss. She missed him. After everything she'd done to him, she missed him. Jazz couldn't say she was surprised. She might not know the ins and outs of India's relationship with her new husband, but she knew there was no chance Bart loved her better than Liam had.

"It feels like a million years ago now," India said, her voice less steady than before. "So how have you been? How are your parents?"

"We're great," Liam said, twirling the ends of Jazz's hair. "My moms have taken up fencing, which is going about as well as you can imagine, and my dad got married." Jazz wondered if India and Bart noticed how he neglected to mention what he was doing, but they didn't seem to.

"I heard your dad got married. His assistant, right? What a cliché. God, you must be pissed about your inheritance, huh?" Bart said with a chuckle that made Jazz's blood boil. Maggie had learned to laugh and let the *gold digger* comments roll off her back. Jazz… not so much. She was banned from two bars because she'd gotten into arguments about it.

Liam's grip on her hip tightened, the only sign that he, too, was pissed at Bart. "Maggie's amazing, actually. I can't imagine anyone better for my dad."

Bart snorted, but India nudged him. "That's great. We're

happy for him," she said, attempting to smooth over her husband's misstep. "We really should head back before my mom thinks we've run away before the exit pictures. But we should catch up when we're back from our honeymoon."

"Absolutely. It was good to see you both." This time, Jazz knew they all knew he was lying.

He didn't let go of her as India and Bart walked away, didn't watch them go. But Jazz did, catching every one of India's split second glances back.

"She's watching," she murmured, turning back to Liam. She brushed his chin with her thumb. "You should kiss me."

Liam's tongue darted out, wetting his lower lip. He cupped her face, his touch like silk against her cheek, lowering his lips to hers.

"Just to be clear, Jasmine," he murmured against her lips. "This isn't for them."

She didn't have time to let his words sink in before he caught her mouth in a kiss. Her hands drifted into his hair, gripping him tighter than she had a right to. Liam didn't seem to mind, leaning his body into hers, his hand roaming over her hip to her back, then down until it was resting on her ass. She gasped, and he took the opportunity to slip his tongue between her lips, tangling with hers, moving as smoothly as he had on the dance floor.

"Disgusting."

They broke apart, turning to find an older woman glaring at them, squeezing her glass of rosé so tightly, Jazz was surprised it was still intact. The woman scowled as she spun around, stomping away from them.

Slowly, Jazz and Liam turned back to each other, eyes

wide. That kiss… Fuck. She couldn't convince herself that *that* was no big deal.

"Maybe she didn't like the stache," she said, nodding to the angry woman in an attempt to diffuse the taut tension growing thicker between them.

Liam released his hold on her face, chuckling. "Impossible. Everyone likes the stache," he said, dropping his hand and twining their fingers together. She screwed up her face and a cocky smile fell over this mouth. "*You* like the stache."

"I don't *hate* the stache," she acquiesced, trying not to remember how soft it had felt when he'd been trailing kisses all over her body. Trying and failing. Pictures flashed through her mind like a film reel, clear as day, despite how much liquor she'd had to drink before they'd climbed into bed together. "It's a weird choice though," she added quickly. "I don't understand why you don't just grow a beard too. You'd suit it."

He squeezed her hand. "Come on, I've had enough of this. Let's head upstairs. My Kindle and your mindless TikTok scrolling are calling our names. I'll tell you the stache story on the way."

CHAPTER SIX

Jazz

Considering how much effort had been put into the design of the estate, it seemed not one person had stopped to think about the layout. There was only a short walk between the building where they held events and the hotel, but the ground was covered in sharp gravel that was a nightmare for anyone wearing heels. Liam's hand was soft and warm in hers as he led her toward the hotel, walking slower than he usually would to keep her steady.

"You promised me a stache story."

Liam laughed, a light breeze ruffling his hair, and Jazz had to look away, staring at her feet—which was probably sensible, given how wobbly she was. "It goes back to when my moms started dating. I was seven, and a really shy kid. Mom —D," he clarified, presumably used to specifying which of his moms he was talking about. But Jazz recognized a subtle shift in his tone anyway, when he spoke about his moms: Danisha was *Mom,* and Eliza was more like *Mum,* as if Liam had picked up a touch of his dad's Irish accent when he was first learning to talk and it had stuck. "She didn't know much about kids, but she wanted to get to know me for my mom's sake. She took me to her favorite place from when she was a kid."

"The art museum?" Jazz guessed.

"Yeah. Her parents used to take her and her brothers when they were younger, and she said she wanted to share a family tradition with me. I loved it, obviously. She let me pick a book out at the gift shop and I chose a book of portraits. When we got home, I asked if we could have a sleepover so we could read the book together before bed."

"She stayed and read to you?" Jazz asked and he nodded. Liam's face always lit up when he talked about his family. Usually, Jazz was a little bitter when she saw people with happy families, but it was hard not to be happy for Liam.

"She did. The book was just portraits, but she made up stories about them all for me. After that, she kind of just moved in." He shrugged. "It's a stereotype for a reason. Anyway, she read that book to me every night for months and I was obsessed with the portraits, but especially the fact that so many of them had mustaches. Obviously, I decided my new life goal was to have a mustache."

"Obviously." They paused outside the elevator, the metal gleaming. Even the buttons were free of fingerprints. Jazz punched the button, rubbing her finger around a little to smudge it. "So you grew the stache because it reminds you of the book and Danisha?"

"Oh no. That's a much nicer explanation. I grew the stache because my second-grade art teacher was the worst. She asked us to draw self-portraits and I gave mine a mustache. She didn't like that and told me to erase it, then gave me detention when I refused—"

"You were seven!" Jazz interjected, incensed on seven-year-old Liam's behalf.

"It was a tough school, and Ms. Bellion was super strict. She said it wasn't realistic and people didn't have mustaches without beards anyway. Which, what the fuck? But I never forgot and I grew this as soon as I could."

"So you're telling me you still have the stache because someone told you you couldn't *thirty years ago* and you never let it go?"

The elevator doors slid smoothly open and Liam tugged her in behind him. "Yep."

Jazz shook her head in disbelief. "Holy shit. That is the pettiest thing I've ever heard. I think I might be in love with you," she joked and Liam turned so he was facing her, a serious expression on his face.

"Thank god. I don't think we can get the deposits back for our Hallowedding at this point." A laugh bubbled out of Jazz's mouth and Liam joined her.

Mirrors lined the walls of the elevator, creating an infinity effect. Jazz's laugh caught in her throat as she looked up, seeing Liam's head thrown back, a grin on his face as he laughed. God, he really was beautiful.

"What?" he asked as he noticed her staring at him.

Jazz's gaze dropped to their hands, held comfortably between them. Liam rubbed his thumb absentmindedly over her skin, and she sucked in a deep breath, holding it and trailing her eyes up his arms, his torso, his full lips, his fucking mustache. His eyes. He knew exactly what she was thinking—he was just waiting for her to say it.

She blew out the breath and tugged him closer. It had been inevitable since the second she agreed to come with him. "Fuck it."

Liam

He wasted no time closing in on Jasmine, his hand slamming against the mirrored wall, fingers dragging down and leaving smudge marks behind. Her lips had been calling to him all day, and one kiss in a room full of people wasn't nearly enough to satiate him. He'd been doing a good job of holding it together, of pretending his brain wasn't cycling through bad ideas on repeat. But then she'd called him baby. *Baby*. Her voice had been just a little breathy, and every last thread of his resolve had snapped.

Liam leaned in, their noses bumping against each other. He trailed his tongue over her lips and her mouth parted in invitation. "Delicious."

Jasmine whimpered, her chest rising and falling rapidly. He was still holding her hand, unable to bring himself to drop it yet, but he drew his other hand down her body and cupped her lower back, pulling her body into his.

"Liam," she pled, the word vibrating through him, straight to his cock. Fuck. She was gorgeous.

He nipped her bottom lip, letting his hand drop lower,

his thumb brushing the perfect curve of her ass. She'd been haunting his dreams since their first night together. The memories were foggy, and his brain couldn't possibly do her justice, filling in the gaps. He needed to get his hands on her bare skin again, needed to feel her legs around him.

The elevator chimed and the doors slid open just as he brushed his lips over hers in a ghost of a kiss. They were both trembling as they walked through the hallway, stopping outside their room. Liam swiped the keycard impatiently. He pulled Jasmine in, tossed the card aside, and pushed her against the door.

She gripped his face, done with his teasing, and captured his mouth in a torturous kiss. The heavenly taste of her flooded his tongue like pure sugar. They'd only had one glass of Champagne each, but he could taste it—deep, bubbly, and sweet, just like Jasmine herself.

Liam's cock strained against his pants as she grabbed his jacket. He didn't have time to breathe before it was on the floor, her fingers working his shirt buttons clumsily. When he tried to help, she pushed his hands away, groaning as she finally unbuttoned the shirt and her fingers made contact with his bare chest.

She was a tornado, her nails roaming over his chest, then scratching down his back. Liam cursed against her mouth, pulling her backward. He almost stumbled over his dress pants as Jasmine pushed them down his thighs, like she couldn't wait a second longer to get him undressed. Far be it from him to deny her. He kicked them away, followed by his boxers, a second before the back of his legs hit the bed.

Jasmine pushed him down into a sitting position, lifted her dress, and straddled his lap. She gasped as his cock brushed against her underwear, breaking their kiss for the first time to look between them. Her pupils swallowed the flecks of gold in her hazel eyes.

"Fuck."

In one word, the air was sucked from the room, like all of his senses were dulled to everything and anything that wasn't Jasmine. She bent her mouth to his neck, trailing kisses across his skin, dragging her teeth over his jaw, and lavishing kisses across his collarbone.

She shifted back, her dress riding up further so the mesh panel exposed her underwear, deep purple lace with a band of pink, purple, and green wildflowers. He licked his lips, trailing a finger over the mesh, and Jasmine's head fell back. There was something beautifully erotic about her being fully dressed, exposed by floral mesh, while his cock begged for her. He lifted the edges of her dress so he could grasp and squeeze her ass, before rolling her hips so her pussy slid over his cock, the lace soft but torturous.

A whimper fell from her lips and he wanted to taste it, needed to feel her mouth on his or he was going to snap, push the violet fabric aside, and press his cock into her without thinking twice. He tilted his head up, brushing kisses across her jaw until she raised her head and her lips met his like magnets.

Her thighs squeezed him, and Liam gasped, his fingers digging into her ass as he moved her over his cock. Soft sounds poured from Jasmine, captured by his tongue as he kissed her fiercely.

Fuck, he was going to come before he'd even got her out of her dress if he wasn't careful. It took every ounce of his self-control to still. Jasmine opened her mouth, to protest no doubt, but it died on her tongue when his fingers found the hidden zip at the back of her dress. The black satin felt like sandpaper compared to Jasmine's soft skin as he pulled the zip down.

The thin straps holding the dress up tied in the back like laces. Liam forced his lungs to breathe slow, measured breaths as he wound the fabric around his finger and tugged. The straps fell away as the laces came undone, the dress slipping down Jasmine's body and pooling around her waist. But with the patience of a goddamn saint, Liam kept his eyes trained on hers as he lifted it over her head, as he smoothed her mussed-up hair.

Then, finally, he let his gaze fall over Jasmine's incredible body. Fuck, his drunk memories had nothing on the real thing. She was breathtaking. Freckles dotted her pale skin, and a large tattoo was splashed across her ribs, curving around her belly in a burst of color. Flowers: watercolor roses, carnations, and morning glories in various shades of turquoise and purple.

"These are gorgeous."

"They're birth flowers," Jasmine replied, breathy. "Maggie's, and my brother and sister's."

Her stomach, thighs, and breasts were lined with stretch marks just begging for him to run his tongue across them, playing connect the dots. He ran a finger over the curve of her belly and she tensed.

"Liam—"

"Give me a second, darling. I'm committing every perfect inch of you to memory."

She was a work of art he could stare at for hours, absorbing every little detail. Liam had visited dozens of galleries, seen thousands of paintings, and Jasmine was a million times more beautiful than any of them.

She sucked in a breath, and he drew his gaze slowly up her body. How lucky he was to have his eyes on her.

Her cheeks were flushed, her eyes bright, when he looked up at her. Liam ran his finger over the point of her chin.

"I think that's the nicest thing anyone's ever said to me," she said softly, her voice thick. She seemed to hear it and gave herself a little shake, clearing her throat before adding, "And that's saying a lot, because you know that old British guy who does the weather on the morning news?"

Liam blinked at the random subject change. "The one with the toupee?"

"Exactly!" Jasmine bounced on his lap, clapping her hands together. Liam sucked in a breath, trying in vain to hold her still. "Well, I ran into him when I was getting a bagel at the airport once and he told me I had, quote, *banging tits*." She put on what might have been the world's worst English accent, and Liam couldn't hold his snort in.

They shook with laughter, clinging to each other for dear life. "Shitty toupees aside," Liam managed between laughs, "he wasn't wrong. You *do* have *banging tits*." His English accent was just as bad, but Jasmine's laughter died in her throat as he leaned in, mapping the edge of her bra with his tongue. She loosened her grip on his shoulders, reaching behind her back to unclip the bra and, as soon as he felt the silky fabric go slack, Liam wrenched it away with his teeth.

"Holy shit," he murmured, his eyes wide. "Are these new? I don't remember these." How the hell hadn't he noticed her nipple piercings through the fabric?

He had his mouth on her before she could answer, a moan spilling from her lips before she spoke. "No, but you were really drunk last time. I got them pierced years ago at the same time as Maggie, when—"

"Please don't talk about Maggie when your nipple is in my mouth," Liam said, but he wasn't willing to pull his mouth away long enough for the words to be anything more than a garbled mess. Jasmine seemed to get the message though, because she said nothing more, just whimpered as he tugged the gold bar with his teeth. He rolled the other between his thumb and finger, Jasmine writhing in his lap.

Every brush of her pussy over his cock felt better than the last. He needed to feel her bare.

He gripped Jasmine's ass as he stood just enough to turn and sit her on the edge of the bed, kneeling before her. She braced herself on her elbows, looking down at him through long, fluttering lashes, as he hooked his thumbs in the thin purple strings holding her underwear up. He tugged them down slowly, Jasmine lifting herself to help him. Tossing them aside, he finally turned, pushed her thighs apart and got his eyes on her.

And his brain damn near short circuited.

"*That* one is new," Jasmine said, her voice breathy. "I got it as an Easter treat for myself."

Liam eyed the gold bar through her clit and fought the urge to bury his mouth against her. "Christ."

"Exactly. 'Tis the damn season," she agreed, and he raised a brow, forcing himself to look away from her piercing and meet her gaze.

"Jasmine."

"Hmm?"

"I don't think I can wait for our Hallowedding to marry you. You're too perfect."

She laughed, a deep, rumbling sound that felt like a hot cup of tea or a warm hug after a shitty day, then raised her left leg and hooked it around his shoulder. "Prove it, baby," she whispered, and she didn't need to ask twice.

Liam cursed her name, leaning in and dragging his tongue over her clit, the metal bar surprisingly cool. He pushed her thighs open further, his fingers digging into her skin. Jasmine's elbows gave way, a gasp escaping her as her body fell back against the bed. Liam couldn't get near enough, couldn't consume her enough. None of it came close to how much she'd consumed him for so many years.

He teased her pussy with two fingers, and Jasmine groaned.

"Is this okay?"

"Yes. *Fuck*, yes."

There it was. Liam pressed two fingers inside her and curled them until she cried out. She was so fucking wet, clenching around him. He fucked her with his fingers, licking her clit and toying with her piercing. They'd eaten a five-course meal that cost more than a week of Liam's wages, had top shelf champagne and profiteroles with literal gold leaf, and none of it tasted even a fraction as good as she did, sweet and rich on his tongue.

She sank her hands into his hair. "Liam," she gasped. "I need your cock inside me now, *fuck.*"

Liam sank his teeth gently into her clit, and Jasmine sobbed, her body twisting on the edge of the bed. He stood up, her legs dropping to the floor with a gentle thud.

"Up the bed, darling."

She shuffled back, her whole body flushed scarlet. Liam plucked his wallet from the pocket of his pants on the floor and pulled out the condom he'd tucked away. He crawled up the bed, positioning himself between her open thighs.

Jasmine snagged the condom from his fingers, tearing open the packet and wrapping her fist around his cock, swiping her thumb through the pre-cum glistening at the tip. She brought her thumb to her mouth, her tongue darting out to lick her lips before she wrapped them around her thumb and licked it clean.

Liam's body shook with restraint, and she took pity on him, her eyes twinkling as she rolled the condom over his cock. He fisted himself, running his tip all over her, his eyes squeezing shut as it brushed the metal bar and Jasmine cried his name. She dropped her head onto the pillow, her red hair fanning around her like flames.

"Please," she begged, and Liam took a steadying breath. He leaned in to kiss her until they were both gasping for air, then pushed inside her with their foreheads pressed together.

Fucking hell. Her pussy drew him in, squeezing him so tightly he wasn't entirely confident in his ability to last all of thirty seconds. And he wasn't even fully inside her yet. Jesus.

Jasmine pulled her lower lip between her teeth and Liam nudged her nose with his.

"Are you okay?"

"I… I, um…"

"Jasmine, darling. Talk to me," he said, pressing a gentle kiss to her forehead. "Do you need me to stop?"

"Absolutely fucking not," she choked out. She gripped his bicep, her fingers shaking. "You feel so good. *More*, please."

Liam twined his fingers with hers, holding her hand against the pillow, and gritted his teeth as he pushed fully inside her, a shuddering breath falling from his mouth as he bottomed out.

"Oh shit," Jasmine moaned, squeezing his hand in a death grip.

Liam counted as he pulled out, *one, two, three*, then pushed back into her, making sure she was comfortable. But Jasmine had other ideas, looping her leg around him and pushing impatiently.

"Message received, darling," he chuckled against her lips. He grabbed her other hand, holding it down against the pillow on the other side of her head, taking care to avoid her hair. "If you need to stop, tell me, okay?"

"I swear to god if you don't fuck me soon, I—*oh*."

Liam couldn't stop a grin from splitting his face as her back bowed, her legs wrapping tightly around him as he fucked her. He used the bounce of the mattress to propel himself, hitting her deeply. Her legs trembled around him, and if he wasn't holding her hands down, he could tell she'd be raking her nails down his back.

Her pussy clenched around him, the sounds falling from her lips increasing in volume and decreasing in coherency. *Fuck,* she was close. Thank god. How was it possible for her to feel so fucking good?

He dragged his lips over her jaw, drawing her lip between his teeth and biting down until she was cursing into his mouth.

"You feel goddamn incredible, Jasmine," he panted and her eyes snapped to his, golden flames sparkling in her hazel irises.

And then, in a split second, she blinked, and they were gone. She slammed her eyes closed, turned her head to the side, and... faked it? She clenched around him, every spasm of her pussy perfectly measured, every cry intentional.

Absolutely not. Not on his watch.

Liam stilled and loosened his grip on her hands, but didn't let go, even when the pins and needles set in. Shit, he hadn't realized quite how tightly he was holding her.

He watched her take a deep breath before opening her eyes and turning back to face him.

"Hey," he said, searching her face for signs of discomfort. There was something there, an edge in her eyes. Frustration? Liam couldn't quite place it. "Are you okay? Did I hurt you?"

She flexed her hands, and he begrudgingly released her, sitting back so he was kneeling. "What? No, why would you have hurt me?"

"Because you faked it."

CHAPTER SEVEN

Jazz

"**B***ecause you faked it.*"

Jazz's heart fell into her stomach. He'd noticed? No one had ever noticed.

"Of course I didn't," she said quickly, playing dumb and hoping her face didn't betray her.

Liam frowned, his brows drawing together. "You did. It's okay, but you never have to do that. If you're not enjoying something, you can tell me. I don't want to do anything that would make you uncomfortable."

He pulled out of her, still hard, and, despite the fact that her orgasm had, once again, disappeared the second she got close enough to grab it, her body was desperate to have him back inside her.

Jazz sighed, rolling the tension from her shoulders. "How the hell did you notice? No one has ever noticed."

"How could I not notice?" Liam replied, like it was the most obvious thing in the world.

"You didn't notice last time," she grumbled, and Liam's eyes widened, a stunned expression falling across his face.

"What the fuck? Are you telling me you also faked it *last time*? And I was so drunk I couldn't even tell." He said the last part under his breath, like he was disappointed with himself.

Jazz flexed her hands just to give herself something to do with them. "It's not your fault."

At this, Liam looked somehow *more* aghast. "Are you kidding me? Of course it's my fault. Clearly I'm doing something wrong and—"

"Liam."

He paused his tirade, and she weighed up her options. She could make some excuse, try and find something to say that wouldn't have him blaming himself for her body's inability to come. But she could see how much he was beating himself up about it, and she hated it. So that left option B: she could tell him the truth. She could finally open up and tell someone, other than her OBGYN, who had been useless anyway, that she couldn't come. Liam wouldn't judge her. It was fine.

She took a deep breath, as if readying herself for battle. "I haven't had an orgasm in ten years."

Liam blinked at her like she'd spoken a different language. "I'm sorry. It sounded like you just said you haven't had an orgasm in ten years."

"I did say that."

"Holy shit." Liam rubbed his face with his hands, shaking his head in disbelief.

"Yep."

"Like at all? Not even alone?"

She shook her head, and he loosed a long breath. "Holy

shit," he repeated and, despite how awkward the whole situation was, Jazz couldn't help but laugh. This, it seemed, just concerned Liam more. He rubbed his temples, shifting so he was sitting with his legs crossed. How the hell did a grown man look so good sitting criss-cross applesauce *naked and hard*? Jesus.

"Are you… okay? Have you spoken to a doctor? There could be some kind of medical reason."

"I'm fine. Frustrated, don't get me wrong, but otherwise all good. I saw my doctor after I realized I hadn't been able to come for a few months, and I mention it every year when I see my OBGYN, but there doesn't seem to be any kind of medical problem." She shrugged. She knew it sounded bad, but she was used to it. It wasn't a big deal. "It's fine. I still have sex—obviously—and I still enjoy it. I just don't finish."

Her explanation did nothing to reassure Liam. If anything, his frown was just getting deeper. "Why didn't you say anything? I get not mentioning it last time, we were both so fucking drunk, but if I'd known I would've—"

"I've never told anyone," she interrupted. "Other than my doctor. Not even Maggie knows."

"Seriously? But you tell Maggie everything."

"The first few times it happened, I wrote it off as stress because I was taking extra classes that semester." Her parents had threatened to stop paying her tuition if she didn't pick up extra classes, and Jazz had barely been juggling her regular class load. "By the time I realized something was wrong, Maggie was dealing with a lot with her parents and I didn't want to worry her. And later it felt like it had been going on for too long." Even to her ears, it sounded like a stream of weak excuses.

The truth was, she wasn't sure why she hadn't told Maggie. It was easier, she supposed, to be the fun friend who planned adventures and pulled Maggie out of her shell —sometimes willingly, sometimes not. It wasn't that she never shared her problems with Maggie, she just didn't share any problems that were more than mild inconveniences. Probably because Maggie wouldn't be on board with Jazz avoiding shit and would insist they deal with whatever it was together. And she couldn't let Maggie help her deal with things, because if she couldn't fix them, Maggie would blame herself.

"You should talk to her about it. Maggie's your person," Liam said and Jazz grimaced. That was twice Liam had caught her not sharing everything with the person she claimed she shared everything with, twice she'd had nothing better than a weak explanation of why she hadn't.

"I'll think about it. But what I'm trying to say," she continued, "is that this isn't a reflection of your... skills." She cringed at the word, and Liam's lips flattened into a thin line. "I'm just saying, it's not you, it's me. Literally."

"No one's faked it with me since high school," Liam said, and Jazz stared at him in disbelief.

"Now that is a level of self confidence even *I* don't possess."

"Obviously there have been people I haven't been able to make come, but they've never faked it. I'm serious. It's kind of my thing." Pink tinged the edge of Liam's ears, and

Jazz got the feeling that he'd be bright red if he wasn't still processing everything she'd thrown at him.

"Making people come is your thing?" He nodded, and she hummed. "So what, you're like a pleasure dom or something?"

Liam tilted his head. "Among other things, yeah."

She raised her brows, impressed. "Damn. What is going on in that Michaelson DNA?" *Pleasure dom* might actually put Daddy Michaelson to shame, and Jazz desperately wanted to know what *other things* Liam had up his sleeve. She also wanted to tell Maggie, but there was no world in which Maggie would want details of Cal's son's sexual proclivities.

Liam wrinkled his nose. "What does that me—actually no, I don't want to know. Never mind."

"What's your record?" she asked, propping herself up on her elbows and pretending not to notice the way Liam's eyes followed her breasts as they bounced.

"Thirty-six in five hours," he said and Jazz whistled.

"Damn. It couldn't be me. Clearly."

Her attempt at a joke fell flat. Liam groaned, running a hand through his hair. His dark brown waves were messy, thanks to her grabbing at them while he went down on her. She'd come close so many times, and Jazz couldn't deny her disappointment that she hadn't quite been able to get herself over the edge. It certainly wasn't for Liam's lack of trying.

"Are you seriously telling me you're okay with the fact that you haven't come in a *decade*?"

"Define okay. Would I like to orgasm? God, yes, but it is what it is. Apparently my body doesn't want to do it."

Liam sighed, lying down beside her and turning onto his side so he was facing her. She mirrored him, their noses mere inches apart. He reached out, running his fingers through the tangles in the ends of her hair before pushing it over her shoulders. "I could try."

She quirked a brow. "Was that not you trying? Because Jesus, that was fucking incredible—lack of orgasm aside."

"Of course I was trying, but we can try something different. Like I said, this is my thing. I have a lot of… techniques, I guess. Not to mention a shit ton of toys at home. I want to make this happen for you."

He spoke so earnestly, his emerald eyes so open and intense, that Jazz's spine tensed. She swallowed, looking away from him. "I'm not a challenge, Liam."

"What? Shit, no, I didn't mean it like that, darling. I'm sorry." He grabbed her hand from where it rested on her stomach and brought it to his mouth, pressing a soft kiss against her palm. "I want to help. You helped me by coming to the wedding, and I want to do this for you."

She should have known that he would take it so seriously, should have known he'd be so damn nice about it. This was Liam, after all. "I love the enthusiasm, buddy, but I think this ship has long since sailed. It's all good, don't worry about. I still enjoyed myself and I can still finish you—"

"Absolutely fucking not." His voice was firm, almost commanding. She'd never heard him like that before.

"I don't get it," she replied with a growl of frustration.

"What's in this for you? And don't just say it's because we're friends and you care about me. Even you aren't that selfless." She wasn't entirely convinced that was true.

"What's in it for me?" Liam's answering laugh coiled through her like an asp, dark and sensual, humorless. "I've been dreaming about feeling you come all over me for *years*. Since that first day when I spotted you at the office, I haven't been able to get you out of my head. It's been fucking torture knowing we were together in February and I can't remember it. And knowing I was inside you but didn't get to see you finish? Unbearable." Her heart stilled, her breath catching in her chest.

"When I say this is my thing, I don't mean that I take it as a challenge to see how many times I can get someone to come. I mean that what gets me off is getting other people off, knowing I made it happen, over and over again until they can't handle anymore. I don't even need anyone to lay a finger on me to make me come. I just need to make *them* fall apart and I lose it. But you? I'm not sure I'd survive making you come, darling, but God, I want to try."

"Oh," Jazz breathed. What was she supposed to say to that? His eyes blazed, emerald flames enticing her to agree. And she wanted to. It surprised her, but she was actually considering it. She'd come closer to finishing with Liam than she had in a decade. If anyone was going to figure out how to make her come, it was probably him.

"Have you really been thinking about this for that long?" she asked and despite making it through an entire monologue about how much he loved making people come, it was *that* that made him blush.

He scratched the back of his neck. "Yeah. After India and I broke up, I really wasn't interested in anyone else. You were the first person who piqued that interest."

"Other than the time you asked Maggie on a date," Jazz pointed out and he glared at her.

"Sure, excluding that, I guess, but that was more me trying to force myself out of my shell, and I'd really love to pretend it didn't happen."

"That's too bad. I will continue to bring it up every chance I get."

"You're a menace."

His low chuckle made heat pool deep within her, bringing her back to the question at hand: were they going to do this? She drew in a long breath, counted to three, and blew it out. Why the hell not?

"Okay, yeah. We can try. But it might take a while."

If Liam was surprised that she'd agreed, he didn't show it. He gave her a reassuring smile. "We're in no rush."

True. She'd waited ten years—she'd been forced to have patience whether she wanted to or not. "Right. But I don't want you to feel bad if I can't come and you do," she replied, gesturing to his still hard cock.

He considered her for a moment before shaking his head. "Nope. That's not how this is going to work."

"What do you mean?"

"I mean until you come, I don't come."

Surely she hadn't heard him correctly. She stared at him, open-mouthed, before finally saying, "You can't be serious."

"I am."

"So what, you're telling me you're not even going to masturbate?"

He shook his head, his eyes sparkling with amusement at her skepticism. "Nope."

"But this could take months!" Years, even. Hell, for all she knew, it wasn't even possible.

"I can wait."

Jesus. He was being serious. Did he have some kind of masochism kink to go along with his orgasm kink? "That sounds like a challenge I can win."

"I'd like to see you try, darling," Liam replied, his emerald eyes twinkling. "Does this mean you're in?"

She blew out a long breath. "You realize how crazy that sounds, don't you?" she asked, but Liam shrugged, as if he couldn't see the problem. "Wow. Okay. I guess I'm in."

She held out her hand for him to shake and he did so, but didn't let go, threading their fingers together and letting their hands rest comfortably on the bed between instead. "Can you seriously come just from making someone else come?" He nodded, an errant curl falling across his forehead. She reached out and brushed it away. "Damn. I really want to see that."

His lips lifted at the corner, his dimples popping out as a smile crossed his face. "Then let's make it happen, Jasmine."

CHAPTER EIGHT

Liam

He should have taken Maggie up on her offer of a day off after driving home from California. But if he said that, she would give him a look that clearly said *I told you so*, and Liam's head was still spinning from the weekend too much to deal with that. He wanted to be curled up on the couch pretending to read while making plans for his first night with Jasmine—their first planned night anyway—but, instead, he was trying not to fall asleep while sourcing options for a client. An incredibly picky client.

Liam read over the criteria they'd sent over for their coffee table again and sighed.

1) Authentic mid-century modern

2) Mint condition, no discoloration, or scratches

3) Rosewood or Walnut

"They're asking for a unicorn," he groaned, and Maggie chuckled from the other end of the couch.

"The Lavines just like the illusion of control. They care more about things looking good than you actually ticking all their boxes. Try to find a couple pieces that meet most of the criteria and then some that don't, but look nicer. I guarantee they'll pick the latter."

This was the third project the Lavine family had hired Maggie Makes Home for, so Liam trusted that Maggie knew them well enough to know what she was talking about.

"Thanks," he replied with a grateful smile.

He could have worked from home, but he was too easily distracted. Maggie gave the team the option of working from wherever they liked when they weren't on site or filming, but they all had keys to the townhouse she'd converted into an office and studio and could work there if they wished.

At his dad's request, neither he nor Maggie brought work home with them, so she spent most days at the office when she wasn't getting her hands dirty on a project. There were several desks and a couple of dedicated office rooms for anyone looking for a quiet workspace, but they mostly gathered in the comfy living room to work on their laptops.

Occasionally, Maggie would head outside to check on a piece she was working on, adding layers of paint or sanding things down. When he needed to stretch his legs or get some fresh air, Liam would join her. It was a far cry from the dark backrooms at the museum—sometimes, in the darker months, he'd work Monday through Friday without seeing daylight. This was so much better, even if he was exhausted from the weekend.

Liam closed his laptop and slid it onto the side table, stretching and yawning. He pulled his sweatshirt over his head and dropped it on the arm of the couch. The coziness was definitely making him sleepier.

He and Jasmine had left California after a room service breakfast, since he hadn't wanted to bump into any of his old friends. He'd had enough looks of surprise mingled with pity to last him a lifetime. They'd taken turns driving up the coast, stopping at a diner for lunch and a drive-thru for dinner, and made it back to Seattle just in time for the sun to sink behind the horizon.

Liam had dropped Jasmine off at her place, ignoring her continued protests when he'd insisted on carrying her bags upstairs, and kissed her on the forehead before dragging himself back out to the car. Exhaustion weighed him down the whole way home, and every step toward his bed had felt like a mile. But instead of falling asleep the second his head hit the pillow, he'd lain awake for hours, with one thing on his mind.

Jasmine.

Or rather, the deal he'd struck with her. What the fuck had he been thinking? He hadn't been, clearly, but any chance of him being sensible had vanished the second she'd explained why she'd faked it. Liam had never had any kind of sexual arrangement with anyone. Before he and India had gotten together, he'd dated regularly, like most people did in their twenties. After India, once he'd been ready, he'd opted for more casual hook ups, avoiding spending more than one night with anyone. It was easier that way.

He couldn't imagine a worse person to start something like this with than his dad's assistant—and Maggie's best friend—who he'd been harboring a secret crush on for two fucking years. Shit.

But he also couldn't imagine that one night being all they ever had. He just couldn't. He would be replaying the memories of her lips on his until he saw her again—while kicking himself for setting the *I don't come until you do* rule. There was edging, and there was *edging*. He must be a goddamned masochist.

But he and Jasmine would figure it out together. And he'd get to spend more time with her, which was quickly becoming his favorite thing to do. It was a win-win in his eyes.

"I'm going to make more tea. Do you want anything?" he asked as he stood up, but Maggie said nothing. When he turned to her, she was staring at him with a raised eyebrow. "What?"

"Jazz has been my best friend for a long time," she said, doing nothing to help his confusion.

"Yes…"

"Which means, even if she wasn't the only person you spent the weekend with, I'd recognize her handy work."

She nodded toward his now-exposed collar bone. Liam frowned, peering down. "What are you—oh." He turned to the mirror and paused at the purple and red bruise decorating his skin. She'd given him a hickey. Jesus. Why was that so hot?

"It's not what it looks like," he said quickly.

"It looks like a hickey."

Liam grimaced. "Ah. Well, in that case, it does appear to be what it looks like."

He absolutely did not want to have this conversation with Maggie. Jasmine probably would want to talk to her about it, and he had no problem with that, but that didn't mean *he* wanted to. But Maggie closed her laptop, which meant they were talking whether he wanted to or not.

"I take it you haven't spoken to Jazz?" he asked, and she shook her head. "And I also take it you're not going to let this go until we talk about it?"

"You know me so well."

Liam snorted, pulling his phone out to check the time. "It's basically lunchtime. Should we talk over lunch?"

"God yes, I'd kill for Italian food."

"That works for me."

Maggie jumped up and headed for the door, sliding her feet into the paint-flecked sneakers she kept there.

Liam started to put his phone back in his pocket when it lit up.

> Am I the only one struggling not to fall asleep today?????

A smile stretched over his face as he read her text. He was suddenly a little less tired.

> Definitely not the only one. Pretty sure I've sprained my jaw from yawning so much.

> I'm going to be good and not make a joke about sprained jaws here.

> Actually...

Speaking of, when are you coming over?

What a segue.

When do you want me?

Days ending with Y?

Shut up.

Stop being so charming.

It's unbearable.

But also I like it.

Tomorrow?

Usually, when people sent every sentence as a new message, instead of just writing a paragraph, it pissed him off, but Jasmine sent them in such quick succession that he was never waiting more than a couple of seconds for the next. She texted like she spoke: like she had too much to say and not enough time to say it. It was adorable.

"Do you want me to pretend you're not just standing there giving my best friend heart eyes through the phone?"

Liam looked up at Maggie and frowned. "I'm a thirty-seven-year-old man. I'm not *giving heart eyes*. What the fuck does that even mean?"

"Wow. You have never sounded more like your dad."

"Are you calling me old?"

"Are you calling my husband old?"

"Yes, Maggie. Your husband is old."

She glared at him. "Liam."

"What?"

"Lunch. Talking. My best friend giving you a hickey. Remember?"

"Right. Yeah, give me a sec."

He looked back at his phone. *Tomorrow?* He swallowed.

Tomorrow sounds good.

He hesitated before sending another.

You gave me a hickey, by the way.

That's hot.

It is. But Maggie saw it and she knows it was you. Pretty sure she's going to grill me over lunch.

Better you than me!

Give stepmommy my best

Enjoy your lunch :)

Liam's heart thudded. A smiley face. That's all it took for him to want to call off work, swing by his dad's office, and steal her away.

Thanks, darling. Have a good day :)

He locked his phone and tucked it in his back pocket, looking up to find Maggie watching him with a concerned expression.

"What?"

She rolled her eyes and sighed dramatically. "You're going to make me my best friend's stepmother-in-law, aren't you?"

Maggie took a long sip of her wine and set it down. Another perk of not working at the museum anymore: a glass of wine here and there with lunch. *Working lunches*, Maggie called them. They usually followed meetings with difficult clients or supplier fuck ups.

"So," she said, folding her hands in front of her. "How was the wedding? I know seeing them must have been hard."

Liam paused, his glass an inch from his lips. He'd been expecting her to jump straight into a conversation about Jasmine.

He took a swig, then swirled the Pinot Grigio around the glass. "It wasn't as bad as I thought it was going to be. The wedding itself was really fucking tacky, and India and Bart… I don't know, I guess seeing them together just made me realize that they're not really the kind of people I want in my life anyway."

"It's their loss," she said, her sapphire eyes flashing with ire for India and Bart. God help them if they ever met.

"It's taken me a while to figure it out, but I wasn't happy back then. I was just forcing myself into a mold, trying to be more like the people I grew up with, and that's not who I am."

Maggie reached across the table and squeezed his hand once. "I'm proud of you. And at least you got a good dinner out of going."

"True," he agreed with a laugh.

"Did you speak to them?"

"Yeah. I was trying to avoid them, but they found Jazz when she was coming back from the restroom, and I figured I shouldn't leave her to deal with them alone." He'd considered it, but he was sure that would have worked out worse for India and Bart than Jazz. "She was amazing," he admitted, feeling his cheeks warm. "She's so effortlessly petty."

Maggie laughed, rolling her eyes. "She's always been like that. I know she did something to my ex, but I haven't been brave enough to ask what."

"Thank god she's on our sides."

Maggie raised her glass. "Cheers to that."

A server bustled over, setting down plates of steaming pasta, and Liam's mouth watered as he breathed in the smoky mushrooms, garlic, and onion in his tagliatelle.

Maggie hummed happily around a forkful of her lunch, chasing it with a sip of wine before saying, "So… Jazz."

He took his time, twirling his pasta around his fork before answering. "What do you want to know? I assume you don't want details."

"Christ, no."

Liam hid his smile behind his pasta as he took a bite. Had Maggie noticed how quickly she'd adopted a little bit of an Irish lilt from his dad with certain words?

"We're just… having fun," he offered, the explanation sounding half-hearted even to his ears.

"So you're sleeping together. Casually." She raised a brow.

"I guess you could call it that."

"Hmm."

"What's that supposed to mean?"

"Casual sex didn't exactly stay casual for me and your dad," she pointed out, and Liam grimaced. He didn't want to think about that.

"We're not you."

"No, you're not. But I also don't believe it's casual for you. I've seen how you look at her—how you've always looked at her. The only person who doesn't seem to know how you feel about Jazz is Jazz."

Jesus, had he really been that transparent? Fuck. "Okay, yes. I have feelings for her. I like spending time with her," he said, carefully. "And by some miracle she likes spending time with me, so—"

"Whoa. What does that mean? Why wouldn't she like spending time with you?" Maggie looked personally offended on his behalf that anyone might not enjoy spending time with him. But Liam still couldn't quite wrap his head around the fact that Jasmine was on board with his proposition.

"Nothing. I'm just saying we like spending time together and we're having fun right now. That's all."

"I don't want to see you get your heart broken again," Maggie said quietly, her face full of concern. A warm feeling settled over him.

"That's not going to happen. You don't have to worry."

"Of course I'm going to worry. I love you both."

"And we both love you. But it's going to be fine. I promise."

Maggie's concerned expression didn't shift, but she nodded, sitting back in her chair. "I have an awful feeling I'm about to learn a lot more about you than I want or need to know. You know Jazz isn't going to keep the details to herself."

He winced. As much as Liam didn't want Maggie knowing anything, he hoped Jasmine would tell her, if only so she finally told her about her lack of orgasms. "Let's just agree that you and I will never talk about it."

"Deal. As long as you're happy."

"I am. I promise." He'd be happier tomorrow, when he finally saw Jasmine. A day apart already felt like a year.

I don't think it's casual for you.

When it came to Jasmine, *casual* wasn't an option.

CHAPTER NINE

Jazz

Jazz spun around, taking in Liam's apartment while Liam made tea and pretended he wasn't watching her, gauging her reactions to his place. She hadn't been here since she'd helped Maggie and Cal pack up Cal's stuff to move out, and Liam had made the place his own.

When Cal had lived in the Seattle penthouse, it'd looked like any old millionaire bachelor's apartment. Now, it looked like Liam. He'd painted the walls a soft, warm brown, covered the mahogany floors with plush rugs, and a giant modular couch took up the center of the room. From its configuration, she could tell Liam used it as a cozy reading nook—he had it set up almost like a bed, with a bunch of blankets and fuzzy pillows. His Kindle was resting on the arm of the couch, and he had no TV that she could see.

Any wall that wasn't lined with a bookshelf was covered in art. Liam didn't seem to favor any particular style— contemporary pieces were hung beside prints of classic paintings. It shouldn't work, but everything he'd chosen complimented each other perfectly. That was his thing, she supposed. She'd never made it to the Seattle Art Museum to see the exhibits he'd worked on before he'd been fired, but she wouldn't know a good art piece from a T.J. Maxx special anyway. What she did know was that Liam had a beautiful eye. Unsurprisingly.

"What do you think?"

Jazz paused her perusal of his bookcases and peered over her shoulder just in time to see Liam setting their tea down on the coffee table. She didn't understand his preference for tea over coffee, and he would never convert her entirely, but she could admit he made a nice cup.

"It feels cozy. Like you. I like it."

Liam smiled, and she ignored the way her stomach fluttered in response.

"No TV?" she asked, taking a seat beside him on the couch and almost groaning with the way her body sank into it.

He nodded toward a summer landscape in a gold frame that was hung on the wall in front of the couch. "That's the TV. But I don't really watch it—I just switch the art up when I want a change."

Jazz sighed, shaking her head at him.

"What?" he asked.

"That should've sounded fucking pretentious, but it just *works* when you say it. Fucking Michaelsons."

"For someone so eager to become one, you sure complain about us Michaelsons a lot."

"No family should be so perfect. I can't even blame the

Michaelson DNA since your moms are perfect too. And Maggie. I bet if you actually tried to marry me, the Ghost of Michaelsons Past would show up the night before and warn you against ruining the family name."

Liam rolled his eyes. "Wow. The Ghost of Michaelsons Past sounds like a judgmental cunt."

"I don't think you're supposed to call your ancestors cunts," she said and Liam just laughed. Her stomach did the weird fluttery thing again, and she looked away. "You have a lot of books." It wasn't a subtle subject change, but Liam didn't seem to notice.

"This isn't even all of them. There's another bookcase in the bedroom. You know how much I read."

"Yeah, but I've never seen you read an actual book. You're always reading on your Kindle."

"I prefer reading on my Kindle so I can change the font, but when I finish a book, I usually end up buying a paperback too. Like a trophy. Besides, a lot of romance covers aren't reading-in-public friendly."

The golden light shining through the floor to ceiling windows illuminated Liam like an angel. A *blushing* angel. From his cheeks to the tips of his ears, he was bright red.

Jazz grinned. "Liam Michaelson, are you embarrassed of the fact you read steamy books?"

"No," he spluttered. "I just don't need to be out there scandalizing the people of Seattle."

"Hmm. I suppose not. You can scandalize me instead. Maybe I'll make you read me a bedtime story."

Liam perked up. "Does that mean you're staying over tonight?"

Jazz rarely stayed over after sober hook ups. If she *could* drive home, she did. She slept like the dead, and even she was sensible enough not to be so vulnerable around people she didn't know. But she knew Liam, she was safe with him, and this wasn't exactly a one-time thing. It was a whole ass arrangement she'd been avoiding thinking about because she still couldn't quite wrap her head around Liam wanting to do this. "Do you want me to stay?"

He nodded. "I do. Sex can be intense at the best of times." Intense wasn't Jazz's experience: frustrating and disappointing were more like it. But that's why she was here, wasn't it? She had no doubts Liam would just end up frustrated and disappointed too, but he couldn't say she hadn't warned him.

"I would prefer to keep you close so I can check on you and make sure you're okay," Liam finished.

It was hard to argue when he sounded so genuine. "Okay, sure."

"I won't force you to cuddle or anything. Although I do like cuddling. You can stay in the guest room while you're here, and I can crash on the couch at your place, if that makes you more comfortable. I just need to know you're okay."

Aftercare *was* the cornerstone of healthy sex, and it wasn't entirely foreign to Jazz. It was better with women, she'd learned over the years. Rarely had a man spent time making sure she was okay after sex—hell, most of the time they didn't reciprocate when Jazz asked if *they* were okay. Even those who liked to cuddle usually did so in silence before falling asleep and leaving her to navigate her way out of whatever messy apartment she'd found herself in.

Of course Liam wasn't like that. They'd both been wasted the first time they'd been together, and he'd still taken the time to make sure she was okay, to rub her back and tuck her in close to him. And despite her lack of orgasm, she'd liked it.

"Cuddling is good with me. At least I know you don't snore," she pointed out.

Liam laughed, rolling his eyes. "Yeah, but you do."

"Oh, I know. But you already invited me to cuddle, so that's your problem now."

"I don't mind. You're a pretty cute snorer."

"Excellent, I'll add that to my resume. Should we set some rules for this… arrangement?" Maggie and Cal had ground rules when they started sleeping together, but Jazz didn't think Liam would want to hear about that. Not that what Liam and Jazz were doing was anything like Maggie and Cal. Those two had been inevitable from the first kiss, and Jazz would be surprised if this thing between her and Liam lasted a week.

"Sure. Did you have any in mind?" Liam asked, finishing his tea and setting the empty cup aside. Jazz snatched hers up before it got cold. She took a sip: lukewarm. This was why she stuck to iced coffee.

She wracked her brain. This was the kind of thing she usually spoke to Maggie about—not that she'd ever done anything like this before. Unless you counted situationships, and she absolutely did not count situationships. But she couldn't exactly call her best friend up and say, *"Hey, I know I said Liam and I weren't going to sleep together again, but we both know I was lying and now we have an arrangement where he's going to help me orgasm after a ten-year orgasm-drought. Any ideas to stop this going up in flames?"*

Instead, she just shrugged. "I can't think of any."

"We can talk things out and add rules as they come up," Liam suggested, and she nodded. At some point, she was going to have to talk to Maggie about this. Probably sooner rather than later.

"Do you have any?"

"Just one. Wait here a sec." Liam stood and strode across the room. With his back to her, Jazz didn't even pretend not to be checking out the long lines of his back. He really was quite beautiful. Tall, but not so tall she had to strain her neck trying to kiss him. He was a little lanky, not muscly enough to suggest he worked out often, but she'd seen him carrying heavy pieces of furniture for Maggie, so he was strong.

He bent down to rummage around in a cabinet in the kitchen and Jazz sat up taller so she could check out his ass. The man could really wear a pair of... cargo pants? Jesus, he was wearing cargo pants. In no world were cargo pants hot, but on Liam? Fuck.

Liam turned around before she had a chance to look nonchalant, a small tote bag clutched in his hand. A smirk danced around the edges of his mouth. "Are you checking me out?"

"Yes," she said, brazenly. No point in pretending when he'd caught her red-handed.

"What's the verdict?"

"Thumbs up," she answered as Liam rejoined her on the couch and set the bag down—up close, she could see it was printed with a black cat wearing a beret and holding a paintbrush.

"A glowing review," he said with a chuckle. From the bag, he withdrew a small chalkboard, a duster, and a box of colored chalk.

"Why do you own a chalkboard?" Jazz asked, hypocritically, since she'd dabbled in chalk art herself. And by dabbled, she meant she'd spent a hundred dollars on supplies, three hours watching YouTube videos, and only ten minutes trying the craft.

"I thought I'd be more likely to stick to a grocery list if I made it more aesthetically pleasing, but I kept forgetting to take a picture before going to the grocery store, so I just do it on my phone now. And I still never stick to my list," Liam replied with a shrug. Honestly, she was impressed that he even made lists. Jazz grocery shopped based purely on vibes. Which is why she ended up ordering takeout so often.

Liam grabbed a piece of mostly intact chalk from the box and chewed the inside of his lip in concentration as he wrote something. He turned the chalkboard around, and Jazz snorted as she read the neat, orange cursive,

"Rule number one," Liam said. "No faking it."

CHAPTER TEN

Liam

He leaned in the doorway, watching Jasmine walk into his bedroom, look up at the ceiling, and stop in her tracks.

"Wow. You know, with anyone else, the combination of the mustache and above-bed mirror would be creepy. Why does it work for you?" She glanced at him with a mock-frown before looking back up. "I need to tell Maggie about this. She and Cal would lov—sorry."

Liam groaned. "Can we make it a rule that you don't talk about my dad and Maggie having sex?"

"We can try, but I'm not going to make a promise I already know I'm going to break."

"Great." He knew her too well to think she'd stop, *could* stop, but it was worth a shot.

Jasmine continued her perusal of his room, her eyes scanning every inch. But as she ran a finger over the spines on his bookcase, Liam realized she was shaking.

"Hey."

Instinct made him wrap his arms around her from

behind, holding her to his chest. It wasn't until she was actually in his arms that he considered they might not be *there*. Yet. If they ever would be.

Fuck it. He'd started digging his hole. He might as well keep going. "Are you okay?" he murmured, his breath making her hair flutter.

She relaxed into his body, and relief flooded him. "Of course. I'm fine," she said, her voice lifting on the last word.

"You want to try that again?"

Jasmine blew out a long breath that vibrated through him. "I am. I'm just a little nervous." She spun in his hold, but didn't move out of his grip. She absentmindedly smoothed a wrinkle in his sweatshirt. "What if I can't do it?" Her voice was small, quiet. When she looked up at him, doubt was etched in her hazel eyes. "We should set a time limit. Or at least a time limit on *you* not coming. I've heard you can die from that."

He hated that she was nervous, but he couldn't help smiling at how fucking cute she was. "That's definitely not true. And you can do it. *We* can do it."

"So you have a plan?"

"Of course I have a plan."

"Care to enlighten me?"

"Nope. Just trust me, darling. I've got this."

He did not have a plan. In fact, he had no idea how he was going to get Jasmine out of a ten-year orgasm drought, but it started with making sure she was comfortable. He hadn't entirely discounted that it might be a medical issue— doctors rarely took women's health seriously—but it was entirely possible it was a mental block. Fuck knows. But he'd be damned if he couldn't do this for her.

"I trust you," Jasmine replied softly, and Liam's blood hummed in response. "So where do we start?"

"We start at the beginning. Talk to me about what you're into."

"What I'm into?"

"Mhmm. I'm, as you so aptly put it, a *pleasure dom*—" The term was corny as fuck, even if it was accurate. "What's your thing? Everyone has that one thing that turns them on more than anything else."

"Oh. Uh…"

He tugged her away from the bookcase, undoing the buttons of her shirt dress as he led her toward the bed. Pushing the dress from her shoulders, Liam tried not to run his fingers all over her the second it dropped to the floor. He failed, of course, but the point was *he tried*.

His legs hit the edge of the bed and he sat down, tugging her onto his lap. Jasmine lifted her legs, and Liam ran his palm along her thighs, her skin silky beneath his hand. He knew they had to take it slow, had to figure out what did and didn't work for her, but god, he couldn't wait to get those thighs wrapped around his head again.

Liam had known what he liked since the first time he'd made someone come. He'd been seventeen, fumbling, and it had taken longer than was probably reasonable for him to figure out where exactly to touch India, but as soon as he'd figured it out, he'd been obsessed.

He and India had been each other's firsts, a one-night summer thing during their trip to the Maldives. They stayed friends through the rest of their high school and college days, but they didn't start dating until their late twenties, and in the decade in between his first time with India and their first date, Liam had fallen even more in love with making people fall apart.

"Jasmine," he prompted, and her eyes flicked from the hand on her thigh to his face. "What's your thing?"

She was quiet for a moment, wringing her hands, before saying, "I like being told what to do, but I like not doing it more."

Liam chuckled, and Jasmine raised a curious brow. "Nothing has ever been less surprising than you being a brat, darling."

"I'm not a brat," she said indignantly, but her hazel eyes glittered. "I just like pushing buttons—especially yours." She punctuated her point by wriggling around on his lap until he gripped her hips firmly, stilling her. He would never admit it, but it wouldn't take much for her to break his *no coming until she did* rule. He was used to fairly regular sex, and even more regular masturbation. Jasmine, sitting in his lap after several days of not coming, was torture. Beautiful fucking torture.

"And you're so good at it," he told her through gritted teeth. "Like I said: *brat.*"

She rolled her eyes, but Liam felt the way she shifted in his lap—no longer trying to tease him, but searching for friction. Jasmine liked being called a brat. Interesting.

"What else do you like?"

"I like pain, especially as a punishment. But I cry easily, which I don't care about, but it bothers some people. I'm good with most toys and anal, and I'm really into bondage, as long as I feel safe with the person. Which obviously I do with you." Obviously. She said it so casually, like it didn't make Liam's heart swell.

He swallowed the lump in his throat, clearing it before replying. "Good. That's all good." She liked everything he did. Of course she did. "What don't you like?"

She rolled her neck, stretching out like a cat, and, though having her sitting on his lap probably wasn't the most comfortable position for them to have this conversation, he wasn't letting go until she did.

"Role-play isn't a *no*," she said. "But I can't take it seriously and it tends to piss people off when I laugh." Liam couldn't imagine her laughing ever pissing him off. "I don't like group stuff. I'm too possessive for that," she continued. "And I really don't like praise, or worship, or anything too… nice. Both inside and outside of bed."

That was interesting. And potentially difficult. Liam usually followed up any kind of degrading dirty talk with praise, but he could adjust. Even if there was definitely something to unpack there.

"I can work with that. Anything else?"

"Oh yeah, I would prefer not to be peed on, but if that's a must, then the shower is my preference."

Somehow, she continued to surprise him. "I'm not going to pee on you. Even in the shower. I promise."

"Perfect. Anything I should know about you?"

"It sounds like we're into the same kinds of things. I like to focus on the line between pleasure and pain a lot. And I can be a little vocal, especially if someone is pushing my buttons." He tapped her on the nose.

Jasmine raised a brow, her eyes glimmering with interest. "Dirty talk?"

"Sometimes, yeah. And I tend to lean on the, uh, firmer side, I guess. So if there's anything you don't like, or I ever make you uncomfortable, please talk to me. You being okay and comfortable is my number one priority, but I need you to talk to me about how you're feeling."

Jasmine wrinkled her nose. "I'm not great about talking about how I feel."

"Rule number two, darling." Liam tilted her chin, hoping it was clear how serious he was from his face. "Talking about how you feel isn't optional."

"Ugh, fine. If I have to."

"You do. I'll add it to the chalkboard later."

She rolled her eyes, and Liam could already tell he was going to have his work cut out for him on that one. Hopefully, with time, she'd be more open with him.

"You listen to podcasts while you work, right?" he asked. They'd listened to podcasts on the drive to California, and Jasmine often talked about her favorites at family dinner.

"Pretty much whenever I'm not in a meeting, yeah. Why?"

"I'm giving you homework," he said, making a mental list. "Having a good idea of what you're into is great, but I want to figure out what gets you closest to being able to come. Like where's the line, you know? I'm going to give you some audiobooks to listen to."

"You're suggesting I listen to erotic audiobooks at work? Where I'm your dad's assistant?" She didn't look remotely put off by the idea. If anything, she curled in closer to him

"How would he find out?"

Jasmine pursed her lips. "True. And I guess, even if he did, he wouldn't have a leg to stand on given everything he and Maggie—"

Liam covered her mouth with his hand, groaning. "No. Absolutely not." When he pulled his hand away, she was grinning. "You did it on purpose that time, didn't you?"

"Maybe I like trying to rile you up."

Her low voice went straight to his cock, and Jasmine smirked like she knew exactly what she was doing. "You don't have to try, darling." He pressed a ghost of a kiss behind her ear and she shuddered.

"Is this graded homework?"

"It's pass/fail."

She sighed dramatically. "Damn. I was hoping for extra credit."

He shook his head, burying his laugh against her neck. "I'll figure something out for extra credit. Anything else you want to talk about before we get started tonight?"

"No," she said, quickly and breathlessly. "What's the plan for tonight?"

"We're getting started on figuring out what gets you close." He patted her lightly on the ass. "Get on the bed and wait for me. I'll be back in a sec."

"Underwear on or off?" she shouted behind him as he walked away.

"Off," he called back, amazed that he kept his voice steady, knowing that she was stripping in his bedroom. God. His bedroom.

He grabbed his laptop from the dining table, the two packages of gummies he'd picked up after work, and headed back to the bedroom. He knew Jasmine favored a joint or an edible over a drink when she wanted to relax.

Liam stilled in the bedroom doorway. Jasmine was lying on her front, her chin propped up on her elbow as she scrolled through her phone. She peered over her shoulder at him. "Are you just going to stand and stare, or…?"

His gaze trailed the curve of her frame. She belonged in a goddamned museum. But saying that would definitely go against her *no praise* rule, so Liam bit his tongue. He took a deep breath, forcing himself to walk into the room and *not* make an immediate beeline for the bed to take a bite of her perfect ass.

"Wild cherry or pink lemonade?" he asked, holding up the bags. He regretted it the second Jasmine turned, and keeping his hands to himself suddenly became a thousand times harder.

"Ooh." Her eyes lit up as she scanned the bags. "Cherry, please."

He tossed her the bag, and she tore the top off while he set the laptop on the bed and pulled his sweatshirt over his head. When she realized he was undressing, she put the bag down and blatantly watched him, his skin warming under her gaze.

She didn't look away until he lay down beside her, when she held up the bag. "Half or whole?"

"Are you still okay staying over?" She nodded. "Whole," he confirmed. "I want you nice and relaxed."

"Open up."

He opened his mouth, and Jasmine dropped a square gummy on his tongue. Sour cherry flooded his senses, and he screwed up his face, quickly chewing and swallowing. "Jesus."

Jasmine smirked, eating hers with ease as he picked his laptop up. "Are we watching a movie? Oh, let me guess! That Pearl Earring one with Colin Firth. I bet that one turns you on."

"It's Colin Firth, of course it turns me on. Who isn't into him? Even my moms love him."

"Straight men?" Jasmine suggested, and Liam shrugged, typing the web address into his browser.

"Surely even straight men find Colin Firth hot? Anyway, no, funnily enough I didn't tell you to take your underwear off so we could watch that kind of movie."

He turned his laptop toward her, and her eyes widened, a sweet laugh bubbling from her lips.

"We're watching porn?"

Liam nodded, setting the laptop on a pillow between them. Though he preferred romance books to porn, it had its place, and his favorite website—a queer-owned, ethical website with a focus on sexual empowerment—had the perfect thing for him and Jasmine to get started with. It was a program designed to help people figure out what kind of porn they might enjoy, and what kinds of things they might want to try out, through short-form videos that started more vanilla and escalated as you worked through them.

He explained the concept to Jasmine, who simply fluffed the pillows behind her and lay back, getting comfortable. "Alright. Let's do this."

Liam threaded his fingers with hers. "You're lefthanded, right?"

"Yeah."

"Perfect. I'm going to hold this hand, and when what we're watching starts to turn you on, I want you to touch yourself with your left." He would be watching her reactions, but he wanted to feel her squeezing his hand when something turned her on.

"I will if you will," she replied, her eyes flicking down his body. She licked her lips and Liam counted to three.

"Fine, but I'm not going to come."

"Yeah, me either," she joked.

"Even if you think you might, you're not allowed," he told her, and her eyes fell to his, her mouth dropping open.

"Not that it's going to happen, but doesn't that kind of defeat the purpose of this whole arrangement?"

"You're supposed to be trusting me, remember?"

She scoffed. "Fine."

"Oh, and other than this," he squeezed their joined hands, "you're not allowed to touch me."

"Worried I'm going to make you come before I do?" she asked with a smirk.

Liam's fingers twitched with the urge to touch her, to put her over his fucking knee. She didn't miss the movement, her smirk widening. Yeah, she knew exactly how to push his buttons. But she could push all she wanted; he wasn't going to break. She was. That was the point of this little exercise. Watching porn, touching themselves, Liam knew it was only a matter of time before she snapped, and he wanted to know what her final straw was. He just had to survive that long.

"Jasmine."

"Hmm?"

"Behave."

"Yes, sir," she sassed, rolling her eyes.

Liam clocked the moment Jasmine moved from just *watching* to *feeling*. They were three videos in, the edibles lulling them into a state of calm, when the actors on the screen started getting rougher, and Jasmine's chest started rising and falling a little faster. Her right hand gripped his a little tighter, and he squeezed it.

She looked over at him, her cheeks just turning pink.

"Touch yourself, darling."

She drew her lip between her teeth. "You first."

Liam fought a laugh, shaking his head. "No. Do as you're told."

Jasmine opened her mouth to protest, but her eyes snapped back to the laptop as the sound of a smack echoed from the speakers. When Liam followed her gaze, it was to see a woman holding her partner over her knee, smacking her ass. The woman being spanked writhed on her lap, and, defiance be damned, Jasmine slipped her fingers between her legs.

Her head dropped back against the pillows automatically, but she caught herself, forcing herself to sit up a little more so she could watch the couple on the screen.

Liam sat up and grabbed a spare pillow from the armchair, tucking it behind her head. She gave him a grateful smile before her attention turned back to the screen. A small whimper bubbled from her lips as she grazed her clit with her fingers. She spread her legs further, her calf colliding with his, and Liam swallowed as he watched her fingers moving over her body. Her deep purple nails were the perfect contrast to her pale skin.

She turned to look at him, staring pointedly at his cock and pausing her movements until he wrapped his fist around it. He almost winced at how sensitive he was. It wasn't going to be easy to hold back.

Jasmine's eyes darkened as she watched him draw his fist up and down his cock.

"Eyes on the screen," he instructed, his voice gravelly. She rolled her eyes, but she looked back toward the screen.

Liam's focus darted from Jasmine to the videos, watching her touch herself harder, faster, during the videos she enjoyed most. As expected, she slowed down during the threesome, and she actively wrinkled her nose at the video of someone jerking someone else off with their feet. It was so cute, Liam fought the urge to reach over and kiss the tip of her nose.

He made a mental note of the things she seemed to like most based on how hard she squeezed his hand.

Anal, spanking, impact play, bondage, degradation, and a little bit of gentle sadism.

It was as he'd expected from what she'd told him, but hearing her tell him what she was into versus seeing her reactions were two very different ballgames. And he had to make sure she wasn't just telling him what she thought he wanted to hear. He'd had partners in the past who'd told him they were into the same things he was, and Liam had been able to tell within five minutes they were uncomfortable.

There was a fine line between pleasure and pain, and making someone come over and over again until they were begging and crying for mercy brought him more pleasure than anything else. But only if the other person was into it as much as he was.

Though Jasmine had been edging closer and closer to him throughout the videos she enjoyed most, her breath caught in her throat as she watched the man on screen slapping his partner's cheek before softly stroking his thumb over the red mark, and, just like that, Liam knew it was game over.

He didn't even have time to blink before she was on him, straddling his hips and cursing against his mouth as her tongue slipped between his lips in a fierce kiss. He groaned at the taste of cherry on her tongue. Jasmine pulled away, running a finger over the head of his cock, the videos playing in the background long forgotten. She positioned herself so she could drag her body along the length of him, and Liam had to fist the covers as the cool metal of her piercing glided over his cock.

Jasmine looked down at him with a wicked smile. She had the upper hand here, and she knew it. He'd made a terrible mistake thinking he could hold off—he was so fucking close already.

He grabbed her hips, his fingers digging into her ass, and pulled her up his body until her knees were on either side of his face. But she sat up on her knees, too far away for him to get his mouth on her.

"Jasmine," he warned. "Are you going to sit down and be good, or am I going to have to make you?"

"Hmm, decisions, decisions…"

"Option B, then." Liam gripped her ass harder and pulled her down onto his face, closing his lips around her clit. Jasmine cried out, her hand slamming against the headboard. Whatever ideas she had to fight back died as Liam flicked his tongue over her clit, and Jasmine rolled her hips against his face, riding him. She was a fucking dream.

Her thighs trembled on either side of his head, her moans falling faster and breathier the closer he brought her to the edge. But Liam was serious about not letting her come yet. He didn't think she was ready, but she was close.

He moved quickly, lifting her from his face and spinning them until she was lying on her back and he was pinning her to the mattress between his thighs. She tried to wriggle her way out, huffing indignantly, but Liam held firm. He reached back to grab his laptop from where it teetered precariously on the edge of the bed, closed it, and set it on the nightstand beside Jasmine's head.

As he leaned down to brush a kiss over her mouth, she stilled for a moment, breathing him in. She knotted her hands in his hair, holding him to her, stealing his breath. It was all a ploy, of course, to distract him enough so she could wriggle out from under him. But Liam saw right through her, his thigh muscles straining to hold her down.

"I think I learned everything I need to know," he whispered against her ear, before calling on every ounce of self-control he possessed and swinging his leg over her, and getting off the bed. "I like chamomile tea before I sleep—do you want some?"

Jasmine glared at him like he'd grown another head. "Are you fucking kidding me?"

"What? It's very calming, and it seems like you could use that."

He laughed as he walked away, and Jasmine threw a pillow after him, cursing him out as it smacked him on the ass.

CHAPTER ELEVEN

Jazz

Liam was definitely onto something with the audiobook thing. Holy shit. Jazz had never had such a fun day at work. She'd spent the whole morning plugged into the audiobook he'd recommended—a dark, BDSM romance that hooked her from the first chapter. Was it a little weird to be sitting in Cal's office, working away on her laptop while listening to a filthy audiobook his son had told her to listen to? Definitely, but as far as Cal was concerned, she was listening to a podcast.

Movement caught her eye and Jazz looked up, knowing who had just walked into the office before she'd even paused the book. Only one person made Cal jump to his feet that quickly, his eyes lighting up. They were like fucking magnets.

Jazz begrudgingly turned the book off and removed her headphones.

"Hi, love," Cal said, standing and tugging Maggie into his arms the second she reached the desk.

Jazz rolled her eyes, smiling at them before looking

resolutely away from Maggie and Cal as they made out in front of her. She was used to this. And she knew why Maggie was here; the longer she spent making out with Cal, the less time she'd have to grill Jazz. Maybe she could use this time to sneak away… But that would only delay the conversation. It was coming, whether she wanted it or not.

"Ahem," she said, when she started to suspect Maggie and Cal were seconds from ripping their clothes off in front of her. "Please be mindful of the other people in the room before you start climbing each other."

Neither of them looked remotely embarrassed when they broke apart.

"Why didn't you tell me you were coming, love?" Cal offered no apology as he took his seat and unabashedly patted his lap in invitation. Maggie looked longingly and sighed before shaking her head.

She held up a bag of subs from their favorite sandwich place. "I can't. I'm here for Jazz, I'm afraid."

"You're afraid?" Jazz replied indignantly, while Cal raised a brow at the bag.

"I thought you seemed cheery this morning," he said. "Good night?" It had been their college tradition for them to debrief their hookups with subs in their cars, and it was a tradition Cal was all too familiar with considering Jazz had once brought subs to the office to debrief Maggie on *their* first night together.

Fucking hell. She fought to keep a straight face as she looked at the father of the man who'd had his tongue all over her last night. "Yep." She tried her best to look noncha-lant. Under no circumstances did Cal need to know about this. She set her laptop on his desk and grabbed her purse from the back of her chair. "Let's do this."

"We'll need to sit in your car. I was working at a site nearby, so I walked over," Maggie said.

"Ah, what a shame. I got a ride this morning." She didn't elaborate—they didn't need to know she'd forgotten to fill her gas tank again. It was bordering on embarrassing how often she forgot. Usually, she had to call Cal and ask him to pick her up on the way to work, but Liam had been more than happy to drive her, promising they'd grab a can of gas and swing by to pick her car up after she finished work. Since he was picking her up anyway, they were going to her apartment tonight, and she would be lying if she said she wasn't hoping he'd spend the night. She'd slept like a damn log in his arms after she'd gotten over her frustration.

And now she had an excuse not to sit in the car with Maggie. If they sat in the kitchen downstairs, she wouldn't be able to ask her about Liam.

"Use my car," Cal offered, grabbing his key fob from the desk and handing it to Maggie. "Do you need a ride home, Jazz?"

"I'm good. Thanks," she said through semi-gritted teeth while Maggie hid her smile behind her hair.

She headed for the door while Maggie and Cal said a highly inappropriate goodbye.

Maggie and Jazz stood in silence as the elevator dropped them down into the parking garage. The silence, awkward on Jazz's side, seemed almost amusing on Maggie's, if the way her lip kept twitching was anything to go by.

The parking garage, while full of cars, was empty of

people. Maggie slid into Cal's driver's seat while Jazz climbed into the passenger's side, closing the door and sighing as the luxury seats enveloped her. She wasn't a car snob, but she definitely *was* a comfy seat snob.

"Before I forget," Maggie began, rummaging around in her bag and pulling out a manilla folder, "Liam asked me to give you this. He specifically told me I wasn't allowed to look, but resigned himself to the fact that you would show me anyway."

Jazz snorted, some of the tension between her and Maggie crumbling. She was being stupid. Maggie knew she and Liam were sleeping together, and she'd had plenty of opportunity since finding out to call and shout at her if she had that much of a problem with it. Would Jazz have answered? Of course not. But voicemails existed.

She and Maggie were best friends, and best friends gave each other shit for who they slept with. But they still showed up with subs to debrief. Girlhood or whatever.

Jazz turned the folder over in her hand, her stomach fluttering as she read the note in Liam's perfect penmanship.

Extra credit, as promised. L x

She opened the folder and withdrew a stapled bundle of printer paper, snorting as she read the contents. It was a kink list, meant for her to rate them on a scale of one to five—one being the least likely to get her close, five being the most.

She scanned the list, whistling. "You definitely don't want to see this." Fuck knows where Liam had found it, but it was extensive. Maggie sighed and held a hand out, despite her warning.

"You listened to me talk about having sex with Cal for weeks when we first started hooking up—"

"It wasn't a hardship."

"—the least I can do is listen to you now. I've just decided to pretend that Liam *isn't* Cal's kid. As much as I can, anyway." She wrinkled her nose, and Jazz felt a wave of warmth for her best friend. She handed the list over, and Maggie's eyes widened as she read over it.

"Christ. Okay. Just how kinky is he?" she asked, flipping the page.

Jazz hummed. "It's complicated."

Maggie looked up at her, raising a brow in the universal sign for *go on.*

It was time. She'd kept this from Maggie for ten years and that was, frankly, ten years too many. She took a deep breath. "Okay, so Liam's a pleasure dom, which means making people come is kind of his thing, which is great except I haven't been able to orgasm for ten years, and no one has ever noticed me faking it, including Liam the first time because we were both so drunk, but he noticed the second time and is determined to help me learn to come again, so we've struck an arrangement where he isn't going to come until I do and he's trying to help me figure out what I actually like, hence the list." She said it all in one long breath and Maggie stared at her, unblinking.

"That is... a lot to unpack," she said finally, tossing the list on the dash. "You haven't had an orgasm in *ten years*? What the fuck?"

"Yeah." Jazz gave her a weak smile. "I'm sorry I didn't tell you."

"God. Is everything okay? Have you seen a doctor?"

Jazz gave Maggie the same rundown she'd given Liam, explaining her long, orgasmless, decade. By the time she was done, Maggie looked exhausted on her behalf.

"I'm so sorry you've been dealing with this. I wish you'd told me. Hell, you know I see you like a sister, but I would've taken one for the team and given it my best shot."

"What are friends for, if not for offering to help each other come during orgasm droughts," Jazz said and the two of them dissolved into giggles. She and Maggie had kissed only once, in their freshman year of college when Maggie had first come out as bi, to see if there was anything more between them, and they'd immediately known they were meant to be just friends.

When they were both able to breathe properly again, Maggie asked, "Is Liam seriously not going to let himself come until you do?"

"Yeah. It's unhinged."

"Completely. But also weirdly sweet?"

"That too," she agreed, leaning back against the headrest and smiling, staring out into the gray parking garage and thinking of how caring Liam had been with her the night before—how he'd held her in his arms as they both drifted off to sleep. Despite how crazy he was driving her by not letting her make him come—was this how he felt about her? —she'd had a great night. And she *was* going to make him come first.

"Jazz."

She started. "Hmm?" When she turned to look at Maggie, her best friend was staring at her with her brows drawn close. "What?"

"It's not just sex, is it? You have feelings for him."

"I—" Jazz's breath caught in her lungs, and she squeezed her eyes together, forcing the anxiety away. *Where the hell had that come from?*

She almost lied, *no* dancing on the tip of her tongue, but she stopped herself. It felt wrong, somehow, to pretend that what she and Liam had was *just* sex. Did she have feelings for him? Of course not. Not like Maggie meant, anyway. It just felt more muddled because she'd already cared about him before they started sleeping together. They'd always had a connection.

Since that first day when I spotted you at the office, I haven't been able to get you out of my head, Liam had said. She hadn't returned the sentiment, but that didn't mean it wasn't true in reverse.

"It's not just sex, no. But I don't know what exactly it is. And I know it's complicated because we're basically family —in a non-incesty way—but I also don't particularly want to stop doing it."

"I'm not asking you to," Maggie promised. "Just be careful, please? I don't want to see either of you hurt over this."

She didn't want to see Liam hurt, was more like it. There was no world in which Liam could hurt Jazz—he was too perfect. She was the wildcard. "No one is going to get hurt."

Maggie grabbed the bag of subs and handed one over to

Jazz. "Alright. Lay it on me. Lack of orgasm aside, how was it?"

Liam

"I swear I filled in the list. I just don't know where it is," Jasmine groaned, leaning down and rummaging in her bag. It was crammed with stuff, most of which Liam could hardly make out, much like her apartment.

He'd expected chaos, this was Jasmine after all, but he hadn't expected *this*. There was stuff everywhere. Not in a messy way—everything seemed to have a place—there was just a *lot* of everything. Mostly, Liam was surprised to see, crafting supplies. Floor to ceiling cabinets were stuffed with yarn and fabric, containers of beads and clay and paint. There was a stack of canvasses against the wall, still wrapped in plastic, and a sewing machine box that didn't look like it had ever been opened. In the years he'd known her, Jasmine had never once mentioned crafting. And when he'd asked her about it, she'd quickly changed the subject.

He ran a soothing hand over her back. "Did you fill it in at your desk? You probably just left it in your drawer or something."

Jasmine sat up like a shot. "Oh no."

"What?"

"I left it in your dad's car."

"What the fuck?"

Before she could respond, Jasmine's phone lit up where she'd dropped it on her coffee table, half hidden by the box of cereal she'd been snacking on while they waited for their takeout to arrive.

She grabbed it, holding it out so Liam could see the confirmation message from Maggie:

You left your list in Cal's car.

The message was accompanied by photographs of the list, Jasmine's answers included. It was unsurprisingly helpful of Maggie, even if Liam hated that she knew what they were doing. Jasmine's fingers flew across the phone:

Did he recognize Liam's handwriting?

Somehow not.

Thank fuck.

Not a big fan of lying to my husband, for the record.

"Shit," Liam said, frowning at the message. "This really isn't fair to her." He didn't particularly care if his dad found out about him and Jasmine, but he knew she didn't want him to know.

"It's not," Jasmine agreed with a sigh. "I'll be more careful so it doesn't come up. I'm sorry." Her voice was a mix of guilt and panic, and Liam ran his hand over her back, surprised. It wasn't like her to worry so much.

"You don't have to be sorry. It was a mistake, it happens."

"It was a stupid mistake." She turned back to her phone.

> I'm sorry. I love you and we owe you big time!!!!!!!!!

I love you too, and it's fine. He was too distracted by the list to ask too many questions. Going to need a blank copy, please.

"Ugh. I don't need to think about my dad filling that in."

> Liam is reading over my shoulder. Pretty sure you've scarred him LOL

That's what he gets for getting me to hand deliver a damn kink list.

He's suffering enough since he's not letting himself come…

Liam plucked the phone from Jasmine's hand, but not fast enough to stop her from sending the message. Perfect.

"Okay, that's enough of that." He pretended to ignore Jasmine's laugh, swiping up the thread until he found the pictures of her answers, but it flooded his senses, warming his blood. That was more like the Jasmine he knew.

He zoomed in, scanning her answers. Everything was as he'd expected based on the night before, but he hadn't given her the list thinking he'd get any new information. She'd asked for extra credit and there was only so much he could suggest she do at work. And the list was helpful to have a note of her limits. He wanted to be clear on what was and what wasn't okay.

"So what do I get as my reward for extra credit?" Jasmine asked as he scanned the list.

"Whatever you want, darling. Within reason," he added, as she smirked. "You're not going to get me to come."

"I want to at least try." She slid off the couch, sinking to her knees before him. Jesus Christ. Someone, somewhere, was testing him.

"Jasmine—"

"You said whatever I wanted," she reminded him, flicking open the button on his jeans and tugging the zip down, torturously slowly.

"Fuck," was all he could say as she pushed his boxers down and freed his cock. She wrapped her hand around him, warm and soft, and Liam closed his eyes, leaning back against the well-loved gray couch.

"I want you to watch," she said, her voice low and Liam begged the universe for a little self-control as he opened his eyes and looked down at her, just in time for her to bend her head and take him in her mouth.

Fuck, fuck, fuck.

His hips strained with the effort it took not to thrust into her mouth, and Jasmine knew it. She looked up at him through her thick lashes as she fisted the base of his cock, taking him as deep as possible. Liam's eyes threatened to flutter close as she neared the back of her throat—he absolutely couldn't handle her gagging. He was already teetering on the edge of a cliff.

Of course, he needn't have worried about her gagging.

This perfect demon of a woman had been put on the planet with the sole purpose of torturing him and *didn't have a fucking gag reflex*. He was fucked.

It was like every inch of his body was being shocked by electricity as she pulled back, dragging her tongue along his cock, then taking him to the back of her throat. Again. Over and over. She ran one finger over his balls and Liam danced too close to his limit. He sat up, lightly grabbing her chin and halting her.

"No more. I can't," he said, and god, he sounded fucking defeated. Jasmine pouted, but sat back on her knees, licking a drop of his pre-cum from her lips. White noise filled Liam's ears, and he couldn't even fault Jasmine's satisfied smirk. She knew exactly what she was doing to him.

CHAPTER TWELVE

Jazz

Eliza and Danisha lived in a white picket fence dream house in the Seattle suburbs. From the outside, it looked exactly like the house in Marysville, Washington Jazz had grown up in, but she knew a lot more love existed in the four walls of Liam's moms' home. The first time she'd visited, she'd watched Liam interacting with his parents with ease and comfort, and wondered what that felt like. It wasn't jealousy, as much as resignation. She was happy for Liam, she just wished... It didn't matter what she wished. There was no point in thinking about something she couldn't change.

It had been Eliza's idea to start twice monthly Friday night family dinners, alternating between their house and Maggie and Cal's place. Though not technically family, Jazz had been included from the first dinner and, unlike her actual family's dinners, she rarely missed one.

Maggie pulled into their driveway and turned her car off. Jazz and Liam were sitting in the back seat, and Cal, sitting in the passenger's seat on a call with his parents back in Ireland, hadn't taken his hand off Maggie's thigh for even a second of the drive. His silver wedding bands, one on his ring finger, one on his pinky, stood out against Maggie's dark wash jeans, and Jazz watched as her best friend's gaze fell to Cal's hand. A smile curved her mouth, and she lifted his hand to her lips, kissing each ring in turn. Jazz looked away, undoing her seatbelt.

Liam reached across the middle seat, dragging a finger across the back of her hand. Jazz looked at Cal, but he was too focused on his call to pay them any attention.

"Are you coming over tonight?" Liam asked softly.

Jazz didn't think twice before nodding. "But I want you inside me tonight," she replied, just as quietly. Though she and Liam had spent three nights together since she'd almost made him come on her couch with her mouth, he was holding back. He'd had his mouth on her, his tongue and fingers inside her, bringing her right to the edge and stopping before she could even consider stepping off. Because even if she could—which she couldn't—she wasn't allowed to come.

"We're taking it slow. I've got a plan, darling," he said, whenever she glared at him. It was killing her.

Liam shook his head, a wicked smile on his face. God, she wanted to lick his dimples. "Not tonight. I've got plans tonight."

"I hate your plans," she grumbled.

"I promise you'll like these."

His voice skittered over her spine, setting the butterflies that had taken up residence in her stomach aflutter.

"Let's go, you two," Maggie said, closing the car door

behind her. Jazz hadn't even noticed Cal saying goodbye to his parents, let alone him and Maggie getting out of the car.

She shook herself. Her phone rang in her bag just as she reached down to grab it from the footwell. By the time she'd found it, rummaging around the messy depths, whoever was calling had been sent to voicemail.

Thank god, she thought as she finally pulled it out and read the notification on the screen:

Mom

Missed Call

Jazz shoved the phone back in her bag and followed Liam, Maggie, and Cal up Eliza and Danisha's picture-perfect stone path to their front door. She'd call her mom back later. Or tomorrow.

But Lilia Cannon was nothing if not insistent, and before Jazz could even step onto the porch, her phone was ringing again. Three heads swiveled in her direction as she cursed, pulling her phone from her bag again.

"It's my mom. If I don't answer, she's just going to keep calling. I won't be long." Hopefully. She waved them on and, though Liam hesitated, the three of them disappeared through the open front door.

"Hey, Mom," she said, forcing the annoyance out of her voice. "Everything okay?"

"Everything's fine." Her mom sniffed through the phone. Fuck. Jazz could practically hear her frown down the line. "You know, Jazz, your brother follows Maggie's husband on Instagram."

"Okay. That's..." Weird. "Nice."

"He's a very respected man," her mom chastised.

Apparently her skepticism hadn't been as subtle as she'd hoped.

"Cal or Xander?"

"Both."

More confused than ever, Jazz rubbed her eyes before remembering, too late, that she was wearing eye makeup. Shit. "Right. Okay. I'm sorry, I don't really know what we're talking about here."

"What we're talking about is the fact that you have time to take pictures with Maggie's husband and attend *her* family dinners, but not ours. Your actual family."

Ah. She suddenly regretted teaching Cal how to use his Instagram story. "I'm sorry, Mom. It's just that Marysville is a longer drive and—"

"That's not an excuse. Your brother and sister make it every month."

"We can't all be as perfect as Xan and Rose," Jazz replied without thinking.

Her mom was silent for a moment. "I'm not even going to justify that with a response," she said, finally. "Your dad and I expect to see you at dinner tomorrow night. Six o'clock at Reveres."

Jazz clenched her jaw. She had every intention of spending her Saturday night at Liam's apartment, somehow tricking him into watching her favorite reality show and then trying to make him come. The last thing she wanted to do was sit in a fancy restaurant while her parents laid out all the ways she'd disappointed them since she last showed face at a family dinner. Not that she cared. "Mom, I—"

"No buts. And that's not all I wanted to talk to you

about. Your dad was in Seattle for a colleague's retirement dinner last week and he ran into Robert Avery."

"Who?"

"His daughter is India Avery—India Heasman now, I suppose. I hear you attended her wedding. With your *boyfriend*." Jazz winced. Shit. "When exactly were you going to tell us you were dating Maggie's stepson?"

She couldn't tell her mom the truth without getting a lecture on lying, so Jazz sighed and said, "I was going to tell you when I next saw you. I was waiting until things were more serious."

"I assume they're serious now, since you're going to weddings together."

She'd walked right into that one. "Yeah, I guess they are serious."

"And Maggie's okay with this?"

Why the hell would her mom even consider that she would go behind Maggie's back? Maggie was her person. She was Maggie's person. Best friends didn't fuck around like that. "Of course."

"And her husband is okay with it?"

"Of course." He'd been okay with the fake dating, at least.

"And do you love this boy?"

"Of course," Jazz repeated without really listening to the question. When she realized what her mom had asked, her heart skipped. Lying about love felt like a step too far.

"How on earth can you love someone your family hasn't even met, Jazz? I'm so disappointed in you." Her mom was disappointed in her? What a shocking twist of events! Jazz could hardly believe it.

Jesus. Last time they'd spoken, her mom had been begging her to settle down. "Xan and Rose met him at Maggie's wedding." Her parents had been on a month-long vacation to the Caribbean and hadn't been home in time for the wedding. Such a shame.

Her mom tutted. "You'll bring him tomorrow."

Absolutely not. "I'll ask him, but—"

"Tomorrow, Jazz. Six o'clock. I'll see you both there." Her mom hung up the phone before she could answer and Jazz clenched a fist around it.

"That escalated quickly," she muttered under her breath, stomping up the porch steps and taking a deep breath before heading into the house.

"I need you to do something for me."

Liam eyed her warily. "At my moms' house?"

Jazz peered around the living room to make sure no one was listening before answering. "It's not a sexual something."

"Oh. Then why are you looking at me all like," Liam gestured to her face, "that?"

"I think this is just my face."

Liam's expression softened. "It's a good face."

How was she supposed to hold it together when he said

shit like that? "Stop trying to butter me up. I'm trying to ask *you* for a favor." Liam gestured for her to go on. "Apparently my dad knows India's dad and now my parents think we're dating. And I might have made it sound like things were really serious between us on the phone, so I need you to come to family dinner with me tomorrow to meet my parents."

"Is that all? Of course I'll come. I'm great with parents," Liam said, and while Jazz didn't doubt that was usually the case, she needed to prepare him for Alexander and Lilia Cannon.

"Not my parents," she warned.

"They can't be *that* bad."

Jazz turned toward where Maggie was sitting, listening to Eliza and Danisha bickering about their vegetable garden. "Maggie."

She looked up. "Yeah?"

"Tell Liam what my parents are like," she said, and Maggie frowned at the mere mention of them. "He's coming to family dinner tomorrow."

"God help you," Maggie said with a shudder. She leaned toward them. "They go around the table and make everyone talk about their biggest achievement from the past month. And if your achievement isn't good enough, they won't move on until you think of a better one. One time, in college, they grilled me for thirty minutes on why I got a B. And they're not even my parents."

"Wait, *you* got a B?" Liam looked more surprised about Maggie's imperfect GPA than Jazz's parents.

"Shut up. It was *one* B," Maggie growled, glaring at him. "You want to compare GPAs?"

Liam's eyes lit up with the challenge. "Let's do it."

"Children," Danisha admonished, as Maggie and Liam readied themselves to see who could one up the other.

"Please don't call them children," Cal begged. "It's already weird enough."

Liam and Maggie really did act like long-lost siblings, which was a little fucked up, given the actual dynamics of their family. But it was also hilarious. Traditional was overrated.

"You wouldn't win. It was her only B," Jazz told Liam. He frowned but didn't protest. "Either way, she's not exaggerating about my parents. They really are that bad."

Liam glanced between Maggie and Jazz in alarm. "What the hell is going on with parents in Marysville?"

"I thought you avoided dinners with your family?" Eliza asked, frowning.

"I do avoid them, but someone, and I'm not naming names—Cal—posted this on Instagram." She held up her phone, showing the room the selfie Cal had posted from the car with Liam and Jazz behind him, complete with cat-ear filter, and the caption *dinner with the fam!*

Maggie turned to her husband. "Dinner with the *fam*? I love you, but you're too old to be saying that."

"Jazz told me to say it!"

"Jazz is also too old to be saying it," Maggie pointed out and Jazz glared at her. She was only thirty. Maggie needed to lighten up. "I still don't see how this led to you and Liam being roped into dinner with your family. Cal's Instagram is private."

"Apparently Xander follows him."

"Oh yeah, we talk all the time," Cal chimed in while Jazz stared at him open-mouthed. "What? We met at the wedding and we like the same books. Do we not like him? Because if you don't want me to talk to him, I won't," he told Jazz, his tone turning serious. "You're family, Jazz. He's just a man."

"Oh my god." Maggie hid her face in her hands, trying not to laugh. Liam didn't even try, and his moms just looked at each other, confused.

Jazz held a hand up. "Okay, I take full responsibility for teaching him that one. It's cool, Cal. My siblings are only a problem when my parents are involved."

She explained the rest of her conversation with her mom, leaving out the fact that she'd told her she was in love with Liam.

"I guess she's pissed off because I come to family dinner with you all, but not my real family."

"We are your real family," Eliza interjected. "You and Maggie are the daughters we never got to have."

"Again, let's not say things like that," Cal muttered under his breath, frowning at his ex-wife, who pointedly ignored him.

"You know, you and Liam could actually get together and make it official," Danisha said, her tone not entirely teasing.

"Oh, we have big plans for that," Liam joked.

Jazz nodded her agreement. "*Big* plans. Our wedding is

going to blow yours out of the water." She nodded toward Maggie and Cal. "One word—"

She and Liam exchanged a look and said, in perfect unison, "Clowns." They cracked up, doubling over, laughing, Liam's parents not far behind them, but when Jazz looked up, her best friend wasn't laughing.

CHAPTER THIRTEEN

Jazz

"Are you okay? You're quiet." Liam wrapped his arms around her from behind, the elevator flying up to the penthouse.

Jazz leaned into him. "Yeah, just annoyed about tomorrow."

Liam pressed a kiss to the top of her head, and Jazz watched in the mirrored wall while her stomach flip-flopped.

"It'll be fine, darling. We just have to sit through a couple of hours and then we can come back here or head to your place, and I'll pretend not to be interested in that god awful dating show you like to watch."

Jazz chuckled, bringing a smile to Liam's face. "I knew you were pretending. Hey, did Maggie seem off to you tonight?"

"I didn't notice anything."

The elevator doors opened and Liam tugged her to his front door. She leaned against the cool wall, a relief compared to the sticky summer evening. "I was probably just imagining things after the call with my mom," she said, offhandedly, as Liam unlocked the door. He pushed it open and followed her into the beautifully air-conditioned apartment.

She wasn't imagining it. Jazz knew Maggie well enough to know something was bothering her about her arrangement with Liam, she just couldn't tell what. And she wasn't entirely sure she wanted to know. Maggie was the definition of having your life together—she was happily married, a homeowner (several times over, at this point), and had a thriving business. Jazz was… Jazz. And she was happy with that, even if she did sometimes worry that Maggie was waiting for her to catch up. It was normal for best friends to move at different paces. Maggie had always been better at having her life together than Jazz. She was used to Jazz's chaos. She wasn't going to get tired of her after so long. Everything was fine.

"Do you want to just have a quiet night?" he asked, and there was no pressure on his face either way. "We could watch a movie or take a bath—or watch a movie *in* the bath."

Jazz drew in a deep breath. A movie in the bath sounded like a dream, but not yet. She needed to distract her racing brain first.

"That sounds nice, but maybe after the plans you promised I'd like," she said, stepping close to him and running her hands up the inside of his t-shirt. Liam's eyes darkened. "I like this one. Who's this by?" she asked, nodding to the painting of the mountain printed on the soft fabric.

"Cézanne. It's one of my favorites. I've always wanted to visit the mountain in Provence."

"Maybe we could go for our Hallow-honeymoon," she joked, lifting the t-shirt over his head and dropping it over the arm of the couch, where Liam had propped the chalkboard up. He'd added their second rule: *talking about how you feel isn't optional*. Jazz dragged a finger over the painting. "Do you miss it?"

"Provence? I've never been."

"The museum," Jazz clarified.

"Oh. I miss being around the art. But working with Maggie and her team is a lot more fun."

"I like hearing you talk about art," she admitted. "I should've visited when you were still at the museum, so I could see you in your element."

Liam smiled at her, his emerald eyes soft and his dimples pronounced. "We could go sometime."

"I'd like that. Have you been back since you…" How did you politely say *had a drunken meltdown and got fired*?

"I haven't," Liam admitted, saving her from having to spell it out. "But if the wedding is anything to go by, I don't mind facing scary things when you're by my side."

"We'll see if you're still saying that after meeting my parents."

Liam laughed as she pulled him toward the bedroom, kicking her sandals off as she went. He stilled her as they passed through the bedroom door, pushing the waistband of her shorts and underwear down. She stepped out of them while he took off her tank top, his fingers lingering over the curve of her stomach.

Jazz wasn't self-conscious about her body, per se, but she was a woman with a body larger than society deemed suitable, and she had her moments when those shitty societal standards got to her. She was only human. Her previous partners had all been kind about her figure, some of them more than kind, but no one had ever looked at her like Liam: like she was a work of art, created just for him. And she had no idea what to make of that.

She reached behind her to unclasp her bra, and Liam wrenched it from her body, tossing it away and nudging her to the bed.

"We haven't talked about safe words," he said, grasping her chin and tilting her face up so she was looking at him. "Do you have one you prefer?"

"Jingle bells," she replied, and Liam released a surprised bark of laughter. "The first time someone asked me to pick one, I was at a Christmas party and Jingle Bells was playing in the background."

"Jingle bells it is. And if you can't speak, snap your fingers. I'll be paying attention, no matter how into it we are. I promise."

"I trust you," she said, and his lips lifted. "What's yours?"

He wrinkled his nose. "It used to be peaches until Maggie and my dad ruined that by giving me a cat sibling."

A laugh burst from her lips. "Holy shit," Jazz wheezed. "You know I have to tell Maggie that."

"I absolutely do not need to know what you tell Maggie about any of this. I can't imagine I'll need to use a safe word, but if I do, I'll borrow jingle bells." He released her chin when she nodded in agreement. "On the bed, darling. Arms above your head, legs spread."

Jazz was intrigued enough to do as she was told without protest, but that didn't stop her from taking her time, crawling up the bed and giving Liam a good look at her ass before lying on her back and spreading her legs.

He watched her until she was settled, his hungry gaze roaming over her body. She raised her arms above her head, arching her back. With the way Liam was looking at her, she should probably have stretched before lying down.

Liam kept his clothes in his giant walk-in closet, so she'd suspected the dark oak dresser in his bedroom was full of the toy collection he'd mentioned. He confirmed her theory when he reached into the bottom drawer and withdrew a set of four padded cuffs. Jazz swallowed, anticipation mingling with that little touch of fear she loved so much when she was tied up.

"Is this okay?" he asked, wrapping one cuff around her ankle.

"Yeah."

He fastened the buckle and repeated with the other ankle. Turning back to the drawer, he withdrew two pieces of thick silver chain with clips on each end. He clipped a chain to each of the cuffs before crouching down. Even with the mirror above her, Jazz couldn't see what he was doing, but she felt it when the other side of the chain was attached to the bed. After clipping the second chain to the bed, Liam ran a soothing palm over her calf.

"Is that comfortable? I can loosen them."

Jazz tested the chains, trying to draw her legs together.

There was very little give, no matter how hard she pulled on them. Just how she liked it.

"It's good," she promised, and Liam kissed her knee before standing and following the same routine with her wrists. The chains were already attached to the headboard, tucked out of sight behind it, and the restraints were just as unforgiving as those holding her legs apart, leaving her entirely at Liam's mercy.

She watched him, her blood thrumming in anticipation, as he unbuckled his belt and slid it through the belt loops of his pants. He made quick work of undressing, and Jazz let out a desperate sigh at the sight of his cock. God, she needed him inside her. She didn't even care about finishing anymore, she just needed to feel—"What's that?"

She tried to sit up to see what Liam was pulling from the middle drawer of the dresser, but the restraints held her down. A curse slipped out of her and Liam turned back just in time to see her pulling at the chains holding her arms to the headboard.

"Not even five minutes," he said, tutting. He turned around and held up a dark purple flogger.

Jazz's breath caught in her throat as he stepped closer to her, running the tails over her torso. They were softer than she expected—not leather. Some kind of nylon maybe.

"This is a beginner one," Liam explained. "It's designed to sting, but not too badly. You okay with that?"

Jazz nodded, because she was sure her voice would come out as nothing but a squeak if she tried to answer verbally, but Liam wasn't satisfied with that. "Words, darling. I'm not doing anything unless you're one hundred percent comfortable with it."

She cleared her throat. "Yeah, I'm good with it."

"Good." Liam leaned in and pressed a sweet kiss to her forehead before standing up straight and, before Jazz even had time to think about it, snapped the tails of the flogger over her breasts.

"Fuck," she cried as the sting ricocheted across her skin. Her back bowed off the bed as far as the restraints would allow. She fell back on the bed, panting, while Liam dragged the tails so softly over her skin they tickled.

"Okay?"

Jazz opened her mouth to confirm before considering. She'd behaved enough. "Is that all you've got?"

The energy in the room shifted as Liam processed her words. A shiver worked its way down her spine. His hand stilled, the tails of the flogger dangling loosely on her stomach. Jazz braced herself for the sting, but it didn't come. Liam leaned over her, his mouth hovering an inch from hers. There was a wicked glint in his emerald eyes as they bore into her.

"Talk back to me again and see what happens." Liam closed the distance between them until she thought he was going to kiss her, but he bit down hard on her lower lip until it throbbed, then pulled back.

Jazz licked her lips. Oh, she *really* wanted to see what happened. "So scary," she mocked as he turned away, her voice dripping with condescension.

She watched Liam's shoulder's rise and fall in a long

sigh, but it was the low, humorless chuckle that made her legs tremble in their restraints. From her tied-down position, she couldn't see what he was doing when he crouched down to the floor. When he stood, he had something grasped in his hand, but he kept it hidden as he took up his spot by the bed again.

"Show me you can snap your fingers in the cuffs," he said, his voice making it clear he wasn't fucking around.

Jazz frowned in confusion but did as he asked. Liam nodded, satisfied. "Why—" H shoved a rolled-up piece of fabric in her open mouth, cutting her off. She squinted at her reflection in the mirror, clocking the red lace. *Was that her fucking underwear?* She tried to protest, but all she could manage were some garbled notes.

Liam looked up, catching her reflection in the mirror with a smirk, the picture of sin. "Better."

He lightly slapped her cheek, eliciting a muffled moan from Jazz, then followed up with a gentle kiss in the same spot. She watched him pick up the flogger from where he'd dropped it on the bed at her insolence, and looked away from her reflection, tensing. Not knowing when the next strike was coming was half the fun, right?

"Remember to snap if you need a break, darling." The way he could slip so quickly from this soft, caring Liam to a darker, harder persona was both impressive and unexpected. Jazz nodded her agreement, and she only had a split-second warning, watching the switch in him, before he brought the flogger down on her inner thigh.

She cried out, biting down on the fabric. Liam didn't let

up—the single strike to test the flogger had been nothing. He flicked the tails against her legs, her upper arms, her breasts. Her skin was on fire, pain mingling with pleasure. Jazz writhed in her bonds, desperate for some friction between her legs. *Holy shit, had she ever been this wet?*

Just when she thought she might sob with frustration, Liam ran his wide palm up her thigh, brushing her clit with a single finger. Then snapped the flogger between her legs.

Jazz screamed through the underwear, the sting of the flogger bordering on agony, but it only took a second before it morphed into fireworks. Liam followed the strike by rolling her clit gently between his fingers and Jazz panted, her heart damn near beating out of her chest. *Fuck,* when was the last time she'd been this close?

Liam was looking her over with a scrutinous gaze, searching, she knew, for any signs of unease. Which made it the world's worst fucking timing for Jazz to feel tears sliding down her cheeks.

He dropped the flogger immediately, rounding the bed to her side and pulling the underwear from her mouth.

"Talk to me, darling. Are you okay?" His voice was tinged with panic, so Jazz nodded quickly, licking her lips and trying to wet her mouth enough to speak. The fabric had leeched every drop of moisture from her mouth.

Liam grabbed her water tumbler from the nightstand—when had he even put that there?—and brought it to her lips, supporting her head with his palm. "Do you need to sit up?"

She shook her head and took the straw between her lips,

taking small sips. She could still feel tears falling from her eyes, entirely outside of her control.

"I'm okay," she said, panting, when she could speak. "Amazing, actually. This just happens. I promise I'm enjoying it. I want to keep going."

It wasn't the first time this had happened, and she knew it wouldn't be the last, but it was the first time someone had trusted her word without question.

Liam nodded, offering her more water and setting the cup aside when she declined. He straddled her, his cock so fucking close to where she needed it. He brushed a cool thumb across her damp cheek, then leaned down and caught her tears with his tongue, gripping her face in a possessive, but not painful way. Jazz trembled beneath him, a whimper falling from her lips.

"Look at you," he murmured, the words vibrating against her skin. "So fucking messy for me. You love this, don't you? Letting me do whatever I want to your perfect. Fucking. Body." He punctuated each word with a kiss, soft and gentle, while his fingers slid back into her hair, his fist closing around it.

He tugged hard enough for it to sting, enough that her fight-or-flight response to kick in, but not enough to make it too painful. *Holy fuck.* She wriggled in his grip, not sure whether she was trying to get away or just desperate to feel him against her pussy.

Liam tutted, shaking his head like he was disappointed in her. "Pathetic. Are you that desperate for me?" He gripped her hair harder, and she moaned, clenching her pussy for some relief. Fuck. If they ever figured out her inability to orgasm—and she was actually starting to believe they might—she was pretty sure he'd be able to get her off just by talking. "Will you beg me for it, darling?"

"Fuck no," she ground out, and Liam's face lit up. He liked her being a brat. Jesus.

"Thought you might say that." He released her hair and searched her face to make sure she was okay before leaning back. He dragged his cock over her clit, just once, just enough to make her gasp. "A shame. I might've let you come tonight." For a moment, Jazz actually reconsidered not begging. She was half tempted, just to see if he could. But where was the fun in that?

So, instead, she took a deep breath and said, "I'd like to see you try."

Liam's eyes flicked over her, almost dismissively. "I bet you would. But only good toys get to come, I'm afraid." *Toys.* That was a new one. Why was it so fucking hot? God, he was really testing her resolve. "Guess I'll just have to bring you to the edge, again, and again, and again."

Jazz whimpered without meaning to, and Liam grinned a sadistic smile. He dangled her underwear over her face. "If I leave these out of your mouth, are you going to behave?"

"Probably not."

Liam took his time folding her underwear, building anticipation before forcing it between her lips. He walked away, humming as he kneeled between her legs, spreading his palms over her thighs. "I'm going to have so much fun getting you in line," he said with a happy sigh. "Brace yourself, darling."

And then, with no warning, he spat on her pussy and pressed two fingers inside her. Jazz clenched around him, forcing her head back on the pillow.

Begging didn't sound so bad anymore.

CHAPTER FOURTEEN

Liam

For the hundredth time since they'd left Seattle, Liam glanced to his right to check on Jasmine. He'd never known her to be so quiet. They were ten minutes out from the restaurant where they were meeting her family, and she'd spent the entire drive staring out the window and fidgeting. It was unnerving.

He'd watched her gradually getting more subdued as the day had gone on. She'd been her usual chaotic self when they'd woken up, if a little more tired after their mind-blowing night. She'd tortured him by doing a virtual yoga class—naked, since she didn't have any workout clothes at his place—and they'd listened to an audiobook together while he made pancakes for breakfast. But by lunchtime, when they headed to her place so she could get ready, her spark had fizzled into a nervous energy.

"Are you okay?" he asked, and she jumped, as if she'd forgotten she wasn't alone.

"Shit, sorry. Yeah, I'm fine. I just feel a little out of it. And I'd rather be doing literally anything else."

"Just a couple of hours and then we'll think of excuses to put them off for the next few months," he promised, reaching across the center console to squeeze her knee. When he pulled it back, she stopped him, clinging to him. He'd never regretted having a manual drive more. He could hold her hand until he had to shift gear, at least.

"Any last-minute advice on impressing your parents?" he asked, and Jasmine snorted.

Her voice was flat when she replied, and Liam hated it. "Don't bother trying. Seriously. I gave up when I was twenty and they chewed me out for refusing to double-major. I've been a hell of a lot happier since."

Something about that niggled at Liam's mind, and he filed it away to figure out later. He was doing a shit job of calming Jasmine as it was. Needling her further was a terrible idea.

"What's with the dress?" he asked instead, and Jasmine frowned down at herself. "You look amazing," he added quickly. "It's just black. You always wear bright colors. I don't think I've ever actually seen you in black—well, except for the wedding, I guess."

The dress in question *was* beautiful. Knee length black linen with a ruffled hem. She looked gorgeous, as always, but wholly unlike herself.

"I call it *Jazz Lite*," Jasmine said with a bitter laugh. "It's how I dress when I need to see my parents, so they can't fuck with my confidence by trashing the clothes that actually feel like me."

Well, that was devastating. And not exactly the subject change he was hoping for. Liam pulled his hand away from

Jasmine's so he could turn into the restaurant parking lot, fighting to keep his face neutral. Jasmine was the last person he expected to struggle with shit like this. She always seemed so sure of herself. The thought of anyone making her feel otherwise…

"What?" she asked. Great. Not only was he doing a terrible job of keeping her calm, he apparently couldn't keep his confusion off his face, either.

"I'm just surprised. You're like the most self-assured person I know. I can't imagine anything shaking your sense of self."

"A little false confidence goes a long way," she replied with a wry smile. "And I have a *lot* of false confidence. Unearned, I might add. Fake it till you make it, right?"

"I believe we have a rule about that," he pointed out, because if he didn't make a joke about it, he was going to turn his Volvo around and head right back to Seattle. How the hell was he supposed to sit through dinner with the people who had made her feel like this? Meeting Maggie's parents had been bad enough.

Jasmine rolled her eyes at the reminder, but she seemed a little brighter, at least. It was something. He released his seatbelt, and brought her hand to his lips, pressing a kiss to her palm. "It's just dinner, and I'll be right here the whole time. You've got this."

She sucked in a heavy breath. "Yeah. It's just a couple of hours. We can manage that."

"Exactly. Rule number three: we're in this together."

A soft smile fell over Jasmine's face, but it was quickly

replaced by a cheeky grin. "Did you get that one from a Hallmark card?"

She scrambled from the car before he could answer. He caught her as she rounded the car and swatted her lightly on the ass. "Brat," he murmured in her ear, before kissing her on the cheek and pulling her into his side, ready to face her parents.

"I finished in the top ten of my half marathon last week." Jasmine's little sister, Rose, beamed proudly at her parents.

"Where in the top ten?"

Rose's smile slipped a little at her dad's unimpressed question. "Eighth. But I beat my best time by fifty-eight seconds, so I know I can do better next time."

Liam felt Jasmine tense beside him as her parents turned away from her sister. The light in Rose's hazel eyes dimmed. She took a deep breath before setting her jaw and looking up like nothing had happened.

Rose, twenty-five, was the carbon copy of their mom—honey blond and lithe, with sharp hazel eyes, and a heart-shaped face. Xander was thirty-six and favored their dad, with darker hair, blue-gray eyes, a square jaw, and a stocky build. Jasmine fell somewhere in the middle, but the thing that struck Liam most about the Cannon siblings was how tense they all were.

"Your turn, Xan," Jasmine's mom said, clasping her

hands on the table in front of her. Jesus. They hadn't even had their entrees yet.

Xander cleared his throat, and Liam wondered if his parents clocked his knee bouncing below the table. "I closed the deal with that East Coast hotel chain I was telling you about. Eight figures."

"Excellent work as always," their dad said, lifting his glass in cheers. Liam wasn't entirely sure what Jasmine's dad's company did, but it had something to do with lumber. Mr. Cannon turned to his middle daughter and sighed. "Anything to share this month, Jazz?"

"Hmm. I did get a parking spot in front of the bank for the first time ever last week, so that was pretty cool."

"On Fifth Avenue?" Liam asked, and she nodded, her eyes twinkling. "Damn. That's very impressive," he told her family, who were frowning at them.

"Isn't that street a no-parking zone?" Xander asked.

"Well, I didn't get a ticket, so I guess that's two achievements." Her family didn't look impressed. "What about you, baby?"

Ah. His turn. He was prepared for this. "I hit my reading goal for the year last week—eighty books."

"But it's only July," Rose protested. "If you already hit your goal, why not make it a bigger goal?"

"I read and set the goal for fun. It's not that serious." Liam shrugged, doing nothing to clear up the confusion on Rose's face.

"But the point of goals is to push yourself to do better. If you already hit the goal, you can do better than that."

Jasmine sighed. "God, Rosie, pull your stethoscope out of your a—"

"Anyway," Liam interrupted, cutting Jasmine off while fighting the laugh that was bubbling up. "I up my goal every year. Just for fun."

"Reading is a great hobby," Jazz's mom said after glaring at her middle child.

"It is," Mr. Cannon agreed. "And if you're reading that much, you must be learning a lot."

"Oh, absolutely. I love… learning." Liam had quizzed his moms on some of their recent favorite reads, so he would have an answer if Jasmine's family asked what he read, but if they wanted to assume he read non-fiction, that was fine with him.

"You could take a leaf out of Liam's book, Jazz. When was the last time you read a book?"

Jasmine gave her parents a saccharine smile. "Actually, Liam and I have been reading a lot together lately. And he generously shares everything he learns."

"I didn't need to hear that," Xander muttered under his breath, quiet enough that his parents, across the table, didn't hear, but Liam and Jasmine did.

Jasmine glared at her brother. "You follow him on Instagram too?" Liam posted the books he read significantly less than his dad did, but he still shared the odd book recommendation, and most of his pictures featured a Kindle or a book somewhere in the background.

"I only followed him after Dad told me you were dating," Xander protested. Shit, Liam hadn't even noticed.

"Maybe if you spent a little less time on Instagram and

more time touching grass, you'd be less of a pain in my ass," Jasmine grumbled, and her brother actually looked a little chastised.

"I'm sorry, okay? I didn't realize they would make you come to dinner. My lips are sealed from now on."

Jasmine sighed but didn't complain further, leaning into Liam as their entrees were served.

The conversation turned to work as Mr. Cannon and Xander spoke about a colleague while they ate. Liam tuned them out, focusing on his own dinner and Jasmine. She was pushing her pasta around with her fork, but not eating it.

"You okay, darling?"

She swallowed, wincing. "Hmm? Oh, yeah. I just don't feel a hundred percent."

It could be the stress of the night making her feel out of it, but her cheeks were paler than usual. Liam held the back of his hand to her forehead and frowned. "You are a little warm. Do you want to try my soup instead?"

She shook her head, leaning into his hand as if she liked how cool it was against her warm skin. "No, thank you. I'm still getting dessert, though. I need chocolate."

"The cannoli?" he asked with a knowing smile. He'd seen the way her eyes had lit up upon spotting them on the menu.

"God yes. I can't wait."

And she shouldn't have to, as far as Liam was concerned. "Excuse me." The server passing by stopped and gave him an expectant smile. "Could we please get a rush order of the chocolate cannoli?"

"Absolutely, sir. I'll get those to you as soon as possible."

"Thank you."

"You didn't have to do that. I was joking when I said I couldn't wait," Jasmine said. Liam tucked a hand behind her, and she sighed as he rubbed her back.

"If you want chocolate, you're getting chocolate. I've got you."

She pressed a kiss to his shoulder. "Thank you."

Jasmine's dad cleared his throat, and Liam forced himself to look away from Jasmine. "I assume you two met through Maggie, but how did this happen?" He waved a dismissive hand between them.

"Oh yes, do tell. I have to say, Liam, I was very surprised to hear Jazz speak about you. She's never been serious enough with anyone to want to introduce them to us before," Mrs. Cannon added, as if she hadn't practically *forced* Jasmine to introduce them. "Not to mention, she's never told us she was in love with anyone, either."

Jasmine tensed. *I might have made it sound like things were really serious between us*, she'd said. That explained that.

"There's not much to tell," Jasmine said, setting her fork down. "We've known each other since Maggie and Cal got together, and we started dating after their wedding."

"Maybe let the romance reader tell the story in the future. That was pitiful," Xander said with a snort, and Jasmine elbowed him.

"There's got to be more to it than that," Jasmine's mom said.

"I met Jazz when I went to visit my dad at work," Liam began, and they all withdrew their attention from Jasmine. "I knew there was something wrong with my dad, and was hoping to speak to Maggie to see if she knew what was going on, but she wasn't there. I had no idea she and my dad had been seeing each other, or that she'd quit her job. But, after a little convincing, Jazz spilled the beans. And, well, I was pretty enamored with her from the moment I laid eyes on her. I was obviously pretty shocked that my dad was in love with someone younger than me, but all I could think about was Jazz."

Jasmine was looking up at him with curious eyes, as if wondering how much of what he was saying was true.

"Pursuing anything seemed like a bad idea, since Jazz and Maggie are best friends, but we ended up spending a lot of time together in the lead up to the wedding, and, when it was over, I realized I didn't want to stop spending time with her. So when the opportunity came up to see each other more, and see what became of it, I jumped at the chance. With Maggie's blessing, of course," he added as an afterthought.

"It took us a little while to figure it out, but I couldn't be happier that we did," he finished. It was the most honest he'd been with Jasmine about his feelings, hidden behind the veil of faking it for her parents. But it felt good to get his feelings out there. And the way Jasmine was looking at him, wide-eyed and a little stunned, he could only hope she was catching up.

"Well, it's nice to see Jazz finally putting some effort into something, at least."

Hurt flashed in Jasmine's eyes, and he watched her close up as her dad's words sank in. Fuck it. Liam had been more than patient with these assholes.

He turned to Jasmine's parents and leveled them with the smile he'd learned watching his dad take people down in court. "I understand you're Jazz's parents and you think that gives you free rein to treat her, and your other children, however you like. I'm not here to debate your god awful parenting skills, but I've been sitting here all night listening to you saying rude things about the woman I care more about than anything in the world, and I think it would be best for all of us if you cut that out going forward."

Four pairs of eyes, ranging from shock to indignation (her parents) and impressed (her siblings), bore into him, but Liam only gave a shit what Jasmine thought. And she was looking at him like he'd just handed her the world on a platter.

"I have an order of chocolate cannoli?"

They all turned to the server standing awkwardly at the foot of the table.

"Perfect," Liam said. He lifted Jasmine's barely touched pasta plate and set it aside. "Just here, please."

The server placed the cannoli in front of Jasmine and scurried away with a deep breath.

Ignoring the stunned silence around the table, Liam leaned in and pressed a kiss to Jasmine's warm, flushed cheek. "Eat up, darling."

Jasmine was quiet on the walk back to the car, leaning on Liam like she needed him to hold her up.

"You want to talk about how terrible your parents are?" he asked, already sure he knew the answer.

Jasmine shook her head, laughing softly. "Definitely not. Even if I didn't feel like death warmed up, what's the point?"

Concerned, Liam ran his eyes over her. She looked exhausted, her skin even more pale than it had been when she'd first mentioned feeling unwell. "What feels wrong?"

"Everything," she replied with a groan. "My head hurts, and my whole body aches. Can I come home with you tonight? I need a good sleep, and I always sleep well with you," she asked almost shyly, as if he could ever say no.

"Of course you can. I wasn't going to give you a choice, actually. I want to keep an eye on you."

He helped her into the car and grabbed her a water bottle from the trunk. She was burning up when he kissed her forehead, and Liam was ninety-nine percent sure she was coming down with something. As he climbed into the driver's seat, he ran through a mental checklist to make sure he had everything he might need to help at home: cold medicine, Tylenol, electrolytes, a small stockpile of tissues because he couldn't pass up a deal at Costco. Hopefully he had everything she might need. Anything else, he could probably rope Maggie or his parents into picking up for him so he wouldn't have to leave her.

Jasmine leaned her head against the window and closed her eyes, and Liam thought she'd fallen asleep until he pulled onto the I-5 and she spoke up.

"Liam?" She sounded sleepy enough that he wasn't entirely convinced she *was* awake.

"Yeah, darling?"

"What you told my family about how you felt about me, about us, how much of that was true?"

Liam hesitated for a moment. He didn't want to scare her off. They hadn't exactly talked about their feelings. They hadn't even discussed what came after their arrangement. But he couldn't bring himself to lie to her. Not about that.

"All of it," he replied honestly and Jasmine sucked in a breath.

"All of it?"

"All of it was true," he confirmed. She was still for a moment, and he almost opened his mouth to apologize, to take it back. But then she reached across the car and set her hand on top of his on the gearshift.

"Good."

CHAPTER FIFTEEN

Liam

Liam shot up, the comforter puddling around his waist, and tried to figure out what had dragged him from sleep. He rubbed his face, pausing when he realized the problem: Jasmine wasn't beside him. The sheets on her side were wrinkled, but empty. Liam swung around so his feet were on the floor, and stretched. God, he was getting old.

He was rolling his neck when he heard groaning from the bathroom, before the unmistakable sound of her throwing up. Shit. He jumped to his feet, raising his fist at the bathroom door, but it wasn't fully closed. "Jasmine?"

He cracked the door. "Don't come—fuck."

She threw up again and Liam didn't hesitate to push into the bathroom, and drop to his knees beside her. She was leaning over the toilet, her legs bent at what looked like a painful angle. Liam gathered her hair in his hand, pulling it gently back from her face as she threw up. When she sat up, there were tear tracks streaked across her cheeks.

Before he could say anything, she doubled over, crying

out in pain. Fresh tears streamed from her eyes and Liam dropped her hair, running his hand over her back as panic spread through him. "Talk to me, darling. What hurts?"

"Everything," she sobbed, clutching her abdomen. She took several deep breaths before she could sit up, tears still slipping down her cheeks. And Liam must have looked as panicked as he felt, because she immediately started to reassure him. "It's fine, I'm fine," she said, wincing with every word. "It's just my period."

Liam grew up with two moms, and he lived with India for several years. He was no stranger to periods. But he'd never known anyone to be in this much pain.

"This seems pretty bad for a period. Do we need to go to the—" He stopped talking as Jasmine gasped in pain again, grabbing her stomach like she was trying to hold herself together.

"—ER?" he finished when she sat back up. He could see how depleted she was, and he shuffled closer so she could slump against him.

"No. I get really bad periods. This is normal for me. I'll be—" She paused, taking a deep breath and swallowing as if trying to convince her body not to throw up. "—fine."

No part of Liam could accept Jasmine being in this much pain as *fine*. Hell, her being in any pain was a problem for him. But his panic wasn't what she needed now. They could talk about why this absolutely wasn't fine once she was better.

"What do you need, darling? I've got you."

Jasmine's face scrunched together as a wave of whatever pain she was feeling swept through her. "Can you bring me my bag?"

Liam helped shift her so she was leaning her weight against the toilet and made quick work of grabbing her bag from his room. When he kneeled down beside her and unzipped it, she looked at it like grabbing even the tank top sitting at the top would be the equivalent of climbing Mount Everest.

"What am I looking for?" he asked, and she gave him a grateful, but weak, smile.

"A black pouch. With turtles on it."

Liam dug through the bag until he found the pouch, unzipping it to find a folded pair of black underwear and a couple of pads. "How many?" Jasmine asked as he pulled one out.

"Only two, but we'll get more. Don't worry."

He didn't ask if she needed help, because he knew her well enough to know she'd push back. Liam unwrapped the pad and stuck it to the underwear, then set it on top of the bag while he helped her up onto the toilet. She'd gone to bed in just a t-shirt, which made getting the underwear on much easier. As he slid it up her legs, she chuckled, then immediately winced.

"What?" he asked.

"Your parents did such a good job with you—oh, fuck."

Liam rubbed her back as she leaned over, a single pained sob falling from her lips. "Let's get you into bed and I'll get you some medicine."

He gently tugged her to her feet, supporting her with an arm around her shoulders.

"No, leave me here. I don't want to bleed on your sheets."

"They're just sheets."

"They're perfect, amazing, rich-boy sheets," Jasmine groaned. "Maggie would understand."

"I don't give a shit about them, but I do care about you. Get in bed. Please."

Jasmine grumbled, but he'd take that over her crying in pain. He got her settled into bed, grabbed painkillers, water, and a heating pad and, by the time he even thought to offer tea to soothe her stomach, she was fast asleep in the fetal position.

Liam sat on the edge of the bed and ran his fingers through his hair. Seeing her in that kind of pain… He was so far fucking gone. His phone showed it was just past five when he grabbed it from the nightstand to send a quick message to Maggie.

Can you call me when you wake up?

Not an emergency.

He sent the second message as an afterthought, even though, to him, Jasmine being in pain was the epitome of an emergency. He should've been surprised when his phone immediately started buzzing in his hand, but this was Maggie. Of course she was awake at this hour.

With a backward glance to make sure Jasmine was still sleeping, he clutched the phone to his chest to muffle the vibrations as he walked into the living room to answer the call.

"Hey."

"Good morning." Maggie sounded as awake as she always did. Liam was a morning person, but normal morning people weren't Maggie.

Liam stopped in the kitchen and sandwiched the phone between his ear and shoulder so he could fill the electric kettle for tea. Though he would be climbing back into bed with Jasmine the second he was off the phone, to keep a closer eye on her, there was no way he'd be able to fall back asleep. "Why are you awake so early?" he asked, stifling a yawn.

"We have a cat," Maggie said by way of explanation. "We're lucky if she lets us sleep past four. She'll be napping on your dad as soon as we're actually ready to get up, but it is what it is. What's up?"

"Jazz is sick."

He heard a rustle of covers, as if Maggie had sat up suddenly. "Shit. Is she okay? What's wrong?"

Liam explained how he'd woken up to find her throwing up and in pain, trying his best to keep the panic from his voice. "She says this is normal, but it can't be, right? Tell me she's not dealing with this every fucking month?"

Maggie sighed down the phone. "Not every month. It used to be, but with her birth control, she only gets her period every few months. But it's always this bad. And her doctor is useless, but she won't find another one. She'll be —" She cut off just in time for Liam to hear his dad shouting in the background:

"Stop biting my toes, you feral little monster. You're

going to make me spill your mom's coffee. Here you go, love. Who's on the phone?"

"Thanks. It's Liam. He has… a friend staying over who's sick. Do you want me to pick stuff up so you don't have to leave her?" she asked, speaking to Liam again, and Liam breathed a sigh of relief. He could've called his moms or asked his dad if Maggie was busy, but that would have required substantially more explanation. Liam had no problem with any of them knowing there was something between him and Jasmine, but that was probably a conversation he should have with her before his dad—her boss—found out.

"That would be amazing, thank you. I have zero idea what she needs, and she's fast asleep again."

"It's cool. This won't be my first emergency Target run. I'll probably be there about ten. I'll bring breakfast."

"You're a lifesaver. I owe you."

"Not this time. Just look after her, okay?"

Liam poured himself a strong cup of tea and grabbed his Kindle from the coffee table, then settled in beside Jasmine, watching the rise and fall of her chest. The pained expression never left her face, and Liam's Kindle stayed untouched on the nightstand.

It was like someone was stabbing her in the uterus with

a blunt axe, repeatedly. Jazz groaned, burrowing into the pillow. The very, very soft pillow… Oh shit, she was at Liam's place.

She forced herself to sit up through the pain. How long had she been asleep? She bled through her pads like crazy on the first day of her period. She was going to ruin his bedding. Fuck, fuck, fuck—

"Hey, it's okay. Breathe, darling."

Jazz jumped, clapping a hand to her chest and immediately wincing at the movement. How had she missed him sitting beside her?

"What do you need?"

"Bathroom," Jazz croaked. Liam jumped over the bed—slowly, as if trying not to shake the mattress too much. Her throat was like sandpaper. Bathroom, water, and, depending on how she felt after that, maybe food.

Liam took her arm and helped her off the bed. She felt steadier than she had when she'd woken up and had to run to the bathroom to throw up. The pain was there, but she wasn't as at risk of doubling over.

"Do you need me to come in?" Liam asked as they paused at the threshold of the bathroom, not a shred of embarrassment on his face. Shit, he'd helped her put her fucking pad on, hadn't he? Jazz's own dad had refused to buy pads or tampons for her and Rose when she lived at home.

"I think I'm okay," she managed, holding onto the wall.

Liam nodded, but didn't look entirely convinced. "Shout if you need me, okay? I'll be right here. I set everything on the counter for you."

Jazz mustered up a grateful smile and hobbled into the bathroom. When Liam said *everything*, he really meant everything. There were several packages of pads on the counter, in her preferred brand, the tampons she favored when she wasn't bleeding as heavily, wet wipes, and a pack of her favorite comfy underwear from Target in black.

He'd called Maggie, clearly.

Jazz grabbed a pad, a clean pair of underwear, and the wet wipes before all but collapsing on the toilet. She would kill for a bath, but she was definitely too weak. Maybe after some food.

She changed her pad and underwear, thankful she'd only bled through a little. And even more thankful she'd taken her favorite turquoise thong off before bed. It wouldn't be as bad if she knew when to expect her period. But it just showed up every few months like a clingy, unwanted ex who couldn't take a hint. At least it followed the same pattern when she did get it, and it didn't last too long:

Day one: Enough bleeding that she would inevitably become concerned she was running out of blood, and so much pain she would have an existential crisis wondering what the fuck the universe had against people with uteruses.

Day two: Less bleeding, but still too much to let her guard down, and significantly less pain. She would eat the entire contents of her pantry and then order three kinds of takeout—and almost immediately throw it back up. The crying usually began on day two.

Day three-four: The approach of the light at the end of the tunnel. She would cry over every little thing, spend a ridiculous amount of money online shopping, then regret it and try to cancel some of the orders.

Day five: Human again, usually pretty horny, but she'd probably still cry about everything.

Day five felt like a fucking lifetime away on day one.

She finished up and pulled herself to the sink, wincing at her reflection. The bruises below her eyes were blueish-purple, and she'd definitely burst a blood vessel or two throwing up—splotchy red spiderweb-like marks dotted her face. Her hair was sticking up at every angle, and her cheeks were mottled with old tear tracks. And Liam had put her fucking pad on. Holy shit, let the ground open up and swallow her whole.

"Jasmine? You okay, darling?"

He was clearly trying to keep the panic from his voice, but Jazz caught herself smiling in the mirror at how thoroughly he was failing.

"Yeah, just finishing up."

The second she stepped out of the bathroom, he was there to take her arm and lead her to the bed. Jazz stopped short of sitting down, taking in the waterproof blanket tucked over the sheets.

"Maggie suggested it," Liam said. "She said you'd be worried about the sheets."

"She knows me so well," Jazz replied with a snort that sent a strike of pain through her. She sucked a breath in through her teeth and sat on the bed before the wave of pain overtook her. Liam sat beside her, rubbing her back softly and murmuring words of encouragement while she breathed through the pain.

When she could sit up again, she swung her legs onto the bed and Liam helped her settle against the pillows. "I'll get you some more medicine and the heating pad. Can I convince you to eat something?" She wrinkled her nose, but he added, "Maggie brought soup," with such a hopeful expression that she couldn't help but nod.

She closed her eyes for what felt like five seconds before he was back. He gave her the water and painkillers first, then set the heating pad on her abdomen, before climbing in beside her and propping his laptop up between them.

Jazz breathed in the soup while he opened the laptop, surprised that her stomach didn't turn. "Are we watching porn again?" she asked and then tried, and failed, not to laugh at her own—hilarious—joke. Laughing was bad. Laughing hurt.

Liam just rolled his eyes. "I thought we could catch up on LoveStruck." He pulled up the episode they'd missed while they were at dinner with her parents and Jazz could have kissed him, if not for the risk of throwing up on him. This was exactly what she needed to make her feel better. Maggie wasn't the only one who knew her well. She was so lucky to have Liam in her life.

She leaned her head on his shoulder in lieu of a kiss. "God, I love you." The words slipped out before she could stop them, and her heart fucking stopped. "I mean, that's not what I, um, I—"

"Uh-uh. Rule number four: no take backs," was all Liam said, before hitting play and digging into his soup, as if she'd said nothing at all.

CHAPTER SIXTEEN

Jazz

"You did *what?*"

Maggie stared at Jazz from where she was sitting at the foot of the bed, open-mouthed.

"I told him I loved him. And then when I tried to explain that's not what I meant, he said *no take backs.*"

Her best friend blew out a long breath and shuffled up the bed, lying on Liam's pillow and facing her. "Shit. I mean, obviously he knows you didn't mean it and was trying not to make it awkward, but… shit."

"Right. Exactly. I don't mean it."

Maggie quirked a brow. "Jazz."

"Hmm?"

"Do you mean it?"

Jazz's lip wobbled before she could stop it. "I don't know what I feel," she cried, tears falling fast down her face. Maggie winced, grabbing a box of tissues from the nightstand and setting it between them.

"Sorry. I forgot day four was a crying day."

"It's fine." Jazz waved her away, grabbing a fistful of

tissues and wiping her face. Maggie was used to her five-day period schedule, and, thankfully, Liam had taken it in stride when she'd cried on him multiple times on day three, before ordering two pairs of boots, fancy cookies from New York, and a soap making kit.

Liam had insisted Maggie take his place watching Jazz while he went into the office to check some tile samples he'd ordered from Italy. Jazz had tried to work from home, but Cal had put his foot down, insisting she rest. So that's what she was doing. At his son's place, and Cal had no idea. It was a constant war of guilt and relief at the fact they were keeping Cal in the dark, but he really didn't need to know who his son was sleeping with, and right now, that's all this was. Kind of.

"Maybe we should wait until you're less hormonal before we try to figure out your feelings," Maggie suggested, rolling onto her back and shooting up. "What the fuck?"

Jazz glanced up and laughed. She hadn't had the chance to tell Maggie about the mirrors on Liam's ceiling yet.

"He has mirrors on his ceiling. Holy shit."

"That's not even the half of it," Jazz said. "I have so much to tell you."

Maggie groaned. "I'm torn between wanting to know it all because it's you, and none of it because it's Liam."

"I can make up a fake name for him, if that helps," Jazz offered, and Maggie shrugged.

"Can't hurt."

Jazz propped herself up on her elbow. "Okay, well Li—shit—Lime?"

"Lime is not a name. It's also basically just Liam."

"Right." Jazz wracked her suddenly empty brain. "I've forgotten every name ever."

"James?" Maggie offered. "Oh shit, no. That's his grandpa's name."

"If we're ruling out Michaelson names, we're going to be here for a while. There are thousands of them." Cal had nine siblings, most of whom were married with kids.

Maggie groaned. "Ugh, just use his name. It's fine."

Jazz gave her best friend a rundown of the night Liam had tied her up, and Maggie's brows climbed higher and higher as she spoke.

"Holy shit. And you still haven't come?"

Jazz growled in the frustration. "Even if I could, he won't let me! He brings me right to the edge and then pulls back every fucking time."

"I thought his whole thing was making people come? That seems like it directly contradicts what he's into."

"I think he's focusing more on what *I'm* into," Jazz admitted with a sigh. "Which, as it turns out, is being a brat and mild sadism."

"Hot," Maggie offered and Jazz nodded her agreement. "It sounds like he's just making sure you're ready. I'm guessing your first orgasm in a decade is going to be a big deal. You'll probably cry."

"I cry anyway," Jazz replied with a snort. "He licked my tears off last time."

"Damn."

"Makes you wonder what's up with Grandpa Michaelson," Jazz mused, "if Daddy Michaelson and Baby

Michaelson are like this. I guess we know why Cal's parents kept having kids. And stayed married for sixty years."

"I think the sixty years has more to do with how crazy in love with each other they are."

"Yeah, well, apparently that runs in the family too. You and Cal are still disgustingly cute."

Maggie raised a brow. "At least I never accidentally told Cal I loved him before we were even dating."

That was a valid point, but two could play that game. "True, but you did almost go on a date with your now-step-son, and ran off for months the second Cal tried to take care of you," she said with a sugar sweet smile and Maggie whacked her with a pillow.

"Touché. And I'd do it all again to get where we are now." Her face took on the same dreamy expression she always got whenever she spoke about Cal. The one that made Jazz's stomach twist uncomfortably. At least this time, she could blame it on residual cramps.

"Like I said: disgustingly cute."

Why was Maggie comparing her relationship to Jazz and Liam, anyway? It wasn't the same. Anyone who spent more than five minutes with Maggie and Cal could have told them they were meant to be together, meant to get married and live happily ever after.

Jazz's eyes snapped to the doorway as she heard the ding of the elevator in the hallway, followed by the sound of Liam's apartment door opening. She swallowed, her heart picking up speed.

"Speaking of disgustingly cute," Maggie muttered with a soft laugh, and Jazz shot her a glare, turning back to the door just in time for Liam to knock and peek his head into the room. It wasn't like that. *They* weren't like that.

"Hey."

He stepped into the room, he and Maggie discussing the tiles, but Jazz barely heard them as Liam immediately crossed to her side of the room and leaned in to kiss her forehead.

Her stomach fluttered: cramps or Liam? Cramps. Definitely cramps.

"How are you feeling, darling?"

"Better," she replied, and he beamed, his dimples popping out. *Fuck.* Tears pricked Jazz's eyes for no fucking reason. *Oh no.* She blinked furiously, looking away from him.

"Are you going to cry again?" he asked, running a hand through her hair.

"No." She hiccupped, the word falling through a sob as the tears started streaming down her face. "Fuck, I hate having a fucking uterus."

Despite Maggie's presence, Liam didn't hesitate to drop on the bed behind her and wrap his arms around her, holding her close to his chest and peppering her face with kisses. "It's okay. Let it out and then we'll have ice cream."

He held her as she cried, while Maggie alternated between sympathetic and bemused smiles. She'd spent years cuddling her and bringing her chocolate when she had her period, so it must be nice to get a break while Liam took a turn.

Jazz was suddenly struck by how, in this moment, she was luckier than she'd ever been. She'd always had

Maggie in her corner, and she'd had more casual friends and her siblings who, at a push, would be there for her. But now, she had Maggie and Liam. And she knew, without a shadow of a doubt, that Cal wouldn't hesitate to take care of her. Eliza and Danisha too. She owed Maggie big time for pulling her into this mis-matched little family, even if she wasn't entirely convinced how exactly she fit into it.

She grabbed the scrunched up, tear-stained, tissues she'd left on the bed and dabbed furiously at her face. Liam took them from her and wiped her cheeks with much gentler hands.

"You guys good if I head out?" Maggie asked, stretching and standing up. "I have to go to work and organize all of our invoices so I can get them to the accountant next week.

"Sounds like a perfect day for you," Jazz said with a watery laugh. No one loved organization like Maggie did. "Did you warn Cal that you're going to be all riled up by the time he gets home?"

Her eyes lit up. "I did. He's leaving work early."

Liam winced. "Gross."

Maggie raised a brow at him. "I was just lying on your bed beneath your creepy sex mirrors."

"Okay, fine. We're even."

"Not even close."

"Thank you for coming over," Jazz said while Maggie shouldered her bag.

"Anytime."

They waved Maggie off and Liam held Jazz tighter, hooking his leg over hers as if he needed to touch every inch of her. "Lunch?" His voice was muffled against her neck, his breath tickling the spot behind her ear.

"I'm not super hungry. Maybe a bath first?"

"I can do that." Liam pressed a kiss to her cheek before standing up and heading into the bathroom. Jazz watched him go, playing close attention to the way his pants hugged his ass. She wanted to take a bite out of him.

"I can feel you staring at my ass, darling," he called as he disappeared from view. She heard the rush of water as he started running the bath, then the crinkle of a package as he sprinkled what she assumed were Epsom salts in.

Jazz groaned and swung her legs off the bed. She was still achey, even if she was feeling a shit ton better. At least she had a few more months before this happened again.

She followed Liam into the bathroom and discarded her t-shirt—well, technically it was his t-shirt, but there was no world in which she was giving it back. It was warm and soft and it smelled like him.

"Will you get in with me?"

Liam gave her a soft smile, the kind she tucked away in the depths of her memories for days she needed a little boost. "Of course I will."

The warm water felt like heaven as she climbed in. It splashed over her as she settled against Liam's chest and he enclosed her in his arms, humming contentedly.

"This is nice," Jazz murmured, laying her head back and closing her eyes. She'd been known to fall asleep in the bath, especially after a glass of wine or two, but she was safe in Liam's arms. He kissed the top of her head, and she felt the tension of the past few days leeching out of both of them.

"Can I ask you something?"

Liam's tone sounded more serious than she liked.

She opened one eye and turned to peer at him. "Depends on what it is."

"Naturally." He toyed at his lip with his teeth before continuing. "What's the deal with your parents?"

Jazz blinked in surprise. She hadn't been expecting that. "What do you mean? You met them. They're awful. They're my parents and for some unknown reason, I love them, even though it probably isn't mutual. That's all there is to it."

She turned away, tears once again threatening her eyes. Jazz was a crier at the best of times, and in her hormonal haze, these certainly weren't the best of times.

"But why are—"

"Liam," she cut him off. "If I'm going to cry, and I am going to cry, it better not be about my parents. Hormonal crying is reserved for shit that doesn't matter, like the existence of capybaras and videos of babies trying lemons for the first time."

"That is... oddly specific." And yet she'd cried over both in the past twenty-four hours. "But fair," Liam continued. "We can talk about it when you're feeling better."

"Or never."

"Rule number two, darling." *Talking about how you feel isn't optional.* Jazz huffed, but didn't bother to protest further. She would, when he tried to talk about it more, but not now. Liam wanted to understand her family dynamic, but he never would. He'd grown up with three parents who loved him so unconditionally it almost made her teeth ache. He would never understand, and Jazz was so fucking glad of it.

Liam brushed his thumb over her cheek. "Can I wash your hair?"

"Is it that bad?" Jazz asked, sitting up quickly and peering at herself in the floor to ceiling mirror behind the door. It was too foggy to see much, but she could see enough to know that her hair was in disarray.

"Your hair is fine. You look perfect as always," Liam assured her, sitting up behind her.

"Liar."

He ignored that. "I know you've had a headache over the past few days, and I thought it might help if I gave you a little massage."

Oh. *Oh.* "Fuck," she said as the tears spilled again, but Liam just chuckled. Apparently Liam being nice to her was her new biggest crying trigger. Maggie had once suggested making a spreadsheet to keep track of all the things that Jazz cried over in a year, and, for the first time, Jazz was actually interested in seeing those stats.

"Is that a yes?"

"Yes, please."

At some point before she'd made it into the bath, he'd set a small pitcher on the side, alongside her favorite shampoo and conditioner, and even the serum she used. Jazz hadn't even noticed them, and she couldn't remember bringing her hair products over. She only washed her hair once a week in an effort to preserve her color and avoid going to the salon more than necessary, so she always just saved hair washing day for when she was home.

"Were those in my bag? I don't remember packing them."

"I saw them in your shower and picked them up so you'd have them here if you needed them," Liam explained, covering her forehead with his hand so none of the water from the pitcher got in her face. He poured the warm water over her hair and Jazz shivered as it coursed down her spine.

"But you can only get them from Sephora."

"I know. I've actually never been to Sephora before but I now have two new colognes, a whole new skincare routine, and a fancy blow dryer I don't know how to use," Liam admitted, a little sheepishly.

He'd gone to Sephora for her. Jesus. She had to start looking around his apartment for a murder lair or some-thing, because there was no way anyone was this perfect. But it was hard to think about that when he was massaging thirty dollar shampoo into her scalp.

Instead, she murmured her thanks and did her best to ignore the way his answering smile made her heart thud.

CHAPTER SEVENTEEN

Liam

For the first time in almost a week, Jasmine was comfortable. She'd been cramp-free for a couple of days, was no longer bursting into tears for no reason, and was wearing her favorite pale pink leggings—which, apparently, was a huge deal, post-period.

Liam was just relieved she was no longer in pain. He could handle the crying when it was over cute videos on TikTok or the end of her favorite chocolate bar (even though she knew he'd stockpiled them for her.) Honestly, Liam found it fucking adorable. She claimed to be an ugly crier, but he'd never seen anyone more gorgeous. What he couldn't handle was her crying in pain. Every one of those cries had felt like a knife in his chest.

Now, she was lying on her stomach, her heels crossed in the air, and her eyes glued on the TV. Liam had his Kindle in his lap, but it had gone to sleep a while ago. His ability to read plummeted whenever Jasmine was around—how the hell was he supposed to look at his book when she was right there?

"Are you watching me again?" she asked, without looking over her shoulder.

Liam busied himself with his Kindle, turning it on just in case she looked back. "No. I'm reading."

"Sure you are, baby," she replied, with a knowing glance at him. She winked and Liam slapped her ass, but pulled his hand back quickly, because he knew he would crumble if he didn't.

It had been more than a week since they'd touched beyond cuddles and chaste kisses. And as torturous as it had been, it was proof that they didn't need sex to spend time together. They were just happy to be in each other's presence. But now that Jasmine was better, they were both ready to end the torture.

She'd warned him she would be ridiculously horny on day five, and that she would try to tempt him, but he shouldn't give in because she would be too tired. And oh boy, had she tried. By lunchtime, Liam had shut himself away in his guest bedroom and made up an excuse for a virtual meeting just so he could breathe.

He knew the leggings were just another temptation, but she was full of energy today. There should've been nothing holding him back, but there was. A throwaway sentence that had stuck in his head on the way to dinner with her parents: *"Don't bother trying. I gave up when I was twenty."*

Ten years ago. Which, by Liam's calculation, was roughly when she'd stopped being able to come. Between that and the knowledge that Jasmine had been running on false confidence for the past decade, Liam had a hunch about why she couldn't let go. He also had a good idea of what they needed to do to get her there, but he knew Jasmine well enough to know she wouldn't be happy about it: they had to talk.

She'd made it clear that she'd gotten closer with him than she had with anyone else, and Liam suspected that had more to do with how much she trusted him than what they were actually doing. Sure, he prided himself on knowing how to make people come, but Jasmine telling him she felt safe with him made him happier than any number of orgasms ever could. He just needed to break through the last of her defenses and help her open up.

He waited for the episode she was watching to finish before speaking. Jasmine had spent most of the episode scrolling through her phone, so it would've been easy to assume she wasn't paying attention to the show, but she had an uncanny (and impressive) ability to pay attention to ten things at once.

He set his Kindle aside and tapped his lap. "Come here."

Jasmine turned the TV off and obliged, though she snuggled in beside him, rather than on his lap. Which was just as well, really. He was only human, and it was already bordering on too warm in the penthouse. He tightened his arm around her and breathed her in. Liam had yet to figure out how she always seemed to smell like the most perfect slushy on the hottest summer day, but he wanted to devour her. Later.

"I wanted to talk to you about something."

Jasmine's face barely changed, but Liam caught the uncertain glint in her eyes before she forced it out. "We could talk," she agreed, snuggling in so close she was practically on top of him. "Or we could take full advantage of the fact I'm better."

So. Fucking. Tempting.

Liam gritted his teeth. "Both great options, but I'm going to go with talking."

"Ugh." Jasmine pouted, and Liam fought the urge to bite her lip.

"I tell you what: we talk first, and then we can do whatever you want."

That piqued her interest. She raised her brows. "Whatever I want?"

Liam nodded, wondering if he'd just dug his own damn grave.

"What I want," she continued, punctuating the words by dragging her finger down his chest, "is you inside me. In my mouth, in my pussy, in my—"

"Then I guess we'd better get to talking then," Liam interrupted, because he couldn't be held responsible for his actions if she finished that sentence. He hadn't been inside her since India and Bart's wedding, and he wanted it just as badly as she did.

"Fine," she said with a smirk, well aware of how much she was tempting him. "What do you want to talk about?"

"Your family."

Her smirk slipped. "That's one way to make me less horny." She sighed, looking away, like she couldn't stand the thought of him seeing her looking vulnerable. "There's not much to talk about it. Like I said the other night, you saw them for yourself at dinner."

"Sure, but I don't actually give a shit about your fami-

ly." That might have been a little harsh—Xander and Rose seemed fine, if stuck under their parents' thumbs too much. "All I care about is how they make you feel."

"They don't make me feel anything," Jasmine protested. "I like who I am and they don't. But I don't care what anyone thinks of me."

"That's a nice sentiment. It's also complete bullshit," Liam pointed out, trying to keep his voice gentle despite the blunt words.

Jasmine's jaw dropped, her eyes flashing with ire. "I don't... That's not... Fuck this. You have no idea what you're talking about. You barely know me, for fuck's sake."

She turned away from him, but Liam held onto her wrist. He was holding her so lightly that it would take no effort to pull away, but she didn't.

"No. We're not doing that. You don't want to talk about your feelings? Reasonable. Talking shit out sucks. But you don't get to pull away just because you're scared. I know you, and I'm not going anywhere."

Jasmine's shoulders seemed to fold in on themselves as she sat back against him. "You're right. I'm sorry. I didn't mean that." Her voice shook. "I'm the fun friend. I'm not used to talking about anything serious, and no one has ever called me on it before."

"Not even Maggie?" Liam asked, surprised. Though Maggie was a recovering people pleaser, he didn't think those tendencies had applied to her relationship with Jasmine.

"Yeah, but that doesn't count. Maggie and I have been calling each other out on our shit since we were teenagers, but neither of us ever actually did anything about it, so we just kind of canceled each other out. It was easier to ignore before she grew up and started going to therapy."

He was taken aback by how bitter she sounded, but that was a conversation for another time. They couldn't tackle everything in one night. "Okay, well keeping shit bottled up for thirty years never did anyone any good, so let's talk."

"I don't know where to start," Jasmine said quietly, wringing her hands. "It all feels so fucking trivial. My parents have lofty expectations. So what? They made sure I had everything I needed, I graduated college debt free, I never had to worry about going without. They weren't abusive or neglectful. They weren't like Maggie's parents."

"Did you really have everything you needed? It doesn't sound like they were particularly nurturing or loving."

"No, but isn't that just what parents are like? Yours are the exception. My parents aren't bad people. I'm just not what they want. They love Xander and Rose. Xan is the perfect mini-me for my dad to turn into a businessman, and Rosie never so much as put a toe out of line growing up." The words streamed from her like water, like now she'd started, she couldn't stop them.

"Xan is the serious one, the innovator, the perfect son. Rose is the younger and prettier one who somehow got the brains, too. And I'm… me. And I'm not saying that to be self-deprecating. I really do like who I am. Mostly. I just don't have a *thing*, like Xan and Rose do. I don't want what they do out of life."

"What do you want out of life?" Liam asked.

"I just want to be happy." Tears rolled silently down her

cheeks, damn near shattering him. "I want a family I can feel like myself in. My job is exactly what I've always wanted—challenging, but not stressful. My apartment is shitty, but I like it. I don't need anything fancy. I just want to be content. What do you want out of life?" She returned the question like she needed a break from thinking about herself.

Liam was still reeling from her answer—it sounded so fucking simple. Fuck anyone who had made her think it was unachievable. He would stop at nothing to make sure she was more than content.

He cleared his throat, threading his fingers through hers. What did he want out of life? *Her.* It probably wasn't the time to drop that in, though. "Honestly? I'm pretty content these days," he said, instead, squeezing her hand.

The tension melted from Jazz's shoulders a fraction, and Liam felt like he could take a full breath for the first time since they'd started talking about this.

"What about long term?"

"I don't know," Liam said with a nonchalant shrug, like he hadn't been falling asleep to visions of a future with her since they'd first met. "I want to be a dad. Maybe have a house with a backyard for the kids to run around in. And I guess I look at my dad and Maggie, my moms, my grand-parents, and I want that, you know?"

"Yeah," she agreed, laying her head on his shoulder. "Me too. But if anyone else asks, I'll lie about it."

He chuckled. "I'd expect nothing less." He wound his arms around her shoulders and tucked her in close to him.

"You have to tell me something at least a little shitty about your parents now to balance this out."

Liam didn't even have to think to know there was nothing to add. "As you've pointed out, my parents are great."

"Come on. They must have done something to piss you off when you were a teenager on the brink of rebellion."

"What kind of teenager do you think I was?" he asked, sounding more affronted than intended. "I never even got grounded, thank you very much."

"Of course not."

Liam hummed, trying to think of a time when he'd been mad at his parents. Something light enough to lift some of Jasmine's tension "Okay, when I was a kid, I was super obsessed with Snoopy. I'm talking bedding, posters, t-shirts, everything was Snoopy."

Jasmine relaxed at the change of subject, and Liam took the chance to wipe her cheeks in case more tears fell. "I was wondering about the Snoopy figurine on the bookshelf," she replied, nodding to the bookshelf in question. Most of his collection was in boxes in his moms' basement, but that figurine had followed him to college and beyond.

"I was so obsessed that I desperately wanted a dog. Not a beagle, like Snoopy, because I did my research and they're a shit ton of work, but I just wanted a dog. My parents said no. They worked all day, and I was at school, so there was no one to stay home with a dog. It makes sense as an adult, but I was pretty pissed about it for a long time."

It was nothing compared to what she'd told him about

her parents, but Jasmine smiled at the story, and he couldn't ask for anything more.

"That's adorable. You should get one now. You can take it to the office with you, and it would be dad-practice."

Liam hadn't considered that he could finally get a dog, now that he didn't have to go to the museum every day. "I could. We should look into that. Thank you for talking to me, darling. I really think it's going to help, and I like getting inside that beautiful brain of yours."

"You're going to make me do this more, aren't you?" Jasmine grumbled, sighing when he nodded. "I miss when everything felt simpler. Do you ever wish you could just go to sleep and wake up twenty again?"

"Definitely not. I didn't know you when I was twenty," he said, simply, and Jasmine looked a little stunned. She recovered quickly, wiggling her eyebrows.

"And if you had? What then?"

"Well, you would have been thirteen, so… I guess I could have babysat you?"

"Shut up. If we'd both met at twenty. What then?"

"Then we'd probably be married with a bunch of babies, living happily ever after with no idea what broken hearts and decades of fake orgasms felt like."

"Sounds like a nice life," Jasmine said, a little wistfully. It sounded like the perfect life.

"We still have time," he promised, and Jasmine laughed like he was joking. Now he just had to make it happen.

CHAPTER EIGHTEEN

Jazz

Her back arched off the bed, almost painfully, as Liam's hands coasted over her thighs, his tongue playing games with her piercing. He was being so fucking gentle, keeping her on edge, building the antici-pation as she waited for him to snap.

God, she loved it when he snapped.

It was possible she loved this more—the anticipation, the lazy roam of his fingers and mouth over her body, the soft spiral into madness. She'd expected him to pounce on her, rough, and hard, and desperate, after a week without this. But Liam was taking his time, like he was savoring her, recommitting her to memory.

He spread her thighs further and pressed his tongue inside her. Jazz fisted the covers. "Fuck, baby," she gasped, clenching around his tongue. Liam's grip tightened on her thighs. He loved when she called him baby, and, though Jazz usually took that knowledge and reserved the term of endearment for opportune moments, sometimes she couldn't stop it from slipping out. Like when he was holding her open, with his tongue in her pussy like she was the goddamn last supper.

Pressure built in Jazz's core and she desperately tried to squeeze her thighs together, to wrap her legs around Liam's head, but he was unyielding, pulling back enough to chuckle. The vibrations made her toes curl, a whimper falling from her lips.

"Liam," she groaned, panting and twisting in the sheets. "You said we could do whatever I want and I want you inside me."

"My tongue isn't enough?" He accented the words by twirling her piercing around the very tip of his tongue until she almost jumped off the bed.

"No," she ground out, and Liam tutted, standing to full height. From this angle, he towered over her, naked and fucking gorgeous. His cock was barely two feet from where she so desperately wanted him, but he turned away. Jazz released a frustrated whine.

Liam peered back at her. "Patience, darling."

"Fuck patience."

He raised an eyebrow, his eyes glinting dangerously, and turned back until he was facing her fully. He leaned over her, his nose brushing hers, the sweet scent of him invading her. His lips were close enough that she could almost reach out and kiss him, but something in his wicked expression held her back. Liam ran his tongue along the seam of her lips and her mouth popped open instinctively, inviting him in. But Liam just smirked.

"You're running your mouth a lot for someone so fucking desperate for me."

Her heart pounded, but she pasted a sugar-sweet smile on her lips and fluttered her lashes at him. "Then I guess you'd better put something in my mouth to shut me up."

His pupils flared and he pulled back, swallowing. He shook his head. "Oh no. You want my cock in your mouth? Then be a good girl and do as you're fucking told. Then we'll see."

He brought his hand down on her pussy, a loud smack echoing through the room. Jazz's head slammed back into the mattress as she cried his name, squeezing her eyes closed against the sudden rush of sensation.

She felt his eyes on her, watching her reaction, making sure she was okay. And she *would* be okay—if he'd stop fucking teasing her. She gave him a short nod to assure him she wasn't tapping out, her blood warming knowing how much he wanted to make sure she was safe and comfortable. Once he was sure, he turned away again and, though Jazz wanted to watch to see what he was grabbing from the dresser, she needed the reprieve to lay her head back, close her eyes, and just breathe.

Liam was silent doing whatever he was doing, but she felt, rather than heard him approach. "Still with me, darling?" he asked, as she felt him kneeling between her legs again.

"You're going to have to try harder than that to break me," she replied, her voice too breathy and desperate for the words to do anything but make him laugh.

He nipped her inner thigh with his teeth, then dragged his tongue over the spot. She expected him to draw his tongue up her thigh, to tease her pussy again, but he didn't. His fingers brushed her clit instead, for barely a second before he was pressing one inside her. He was gentle, taking it slow to make sure she wasn't tender after being in so much pain for days.

But Jazz didn't want gentle. "More," she moaned, and Liam obliged, pushing a second finger inside her and curling them, massaging her G-spot until she was trembling. Every nerve ending on her body felt like a live wire, electricity crackling over her skin.

Liam withdrew his fingers and she opened her mouth to protest, but it turned into a whimper as he dragged them down and pressed them against her ass. "I believe," he began, circling the rim with a ghost of a touch, "that you wanted me in your mouth, in your pussy, and here. Was that right?"

"Yes," she gasped.

"Well, we've already established you can have me in your mouth when you stop running it." He pressed one finger, wet from being inside her pussy, into her ass. Her body protested for only a moment at the initial sting. Though she was no stranger to anal, it had been a while. But Liam kissed her knee and she relaxed, taking deep breaths. He drew his finger out and pressed it in again, slowly, until she was on the verge of begging for more again.

She moaned as he pulled out entirely, and she heard a cap opening. The lube was cold when he rubbed it over her with two fingers and Jazz gasped, but it was quickly swallowed by a cry as he pressed both inside her. Her body adjusted faster this time, her muscles relaxing around him as he fucked her with his fingers.

Pleasure ricocheted through her whole body. *Holy shit, was she actually going to come?* The cliff's edge teetered closer and closer but, before she could leap, Liam pulled out of her again. He replaced his fingers with his tongue, circling her ass with the firm tip before sitting back on his knees.

"Since I can't have my cock inside your ass and your pussy at the same time, we'll have to make do with this for now."

Jazz didn't get the chance to sit up to see what *this* was before she felt the cool metal plug against her ass. Her breath caught in her throat as Liam drizzled more lube over the plug, spreading it around so it was fully covered before pressing it into her. Jazz let out a long moan, her body instinctively struggling against the intrusion as the plug reached its widest point inside her.

"Breathe, darling," Liam whispered, his breath tickling her thigh. Jazz sucked in a deep breath and Liam pushed the plug in the rest of the way. She swallowed down her whimpers, clenching around the plug. It was torture, having it inside her, completely still. She needed movement; she needed friction.

"Move up the bed."

For once, Jazz did as she was told, crawling up the bed and relishing in the sound of Liam cursing softly.

"Do you want me on my back or on my knees, baby?"

"Your back," he replied, his voice like gravel.

When Jazz turned to lie down, Liam was still kneeling at the end of the bed, like she'd caught him mid prayer. He stood up, his eyes flicking over every inch of her. He shook his head, his expression almost stunned.

"What?" she asked, and he drew his gaze to her face.

Liam followed her up the bed, kneeling between her open thighs, so close that his cock rested on her belly. He cupped her face with his hand, his expression blazing. "I know you hate praise, but... Fuck, Jasmine, you can't expect me to see you like this and not tell you that you're the most beautiful thing I've ever had the fucking privilege to lay eyes on. You belong in the Louvre."

"Oh," she breathed, her eyes burning, because how the hell was she supposed to respond to that?

He said *the Louvre* with a perfect French accent and Jazz filed that knowledge away for later. Did he speak French? Had he visited Paris? There was so much she didn't know about him, and she wanted to know everything.

Jazz had always obsessed over things—hobbies, tv shows, celebrities, niche interests she absorbed in excess, learning as much as she could before the swell of interest dissipated and she moved onto something else. But she'd never wanted to absorb something as much as she did Liam. She wanted to take a walk through his brain and learn everything there was to know about Liam Michaelson. She wanted him to consume her.

As if he saw that in her eyes, Liam leaned in and kissed her. She could get drunk on the taste of him, the taste of *her* on his tongue: sweet and salty and perfect. His tongue danced with hers like he was imprinting himself on her.

"Please, Liam," she begged, and Liam brushed his lips over hers once more before sitting up. He reached across the bed and slid open the nightstand drawer, but Jazz stilled him with a hand on his arm.

The emerald in his eyes was almost black when he met her gaze, desperation etched in every line on his face.

"I don't want to use a condom. I want to feel you as close as I can," Jazz whispered. "I'm on birth control and I get tested regularly. But if you want to use one, we should."

"I get tested too," Liam said, closing the drawer. "And I'll always want to be as close to you as I possibly can be."

Jazz ran her finger up his arm and over his chest, lingering over his heart, before trailing it down his stomach and watching him shudder as she brushed his cock. Liam sat back, fisting his cock.

And when he pressed inside her, they weren't brat and dom, darling and baby, best friend and stepson. They were Jazz and Liam. *Jasmine and Liam*, Jazz mentally amended when Liam groaned her name, stilling inside her.

The strain of not coming for so long was clear in the tension in his muscles, and Jazz was determined that he wouldn't be waiting any longer. Even if she couldn't come, he'd been waiting long enough. He'd been so good to her, and sure, he'd be pissed to be the one coming first, but she would make it up to him by making him come time and time again. She needed him to fall apart, needed to know she was the one making it happen. Perhaps she understood the *pleasure dom* thing more than she thought.

Jazz felt impossibly full with both him and the plug inside her, but she squeezed her pussy around his cock and Liam's hand flew out, slamming against the headboard. "Christ," he cried, his breathing labored. "Jasmine, darling, do you think I don't know what you're doing? It's written all over your beautiful face."

He covered her body with his, his arms bracketing her head, his forehead pressed to hers. "I know you want to make me come. And you can. When *you* come." He pulled out of her and thrust back inside, once, twice, Jazz lost count as flames engulfed her body.

"Rule number three: we're in this together, remember? You want me to let go? You first."

It wasn't a challenge, but it sure as hell sounded like one. But Jazz could hardly focus on anything Liam was saying. Every stroke inside her made her more sensitive than the strike of the flogger had.

Liam leaned back, gripping her hips and using the spring of the mattress to fuck her. Unable to reach his back, Jazz's nails raked over his thighs, and she threw her head back, the blood rushing in her ears all she could hear. Until Liam's voice broke through, and she forced herself back into the present, a spring coiling in her belly at the sight of his smile, strained but soft.

"There she is. Look up, darling."

Jazz frowned but followed his direction, gasping as she realized why he'd suggested it. She'd forgotten about the mirrors. With Liam sitting back, she could see every inch of his cock disappearing inside her. She took in the full picture: her thighs and stomach wobbling with every thrust, her breasts bouncing, her hair splayed around her like flames on the white pillowcase, her pale skin slicked with sweat and burning red. But it was like she was seeing herself through

Liam's eyes, seeing the beauty in her body—the art they made together.

She met his eye in the mirror, their reflections amplifying every brush of his skin against hers. He released his grip on her hips, one hand grasping the back of her thigh to give him more leverage, opening her wider to him. Jazz cried out as he hit her deeper. Her body felt like it might burst, the pressure from the plug only serving to make everything more sensitive.

Liam brushed his thumb over her clit and Jazz's vision blurred at the edges, a soft haze the color of his eyes creeping across the room. She was no longer in control of the sounds falling from her lips like cascading dominos, of the way her body shook and trembled beneath him, lashes of fire and electricity striking every inch of her. Her fists and toes clenched, her palm stinging as her nails dug into her skin.

Breathing became a struggle, short, sharp bursts trying to force oxygen into her lungs between cries and curses and whimpers of Liam's name. His fingers shook where he gripped her thigh. Jazz could tell his control was faltering. Though he'd had a steady rhythm when he started playing with her clit, his movements were becoming jerky, hard, then soft, his thrusts becoming merciless.

She was so close she could cry. She'd forgotten sex could feel like this—shit, had sex ever felt like this? No. It was just him. Liam. The man who saw her, inside and out, and still liked her.

In the same second that thought crossed her mind, Liam pinched her clit and breathed her name, and Jazz didn't so much as leap from the cliff as explode like a fucking supernova.

Her vision went black, every sound dying in her throat, her body suspended in a moment of perfect stillness that simultaneously felt like it lasted for a split second and an hour. And then the wave crashed over her.

It was like being doused in a pool of glitter, shimmering stars falling around her as fireworks burst behind her eyelids. She was vaguely aware of Liam's body covering hers, his lips pressed against her jaw, tears slipping down her cheeks. The comedown was a slow fall, rather than a crash, and Liam coaxed her through it, murmuring soft words she couldn't distinguish in her ear. Her heart was still racing when the shockwaves dissipated, her lungs still screaming for air, but Jazz managed to pry her eyes open.

Liam was staring at her, his eyes brighter than any emerald she'd ever seen, a mix of shock and pride on his face. "Jasmine," he said, panting and enclosing her face in his hands. "You fucking did it, darling."

He pressed his lips to hers, grinning from ear to ear through the kiss. But when Liam started to pull away, trying to alleviate his weight from her, Jazz held him close to her, buried her face against his neck, and sobbed.

CHAPTER NINETEEN

Liam

He was so fucking proud of her. Liam held Jasmine in his arms, brushing and kissing her tears away, just letting her let it all out. He could feel the exhaustion in her body, her grip on him weak, but she refused to let go, as if she was worried he was going to pull away. Like he ever could.

With his chest pressed against hers, he could feel her heart racing, then slowly calming as she cried it out. "You're okay, darling. I've got you."

When her cries softened into sniffles, and she seemed a little steadier, Liam tried to pull away, but she clung to him. "No. I don't want to let you go yet," she murmured sleepily, and, though Liam wanted nothing more than to fall asleep exactly like this—still inside her, cum leaking all over them both, panting and spent—she needed water, at the very least.

He kissed her forehead, her eyelids, the tip of her nose. "Let me take care of you first. We'll get ready for bed, and then I'm going to hold you all night."

"But I want to fall asleep with you inside me," she

grumbled, and, though it took Liam's brain a second to register the words, his cock picked up on them right away. Had he ever been hard again this quickly? Jesus.

Jasmine must have felt him, because she suddenly perked up, but, as much as Liam was already ready for round two (and three and four and beyond), they needed to rest.

"I promise we can still do that," he said, with one last kiss to her nose before pulling out. "But we need to get ready for bed first." Jasmine sighed and pouted, but didn't protest. She was so fucking cute.

His muscles protested as he climbed off the bed. He grabbed a warm washcloth from the bathroom and a glass of water, which he handed to Jasmine first, making sure she drank some, before turning his attention to the mess they'd made. Liam willed his cock to calm down as he took in the sight of Jasmine glistening with his cum. He took a deep breath and focused on the plug.

She whimpered when he tugged gently on it. "Deep breath," he instructed, and he heard her taking a big gulp of air as he slid the plug from her. He cleaned her up with the washcloth and she hummed in thanks, taking small sips of the water. When he was done, he rinsed the cloth and plug in the sink, tossed the cloth in the laundry basket, and set the plug aside to clean properly tomorrow.

As turned on as he was, sleep dragged him down. The temptation to just climb into bed and fall asleep beside Jasmine was strong, but they were too old not to know better. He knew he'd regret it if he didn't drink some water and take his vitamins before bed.

"You go get ready in the bathroom first," he said, offering a hand to Jasmine, who reluctantly took it and sat up. She looked dazed as he helped her to the bathroom, and who could blame her? Liam was fucked after just a few weeks without coming. Ten years? He was surprised she could stand.

Jasmine was always beautiful, especially in the quiet moments she wasn't trying to be anything but herself; first thing in the morning, before he brought her coffee in bed, when she had sheet marks on her skin and her hair was chaos; when she took the first bite of something she loved, usually involving chocolate, and a flash of bliss crossed her face; when they were just lying on the couch together and she really relaxed into the moment.

But Jasmine post-orgasm was effervescent, and Liam was well on the road to getting hooked on making that happen. Perhaps he already was.

While Jasmine was in the bathroom, he stripped the ruined blanket from the bed and tossed it in the closet to deal with later. He wasn't entirely sure it was cleanable, but he'd give it a shot. He usually put a waterproof blanket on the bed, but he hadn't been expecting *that*.

He filled Jasmine's water tumbler and got a glass for himself, before turning off all the lights and making it back to the bedroom just in time for her to walk out of the bathroom, rubbing her eyes. She got settled in bed while he sped through his nighttime routine: teeth, vitamins, mustache oil, and moisturizer, so he didn't wake up with a face that felt like sandpaper.

He half expected her to be asleep when he finished, but

Jasmine was sitting up, squinting at her phone screen. "What are you doing?" he asked, climbing in beside her.

"Booking a yoga class for the morning. I can already tell my muscles are going to be screaming. You want to come?"

Liam winced. "Definitely not. I can't imagine you still being attracted to me after witnessing me trying to do yoga." Jasmine snorted as she booked her class and set her phone aside. "Why yoga? Wouldn't a massage be better for your muscles?"

"I like yoga," Jasmine said with a shrug and a yawn. "And I don't want anyone else's hands on me but yours."

Before Liam even had time to blink at her words, she lay down, tugging the covers up over her naked body, hiding after saying something vulnerable. Liam lay down beside her, pulling her back against her chest and pressing a kiss to her neck. He didn't address her comment, but it sank into him, nestling nicely alongside his heart.

"Jasmine."

"Hmm?"

"I know you hate it, but can I have a free pass to say something praise-adjacent?"

She snorted, wiggling her ass against him. "Just this once, but I believe you made me a promise first."

"A promise is a promise." Liam tugged her closer and slid his cock inside her. She whimpered, her head dropping back against him, her pussy hugging his cock. "I assume asking if you're going to behave is a waste of time?" he murmured in her ear and she shivered as his breath tickled her ear.

She squeezed around him, and he sucked in a breath.

 208

"Aww, are you worried you can't handle me?"

He ran a thumb down her throat before wrapping his fingers around her neck and applying light pressure. She moaned, her breaths picking up. "I think I've more than proven I can handle your bratty ass, darling. Now behave and let me be nice to you for a second, for fuck's sake."

"Fine," she grumbled, but a smile fell across her face. Liam leaned in and kissed the very corner of her mouth as he released her throat.

"You let me in. You trusted me enough to let me in, *and* to let go with me. I'm so fucking proud of you, Jasmine, but I'm also so honored and grateful that you could do that with me. Thank you."

He couldn't see her face—intentionally on his part, because he knew this would be easier for her to hear if he wasn't looking her in the eye—but he felt the sharp intake of breath that caught in her chest.

She was silent for a moment, and, when she answered, he knew she was forcing her voice to sound calm and collected. "Does this mean I've earned your cock in my mouth?"

Christ. "Behave tomorrow and we'll see what happens when we get home."

"Home from where?"

"It's a surprise," he said, nipping her earlobe. It was a surprise for both of them, considering he hadn't actually planned anything yet. But he wanted to take her out, needed to take her out. As much as he loved being tucked away behind closed doors with Jasmine, he never wanted her to feel like this was all he wanted.

"Liam?"

"Yeah?"

Jasmine let out a long breath. "I'm not used to believing people when they say nice things to me. Mostly, I think they're just saying it out of obligation and don't actually mean it. But you… I believe you when you say it. Thank you. You know Maggie will always be my bestest best friend, but you're a very close second."

Liam held her tighter, his heart thundering. He was constantly toeing a line of wanting to scream about how obsessed with her he was and playing it cool so he didn't scare her off. "I would never dream of trying to take Maggie's spot, but I'm happy to be next in line. Even if you hold my top spot," he added with a faux-dramatic sigh, and she laughed, kicking his shin and then gasping when it caused him to shift, his cock pressing deeper into her.

"I don't suppose there's any way that you don't think there's a correlation between me talking about my feelings and finally having an orgasm?"

"No, there's no way. It's one hundred percent that and we're going to keep talking shit out."

"Fuck."

"I tell you what," he began, running his fingers through her hair. She'd brushed it before bed and his fingers glided straight through. "Before we have sex, every time, you tell me something, and I'll tell you something."

"Rule number five: conversing before coming."

Liam laughed, and Jasmine tightened around him as she felt the vibrations. "That certainly is a way to put it."

"I expect everything you share to be as cute as you being obsessed with Snoopy, for the record."

"I'll see what I can do. Now it's sleep time, darling. I've got big plans for you tomorrow night and I need you nice and rested."

"Promises, promises," she sassed, bringing his hand to her lips and kissing it.

Jazz

Jazz rolled her neck and shoulders as she stepped out of the yoga studio into the streaming Seattle sunshine. God, she'd needed that. Liam had well and truly put her body through it the night before. If they were going to keep this up (and she really, *really* hoped they were), she was going to have to make Sunday morning yoga a regular thing. She just needed to convince Liam to come with her. She needed to see him bending over in front of her in tight pants with calming music in the background.

She glanced at her phone, checking the time and weighing her options. It was just before ten, and Liam had gone to his moms' for breakfast since she'd been at yoga. She was already counting down the hours until she'd get to see him for whatever he had planned—eight hours, thirteen minutes to be precise, and she was well aware that she was acting a little clingy and codependent, but as long as she didn't *show* it, what was the harm? She could manage a morning and afternoon without him. Besides, she had a lot to update Maggie on.

Her best friend answered on the second ring. "Hey, you're up early."

"I had an eight-thirty yoga class. Do you want to grab brunch this morning? I'm not far from your place."

"Brunch sounds amazing, but I can't. I'm just heading out to meet up with Nadia. We're getting breakfast and meeting a couple of her colleagues for an early matinee of some Italian play thing."

"I don't know what to say to that," Jazz said, dumbfounded.

"I know, I know. It sounds awful. Why do you think I didn't invite you? I'm only going because Nadia's celebrating starting her new business. Did you know she has three now? She has her realtor business, her website where she sells courses for other realtors, and she just opened this gorgeous online stationery store. You'd love her notebooks. They're beautiful. She's even in talks for a book deal. I don't know how she does it all. Just give me a sec to say goodbye to Cal."

Jazz rolled her eyes. If only everyone was as perfect as Nadia was. She started down the sunny street, the bag and mat slung over her shoulder knocking against her back. Though most parking in Seattle was free on Sundays, it was still a nightmare to find a spot. She'd gotten lucky finding one a ten-minute walk from the yoga studio, and there was a cafe on the way back to her car. Even if Maggie couldn't make it, there was nothing stopping her from getting breakfast by herself. She was great company.

She stopped between the cafe and a tattoo parlor, leaning against the wall just as Maggie picked back up and she heard her front door closing behind her. "Sorry about that. You know what he's like with goodbyes." Even if Jazz didn't know what Cal was like, Maggie being so breathless was enough to put two and two together.

"I'll never begrudge you making me wait so you can make out with your sexy ass husband," Jazz replied, just thankful they were no longer talking about Nadia and her laundry list of achievements, and Maggie laughed.

"Can you still call Cal sexy when you're sleeping with his son?"

"I would call Cal sexy to Liam's face. His moms too. Actually, I'm pretty sure I have."

"Poor guy. He really does have his work cut out for him with you, doesn't he?"

Jazz knew she was joking, but Maggie's words stung. "He says he likes that about me," she said, a touch more defensively than she would have liked. She hated how close to the surface the doubt was, that Liam was going to wake up one day and wonder why the hell he'd wasted so much time hanging out with her. It had been easier to hide from the inconvenience of insecurity before he'd been so nice to her.

"Obviously he likes that. It's you. What's not to like?" Maggie said, the words doing nothing to stop the dark cloud that had been creeping over her since Maggie told her about Nadia. "How are things going with him? Any closer to an orgasm?"

"Nope," Jazz replied, the word surprising her as it

slipped out without a thought. She'd planned to tell Maggie over brunch. What difference did it make doing it over the phone? But something in the back of her mind told her to keep it to herself. "But it's going well. We're having fun."

Maggie hummed, concern clear in her voice. "Are you sure you shouldn't get a second opinion with another doctor? Maybe this has something to do with your awful periods."

"I'm not super worried, but I'll keep it in mind," she answered dismissively.

She knew that if Maggie found out that talking about her parents had been the key to helping her let go, she would have exactly one recommendation: therapy.

It was a universal truth, in Jazz's experience, that whenever someone you knew started going to therapy and found it helped, they wouldn't stop until everyone they knew was in therapy and thriving. Sure, she'd seen the incredible changes in Maggie since she'd started seeing her therapist, but that didn't mean it was for everyone. She didn't even like talking about shit with Liam.

"Hmm. Well, as long as you're having fun and Liam's being—shit. Nadia's calling. I need to answer in case it's about breakfast. Can I call you tonight?"

"Liam and I are going out tonight, but we can catch up next week."

"Perfect. Love you, bye!"

The call cut off and Jazz let her hand drop to her side, clutching her phone with more force than necessary. It was fine. Maggie was doing better than ever. She had new friends—grown-up friends who did things like going to

Sunday matinees, juggling incredible careers, and families. She was happy, and that's all Jazz wanted for her. Just because Jazz wasn't there yet didn't mean Maggie wasn't interested in her anymore. She didn't want those things anyway. She had plenty of time to figure it all out.

A buzzing sound caught her attention as the neon sign on the door of the tattoo shop lit up:

Open. Walk-ins welcome!

Jazz pushed off the wall, peering in through the window of the shop. Their work was beautiful—detailed portraits and color work to die for—but it was one little tattoo in the corner of a flash sheet that caught her attention. It was stupid and reckless and completely unhinged, but it had been a while since Jazz had done something like that.

She was overdue a little chaos.

The bell above the door jingled as she stepped into the tattoo shop. A girl with bubblegum pink hair and a matching gemstone on her front tooth smiled at her from the desk.

"Hi," Jazz said, pasting on a smile. "Do you have any space for a walk-in? I'd love one of your flash designs from the window."

CHAPTER TWENTY

Liam

Was it still a date if you didn't technically ask the other person to go on a date with you? Probably not, but Liam was taking it as such anyway, and holy shit, he was on a date with Jasmine. Language and labels seemed like a moot point when they spent more or less all their free time together, and all of their nights in either her bed or his. They'd gone way beyond their initial pact, way beyond friends with benefits. As far as he was concerned, they were well on their way to their hypothetical Hallowedding not being so hypothetical.

He might be getting a little ahead of himself.

Could he have just asked Jasmine on a date? Sure, but they were twenty-four hours out from her being more vulnerable with him than she had been with anyone in years, and the last thing he wanted to do was overwhelm her.

"What are you thinking?" she asked, nestling into his side and scanning the menu in his hand, even though there was one sitting on the table in front of her. He slung an arm around her shoulders so she could snuggle in closer.

Never, in years of dating India, had they shared the same side of a booth in a restaurant, but Jasmine had slid right in beside him like it was second nature.

"I'm torn between the buffalo bites and the mini tacos. What about you?"

"Everything looks delicious," she mused, and Liam's gaze fell to her lips. "Why don't we order both and split them? And maybe a side of crispy potato skins?"

"Good plan. Let's do that."

Sharing dishes: something else India would never have done. Liam wasn't sure why she kept crossing his mind. He supposed if they were counting this as a date—and he was—then it was technically his first date since they'd broken up. There had been the almost-date with Maggie but, after she'd called it off, and he realized he wasn't ready, he'd just never asked anyone out again, sticking to casual hookups instead.

Liam had loved India, but things had never felt as natural with her as he did with Jasmine.

"Are you going to tell me where we're going after dinner yet?" Jasmine asked when they'd placed their order.

"Nope. It's a surprise, but I promise you'll love it."

"I assume whatever it is involves getting messy, since you told me to wear clothes I didn't mind ruining." There was an eager twinkle in Jasmine's hazel eyes. Between that and the flecks of gold, it was like her eyes were full of stars, sparkling constellations prettier than anything in the sky.

"Very messy," he confirmed.

"Excellent. I guess that means we get to shower it all off later, and that's exactly why you picked it."

Visions of Jasmine's wet, naked skin beneath his fingers as the shower beat down on them both hadn't been his motivation for picking their first date activity, but it certainly didn't hurt. "That's a bonus."

A server brought their strawberry mojitos, and Jasmine held up her glass.

"What are we toasting?" he asked, following suit.

"To orgasms," she announced, garnering a scandalized look from the group at the table beside them.

"To orgasms," Liam agreed, and they clinked their glasses and sipped. The taste of sweet fresh strawberries and tart lime flooded his senses. He didn't drink often, but he couldn't wait to taste the sugar on Jasmine's tongue later.

"This is nice," she said with a happy sigh. "I love spending time in our apartments, but it feels good to get out for a night."

"We should do this more often," he agreed, and she nodded, with a grin that set his stomach fluttering.

Liam fell somewhere between an extrovert and an introvert, but Jasmine was definitely the former. The restaurant wasn't busy. There were maybe a dozen tables full and twice as many empty, but he'd felt the shift in her as soon as they'd walked in. It was like she absorbed the energy of those around her, amping herself up.

He didn't really care where they were, he just liked holding her hand, asking her about her day. Liam opened his mouth to do just that, but Jasmine spoke first.

"How was breakfast with your moms?"

Liam snapped his mouth closed. He knew he shouldn't compare, but... When had India ever shown a genuine interest in things like that? She was a pro at asking all the right questions, but they always felt like more of an obligation than her actually caring. Jasmine's expression was genuinely curious, but it morphed into concern the longer he stayed quiet.

"Are you okay? You're being kind of quiet tonight."

Shit. "Sorry. I'm just happy to be spending the night with you and I'm soaking it in," he said, and her expression softened. "Breakfast was good. My moms are thinking of converting their garage into a sauna room."

Jasmine clung to his every word, and Liam vowed not to let India cross his mind again for the rest of the night. But that became substantially more difficult, an hour later, when they were putting down their forks from the fudge cake they'd shared, and his phone lit up on the table. India's name flashed on the screen, and both Jasmine and Liam just stared at it silently for a moment.

"Are you going to answer it?"

The thought hadn't even crossed his mind. "No. I really have no interest in speaking to her." The words weren't bitter or angry, they were just matter-of-fact. There was no lingering heartbreak in his chest.

The phone rang out and the screen went black. "Has she called before?"

"Not since we broke up," Liam told her, frowning at the phone in confusion. "And I can't think of any reason she'd need to call now. It's not like we have mutual friends or anything."

"Maybe a pocket dial by mista—or not," Jasmine finished as his phone lit up again.

India

(1) New Message

Jesus, had just thinking about her summoned her? He flipped his phone over, screen-side down on the table, and turned his attention back to Jasmine, who was looking between him and the phone, aghast.

"Liam!"

"What?"

"You have to check it."

He cupped her chin between his thumb and forefinger. "Jasmine, darling, I cannot stress enough how little interest I have in anyone else in the world when you're sitting beside me."

Her eyes widened, and she sucked in a breath. "That is a very nice thing to say," she murmured.

"I mean it."

Jasmine gave him a wicked smile. "I know. And I am going to need you to let me thank you properly later by coming in my mouth." A woman at the table beside them choked on her drink, but Liam was getting used to the chaos that fell from Jasmine's perfect lips. His blood thrummed. "But Liam?"

"Hmm?"

"We have to look at the message. It will haunt me for the rest of the night if we don't—I'm too nosy for this."

Liam laughed, shaking his head and unlocking his phone before handing it over without even glancing at it. "Have at it."

"Wow, you really don't care, do you?"

"Not at all."

Jasmine swiped open his messages, and her smile dimmed as she scanned the screen.

"Bad?"

"Oh, no. It's not bad."

She turned the phone to face him.

> Hey Liam, hope you're doing well. I'd love the chance to speak to you. Can you give me a call when you have time?

Well, that was vague. And he definitely wouldn't be calling her. His eyes drifted up the screen and he realized why Jasmine's smile had faded. Ah. His last message to India, sent just twenty minutes before he'd walked into their apartment and found her in bed with Bart.

> Heading home early. I think I must have caught that cold your dad had at the weekend. Do you want to order from Zerroni's tonight? Love you <3

It was like reading something a stranger had written. It was, in a way, he supposed. Liam didn't think he would recognize himself if he looked back now. That Liam had no idea he was about to turn his life upside down. He had no clue how thoroughly broken he would be for the next six months, how hard he'd have to claw himself out of his own head. He had no idea how long he would spend blaming himself, convinced that he must have done something to make them betray him like they had.

But that Liam hadn't met Jasmine. And present-day Liam was far happier in this moment, tucked in a restaurant booth with his arm around her than he ever had been back then.

Liam opened India's contact page and scrolled down, hitting *Block Contact*.

"You're not going to call her?" Jasmine asked.

"Nope."

A laugh bubbled out of Jasmine's mouth as she read the sign.

Welcome to Chaos!

"Nice of you to bring me somewhere I'll fit right in," she said, bumping his hip with hers. "What exactly does chaos entail?" Her smile was infectious.

"You'll see, darling."

He left Jasmine by the door as he gave his name to the man at the front desk, who handed him a key and gave him a quick rundown of the room he'd booked. He dangled the key on his finger and beckoned Jasmine over. She wrapped an arm around his waist and raised a brow at the key.

"Chaos is giving kind of seedy vibes."

The key did closely resemble an old motel key, red plastic, printed with the Chaos logo and the *Room 2* in black block letters.

The man at the desk cleared his throat. "Just so you know, there are cameras in the rooms."

This just confused Jasmine more. "Without any context, I don't know what to make of that. Kinky or creepy?" she asked Liam as he thanked the man at the desk and tugged her down the corridor.

"Neither. Although if you're into that, we can revisit it another time." He couldn't remember how exhibitionism had scored on her kink list, but he would happily show her off like the work of art she was.

"I know a place we could go for that. Shit, actually, no, I can't tell you about that."

Liam frowned before realizing that probably meant it was something to do with his dad and Maggie. "Jesus Christ. Burning that from my brain. Okay, this is us."

He unlocked the door and felt around the wall for a light switch. He flicked it on and color assaulted his eyes. Paint splattered the room in every color of the rainbow and beyond. Only one spot was clear: the giant canvas hanging on the wall, waiting for them to cover it. A long table held bottles of paint, containers of glitter, bowls full of fabric and paper scraps, glue, and pompoms. There were no paint brushes, but there were plain white overalls and gloves to give the illusion that they might not be walking out of here covered in as much paint as the canvas.

"Holy shit," Jasmine squealed, spinning around and taking the room in. "This is amazing. I swear, this is what the inside of my head looks like at all times—sexy, mustached man and all," she added with a wink. "Do we put these on?" She held up a set of overalls before Liam could respond to the *sexy, mustached man* comment.

When he nodded, she tossed a set to him and pulled the

overalls on over her denim shorts and t-shirt. Liam was around people in overalls every day at work, but he'd never considered them hot until they were on Jasmine's body. He begrudgingly looked away so he could step into his set and, by the time he looked up, she already had a bottle of bright turquoise paint in one hand and a container of silver glitter tucked under her arm.

Most people would look unsure, maybe even question the lack of painting tools, having lost their sense of curiosity and chaos somewhere before high school. But Jasmine wasn't most people. She clapped her hands together, not even flinching when paint and glitter flew all over her overalls, face, and hair.

"So do we have a plan here or are we just going for it?"

And as Liam watched the turquoise paint sliding down her cheek, dripping onto the floor, his breath caught in his throat. Because love wasn't trying to squeeze himself into a box to be the perfect boyfriend for India, and it wasn't either of their faults that they hadn't been right for each other.

Love was beautiful chaos, and he was deeply and desperately in love with Jasmine.

CHAPTER TWENTY-ONE

Jazz

Liam had been quiet all night, but not in a distant way. In fact, he'd been almost unnervingly present. Unnerving in the sense that Jazz liked it.

Throughout dinner, he'd kept an arm around her shoulders, paying more attention to her than their food. He hadn't even wavered when India had called and texted, and Jazz actually believed he didn't care. Which made zero sense, because she could (and would, if requested) recite the name of every lover who'd ever wronged her and would kill to run into any of them so she could use some of the carefully rehearsed comebacks she hadn't thought of in the moment.

After dinner, he'd taken her to a place that was a perfect combination of the two of them, and watched everything she'd done with a look of wonder. Every splash and smear of paint, every drop of glitter, every pompom thrown at the wall like a snowball. It was like she was creating a goddamn masterpiece and every step fascinated him.

Their final painting hadn't been close to a masterpiece, but she couldn't wait to see it once it had been sealed and varnished. Jazz had found an old red lipstick in the bottom of her purse and pressed a kiss mark above her signature, then forced Liam to do the same. It might not be a grand work of art, but it was theirs.

Between dinner, painting, and Liam's undivided attention, the whole thing had felt almost like a date. Except a date where the other person was actually interested in getting to know her and not just what was between her legs. It had been the perfect night, and Jazz's heart was a tangled, confused mess.

She pushed that aside as Liam followed her into her apartment, choosing to focus on the rest of her body: *those* feelings were loud and clear.

"Shower?" Liam asked, dropping her purse and the bag of leftovers from dinner on the couch. They'd ordered extra dessert, fully intending to work up an appetite when they got home.

"Shower," she agreed, leading him to her bedroom.

The overalls had done an okay job of protecting their clothes, but they were both still covered in paint, glitter, and assorted crafting materials Jazz didn't even remember seeing. She plucked a feather from Liam's hair, causing glitter to sprinkle over his face.

He swiped at his face. "I'm pretty sure we're going to be covered in this for the rest of our lives."

"Whoops." She had been just a touch overzealous on the glitter side of things.

She lifted her t-shirt over her head and tossed it on top of her laundry pile. It was relatively unscathed, but if the flecks of paint that had slipped under the overalls stained, she didn't mind. Her shorts were totally paint free, and she kicked them off, turning around to check out how much paint was on her skin in the full-length mirror.

"What's that? Are you hurt?"

"What?" Jazz followed Liam's gaze down to her hip and stilled. Fuck. How the hell had she forgotten that? And how was she supposed to explain it? "Oh. It's nothing. I'm fine."

Liam squinted at the white bandage, barely hiding the clear tattoo covering. "Is that a new tattoo? When the fuck did you have time to get a tattoo? I literally saw you naked this morning."

Jazz stepped back, wringing her hands. "It's possible I made a really impulsive post-yoga decision."

"And forgot to mention it?"

"Maybe," she replied with a grimace. "Okay, here's the thing: it's really unhinged, and I know it's really unhinged, but I saw the design in the window and I was thinking about how amazing last night was and how you got me to open up to you, and you opened up to me and I—" She cut herself off, her sentences were running together into one big jumble. "Okay, it's probably easier if I just show you, but again, I know this is a highly questionable decision."

Liam watched warily as she peeled the white bandage away. She watched his face transform, his eyes widening, jaw going slack, as he dropped to his knees to look closer.

"Holy shit," he murmured, brushing the skin around the tattoo with his thumb. "This... I don't even know what to say."

She winced, rubbing her forehead with paint-flecked fingers. "In my defense, I can't really be held accountable for my behavior less than twenty-four hours after you made me come for the first time in a decade and—what are you doing?" She stilled as Liam hooked his thumbs in the waistband of her underwear.

"Hold on to the wall, darling."

"The wall? Wha—oh fuck."

Liam

Snoopy. She'd tattooed goddamn Snoopy on her hip *for him*. Liam was careful not to touch the still fresh tattoo as he gripped her hips, burying his face against her pussy and devouring her.

It was covered by protective plastic film—which was probably just as well considering there had been a chance of it getting covered in paint—but the skin around the dainty design was red and tender looking. It wasn't a big tattoo—maybe two inches tall, with Snoopy sitting down, holding a book. Though most of it was just black line work, Snoopy's book featured a pink heart. A romance book.

What the hell did this mean for what Jasmine felt about him? He wasn't entirely sure, but it could only be good.

He nudged her back against the wall, lifting her leg over his shoulder, opening her wider to him. He was relentless, unable to get enough of her. She moaned, shaking in his grip, while he circled her clit with the flat of his tongue, fucking her with two fingers. Seeing her come last night had been incredible—but now he wanted to taste it.

She jumped when he grazed her clit with his teeth, his name spilling from her with a slew of curses.

Jasmine knotted her hands in his hair. "Liam," she groaned, tugging him just hard enough that he pulled back. "What about rule number five?"

"Now you want to follow the rules?" he asked, dragging his gaze up her body. Her skin was flushed, her chest rising and falling as she panted. He hadn't noticed, but, at some point, she'd taken her bra off, and her nipple piercings glinted in the light.

"You told me I had to behave in order to get your cock in my mouth. This is me behaving," she said through gritted teeth.

"Wow, I hardly recognize you."

She growled at him, but it turned into a whimper, her mouth dropping open and her head falling back as he curled his fingers inside her.

"Okay, let's stick to the rules. Tell me about your exes. Anyone serious? Anyone I'm going to have to fight off if they come trying to win you back?" It seemed fitting, given that she knew all about his ex—and since said ex had come out of the woodwork.

"You want me to talk about my exes while you—*fuck*—fucking finger me?"

"Give me some credit, darling. I can multitask. I'm still listening." He winked and didn't give her the chance to argue before leaning in and running his tongue over her clit.

"Oh fuck. Okay. Um… Shit, there's really no one worth

mentioning." Her words were slurred slightly, her voice breathy and jumpy. "I've never really had anything serious, just people I've dated for a few months here and there who weren't looking to commit to anything."

"Why?" he asked, pulling back just enough to ask before turning his attention to her pussy again. He withdrew his fingers, replacing them with his tongue and pressing one finger slowly inside her ass.

Jasmine cried out, clenching around his finger. "Why have I never had anything serious or why has no one ever wanted to commit?"

"Both," he managed without pulling away. He was pretty sure he'd never tasted anything as fucking perfect as Jasmine, and he wasn't interested in giving up a single second more than he had to.

She must have been able to make it out, though, because after a moment, she answered. "I don't know… I mean, I'm not great with expectations since I never seem to be able to meet them, so I guess I've been drawn to people who have low expectations of me."

Jesus, he despised her parents.

"And it's been hard to have anything serious when I haven't been able to trust anyone to tell them about the orgasm thing—until you." Her voice cracked, the last word falling away with a whimper. *Until him.* That deserved a reward. Liam pressed a second finger inside her ass and she gasped.

"And okay, sure, I've spent years telling everyone I didn't want anything serious, but I'm pretty sure I've been lying to myself. It's just scary to say I want something like that in case no one wants me like that—oh fuck, baby. *Fuck.*"

Jasmine's whole body tensed, the orgasm ripping through her when Liam brushed a finger over her clit. He was right: as beautiful as she looked when she really let go, she tasted even better. He only let up when her body slumped against the wall and he wasn't entirely sure she could hold herself up.

Liam's body ached as he stood up—maybe he should have taken her up on the offer to join her at yoga. But then she wouldn't have the tattoo. He trailed his fingers lightly across it as he took her in his arms, swallowing down the emotion thick in his throat.

"Are you alright?"

"Mhmm," she replied sleepily.

"Feel better getting it out?"

Her eyes fluttered open, hazy and dark. "Talking about my feelings is unsurprisingly better with your tongue inside me."

"Oh no, I guess I'll have to do that every time. Such a hardship," he joked with a smile, and Jasmine laughed, brushing a finger from one dimple to the other, across his lips.

"My turn to ask you something."

He tucked her hair back behind her ear. "Before you do, I find it completely unbelievable that everyone you meet doesn't want you like that, darling. You deserve everything you want and so much more." *And I want to be the one to give it to you.* He couldn't tell if she heard the unspoken words, but her shoulders tensed for a split second before she relaxed back into him. "Now it's your turn. Ask away."

She tilted her head, searching his face as she asked, "If you'd picked up the phone earlier, and India told you she'd made a mistake and she wanted to get back together, would you take her back?"

"No." He didn't even need to think about it.

"Why?"

Because she's not you. But it wasn't that, not entirely. Even if Liam hadn't started falling for Jasmine the second he'd laid eyes on her in his dad's office, he wouldn't have taken India back. She'd broken him completely without breaking a sweat, and for what? Neither of them had been as happy as they pretended to be when they were together.

"I don't miss her. At all. I miss parts of the life I had back then—the museum, mostly—but I don't even think she's crossed my mind since just after the wedding. What we had wasn't like this. It wasn't comfortable, and easy, and trusting. It was just all we knew."

"I hate her for hurting you," Jasmine said, laying her head on his chest. "But I'm glad I got to meet the version of you who knows he deserves better than that."

"Likewise."

"Now about me behaving…"

Jasmine stepped away and dragged him toward the bathroom, tearing his clothes off while the shower warmed up, then tugged him under the spray. The water spilled over their bodies, and Liam watched the light reflecting on the water droplets as they drizzled down Jasmine's skin. He wanted to lick each and every one of them off, but she didn't give him the chance, falling to her knees and pushing him back against the wall.

"You called me your *toy* once," Jasmine mused, wrapping her fist around his cock and drawing a grunt from his lips.

"And you liked it."

She licked her lips. "Maybe. But words are just words unless you back them up. You want me to be your toy, baby? Then fucking use me like one."

She was going to be the death of him. Liam leaned down and clasped her chin. "Be careful what you wish for. You think you can handle that?"

He brushed his thumb over her lips and she caught it between her teeth, biting hard enough that Liam pulled it back.

"You don't scare me."

"We'll see." He released her chin and slapped her lightly across the mouth. "Open up."

Jasmine's eyes glittered as she opened her mouth, her lids fluttering as he slowly pressed his cock between her lips. She moaned, moving her tongue side to side over him as he pushed to the back of her throat. It was an exercise in control to take it slowly, easing her into it. But Liam knew Jasmine well enough to know she wouldn't tap out if she was uncomfortable. She was too fucking stubborn for that, so he watched her reactions like a hawk, testing the back of her throat with the head of his cock.

Of course, this was Jasmine he was dealing with, and patience wasn't in her wheelhouse. Her eyes flashed in frustration and she tried to move her head, taking him further.

Liam fisted her hair, pulling his cock back until he was resting on her tongue.

"Uh-uh. Good toys hold still, Jasmine. Do you want me to fuck your mouth? To treat you like the desperate little brat you are?" His voice was low, breathy, every word a fucking challenge not to just fuck her.

Jasmine's eyes widened, her expression somewhere between fear and delight. She nodded as much as she could while he was holding her hair so tightly.

"Then fucking behave," he warned, tightening his grip and thrusting hard into her mouth. Jasmine moaned around his cock, struggling against his grip and looking damn happy about it.

The water pounded on them, mingling with the tears streaming from Jasmine's eyes. She breathed in through her nose, spluttering and choking on his cock as she inhaled the water. But she didn't falter. If anything, she sank deeper and deeper into her pliant state.

"God, I fucking love it when you cry for me. So fucking pretty," Liam groaned and Jasmine's eyes flamed in a challenge. He'd teetered too close to praise.

She ran her hands up his thighs. He expected her to scratch him as a punishment. She wouldn't edge him. He knew she wanted his cum as much as he wanted to give it to her.

He didn't expect her to press a finger into his ass. Liam's head snapped back, connecting with the wall as Jasmine curled her finger inside him. She had small hands, and there was barely a sting as she massaged him. With her other hand, she cupped his balls, squeezing hard enough to make him curse, but not so hard it was painful. He clenched around her finger, his fist shaking, tugging hard on her hair.

Jasmine hummed, and he lost it, coming down her throat with a garbled cry that sounded something like her name as fire washed over him. She'd fucking obliterated him.

When his hold on her hair loosened, his muscles giving way, she released his balls and gripped his hip, holding him to her face, drinking him down. She didn't stop sucking him, lapping at him, fucking him with her finger, until there was nothing left of him.

When she pulled back from him, he collapsed to his knees, grasping her face and ignoring the saliva and cum dripping from her mouth as he kissed her fiercely. He held her to him in a vise grip, breaking their kiss but pressing their foreheads together.

"Fuck, Jasmine," he whispered, utterly spent.

Jasmine laughed through panting breaths, grinning from ear to ear. "I really should behave more often."

CHAPTER TWENTY-TWO

Jazz

"Hey you."

Jazz jumped as someone slid her headphones off, the familiar voice murmuring in her ear, lips grazing her cheek. She spun around in her chair, knocking her elbow on Cal's desk. She was working on her laptop with her headphones in while he was in a meeting downstairs, listening to another of Liam's audiobook recommendations. Cal's office was calm and comfortable. Her being there had absolutely nothing to do with the fact she was hiding from Sierra, who had become suspicious of Jazz's good moods and achey muscles and was pestering her to find out who she was hooking up with.

"Hey. This is a nice surprise. Are you here to see your dad?" she asked, looking up at him. Liam stepped closer, leaning down to plant a quick kiss on her lips.

"I'm here to see you. Want to grab lunch?"

Her brows knit together, and she frowned at him. Suspicious. "What's the occasion? Is something wrong?"

"The occasion is that I want to spend time with you."

"Ah, of course. Because you never see me outside of working hours. You're so deprived of my company, I honestly don't know how you're still functioning. I would be curled up in a ball, crying in the corner, if I were you."

"Jasmine." His mustache twitched.

"Hmm?"

"Get your ass off that chair so I can kiss you properly."

She took her sweet time standing up, but as soon as she was out of the chair, Liam pulled her to him, catching her lips with his and giving her a little bite for talking shit. Her toes curled in her shoes, her hands immediately finding purchase on his ass as his tongue danced along hers.

His hand crept up the back of her shirt, and, though his fingers were warm, the movement doused her in cold water.

She placed her hand on his chest, breaking their kiss and gently pushing Liam back a couple of steps. "We can't do this here. Your dad could walk in at any second."

"You know I'm thirty-seven, right? My dad knows I kiss people. I'm not going to get grounded or anything."

"But your dad doesn't know you kiss me," she reasoned, and Liam's lips turned down at the corners. "What?"

"Do we need to be so secretive about this? I know we hit our goal of making you come, but I don't want to stop doing this, and you don't seem to either."

"I don't. But do you really want your parents to know that we're sleeping together?"

Liam frowned. "This isn't just sex. I think we both know that."

Maybe, but it was the first time either of them had said it out loud. And it wasn't exactly a conversation she wanted to have in his dad's office—or ever, if she could help it. Not talking about it was easier. Not talking about it was safer.

"Okay, fine. Do you really want your parents to know we're casually seeing each other?"

"Uh, yeah. I do. Why are we keeping it so under wraps? Do you not want people to know you're with me?" His voice was small, insecurity creeping into his emerald eyes. Shit.

She crossed the distance between them, wrapping her arms around his middle. "Whoa, baby, it's nothing like that. You're perfect. But your parents… You're their pride and joy. Their only kid. And I love them so much. I love how they've accepted me into their family, but there's a big difference between me being in the family as Maggie's best friend, and me sleeping with their son."

The worry in Liam's eyes morphed into confusion. "Why would they have an issue with that?"

"I'm not exactly the kind of person parents dream about their kid being with."

"What the fuck? Jasmine, you're incredible. My parents love you."

"I know! And I don't want that to change."

Liam crossed his arms and narrowed his eyes. "You're not very nice to yourself. I don't like it."

Jazz opened her mouth and closed it. She loved herself. It wasn't her own perception of herself that was the problem. It was how everyone else perceived her. *She* thought she was great. And she didn't care what anyone else thought.

Except Liam's parents. And, she supposed, her own

parents, deep down, but that was purely a biological urge and it wasn't her fault. There was also her newfound worry about Maggie outgrowing her, but everyone worried about that kind of shit when they turned thirty, right?

Sometimes she worried that the people she worked with didn't respect her as much as they had Maggie. She knew she was good at her job, but she wasn't Maggie. And she'd drifted away from all her old college friends when they went on to do amazing things with their degrees and she hadn't, but Maggie drifted with her, and Maggie… Well, Maggie had needed therapy to learn to love and value herself. Shit.

Panic was rising through her, her blood rushing faster through her veins, her lungs searching for air that just wasn't there.

"You still with me?" Liam asked, watching her with concern. She must have looked as panicked as she felt, because he swiped a gentle hand over her back and pressed his forehead to hers. "Hey, I've got you. Breathe, darling." His breath was warm against her face, and she copied him: in and out and in and out.

Her brain swirled. "I'm okay." She swallowed, sucking in a big breath. "Just unpacking some shit."

"Care to share with the class?"

"Nah. I think I'll save it so I have something to earn my next orgasm with," she said, and Liam shook his head, smiling. He cupped her face with his hand, rubbing his thumb over her cheek.

"I think we need to have a talk about what this is," he gestured between them. "And what we want. Soon."

Jazz nodded, her anxiety calmer but still fluttering in her stomach. He wouldn't be smiling as he said it if he was going to call things off—hell, not even five minutes had passed since he'd said exactly the opposite, but the little voice in the back of her head couldn't help but expect the worst.

"In the meantime," Liam continued, "no more being mean to yourself, please. I instinctively want to fight everyone who's mean to you and you being mean to yourself makes that complicated."

"Be honest with me: have you ever fought someone before?"

"No, but I would," Liam said, a shade defensively. "For you, I would."

He deserved a tighter hug for that. Jazz squeezed him, then rose on her tiptoes to kiss him. "I would fight someone for you too."

"Oh, I believe that," Liam said, smiling against her lips. "But I also believe you'd fight someone just for fun."

"Duh. I'm a Scorpio middle child through and through, baby: rebellious, domineering, hot-tempered…"

"Don't forget charming, sensual, and loyal. Coincidentally, all of my favorite things."

She gaped at him.

"Oh, don't be too impressed. I know next to nothing about astrology, but I asked my dad for your birthday and looked it up when we first met. I've been waiting years for the right time to pull that info out."

She had never been more attracted to him. Jesus. Jazz wanted nothing more than to show him just how much that turned her on, but the elevator dinged, and though she hated herself for doing it, she jumped out of his arms. The flash of hurt on Liam's face lasted only a split second, but it lanced through her like a knife in the chest.

"Hey you two," Cal said with a wide smile as he walked into the office. "What are you up to?"

"We were going to grab some lunch. Ethel's?" he suggested, and Jazz nodded her agreement. Ethel's was the diner closest to their office building, and a favorite of the Michaelson and Hicks' team.

"Sounds perfect. You want to join us, Cal?" Asking was the polite thing to do. It had nothing to do with avoiding any kind of serious conversation with Liam over lunch. Of course, Liam raised a brow that told her he saw right through her flimsy invitation. That was fine by her—she was quite sure she'd enjoy paying for it later.

Frustration and pleasure built side by side within her as she clung to the headboard. Her wrists were cuffed, but she had enough leeway to wrap her fingers around the wooden posts and hold on for dear life as Liam fucked her mercilessly, her ankles on his shoulders.

The thrust of his cock inside her, deep and rough, was accented with soft kisses to her calves, and it felt incredible. Embers sizzled all over her body, but she just couldn't get her brain on board. She pinched her eyes closed, drawing in a watery breath, and Liam stilled immediately.

"Darling—"

"Fuck," she interrupted, turning her head to hide her face in her arm. Had she always cried this much? Jesus. "It's just… It's not going to happen. I'm sorry."

Liam made quick work of setting her legs down and unbuckling her cuffs. She immediately covered her face with her hands, trying desperately to suck her goddamn tears back into her eyeballs. What the fuck was wrong with her?

"Look at me," Liam pleaded, his voice soft. He laid his palm on her shoulder, warm and comforting, but not invasive, like he was trying to give her space. A few months ago, Jazz would have relished in the space to work through her feelings. But now, she needed to be close to him like she needed air.

She flung her arms around his shoulders and burrowed into his chest, breathing him in. Sweet, spicy, warm, safe. Liam wrapped her in his arms, pressing his face to the top of her head.

"I'm sorry," she repeated, the words muffled because she had no intention of moving away from his chest.

"Sorry for what? You haven't done anything wrong," he replied, running his hand down her back.

"I thought I could finish. I *wanted* to. I just couldn't focus."

"It's okay. You never have to be sorry for that. It won't happen every time. That's completely normal. If you're not feeling something, we can switch it up and try something else, take a breather, or stop. No questions asked."

Jazz pulled back, wiping at her tear-streaked cheeks.

"But this is your thing. And you've made everyone else come so obviously I'm the problem."

"I said no one has ever faked it with me, not that I've never not made someone come," he said with a soft chuckle, cupping her cheek and nuzzling the edge of her nose. "Women only come during sex something like 50 to 80% of the time. And we literally just started unpacking everything. It's going to take a while for you to feel totally comfortable with it all."

"I can't believe you just had that statistic ready to go," she grumbled, even though she definitely believed it. "And yes, that makes logical sense, but still: I'm sorry."

Liam frowned. "Say sorry one more time and I'm going to edge the fuck out of you next time and not *let* you come."

"Rude." She flopped back against the pillows with a dramatic sigh.

Liam snuggled in beside her, offering his arm out so she could tuck herself into his side. "You okay?"

"Yeah," she murmured. "Frustrated, but I'll survive."

"You better." He kissed her forehead, then reached over her to snag his phone from the nightstand. "I know something else we can do that's just as fun."

"We already did the daily crossword today. Eight across: Monet, remember?" She didn't know how he could forget. He'd been mad as hell when she'd figured out the art clue first, even if he had tried to hide it.

"Not that, and I didn't forget," he replied with a huff. "Help me pick a dog from the shelter website."

"Seriously?"

Liam held his phone up and Jazz squealed as she took in

the thumbnails on the screen. "Oh my god, they're all so cute. How can you possibly pick just one?"

"This is why I need help. I've been looking, but I want them all."

They scrolled through the website, clicking into each dog's profile to learn more about them. Liam was open to any breed or age, though he was hoping for someone on the smaller side since his car wasn't huge.

"That one looks like he would try to eat you if you ever fell asleep on the floor," Jazz said, pointing out a small Chihuahua mix.

"That's a no from me. This one looks friendly. Lacey." He clicked into the profile of a black and white fluffy pup, with her tongue hanging out of her mouth in the picture. "Hmm, it says she's not good with kids."

"You don't have kids."

Liam eyed her. "Yet. We're having at least four, ideally six. We talked about it at my dad and Maggie's wedding, remember?"

Jazz rolled her eyes, smiling as she tried to remember the details of the conversation they'd had. They'd both been absolutely wasted. "Vaguely, but if we're having six kids, we should probably get a move on. I'm not getting any younger," she joked.

"I'm ready when you are," Liam added, sounding significantly *less* jokey than she had. Jazz wasn't willing to unpack how exactly her body *and* her heart responded to that. "But I guess Lacey's out." He swiped out of her profile and scrolled down.

They both saw the listing at the same minute, Liam

sucking in a breath and Jazz grabbing for the phone. "Holy shit, that is the cutest dog I've ever seen. Look at his little face, and his floppy ear, and—oh my god, his fluffy little butt," she gushed, zooming in on the picture of the tiny puppy.

He looked like some kind of corgi mix, with dark gingery fur and a white nose and belly, and he couldn't have been older than twelve weeks old. She knew he was a little younger than Liam had been hoping for, but he was so fucking cute.

"He's adorable," Liam said, and she could already tell from his voice that he was in love. She swiped to the next picture, which showed the puppy's face more clearly, and gasped. "Is that what I think it is?" Liam asked.

Jazz zoomed in closer to the little V-shaped patch of dark brown fur right below his nose. "It is. He has a mustache. It's meant to be."

"He has a mustache like me, he's a redhead like you and look, his profile says he's cheeky and loves cuddles. He's basically us in puppy form."

"Damn, I'm about to get replaced by a puppy."

"Never." Liam grinned and tapped her on the end of her nose.

"It looks like he was only listed this afternoon. His profile isn't even complete yet. That probably means he's still available."

Liam was way ahead of her, clicking on the *Adopt Me!* button and typing in his information. He sent off the form and a pop up promised that he'd hear back within forty-eight hours.

"You're going to be a dad," she said, squeezing his hand.

"I am. You're not allowed to call me daddy, though," Liam warned.

"Oh, because of your dad and Maggie? I'd never. You know about that?"

He narrowed his eyes. "Know about what?"

Oh. Oh no. There had to be nothing worse than finding out that your dad's wife, who was seven years younger than you, called him *daddy*. And as much as Jazz loved giving Liam shit, she didn't want to be the one to scar him with that.

"Nothing!" she said too quickly, as she watched the realization sink into Liam's eyes. He scrunched his face up in disgust.

"Oh my god. That's… Ugh. Is that where the hand painted *World's Greatest Daddy* mug he has came from? I knew I didn't paint that for him."

"I painted that for him. As a joke, obviously," she admitted with a guilty smile.

"I'm never going to be able to look at them ag—what are you doing?" he asked, as Jazz lifted the covers and crawled beneath, kneeling between his legs.

"Apologizing for putting that thought in your head. Your turn to hold on to the headboard, baby."

CHAPTER TWENTY-THREE

Liam

When Liam let himself into his dad and Maggie's house, Peach immediately ran up to the front door to greet him. She was a fickle thing. Sometimes she loved cuddles and company, and other times she hissed at you for so much as looking at her. But she stamped her little paws on Liam's foot, which he took to mean today was a cuddling kind of day.

"Hi, sweet girl," he cooed, reaching down and bundling her into his arms. She cuddled into his chest, rubbing her fluffy little head on his chin. He kissed the top of her head and she leveled him with a warning look. Peach despised the mustache. "My bad. Where's your mom?"

"Meow."

"Helpful. Very helpful. Maggie?"

There was no answer, but he knew she was here: her phone was sitting on the kitchen table, and her water tumbler was sitting open by the sink, as if she'd started to fill it, but something had distracted her. Peach leaped out of his arms and padded along the counter to the tumbler, where she immediately started licking the straw.

Liam grimaced. "How many times have you done that without being spotted? Gross." He lifted her from the counter, rolling his eyes at her protesting hiss.

He wasn't a cat person, but he *was* excited about finally getting a dog. Thank god dogs didn't jump up on the kitchen counters to lick straws.

Although Liam loved his dad and Maggie together, he couldn't pretend he wasn't relieved that the only children Maggie wanted were four-legged. Having a human sibling almost forty years younger than him would be more than a little strange, especially since he'd been an only child his whole life.

Peach wound around his legs as he checked for Maggie in the living room, before heading upstairs to her office. Although his dad had a rule against working from home, she still had an office in case of emergencies (and Liam knew she snuck in there to work when she couldn't sleep).

Maggie's office door was wide open, with no Maggie to be found, but their bedroom door was closed. Liam knocked, in case she was changing or something.

"Maggie? You in there?"

He heard a muffled curse through the door before Maggie answered. "Yeah?"

"Are you busy?"

"A little. Is it an emergency?"

What kind of question was that?

"Define emergency," he called back. "Are you going to be long?"

Maggie said something that sounded suspiciously like, "For fuck's sake," before shouting, "I'll be out in a minute."

Sure enough, a moment later, Maggie exited the bedroom, closing the door behind her and adjusting her shirt. Her cheeks were red, her hair tied in a messy knot on top of her head.

"What were you doing?" he asked as she led him down the stairs.

She looked over her shoulder at him and glared. "I was *trying* to do your dad, but your son having a conversation with your wife while you're inside her is kind of a turn off, wouldn't you say?"

Liam shuddered. That was the last thing he needed to hear after what Jasmine had let slip the night before. "Please don't talk about having sex with my dad."

"Then take a hint and don't interrupt me when I'm having sex with your dad," she hissed under her breath, sounding strangely like Peach. She took a deep breath. "But also, it's nice to see you. I just wish you'd shown up a couple of hours later."

"A couple of hours? Christ. That's still way more information than I need about your sex life."

Maggie shrugged. "I'm sleeping with your dad. You're sleeping with my best friend. It is what it is. Do you want tea, even though it's like three billion degrees out?"

"I'm good. But you know hot drinks actually cool you down in hot weather."

She gave him a skeptical look. "So you say every summer, but I'm going to stick to iced coffee and water, thanks."

"You need to re-wash your straw, by the way. Peach jumped up on the counter and licked it," Liam told her, and Maggie turned to glare at Peach.

"Peach Penelope Michaelson, you know you're not allowed to lick straws." She slumped into a chair, fanning herself, and turned her attention back to Liam. "This is a reoccurring problem. I don't even want to know how many times she hasn't been caught. Anyway, what's up?"

"Is my dad coming down soon?"

"I doubt it. He was running a bath—that we were supposed to take together, thank you very much—and I told him not to let it go to waste."

"Perfect," he said, ignoring the bath part. "I wanted to talk to you about Jazz."

Maggie clapped her hand to her chest. "You're kidding. I would never have guessed, considering you've spoken about literally nothing but Jazz for the past month."

"It's not my fault she's so…" Liam trailed off, gesturing in the air as if a single word to sum up how incredible Jasmine was might magically come to him.

"Eloquent," Maggie replied with a laugh, but she gave him a warm smile. "But seriously, nothing makes me happier than someone finally seeing her for how amazing she is. It's about time."

Liam knew he and Jasmine didn't technically need Maggie's approval to do whatever it was they were doing. Checking in with her had been the right thing to do initially, but they were all adults. Still, he couldn't deny it felt good, knowing that the most important person in the world to Jasmine was on board with them.

"She is amazing," Liam agreed. "That's actually what I wanted to talk to you about. I stopped by the office yesterday and she was acting super insecure about my parents. She's convinced they're going to be upset if they find out we're together, like she's not good enough for me or something, and I have no idea how to convince her otherwise."

Maggie's face pinched with concern. "I wish I could say I was surprised, but I'm really not. Jazz does a great job of acting like she's super confident, but it's not real, and she shuts down whenever I try to talk to her about it."

So Jasmine's false confidence hadn't gone entirely unnoticed. But Liam couldn't blame Maggie for not getting through to her. Maggie had been dealing with enough before she started working on herself.

"I've managed to get her to open up a little," he admitted, and Maggie raised her brows, looking impressed. "We still have a lot to work through, but I think it's getting easier for her." Orgasms were a wonderful incentive. "But yesterday I dropped by the office to see if she wanted to grab lunch, and she freaked out a little."

"About grabbing lunch?"

"About my dad potentially finding out we're together. Maybe I'm not objective enough considering I've only ever had amazing parents, but you know him: he'd be fine with it, right?"

"Of course. He loves Jazz and so do your moms. Do you have any idea how many times your dad has mentioned that he thinks you'd be a good couple? I had to stop him from matchmaking last Christmas."

Liam blinked in surprise. "Seriously?" Maggie nodded with the fond smile he had learned was reserved for thoughts of his dad. "Shit. I'm guessing you've never mentioned that to Jazz? Because that'd probably solve a lot of her anxiety."

"I didn't want to meddle. Jazz can be… flighty. She's never been in a serious relationship, and it's not for lack of trying from her past partners. I've seen people tripping over themselves trying to show her how much they cared, and I genuinely don't think she noticed a single one of them." That was the opposite of what Jasmine had said, but Liam didn't find it hard to believe that she truly thought no one had wanted her wholly.

"I think it would help if you talked to her about this. We're working through things, and it's going well, but I think she's going to need more than me telling her shit to believe it. And you're her person."

"I'll talk to her," Maggie promised. "Speaking of talking, is there any chance you can convince her to get a new OBGYN for a second opinion?"

"About her periods? Yeah, I've been thinking about that. She shouldn't be in that much pain."

"Right? That and the orgasm thing. A decade of trying with no results can't be good, especially now that she's told you and you're actively working on it."

Liam tilted his head, confused. "She didn't tell you? We figured that out."

Maggie's jaw dropped. "Seriously? That's amazing. When did that happen? She didn't mention anything."

"Last Saturday, once she was feeling better," Liam explained, and Maggie's brows knit together. "What?"

"Nothing, it's just… I spoke to her on Sunday morning, after she'd been to yoga. I actually asked her if you were any closer and she said no. Why would she lie about that?"

Shit. Guilt toiled in Liam's stomach. Had Jasmine not wanted her to know for some reason? He'd half expected her to roll over when they were finished and call Maggie immediately, if he was being honest. There must be something wrong if she hadn't told her at all. Liam filed it away, something for them to talk about later. "Maybe she wanted to tell you in person," he reasoned, but Maggie looked no less concerned.

"I've seen her like three times since then. Weird. I'll try to grab her for lunch tomorrow."

"Thanks," Liam said, relieved. "And maybe we could all do dinner with my moms this weekend or something? I don't want her to feel uncomfortable around them and my dad."

"That sounds good. Hey, earlier, when you were talking about Jazz being worried about your parents finding out, you said *together*," Maggie said, with a weighted expression. "What does that mean, exactly?"

"It's… complicated," he admitted, drumming his fingertips on the dark wood table. "It's definitely more than sex for both of us. We just haven't talked about it."

"You mean aside from when she accidentally said she loved you while she was sick and you said no take backs?"

At least she was telling Maggie some things. "You can't deny that's going to be a cute story to tell our grandkids someday." Sure, it hadn't been a real *I love you*, but it definitely implied that she saw him as more than a friend she was sleeping with.

Maggie laughed, rolling her eyes. "True. What's your plan? As a fellow woman with more baggage than an airport who has been wooed by a very charming, if a little intense, Michaelson man, I'm going to suggest you take it slow."

"Only a *little* intense? Wow, we really need to do better than that. But yeah, slow is the plan. We went on a date on Sunday."

Maggie sat forward, her hands flat on the table. "Are you kidding me? Fair enough keeping her sex life to herself, considering you're my… you know, but she didn't tell me you went on a date?"

"In her defense, I didn't tell her it was a date," Liam added quickly, and Maggie narrowed her eyes at him.

"Oh. That's… unconventional. But this is Jazz we're talking about, so it makes sense, I suppose. Was it a good first date, at least?"

Liam couldn't stop a smile from spreading over his face. "The best."

Maggie reached across the table and squeezed his hand. "You look really happy, Liam. And I'm happy for you, but be careful. Please. You're two of the three most important people in the world to me and I just… Please be careful."

"I will. *We* will, I promise."

Maggie nodded, looking reassured, and stood up. "This was a lot. I need coffee. So, tell me all about this date," she said, grabbing two glasses from the cabinet. "But for the love of god, leave out the dirty parts. I can just about handle hearing them from Jazz."

CHAPTER TWENTY-FOUR

Liam

"I'm in the bedroom!" Jasmine called when he closed the front door behind him.

Liam yawned as he stepped over her purse, discarded by the door, and headed down the hallway toward his bedroom. It had been a long day of dealing with difficult clients who wanted bespoke pieces, without bespoke price tags, and he'd barely spoken to her all day, other than a quick message at lunch to ask if she wanted to stay at his place or hers. There was no question of them spending the night apart at this point. Anytime they did sleep alone at their respective apartments, they both slept like shit. He missed her too much.

He smiled at their chalkboard, hung on the back of his bedroom door at Jasmine's suggestion:

Rule number one: no faking it.

Rule number two: talking about how you feel isn't optional.

Rule number three: we're in this together.

Rule number four: no take backs.

Rule number five: conversing before coming.

It was filling up fast, a snapshot of the days they'd spent together since starting their arrangement.

"Do you want to go out for dinner ton—" Liam stopped in his tracks as he pushed the door open, every thought emptying from his head. Jasmine was lying on the bed, not a scrap of fabric on her.

"I think we should stay in," she told him with a wicked smile. And then she spread her legs.

He strode forward, reaching for her, but she held up a hand. "Nuh-uh. I remembered something this morning— something you told me a while ago that I never got to see." She nodded to something behind him, and Liam realized she'd dragged a chair in front of the bed. "Get undressed and sit."

She'd never taken control like this, but Liam was quickly learning that, as dominant as he was, he could be into just about anything where Jasmine was concerned.

He did as he was told, stripping off and taking a seat. Then narrowed his eyes as he realized how far away he was. "I can't reach you."

"Exactly," Jasmine replied, eyes twinkling. She reached back and picked up three toys: a beaded metal dildo, a slim lilac vibrator, and a clear glass dildo with a bulbed head. "Which one?"

"Are you using it on yourself or me?" Liam asked, resting his elbows on his thighs and leaning forward.

"Me. For now."

Jesus. Liam sucked in a breath. "The glass one."

Jasmine dropped the others on the bed before rolling the head of the glass wand over her clit.

"You told me you could come just by watching someone else come," she reminded him, and Liam tried to focus on her words and not on the glass he would very much like to replace with his mouth. God, it felt like a lifetime ago he'd said that, on the night of India and Bart's wedding. It was funny when he thought about it. He'd spent years with India. Barely a month had passed since he and Jasmine had struck their deal, and he'd needed much less time than that to know he was going to be with her forever. He just needed to get her on board with that little plan.

"I did say that." He watched her, licking his lips.

"Time to prove it, baby. No touching. Me *or* yourself."

This was going to be fucking torture.

Jasmine dragged the toy over her skin, teasing her pussy. "Shit," she said, barely pressing the head inside her. "I forgot lube. Care to help out?"

She didn't need lube—he could see how wet she was from his chair, the glass dildo already glistening. But Liam knew what she wanted.

He rose slowly, Jasmine tracking his every movement as he stepped close to her and lowered his head.

"Don't touch," she warned and Liam had to ball his hands into fists to resist the temptation as he spat on her pussy. Jasmine whimpered, swirling the toy around his spit and pushing it inside her. Her name spilled from his lips, but she just raised a brow. "Good boy. You can sit back down now."

Liam retreated to his chair, but not before shooting her a

look that made it clear he would play by her rules now, but she'd pay for it later. Which was almost certainly her intention.

She made sure he was watching her before she continued fucking herself with the glass wand, as if he could look anywhere else. Liam's eyes drank in the details—the rise and fall of her chest, the soft wobble of her stomach and thighs as she shook, her dark lashes fluttering, her teeth clamped around her lower lip. With her head thrown back and her back arched, she wouldn't have looked out of place in a Courbet painting.

Jasmine gasped his name, and he knew she was close. Her breaths were ragged, her movements jerky, and he wasn't fucking close enough to her. He stood and crossed the distance between them with one step, leaning over her, his hands on either side of her torso. Her eyes snapped open, hazy like a foggy morning.

"I'm not touching," he murmured, though it wasn't strictly true. He was leaning over her enough that his cock lay, painfully hard, on her stomach. Because he'd be damned if he came anywhere but all over Jasmine. *His* Jasmine.

From his new angle, all he could see was her face, and that's exactly what he wanted. She whimpered his name and her whole body tensed. Her mouth fell open in a soundless scream, her orgasm ripping through her. Liam was so focused on her perfect face that his own orgasm took him by surprise. His elbows buckled, and he caught himself just in time to stop his body weight collapsing on her.

Jasmine gasped, staring down her own body in wonder

as Liam came all over her stomach without so much as lifting a finger. "Holy shit."

"I told you so," he said, panting.

She swiped one finger through his cum and brought it to her lips. She sucked it, cum dribbling over her lips and spilling onto her chin. If she wanted him hard and even more desperate for her, it was working. But this was Jasmine, after all—everything made him hard and fucking desperate for her.

Liam stood up enough to take her in. She still had the glass wand inside her, and he wrapped a hand around the end, pulling it out torturously slowly. Jasmine moaned, her eyes widening when he brought the wand to his mouth and drew it between his lips. Liam closed his eyes, wrapping his tongue around the sweet, intoxicating taste of her. The wand was warm from being inside her, and Liam couldn't wait to replace it with his tongue, fingers, and cock.

Jasmine sighed, raising her arms above her head and stretching. His cum dripped down her stomach. She peered down, tutting. "Seems like such a waste."

And they couldn't have that. Liam dragged the toy through his cum and brought it to her lips. She licked it, swirling her tongue over the head and drawing it between her lips. Liam pulled it out of her mouth with a pop, swiping two fingers through the cum. He dragged it over her clit, her pussy, her ass, covering her in it. He pressed his fingers inside her pussy, savoring her little whimper as he pumped them, using his cum to massage her G-spot. "Not a waste anymore."

"Liam," she moaned, fisting the covers, her whole body flushed crimson.

"Did you like pretending to have control, darling?"

Her eyes snapped open. "Pretending?" Her tone was mocking. Bratty Jasmine was back in full force. Perfect.

"You might have been holding the reins for a second," he said, curling his fingers inside her and watching her back arch with a satisfied smile, "but it's *my* cum you're covered in. My fingers you're clenching around." He leaned in and pressed a kiss against the corner of her mouth. "It was my name you cried when you came. You really think you're in control here?"

Liam pulled his fingers out of her pussy and shoved them in her mouth, laughing at her protesting growl. "Be a good girl and lick them clean," he instructed. So, naturally, she bit him. He yanked his fingers back. The pain was fleeting, but it went straight to his cock. He was going to be ready to fuck her in no time.

"Oh, you're going to regret that."

He gave her a split second's warning before he grabbed her by the ankles and pulled her down the bed. He tugged her to her feet, steadying her when she stumbled, blinking in a daze. She didn't have time to fight against him as he sat back in the chair and immediately put her over his knee.

"*Fuck*," she cried out, struggling in his hold. The chair was tall and cushioned, and he pulled her just far enough over his lap that her feet couldn't touch the ground. She kicked them, trying to wriggle out of his grip.

"Behave." He brought his hand down on her ass and she

moaned, her body falling still. "Do you want me to be gentle?" he asked, already well aware of her answer.

"Fuck no."

"You want it to hurt? You want me to punish you like the filthy brat you are until you're begging for mercy?"

"I don't beg," Jasmine promised.

He chuckled, running his hand over her ass. "We'll see about that."

Smack!

Jazz cried out, her legs kicking aimlessly before she fell limp over Liam's knee.

Over.

And over.

And over.

He alternated, giving each ass cheek equal attention, his palm connecting with her ass again and again like he couldn't possibly leave a single spot unpunished. Her skin was burning, each strike of his hand like an electric shock leaving a trail of fire in its wake.

"Ready to beg yet, darling?"

Jazz whimpered, not sure she would be able to find the words even if she wanted to give him that satisfaction. And she absolutely did not. Yet.

She'd been tense for the first few smacks, but he'd

slapped every ounce of tension from her body. She didn't even have it in her to tense as she felt the air rushing toward her in anticipation of another strike. Her body craved this—there was no point in pretending otherwise.

She was dripping wet, sticky with his cum and her own desperation to get him inside her. Jazz wasn't sure how long he'd been spanking her for—it could have been five minutes or five hours for all she knew—but she wasn't sure how much longer she could hold out without some sense of relief. How the fuck did Liam have the patience for this?

His palm came down on the top of her thighs, the new spot jolting her body out of its pliancy. She cried out, her hand slamming against the side of the chair. "*Ow.*"

Liam ran a flat hand over the spot he'd spanked her, gentle and soothing. And it was so much fucking worse. He was so close to her pussy, so close to the spot she so desperately needed him.

"Please." Her lips formed the words, but barely a sound fell from them. It was enough for him to hear her, though. Liam's hand stilled.

"What was that?"

She drew in a shaky breath. "Please," she repeated, her voice scratchy and weak.

"Please what, darling? Tell me what you want."

He'd won the second he'd thrown her over his knee. Hell, he'd won the second he'd walked through the goddamn door.

"Fuck me, baby. Please. I'm begging."

Liam ran his thumb over the curve of her ass, so close, but so fucking far. And then, without warning, she was on her feet, and he was practically throwing her down on the bed. Her head was spinning, her desperation to feel him overtaking every one of her senses.

"Are you okay?" Liam said in her ear, stroking his hand through her hair, his fingers and voice gentle. Temporarily if she had anything to say about it.

"Yeah," she said, breathing hard. "Don't stop. Please don't stop."

"Turn your head and look up."

"Make me."

Liam didn't even hesitate to wrap her hair around his fist and roughly force her head, but he leaned in and peppered her temple with soft kisses. He toed the line between hard and soft so fucking beautifully.

Jazz flicked her eyes up toward the mirror and gasped. Her ass was red raw.

"You're going to be wearing my handprints all week," Liam promised, swinging a leg over her thighs and trapping her prone beneath him. She whimpered as she watched him in the mirror, her neck straining. Liam fisted his cock, his jaw tense as he pressed inside her—like he wanted this just as much as she did. He started slowly, then, as suddenly as he'd thrown her on the bed, he was deep inside her, Jazz reaching out and grasping the covers for dear life.

Liam was unrelenting, pinning her to the bed as he fucked her, hard and merciless. Jazz gulped in air when she could, gasps mingling with sobs, the friction of the blanket against her nipples unbearable. She couldn't escape him, even if she wanted to, he was holding her down so fucking thoroughly.

Pressure built faster than she could cling to reality, washing over her and dousing her in an orgasm so strong she might have blacked out for a moment. Every part of Jazz's body tingled. From the tips of her hair to the soles of her feet, she was on fire. Liam grunted as her pussy clenched around him.

Before she even finished falling from her high, he shoved a hand roughly underneath her, pinching her clit between his thumb and forefinger. "Give me one more, Jasmine. I want to see you break."

His voice, low and gruff, was her undoing. Jazz splintered, her body fighting Liam of its own accord. She kicked and twisted, pulling at the covers, desperate to get away from the assaulting pleasure as he fucked her and rubbed her clit. It felt like she was coming out of her skin, like she was fixed to the ceiling with the mirror, staring down at them. Her face was drenched with tears, wave after wave of bliss exploding over her like fireworks.

Liam gasped her name, his knees giving way as he came inside her. His body covered hers like a safety blanket, and he pressed breathless kisses to the back of her neck while his cum spilled out of her.

He only gave himself a few seconds to catch his breath before pulling out and gathering her into his arms, alternating between peppering kisses over her face and searching her eyes.

"Are you... Fuck, are you okay?" he panted, running a shaking hand over the back of her head. His eyes were wide. Stunned.

It hadn't just been intense for her. Liam was trembling, and he was still fully focused on making sure she was okay.

She cupped his face, stroking her thumb over his cheek. "I'm fine. Are *you* okay?"

His body folded into hers, his head dropping onto her shoulder. "Yeah, I…" His voice shook, his arms tightening around her like a vise. "Shit, I don't know what's wrong with me."

Jazz ran her hands up his bare back. "It's just the come down from the adrenaline. Breathe, baby. I've got you." She slipped her finger into his hair, lightly scratching his scalp, and he sighed contentedly.

"That's nice," Liam whispered, his breath tickling her neck.

"Lie on your front. Let me give you a massage."

"But you're tir—"

"Let me take care of you. Please."

Liam looked uncertain as he nodded, twisting and lying on his front, his back rising and falling as his breaths slowed. Jazz's body ached, but it was worth a little extra pain when she closed her fingers around Liam's shoulders and he moaned. She moved closer to him, taking her time, kneading his muscles until his breathing was slow and even. Why the hell had she waited so long to do this? Liam letting her take care of him was almost better than the sex had been. He was so thoughtful, so caring, doing everything he could to make sure she felt safe and seen, and Jazz had barely reciprocated. She wanted to do more for him, needed to do more to show him how glad she was to have him in her life.

For a moment, she thought he'd fallen asleep until he reached for her, threading his fingers through hers. "Lie down with me? I need to see you. I need to know you're okay."

"I promise I am," she assured him. She lay down and Liam turned onto his side, rolling his neck.

"Come here." He held out an arm and Jazz snuggled into him, his skin burning against hers. He pressed his lips to her forehead. "Thank you for taking care of me," he mumbled, his eyes fluttering closed.

And before she even had the chance to reply, Liam was fast asleep.

CHAPTER TWENTY-FIVE

Jazz

"You can't keep ambushing me like this," Jazz grumbled as she trailed Maggie through the parking garage to her car.

She'd shown up the second Jazz and Cal's last meeting had ended, kissed her husband, then dragged Jazz into the elevator.

"It seems to be the only way I can get you to actually talk to me," Maggie said as they climbed into her car.

Jazz frowned at her best friend. Sure, she'd kept a couple of things back lately, but she thought she'd done a good job of hiding it, considering how observant Maggie was. "I talk to you every day."

"Then why did I have to find out from Liam that you finally came?"

"Oh." Jazz looked down at her lap. "That."

"Yeah. That."

Maggie handed her a sub and unwrapped her own, taking a bite before giving her an expectant look. "Should we start with the orgasm, or with the fact you lied to me and told me it hadn't happened when it had?"

Jazz sighed and unwrapped her sub, ripping the corner of the paper into tiny pieces and squirming in her seat. Her ass was on fucking fire, and Maggie's car wasn't nearly as comfortable as Cal's.

"I didn't mean to lie to you. I was going to tell you, I just… I don't know why I didn't. You know, you were busy heading to meet your other friends, and it didn't seem like the right time—"

"Are you pissed off that I was hanging out with Nadia?" Maggie asked carefully, with no judgment in her tone.

"No," Jazz replied, a little defensively. Maggie raised a brow. "It's not that you're hanging out with other people, it's Nadia. She's great, she's perfect, she's got it all together. She's the polar opposite of me, and I love that for her, but she seems so much older and grown up than us." By *us*, Jazz meant *me*.

"She's actually a year younger than me," Maggie said, and Jazz groaned. Of course she was. "And yes, she totally has her life together but Jazz, we *are* grownups now. We have big girl jobs and bills to pay, and I have a husband."

"I know, but you're not even thirty," Jazz protested. "And I'm barely thirty." Technically, she was closer to her thirty-first birthday than her thirtieth, but that was neither here nor there.

"Thirty is grown up. I really think you'd like Nadia if you got to know her. She's a lot of fun. But," she added quickly, as Jazz opened her mouth to protest, "I'm not going to force you to be friends with her. And I'm also not going to stop hanging out with you because I spend time with her sometimes. We mostly do work related shit anyway."

"I get it, Maggie, it's fine. You're allowed to have other friends. I just get stuck in my head sometimes."

"I know, but I don't want you to think anyone is ever going to come before you. Even Cal knows that if you call, I drop everything. You're my number one. Always."

It wasn't that Jazz didn't believe Maggie, it was that she couldn't. Maggie had told her time and time again that she loved her and accepted her exactly as she was—hell, she'd shown her time and time again—but Jazz couldn't wrap her head around it. Not now that it felt like Maggie had skipped ten steps ahead in life and she was still drowning in quicksand.

She couldn't say that, though.

"Same," she said, instead. "You're my number one always too."

"Too right I am." Maggie brushed the breadcrumbs from her pants onto the car floor. "Speaking of Cal, Liam came to see me last night."

"And presumably spoke about our sex life—which is super weird, for the record."

It was the first night she and Liam had spent apart in a few days. In the interest of trying not to appear too clingy, she'd lied and told him she and Sierra were hanging out at her place after work. Well, it had been a lie initially, at least. Convincing Sierra to hang out had taken nothing more than the promise of Thai food and hazelnut truffles from her favorite pot shop downtown. It had been nice, actually, to spend time with her outside of work. It had been the first time they'd hung out since Maggie's bachelorette party, and Jazz had forgotten how much she liked spending time with her.

Sierra had fallen asleep on her couch, while Jazz had tossed and turned in a cold bed, unable to sleep.

"We weren't talking about your sex life." Maggie rolled her eyes. "The orgasm thing just came up."

"Shit, does Cal know now?"

"No, but I wanted to talk to you about that. Liam told me you were worried that Cal, Eliza, and Danisha would have a problem with the two of you being together. What's up with that?"

"What's up with that is that Liam has a big mouth," Jazz said through gritted teeth. If Liam wasn't so cute, and she hadn't missed him so much overnight, she might be more pissed off about it. "But as I explained to Liam, he's an only child and their entire world. I'm personified chaos. That's not exactly what most people want for their kids—ow." She rubbed her arm where Maggie had whacked her with a little package of pretzels. "What was that for?"

"For giving my husband so little credit. What the fuck, Jazz? Cal loves you. Not just because you're my best friend, but because you're you. Eliza and Danisha too. Liam's parents are not our parents—and yes, I recognize that's a weird thing to say, considering I'm married to his dad."

Jazz covered her face with her hands and groaned. "This situation is all so fucking messy."

"It doesn't have to be." Maggie tugged her hands away. "What do you want here? Taking everyone else out of the equation except you and Liam. Do you want to be with him? Like really with him?"

"I have no idea. This wasn't supposed to happen. It was supposed to just be sex." She dropped her head back against the headrest and closed her eyes, her temples pounding. "But it's not. Just sex, I mean. Maybe it was at first, or maybe it never was. I don't fucking know."

"It's never just sex."

Jazz loosed a humorless chuckle, opening her eyes and turning to face Maggie. "I got a tattoo for him."

To Maggie's credit, she hardly blinked. "Okay. That definitely has some implications, but you do also have tattoos for a bunch of people."

"I'm not sure you and my siblings count as a bunch of people." The bouquet on her ribs was made up of roses for Rose, carnations for Xan, and morning glories for Maggie. She'd been playing around with the idea of adding Cal, Eliza, Danisha, and Liam's birth flowers too.

"It was supposed to be comforting. What did you get for him?"

"Snoopy reading a romance book on my hip. He was obsessed with Snoopy as a kid."

"Of course he was. That is pretty adorable." Jazz sighed her agreement. "You could just… be with him? Marry him, pop out a couple of the world's cutest babies, grow old together," Maggie joked. Or at least, Jazz hoped she was joking.

That sounded simultaneously perfect and terrifying.

How the hell was she supposed to decide if she wanted that? And then commit to it? She couldn't even stick to one fucking hobby. Maggie didn't get it. Sure, she'd run away when confronted with her feelings for Cal, but even at her lowest, she always had it together. And once she had him back, she'd done everything right: she'd gone to therapy, walked away from her family, started a badass business.

Jazz had only gotten her job because she was Maggie's friend, and no matter how much being around them stung, she loved her family too much to walk away.

"I'm not you Maggie. I don't bounce back when shit goes sideways. I can't just call it quits with my parents and ride off into the sunset with someone because he's the first person to treat me well." The words shot out of her mouth like bullets, each one heading straight for her best friend.

Maggie shrank back, hurt flashing in her eyes and horror filled Jazz. Why the fuck had she said that?

"Oh my god, Maggie, I didn't mean that. I don't even know where that came from, I don't think any of that. Fuck. I'm so sorry."

Maggie pursed her lips, nodding once. "It's fine. I know you don't mean it."

"It's not fine. There's zero excuse for me to lash out like that. I know you're just trying to help."

Maggie reached out and rubbed her shoulder. "We've said worse to each other over the years. It's fine. Seriously. For what it's worth, I wouldn't be talking about this if I didn't think this thing between the two of you was worth it. He's a good guy, Jazz."

Like that was the problem. Liam wasn't just a good guy

—he'd raised the bar so damn high she knew no one would ever be able to compete. Liam would never lash out at a friend like she had. Liam would never lie because he couldn't handle talking about his feelings. Liam would never give up just because something was a little tricky. Which meant Liam wouldn't give up on her, even when she gave up on herself, time and time again.

"I like him. More than like probably. And I want more with him. I want everything you said and more, but I'm scared. I don't think I'm ready to deal with it all right now."

"He's not rushing you. He just doesn't want to hide you away. And you deserve better than that, anyway." Doubtful.

But Liam had already done so much for her. Even if it made his parents look at her differently, she could do this for him. "Fine. I don't mind if his parents find out, but I really don't want it to be a whole big thing."

"We can tell them over dinner this weekend. We'll casually mention that you're seeing each other, and they'll be fine with it. I promise." Maggie gave her a reassuring smile that did nothing to soothe the anxiety coiling in her stomach.

For Liam. She could do this for Liam.

Liam jumped out of his car on cloud fucking nine, walking up the stone pathway to his dad and Maggie's place. He had thirty minutes before he had to leave to pick Jasmine up from her yoga class, and got to tell her the news in person, which gave him just enough time to tell his dad and Maggie.

"Knock, knock," he called as he stepped into their hallway.

"In the living room," his dad shouted back.

Liam headed in, finding his dad and Maggie sitting side by side on the couch, Peach curled up with her head on Maggie's lap and her tail on his dad's. It didn't look comfortable, but she was snoring softly.

"Hey," Liam said, sinking into the seat opposite them, practically vibrating with excitement.

"You look happy," his dad commented, while Maggie narrowed her eyes suspiciously.

"I have exciting news."

"Go on."

Liam took a deep breath. "You're going to be grand-parents!"

He realized his mistake the second the words left his mouth, as the blood drained from both of their faces.

"Maggie's too young to be a grandma, she's not even thir—"

"JAZZ IS PREGNANT?" Maggie jumped to her feet, Peach rolling onto the plush carpet and meowing begrudgingly. "My best friend is pregnant and *you're* the one telling me? Are you kidding me?"

Liam rose slowly to his feet, holding up his hands. "Jazz isn't pregnant." This was, without a doubt, the worst way he could've phrased it.

Genuine rage filled Maggie's face. "You got someone else pregnant? What the fuck, Liam? What happened to the best date of your life? What happened to a fun story to tell your fucking grandkids one day? I vouched for you. I told her you were a good—"

"No one is pregnant," he said, raising his voice enough to be heard over Maggie's tirade. She stopped pacing in front of the couch and glared at him.

"What does that mean?"

"It means I'm not sleeping with anyone other than Jazz, and this is not the cute way to tell you I'm adopting a puppy like I thought it would be."

"A puppy," his dad repeated, staring at him, shell-shocked.

"Yep." Liam held up his phone, showing them the picture from the shelter's website. "This is him. Cute, right?"

"Oh my god." Maggie folded in on herself, collapsing on the couch, covering her eyes. "The two of you are aging me, you know. I'm younger than both of you and you're aging me."

Liam grimaced. "Sorry. I didn't think this through." It was nice to know just how seriously Maggie took defending Jasmine, though.

"You know, your moms and I always swore that if you ever got someone pregnant, we would react better than our parents did, and I have to say, I think I handled that pretty well," his dad chimed in, though he still looked like he'd been clubbed over the head.

Peach hopped up on the couch again, and Maggie

grabbed her, holding her to her chest and breathing deeply. "I could probably have handled it better," she admitted. She brandished a finger at him. "But let that be a warning if you ever do hurt her."

"Consider me warned. This one was on me."

His dad cleared his throat, glancing expectantly between Maggie and Liam. "Clearly I've missed a chapter. You and Jazz are what—dating?"

"We haven't really talked about what it actually is so…" Liam trailed off.

Maggie sighed. "They're casually seeing each other. But like *we* were casually seeing each other, you know?"

"Ah, I see."

"I'm going to marry her," Liam said without thinking, because apparently his mouth was no longer connected to his brain. "But we're taking it slow for now. We've only gone on one date."

"And Jazz doesn't know it was a date," Maggie pointed out. Semantics.

"That sounds very complicated," his dad said, before shrugging. "But I'm on board. You and Jazz would be great together—haven't I been saying that, love?"

"You have," Maggie replied, some of the stress on her facing melting away as she smiled at his dad.

"Jazz is great, Liam. She's perfect for you, and I'm happy for the two of you."

"Thanks, Dad. Could you maybe mention that to Jazz? She's convinced you're going to think she isn't good enough for me."

"Really? I love her. She knows that, doesn't she?" He

directed his question to Maggie, who released Peach to take his hand.

"She does, don't worry. It's just her parents—"

"Say no more. I'll make sure she knows I'm happy for you."

"Thanks," Liam said. It wasn't exactly the low-key dinner they'd planned for telling his parents, but there was always a silver lining: telling his moms couldn't possibly go any worse.

"Can we see the puppy now?" Maggie asked, and Liam handed his phone over, happy to be back on steady ground. She squealed. "Oh my god, look at him. He's so tiny."

"Aw, Liam, he's lovely," his dad added when Maggie turned the phone in his direction. "What's his name?"

"He doesn't have one yet. I want to talk to Jazz first but I was thinking, since he's technically my first baby, I could do what you did and give him my middle name: Bray." Liam's first name came from his dad's middle name, Uilliam, and his middle name had come from the town in Ireland his dad had been born in. He'd always loved it. Though he didn't spend much time in Ireland these days, once or twice a year at the most, he always felt completely at home there.

"He looks like a Bray," Maggie agreed. "God, he even has your mustache."

"And Jazz's hair," he pointed out.

Maggie gave him a pointed look. "Liam."

"What?"

"Is Jazz aware that you're considering her the puppy's mom?"

"Well, explicitly stating that doesn't feel like it would count as taking it slow, but you know she's going to take one look at him when we pick him up next week and be completely obsessed with him."

And if she wasn't… Well, he could probably return the *Proud Dog Mom* coffee cup he'd ordered.

CHAPTER TWENTY-SIX

Jazz

"Jazz."

"The answer is no," she said with a sigh before looking up into Cal's face. "Look, you know I love you, but as much as I appreciate you giving my best friend multiple orgasms every day for the rest of her life, I can't keep clearing your schedule so you can go home and have sex with your wife."

"Come on, Jazz. The man's in love. Throw him a bone," Sierra chimed in from beside her. Jazz just rolled her eyes at her assistant, while Cal dropped into the chair opposite her desk.

"Valid points from you both, but surprisingly not what I was going to say for once."

"Oh. In that case, what can I do for you?"

"Do you want to come over to watch the season finale of LoveStruck tonight, since Maggie and Liam have that work dinner?"

Ah, yes. The *work dinner*. With Nadia. If it wasn't bad enough that she had to deal with Maggie talking about her, now she had Liam telling her all about Nadia's laundry list of achievements.

She knew, deep down, that it wasn't about Nadia. Nadia was fine. More than fine, she was great. But even though Jazz was well aware that jealousy wasn't a good look on her, she just couldn't shake it. She'd planned to sit on her couch and stew all night, but trashy reality TV sounded better.

"It's already the season finale?" she asked Cal, who nodded excitedly. Jazz had always been hopeless at keeping up with TV shows. It wasn't unusual for her to accidentally skip episodes or suddenly realize she was watching the same thing for the second time, ten episodes in.

"Yeah, I was going to wait for Maggie so we could watch it tomorrow, but I don't want to get spoiled on TikTok." Jazz didn't dare suggest he just stay off TikTok. Maggie had gotten him hooked on reality shows when they'd first started hanging out outside of work, and Cal hadn't looked back since. "And there's something a little sad about a fifty-eight-year-old man watching a reality dating show at home alone on a Friday night."

"100%, that would be super weird. I'm in. Ooh, we should make cocktails."

Cal's eyes lit up. "We still have the edible glitter Maggie got for your Galentine's thing."

"Perfect."

"This little friendship thing you two have is so cute," Sierra said, leaning in and whispering, "Do you think that'll change when he's your father-in-law?"

"Sierra!"

"What? I thought it was common knowledge now."

Common knowledge was a stretch. Cal knew, and Jazz and Liam were planning to tell his moms they were seeing each other over dinner. The only reason Sierra knew was because she'd spied him kissing her goodbye when he dropped her off for work.

"It's not going to change," Cal confirmed, not even flinching at the *father-in-law* comment. They weren't technically even dating. "Do you want to come over, Sierra? We can catch you up if you haven't watched the rest of the season," Cal promised.

"Oh, I've watched it. LoveStruck is huge in the Hayashi family and we go all out for the finale. My dad ordered a cake from our favorite bakery, they decorate the house, and my brother and his partners are coming into town all the way from Tacoma."

"Tacoma's like a thirty-minute drive. It's not exactly Antarctica."

Sierra shrugged. "It was a bigger deal when they lived in Portland. Oh, I almost forgot, my dad made t-shirts. I'll send you pictures."

God, Jazz couldn't imagine her family ever doing anything like that. Their Christmases weren't even that festive. She hoped Sierra knew how lucky she was to have a family who enjoyed spending time together. Fuck, Jazz would settle for a family who wanted her around as she was, instead of some character she played, trying to fit in. She wasn't asking for parties and t-shirts—although that would be nice.

"I hope you're taking notes here, Jazz," Cal said, pulling

her attention back to them. "We're going all out next year. A party, T-shirts, everything. We can even get t-shirts for Peach and Bray, get the whole family involved."

The whole family. Jazz swallowed, her throat suddenly thick. "That sounds nice."

Jazz handed Cal a glass of shimmering pink vodka and sank onto the couch, tucking her feet under her legs.

"Thanks," Cal said, setting the big bowl of popcorn he'd made between them and immediately lifting it up again when Peach jumped up to inspect it. "How are you doing?"

"Me?" Jazz asked, and Cal raised a brow.

"I don't think Peach is going to answer."

"Right. Yeah, I'm fine. Why wouldn't I be?"

"You know, with everything going on with Liam. He mentioned you were a little worried about me and his moms finding out."

Liam might as well have taken an ad out on the front page of the paper. She wouldn't be surprised if she showed up at work on Monday and Sierra somehow knew that she'd been worried about that.

"It's just complicated," she replied with a sigh. "And it changes things—it changes our whole dynamic."

"It doesn't have to change anything." Cal offered a reassuring smile. "I'm happy for the two of you, and I know Eliza and Danisha will be too. Whatever this turns into, we're all on both of your sides."

"Thank you." Jazz knew Cal really believed what he was saying, but if something went sideways between her and Liam, she knew it would be her fault, and they'd all be on his side—as they should be. "I guess I just don't want to mess up something good, you know?"

"I get it, I promise. Do you remember what a mess Maggie and I were at the beginning? We would never have figured everything out without you."

"Yeah, but Liam and I aren't you and Maggie. *I'm* not Maggie."

"I know," Cal said, gently. "You and I are a lot more alike than you and Maggie. But that's how I know you're going to figure it out and be okay."

Jazz let Cal's words sink into her. She'd always thought that she and Maggie were two peas in a pod, in so many ways—shitty parents, stubbornness, protectiveness. But when things went wrong, Maggie scrambled to fix them. She pushed through them and believed, without a doubt, that there was nothing she couldn't do if she just worked hard enough. Jazz gave up, and, though she might put on a decent show, she wasn't entirely sure she could see *anything* through completely. Not to a high enough standard, anyway. She just wasn't good enough, and she'd made her peace with that. She was okay with not being enough.

But she wanted to be enough for Liam. She wanted to be enough to earn her place in this family they'd built.

"I guess Maggie has a type," she said after a weighted silence. Cal had been convinced he wasn't enough for Maggie for months before they'd officially gotten together.

"That she does," he said with a wry smile. "Listen, I'm

saying this as your friend, not Liam's dad: you are good enough for him. And he could be good for you, if you let him."

"Yeah." He already was good for her. She'd already grown so much in the time they'd spent together, but could she ever grow enough? Could she ever actually settle down and be the sense of peace and calm for him that he was for her? She didn't want to be someone he had to take care of, always waiting for her to get scared and fuck things up enough to make everything come crashing down, like some twisted game of dominoes.

But she had no idea how to be anything else.

"Christ. How much did you two have to drink?" Maggie asked, as Cal grabbed for her and pulled her into his lap. Liam pointedly looked away as Maggie smacked Cal's hand away from her ass.

"Enough that we're going to regret it tomorrow, but I feel amazing right now." Jazz giggled, standing up on wobbly feet and reaching for Liam. "Hi, baby."

"Hi." Liam's mustache twitched, his dimples popping out, and he fought a laugh. She wrapped her arms around his neck and planted a kiss on his lips. "Wow, you really do taste like a liquor store."

"Drink up," she murmured against his lips, momentarily forgetting that his dad was sitting a few feet away from them.

"They're so cute. Aren't they so cute, love?" Cal whispered loudly.

"They're adorable," Maggie replied. "But let's get you up to bed, yeah?"

"How about I get *you* up to bed?" Cal said, and Maggie turned to Liam with an apologetic expression.

"I am so sorry. He's going to pass straight out once he gets into bed, don't worry."

"*We're* not going to pass straight out," Jazz piped up, running her finger along the buttons on Liam's button-down.

"Yes, we are. Well, after you drink a lot of water."

"Boo," Jazz shouted as he tugged her into the kitchen. She'd left her water tumbler sitting on the table—who needed water when you had vodka?—and Liam filled it before threading his fingers through hers and walking her slowly up the stairs. Which was just as well, because her head was spinning.

"Goodnight," he called down the stairs, and she copied him, before they paused in front of the doors to Maggie and Cal's guest rooms.

It wasn't unusual for both Liam and Jazz to crash at their place, and two of the four guest bedrooms had been assigned to them. The two of them glanced between the doors.

"This must be what it's like when step-siblings start dating and go home to their parents' house for Christmas, not sure where to sleep."

Liam peered down at her, sorting through her slurred words, before replying, "It's not like that."

He pushed open the door to the room on the left—her room—and pulled her inside, depositing her on the bed.

"Drink up, darling. It'll hurt less in the morning if you do."

Jazz grumbled, but accepted the water tumbler and circled the straw with her lips. At least she had a good show while she sipped at the water, watching Liam undress and fold his clothes on the chest at the end of the bed.

She sighed happily. "God, I love your body." She reached out a hand in a *gimme* motion, and Liam obliged her, stepping forward with an amused smile. He let her run her hands all over his torso. She wanted to lick his stomach, but she wasn't quite drunk enough to justify that. "You're so hot. I hate it," she whined. "How am I supposed to resist you when you look like this *and* you're so nice?"

"Who said you had to resist me?" Liam asked. "Arms up."

Jazz set her tumbler aside and raised her arms so Liam could pull her shirt over her head. "Do you want a t-shirt to sleep in?"

"I want to sleep naked."

"Fine, but I'm not touching you while you're this wasted," Liam warned with a laugh, pressing the tumbler back into her hands. "Drink and get ready for bed."

"Boo," she muttered, kicking off her leggings and underwear while she sipped the water. "You're so fucking good. Can't you just have *one* red flag?" She stomped to the bathroom, then turned in the doorway and gasped. "Oh my god, what if your lack of red flags *is* the red flag and you actually have a bunch of bodies stashed somewhere?"

"That's confidential," he answered with a wink.

Jazz hurried through her nighttime bathroom routine, skipping her skincare. By the time she was done, Liam had turned down the bed. She climbed into her usual side and he kissed her on the forehead before heading into the bathroom to get ready.

"Did you have fun with my dad tonight?" he asked when he returned, climbing in beside her and offering his arm out for her.

"I thought you weren't going to touch me."

"Don't be a brat. Get in here."

Jazz wanted to cuddle too badly to argue further. She snuggled into his side, and Liam switched off his bedside lamp, plunging the room into darkness.

The darkness sobered her slightly, sleepiness settling into her bones. "We had fun," she told him with a yawn. "Although your dad was pretty pissed when his favorites didn't end up staying together. How was your dinner?"

"It was good. The food was just okay, but the restaurant did a quiz thing and that was fun. Maggie is scary competitive, though."

"Yeah, she's a lot. She always wins too."

"Not tonight," Liam said. "Nadia got literally every question right." Jazz tensed. "What?"

"It's nothing."

"It's not nothing. You don't like Nadia?"

"I don't really know Nadia." It wasn't a lie, and it sounded better than letting the jealousy coursing through her spew out.

"You should try to get to know her. I really think you'd get along. She's intense, but she's nice."

"I'll think about it," she lied. "I'm tired. I missed you tonight," she added sleepily, nuzzling into the crook of his neck.

"I missed you too, darling."

"We should go out again soon, like we did a couple of weeks ago. Grab dinner, maybe go bowling or to an arcade or something. Next week?"

"It's a date," Liam said, and she could hear the smile in his voice.

She was on the precipice of sleep when his words really registered.

"Liam?"

"Yeah?"

"Was it a date? Last time, I mean."

Liam was quiet for a moment, but she heard his breathing quicken, felt his heart racing. "It was," he said, finally. "It was a date. Are you okay with that?"

It was just a date. One date. And he was still here. He still wanted to be around her. She hadn't fucked it up.

"I am okay with it, I think."

Liam loosed a relieved sigh. "Good. I'm glad."

"Maybe we could do more of that."

"Going on dates?"

"Yeah. I'd like to."

"Then we will." He brushed her lips gently with his, and Jazz breathed him in. "Sleep time. You're already going to be feeling rough in the morning, but I'll take care of you."

CHAPTER TWENTY-SEVEN

Jazz

Jazz squinted between a flickering parking garage light, and Liam, sitting with his eyes closed in the passenger seat of her car, wondering if she'd made a mistake bringing him here. Or, at the very least, surprising him. She'd considered blindfolding him, but they were already running later than planned (her fault) and she knew that bringing a blindfold into the mix would only delay them further.

"You can open your eyes."

Liam's emerald eyes fluttered open, his gaze falling to her face first, a soft smile on his lips. He must have recognized the parking garage in his peripheral vision, because his eyes immediately widened. Jazz drew her teeth between her lips.

"We're going to the museum?" Liam asked, and Jazz couldn't tell if he seemed happy or horrified by the date she'd planned. She swallowed.

"You said you missed it and I thought maybe if you

didn't have advance notice to stress about coming back, it would be better. But if you don't want to—"

"I want to. This is perfect. Thank you," Liam said, and Jazz let out a relieved breath.

"In that case…" She leaned down to rummage in her purse, in the footwell by Liam's shoes. Confusion filled his eyes when she withdrew a crumpled old Washington State University ball cap and placed it on his head. "It's your disguise," she explained. "You know, in case you run into any of your old colleagues you don't want to talk to. I know mustaches are the traditional disguise, but I didn't think that would work."

Liam chuckled, tugging on the brim until his face was hidden in shadows. "What's the verdict?"

She looked him over, her fingers aching to reach out and grasp his face. How did he always look this good? "God damn it," she answered with a sigh.

"Let me guess—*fucking Michaelsons*?" His mouth quivered on the edge of a smirk.

"Something like that," she grumbled. "Come on. Let's go in before we do something illegal in a parking garage."

Liam trailed her to the elevator, wrapping his arms around her from behind as the doors slid closed, and resting his chin on her head. "I'm glad we're doing this."

"The museum?"

"The date," he replied, tilting his face to kiss the top of her head. "But the museum too."

Jazz swallowed, unable to ignore the contentment in his voice. Liam had been taking care of her for weeks, making her feel safe and comfortable and cared for, and he seemed to do it all with ease. It shouldn't have taken her so long to do something for him.

A wall of noise assaulted them when the elevator doors slid open, chattering families and squealing children running around the entrance hall. The line at the ticket desk was almost to the door, and Jazz was grateful she'd had the foresight, for once, to buy their tickets online.

"Is it always this busy on Sundays?" she asked Liam, flashing the QR codes on her phone to the ticket attendant. He scanned them and waved them through.

"Yeah, but it's really just the family exhibits that are busy. The rest is usually quiet."

Jazz nodded, staring up at the grand staircase in awe. Sunlight streamed through a wall of windows, illuminating a stunning arched ceiling, smooth stone sculptures, and steps leading to the third floor.

"Pretty impressive, right?" Liam asked, correctly interpreting her wowed silence.

"It's gorgeous."

"What do you want to see first?"

She smiled up at him, certain she was already looking at the most impressive work of art in the place. "I want to see your favorite piece."

Liam scrunched his brow like he was thinking hard. "There's probably a mirror around her somewhere so you can see yourself—hey!" Jazz whacked him with her purse, but she could see him fighting a laugh. "Too praise-y?"

"I suppose not," she admitted with an exaggerated sigh.

Liam cupped her chin and dropped a quick kiss on the

tip of her nose. "Come on. My favorite painting's on the fourth floor."

He led her up the stairs and through several corridors, pointing out various sculptures and paintings as they passed and telling her all about them and how they came to be in Seattle. Jazz had never been an art person, but she could spend days listening to Liam talk about it. She clung to every word, interested in the facts behind the art, but mostly in his feelings. She filed away his likes and dislikes, and the whys behind them, adding building blocks to the picture of the man that was quickly becoming a permanent fixture in her brain.

"My favorite's just over there," Liam said as they entered a hushed gallery room. He hadn't been kidding when he said the rest of the museum would be quiet—without the families, it was perfectly peaceful.

Jazz spun around to face him before they reached the painting, and he raised a questioning brow. "I want to see it like you do—experience it like an art person. How do I do that?"

Surprise lit Liam's eyes, like he was happy she was interested. "Close your eyes." She did so, and he grasped her shoulders, spinning her around and walking her slowly forward. "When you open your eyes," he said, holding her still, "just say the first thing that comes to mind when you see the painting."

"I can do that."

Liam squeezed her shoulders, and she opened her eyes, stepping back into his chest as she realized how close to the wall they were. She took in the painting with a small gasp. It wasn't what she'd expected. Dreamy pink and blue clouds surrounded the bones of a house consumed by blue flames, a couple embracing on an ash-covered bed at the centre while it burned down around them. The gleaming brass plaque below read:

Nothing Lasts Forever, 1889

Oil on canvas

She didn't recognize the artist's name.

"It's sad." She didn't mean to whisper, but there was something about the painting that demanded the hush. "No —beautiful. Tragic? All of the above." This was Liam's favorite. She wanted to get it right.

"This isn't school, darling. There's no right answer," Liam said, reaching for her hand and threading their fingers together. "But that's how I see it too. Beautiful but tragic."

"Is there a story behind it?"

"It's a weird one. The artist isn't well known—he only painted a half dozen paintings before he died, and there's no record of the stories behind them. But art people love to speculate, so we have theories. All six paintings feature the woman on the bed. The first two were painted in the shades of blue and pink you see in the sky, and they gradually got darker. Until this one. This was the last painting. They found it in his studio in Toulouse after he died. The theory is that he loved the woman, but she was promised to another, and this painting shows he would rather he and his lover burn together than be apart. They say he died of a broken heart."

"Wow. That's so…"

"Romantic?" Liam suggested and Jazz snorted, turning to look at him.

"I was going to say dramatic. But yeah, it's pretty romantic too. I understand why you love it so much. It's the perfect balance of light and dark, peace, and chaos."

His face lit up with excitement, as if she'd interpreted the painting like he did. "Exactly. I knew you'd—"

"Liam? Is that you?"

Liam's whole body tensed, and Jazz knew who the voice belonged to even before she looked up over his shoulder and into the icy blue eyes of his ex-girlfriend.

Liam turned to face India, threading his arm around Jazz's waist, and she pasted a wide smile on her face. "Hi. It's good to see you again. How are you?"

India dragged her gaze over Jazz. It didn't feel like a judgmental glare, like the kind Jazz's mom had perfected, but more of an appraisal. When her eyes returned to Jazz's face, they were hesitant. "I'm good. How are you guys?"

"We're great," Jazz said, looking up at Liam. He wasn't even looking at India. His perfect dimply smile was trained on Jazz. And, when Jazz turned back to look at India, she knew it hadn't gone unnoticed.

"That's nice. Liam, I called a couple of times. I left some messages. Did you get them?"

"I did," Liam confirmed, finally looking at India.

She waited expectantly, but Liam didn't elaborate. India swallowed, standing a little straighter. "I was hoping to talk to you."

"Alright."

Jazz bit her lip, trying not to laugh as India looked between the two of them.

"I was hoping to talk to you *alone*."

Liam tucked Jazz closer to his side. "Jazz and I are a package deal."

India's face fell, a perfect curl of blond hair slipping from her ponytail as she dipped her head, staring at the polished floor. She took a deep breath and squared her shoulders, looking up again. "I made a mistake. Obviously, but I mean…" She toyed with the silver pendant hanging around her throat. "I love Bart. I've always loved Bart. You know how it was with the three of us. But it's not what I thought it would be. He's not you, Liam. It's always been you."

Jazz's stomach twisted as India pleaded. *It's always been you.* How many times had she heard those exact words in the audiobooks she'd listened to since Liam had started recommending them? The people saying it in the books always got back together. How the hell was she supposed to compete with that?

"I need to know," India continued, "if there's any chance we—"

"No."

Jazz started as Liam interrupted, his voice firm but not unkind.

"There's no chance. You gave up that chance when you slept with my best friend." India winced. "But even if you hadn't, we were on borrowed time. It was never going to work out between us. I hadn't met Jazz yet, and once I did…" He turned to face Jazz, looking at her like India wasn't even in the room.

Holy shit. There was no need for him to finish that sentence. The implication was clear enough: India wasn't Jazz.

Liam might have forgotten India was standing before them, but Jazz hadn't. She resisted the urge to give the woman who'd broken Liam's heart an *I win!* smirk—she was petty, not an asshole—and India mustered a weak smile for her.

"You've got a good one. Don't do what I did and mess it up."

"I would never do what you did," Jazz said instantly. So maybe she *was* a little bit of an asshole. India gave Liam one last longing look and spun on her heel, fleeing the gallery room.

Jazz blew out a breath. "Are you okay?" she asked Liam.

"I'm fine. At least you're not wondering what she wanted when she called now." He slipped his hand over her ass and squeezed. Well, then. He really did seem fine. How was he so unfazed? "Are you okay?"

Jazz nodded. "I think she bought it."

Liam raised a brow at her. "Bought what?" He had a pleased little smirk on his face when he turned back to look at the painting, because he knew exactly what she meant. *I hadn't met Jazz yet, and once I did…*

And she knew exactly what he was implying: it wasn't an act. He'd made his feelings pretty damn clear. She just didn't know what to do with them.

And maybe India interrupting them by calling at dinner, and again at the museum, was a sign from the universe that Jazz had no business going on dates with a man like Liam. But she was nothing if not spiteful, and, frankly, the universe could go fuck itself.

CHAPTER TWENTY-EIGHT

Jazz

Jazz pushed a roasted tomato around her plate with her fork, trying to look engaged in the conversation she was supposed to be involved in. Maggie had texted Jazz as she and Liam were walking out of the museum to invite her to brunch with her and Nadia. And, after seeing how well Liam had handled India, Jazz had figured she could try to be friendly with Nadia.

She'd spent minimal time with Nadia since she and Maggie had become friends, mostly around Maggie's wedding, when Jazz had been too busy with her maid of honor duties to get to know her much. That hadn't stopped her from building up a picture of Nadia in her head, a picture that Nadia, in person, was tearing to shreds.

Why did she have to be so fucking nice?

She'd greeted Maggie and Jazz with hugs and given Jazz three compliments before they'd even sat down. And not one of them was a simple, "I like your shoes!" It was things like, "Oh wow, Jazz, that necklace really brings out the gold in your eyes, it's gorgeous," and, "You have the most infectious laugh. I love it."

Jazz really fucking hated being wrong. But Nadia being so nice didn't make her feel any less threatened. Instead, she was more convinced than ever that she was going to lose her best friend to someone who was clearly a better fit for her.

After Friday night, she'd planned to take the weekend off from drinking, which meant telling Liam's moms they were seeing each other sober. Eliza and Danisha hadn't seemed surprised in the slightest, and they'd played it pretty cool, but Eliza had given her more hugs than usual, and Danisha had given her the biggest slice of the apple crumble cake she'd made. Jazz took that as approval on their parts.

She longingly eyed the servers passing with trays of mimosas. Brunch without a mimosa was sacrilege, but she couldn't trust herself not to be an asshole to Nadia with so much as a drop of alcohol in her system. Instead, she grumpily sipped her hazelnut iced mocha.

"So, Jazz," Nadia began, giving her a warm smile. "You must be super busy at work right now. Maggie was telling me about the pay discrepancy case you all have been working on?"

"Yeah, it's been a lot, but we have a ton of good people on the case, so we're getting there."

"That's great. I know Maggie used to work like really long days when she was doing your job, and trust me, I know what that's like."

"I have a pretty good work-life balance," Jazz replied. "Cal doesn't like us to take work home and I have an amazing assistant, so it's not so bad."

Nadia raised her brows and whistled. "Good for you, girl. I could do with taking a leaf out of your book. I swear I don't remember the last time I just sat down for some me time."

"Give yourself some credit, Nad. You have twin toddlers and three jobs. You're killing it," Maggie said, patting Nadia on the hand.

"It'll be worth it when the kids are all grown up and I have my empire," Nadia said with a wink. "Do you want kids, Jazz?"

Jazz stilled, her fork halfway to her mouth, and dropped the same tomato back onto her plate. "One day, yeah. Probably not for a while, though."

"You're doing the right thing waiting until you're totally ready. I love my kids, but we had them young because I was convinced I could do it all: the kids, the husband, the career. And sure, I'm doing it, but at what cost? If I could go back in time, I'd do it like you."

Jazz was sure Nadia's statement was supposed to be positive, but all it did was make her wonder what the hell she'd been doing with herself for the last ten years. Nadia was three years younger than her and had all that.

She pushed back from the table, her chair legs dragging across the floor. "I'll be back in a second. I have to use the restroom."

Concern flashed over Maggie's face, but Jazz didn't give her the chance to follow as she crossed the restaurant and barricaded herself in a stall. She sat down, letting her head drop into her hands.

She was only thirty. But wasn't that what she'd been telling herself for the past decade?

She was only twenty: she didn't have to know what she wanted to do with the rest of her life.

She was only twenty-two: didn't everyone struggle to figure shit out after graduation?

She was only twenty-four: it wasn't a big deal that she kept bouncing around from job to job, she had time to figure it out.

She was only twenty-six: just because half of her high school classmates were settling down and having babies, didn't mean she had to worry about it yet.

She was only twenty-eight: just because Maggie had found her happily ever after didn't mean she was going to forget Jazz.

She was only thirty: she was going to feel ready for it all at some point. Right?

That's what she'd been waiting for—that moment where everything clicked into place, when she woke up one day and knew she was ready to settle down, to find the person she wanted to be with, to become a mom.

But what if she couldn't? What if she was too late? She'd long suspected having kids might not be as easy as making the decision and coming off birth control. There was obviously something wrong, given how bad her periods were. But she kept telling herself she'd cross that bridge when she came to it. Just like she'd told herself she'd paint a picture, make herself a dress, finish a goddamn bracelet. And she hadn't done any of it.

She was thirty years old, and she had absolutely nothing to show for it.

Jazz sucked it in a shaky breath, and when she blew it out, tears fell with it. She wrapped her arms around her middle, as if she could hold her heart in her chest. Her breath hitched as she forced oxygen into her lungs. A blurry film crept over her vision as her skin tingled, the tips of her fingers going numb.

Her phone buzzed from where she'd dropped it on the floor and she jumped, reaching for it and wiping her tears away as they continued to spill down her cheeks.

> Can I pick you up from brunch or do you have plans with Maggie after? I have a surprise for you. Miss you :)

She read the text over, and again, and again, in Liam's voice, trying to soothe her racing heart. Before she could stop herself, she hit the call button and held the phone up to her ear.

"Hey, darling."

"Liam."

A sharp intake of breath sounded down the phone. "What's wrong?"

"I just… I just needed to hear your voice," she sobbed. It wasn't working. Why wasn't it working?

"Where are you? What's going on?"

"I'm in the restroom. I don't know what's wrong. I just can't… I started panicking and I couldn't breathe and I—"

"Hey, hey, it's okay," Liam said, his voice low and slow. "You're having a panic attack. It's okay, we can work through it. Everything is going to be just fine. Take a deep breath with me, Jasmine." Liam took a deep, loud breath and Jazz copied him. "And another one."

Gradually, as she followed along, listening to Liam's calm breathing and comforting murmurs, she stopped shaking so much. "I think… I think it's passed," she said, lifting the hem of her shirt to wipe her face.

"Take it easy. Do you want me to call Maggie—"

"I don't want her to see me like this. I'll be fine." That was the last thing she needed. She couldn't talk about this with Maggie. That wasn't an option.

She sighed, pulling her phone away to check the time. She'd been away from the table for too long. "Liam."

"Yeah?"

"Can you do me a favor and pretend you don't hear me peeing while we're on the phone? I don't want to hang up yet."

"Of course," he said gently. "Did something happen? Do you want to talk about it?"

Jazz sandwiched the phone between her ear and shoulder as she stood up enough to pull up her skirt and push down her underwear. "It's a long story. And I don't think I can talk about it and stay calm."

"That's okay. We can talk later, or whenever you're ready. You want me to come pick you up? I can be there in fifteen—maybe even ten if traffic is okay."

"No, I… I have to go back out there. I'll be fine." She wiped, flushed, and flinched as she stepped out of the stall and took in her reflection above the sink. The paper towels were rough, but they were better than nothing. She wet one with cold water and dabbed below her eyes, trying to de-puff.

"You sure?"

"Yeah. I feel a little better. Thank you. I needed this."

"Anytime, darling. You know I'm always here."

Fuck, she didn't deserve him. She took a deep breath, pushing that worry aside for now. She couldn't handle something else. "I don't have plans with Maggie after brunch, so you can pick me up if you still want to."

"Good. You're going to love what I have planned."

"Any hints?"

"Hmm… Well, we'll have to stop by the pet store before we go."

Jazz gasped. "We're picking up Bray? I thought the shelter said we couldn't get him until tomorrow."

"They called an hour ago to say we can pick him up today. In a couple of hours, we're going to be parents," he teased, and despite how knotted her insides were, Jazz smiled.

"You're going to be a dad," she corrected. "I'm a bonus mom at best."

"It won't be that when he likes you better than me. I'll pick you up in an hour?"

"Yeah. Thank you. For all of this."

"Nothing to thank me for. Call me if you need me to come pick you up early, okay?"

"I promise. See you soon."

She hung up and took a deep breath, her heart still racing, before heading back into the restaurant. There was nothing she could do about her eyes. God, she was tired.

Maggie was sitting alone, her tongue poking out as she read through something on her phone. She looked up as Jazz approached, her eyes widening. "Are you okay? You were gone a while. Shit, have you been crying?"

"Hmm? Oh, no, don't worry," Jazz waved her away. "I had an eyelash in my eye that I couldn't get out and Liam called to talk about Bray. That's why I took so long. We're getting him from the shelter today, so he's going to pick me up after brunch." Maggie didn't look convinced, so Jazz quickly changed the subject. "Where's Nadia?"

"She ran outside to take a client call."

"On a Sunday?"

"No rest for the wicked. Hey, I was thinking and we should go out next weekend."

Jazz eyed her warily. "You, me, and Nadia?" She didn't need a repeat of today.

"No, just you and me. We can go to a bar, just like old times."

"That sounds great," Jazz replied, her stomach calming a little. Maybe this was what they needed to get back to how things were. Liam was right—everything was going to be just fine.

"Does he look smaller in person, or is it just me?"

"He definitely looks smaller," Liam agreed. "The shelter said he was smaller than the other puppies in the litter, but he should catch up."

Bray was sitting on the rug in front of the couch, looking up at them both with an expectant expression. Jazz had expected a little anxiety from the tiny pup, but he didn't seem fazed in the slightest to have left the only home he'd ever known.

"What do we do with him?" she asked Liam, and he shrugged, looking as uncertain as she did.

"I don't know. Play with him? Feed him? Love him?"

Jazz clasped her hands and leaned forward, looking Bray in his dark brown eyes. "Do you want some toys?" He tilted his head to the left. "Food?" And the right. "Cuddles?"

"Ruff."

Well, then. "Alright." Jazz reached down and picked him up gently with one hand. She settled him on her shoulder and snuggled into Liam, so Bray could sniff both of their faces. He did just that and, apparently happy with what he smelled, licked both of their cheeks.

"Oh my god," Jazz whispered, trying not to scare him as she smiled at Liam. "I think he likes us."

Liam was watching Bray with so much love in his eyes that Jazz's heart skipped a beat. "I think I would die for him," he said, offering a finger to the puppy. Bray rubbed his head on Liam's finger and Jazz practically melted.

"Same." She scratched the top of his head while Bray rubbed his face on Liam's. "Do you love your daddy?" she cooed, and both Liam and Bray turned to her and scowled. How Bray knew the D word was off limits, she had no idea. She held up her hands. "Sorry. Do you love your papa?" she tried and Bray barked his agreement, spinning around to boop her nose with his.

"Papa it is," Liam chuckled. "And that makes you mama."

"I'm not his mom," Jazz said, but the words were muffled as Bray stepped right in front of her face and sat down on her chest.

"Try telling him that."

Bray gave her literal puppy dog eyes, and she sighed. "Fine. I'm your mama."

Liam wound his arm around her shoulders and leaned his head against hers, both of them staring down at Bray. "I think he's happy to be home. We make a cute little family."

Bray agreed with a little chirp, then promptly lay his head down and started snoring. Liam picked up his Kindle turning his attention to his book like what he'd just said was no big deal. *Family.* Jazz looked between both of them, her heart damn near beating out of her chest. Is that what this was? A family she actually felt comfortable in?

Something warm spread through her, but it was no match for the panic that always seemed to be right at her fingertips these days.

CHAPTER TWENTY-NINE

Liam

Jasmine tightened around his fingers, her teeth sinking down on his shoulder in an attempt to mute her scream as she came. The bite burned, and Liam fucking loved every second of it.

"That's one," he said, when her breathing slowed again. "Lose count and we start over."

"Oh fuck."

He spun her around and laid her on her back, moving down her body and kissing everywhere he passed. Their record, so far, was five, and they were determined to obliterate it.

It was Monday, and they'd both taken the day off from work since they'd planned to pick Bray up that morning. Liam had the whole week off, at Maggie's insistence. *"Pawternity leave,"* she'd called it.

His dad had tried to get Jasmine to take the same, but she'd refused, claiming she had too much to do because of some case they were working on. Liam was pretty sure it had more to do with staying busy, so she could spend a little less time in her head, but at least they had the day together. Not that they needed the time to get used to being puppy parents: Bray had claimed a spot on the arm of the couch and seemed content to sleep for as long as physically possible.

Which was fine with Liam: he had plans to make Jasmine come at least six times, and, once she was nice and relaxed, broach the topic of her panic attack yesterday.

He'd been ready to jump in his car and break every traffic law to get to her when he'd answered the phone and heard her crying, struggling to breathe. But by the time he'd picked her up, she'd seemed fine. A little worn out, maybe, but otherwise just happy to see him. Words couldn't describe how relieved he'd been to see she was okay, but that hadn't stopped his worry about why she'd had the panic attack in the first place.

That was a topic for later, though. For now…

He caught her clit in his teeth and she cried out, fisting the blankets. Though he loved to see her struggle against the cuffs when he restrained her, he wanted her to fight against every single orgasm this time.

"I'm going to make you come over and over, darling."

"Promises, promises," she gasped, moaning as he roughly parted her legs and slapped her pussy.

He'd been planning to build her up slowly, make her come on his fingers, his tongue, maybe a toy or two, before pressing his cock inside her. But he couldn't wait.

He lined his cock up and thrust inside her, Jasmine's eyes flying open in surprise. Good. It wasn't going to take much. He could feel how close she was in the way her pussy hugged his cock, in the way her thighs trembled. But she was fighting it, her jaw set, her fists clenched.

Game fucking on.

"You think you can hold back? Think again, Jasmine. I'm not asking nicely for you to come," he said, his voice low and rough. "I'm fucking making you." He fucked her harder, and she cried out, her head twisting on the pillow as he fucked her harder.

"Is that all you've got?"

Liam leaned in closer so he could grip her face and force her to look at him. He brushed his thumb across her lip. "Admit it, darling. You're desperate for it. You love being my filthy fucking toy and making a mess all over me. You love that I can make you do whatever I want." She whimpered, her eyes glazing over, her resolve slowly shattering. "Now fucking *come*." He gave her a feather-light slap on the cheek and she splintered, the strength of her orgasm taking him by surprise. He pulled out of her and cursed as she squirted all over him. Holy shit. Liam had to squeeze his eyes together and take several deep breaths to stop himself from coming on the spot. They had a long way to go before he got to come.

He kissed the cheek he'd slapped as Jasmine came down slowly, eyes wide and panting. Liam stood up, walking backward to the dresser where he'd laid a bunch of stuff out before they'd started. Her body shook with the aftershocks. "Count, Jasmine."

"Two," she said sleepily, then shot up, gasping as Liam pressed a vibrator to her clit and turning it on low. "Liam! I can't, I—*Fuck*."

"I know you have more than that in you. Are you tapping out?"

"Never," she promised through gritted teeth. "I can take it."

"Prove it," he said with a low, wicked laugh, and cranked the vibrator up to full power.

"Can we talk about what happened yesterday?"

Jasmine turned her head to look at him, her hair tickling his nose. "I thought we were supposed to talk about shit before sex."

Liam plastered what he hoped was an innocent expression onto his face and shrugged. "I forgot. What can I say? You're just so distracting and—"

Jasmine sat up in the bath, water and bubbles rushing down her body. "Liam Bray Michaelson, did you butter me up with eight orgasms just so I would be more inclined to talk?"

They'd both tapped out at eight—Jasmine spent, and him so desperate to come inside her, he just couldn't wait any longer. They were having so much fun making up for all the years Jasmine couldn't come. He was shooting for ten next time.

"On a scale of one to ten, how pissed would you be if I had done that?"

Jasmine considered him suspiciously. "I would be reluctantly impressed, to be honest."

"In that case, yes, I did do that."

She breathed out, her nostrils flaring. "You're lucky you're cute."

"You weren't calling me cute when you were begging for mercy a half hour ago," he murmured in her ear as she lay back down, letting him run his hands over her soapy body.

"What can I say? You're just *so* distracting," she teased and Liam chuckled, squeezing her in his arms. If he had his way, they'd lie like this forever and he'd never have to let her go, not even for a single second. This was exactly where they belonged—wrapped around each other.

Bray padded into the bathroom, dropped a sparkly pink dragon toy on the bathmat, and barked at them. He'd woken up as Liam was running the bath and he'd wandered in and out, bringing them every toy he owned. Which was, Liam could admit, a lot of toys, considering they'd only brought him home yesterday. They'd gone a little overboard at the pet store, and both Liam and Jazz had started online shopping the second Liam had been given the green light from the shelter.

"Good job, buddy," he told Bray, who stuck out his tongue, wagged his tail, and ran off, butt wiggling, presumably to fetch another toy. "Is this normal behavior for a puppy?"

"Fetching? I think so, but I've never had a dog. Maggie's family had dogs when she was growing up, so she might know," Jasmine offered, and Liam ran a wet hand through his hair.

"I should've done more research. I feel like I have no clue what I'm doing here."

"If you can handle me, you can handle anything," Jasmine said, squeezing his hand. "And I will begrudgingly admit you're pretty good at handling me."

"Handling you is my favorite thing to do." He ran his hands all over her body and Jasmine sighed a happy sigh, relaxing into him. "And speaking of you…"

"Ugh."

"Talk to me, darling. What happened?"

Jasmine was quiet, skimming her fingertips over the top of the water. Finally, she huffed, and said, "Nadia was just talking about her life and she's achieved so much. It's incredible how much she's done, but I don't know. It just made me spiral. Do you ever just feel like you're completely wasting your life?"

"Not recently, but in general? Sure."

"Seriously?" Jasmine sounded skeptical.

"I lost the woman I thought I wanted to marry, all my friends, and got fired from my dream job. Not to mention, my parents are super impressive people with amazing careers, and I went to art school," he said with a wry laugh. "Don't get me wrong, I'm really content these days, but I'm still not exactly where I thought I'd be at thirty-seven."

"I'm not where I thought I'd be either," she replied, her voice tinged with sadness.

"Where did you think you'd be?"

"I have no idea. I've never been able to picture my future—what's the point of picturing anything when I never actually fucking follow through?" She laughed bitterly. "But

I guess I thought I'd figure it out someday. Yet here I am. It's like time moved on for everyone else and I'm still seventeen, sitting in the guidance counselor's office with no answer when they asked me where I wanted to be in ten years."

Her voice cracked, the sound unbearable to Liam. He swallowed. "Can I ask you something?"

"Sure."

"Do you really not know what you want, or are you just scared to want it because you don't think you can get it?"

Her spine tensed, her breath shaking as she drew air into her lungs. "I don't know. I'm not sure I've ever actually managed to do anything I really wanted to. My parents forced me to get my degree. I didn't actually care about it. And even then, I only managed it because Maggie helped me. Your dad practically handed my job to me. I didn't earn it, and then Maggie and the rest of the team had to help me figure it out. Anything I've tried to do by myself, I've given up on. You've seen all the craft shit at my place. I've never finished any of those projects—not even a tiny fucking bracelet. I couldn't even make myself come. I needed *you* for that."

Did she really think achievements only counted if she did them alone? Liam wouldn't have been surprised if that was one of her parents' dinner stipulations. It was bullshit.

"I didn't tell you why I loved Snoopy so much, did I?"

"No, just that you were obsessed."

"One of my mom's friends got me this Snoopy children's book collection for my fifth birthday. There were twelve books, all for a first grade reading level. I couldn't read them, but I memorized them because my parents read them to me every night. And they're the only books I read by myself for the next four years, because I couldn't read properly."

Jasmine pulled away from him so she could turn around to face him fully, eyes wide. "Really?"

"Mhmm. I was fine with everything else in school, but not reading. I knew there was a problem because all of my friends were flying through books, but I didn't tell anyone because I was embarrassed. I was also really resourceful, and I have a great memory, so I mostly just memorized shit and I managed to keep it under wraps until third grade, when it became really clear that I could barely read."

It was why he'd fallen in love with art as a kid. Art didn't need words. Liam could feel the emotions and craft a story in his head without having to read.

"I had an amazing teacher, and she spoke to my parents. There was a bunch of testing and they figured out pretty quickly that I'm dyslexic. I got lucky. My parents paid for intensive tutoring with a specialist and he gave me tons of techniques and resources to help me catch up with my classmates. I was pretty much on par with everyone else at school by sixth grade. I love reading now, but I still use most of the techniques I learned when I was ten—that's why I read mostly on my Kindle, so I can change the font."

"Holy shit. I would never have guessed," Jasmine said. "That's so impressive, Liam. You're amazing."

"It is impressive," he agreed. "It's the thing about myself I'm most proud of, actually. But I had help. I couldn't have done that on my own. And that doesn't make it any less of an achievement, does it?"

She frowned, as if she couldn't fathom why it would. "Of course not. It's an amazing achiev—oh. I see where you're going with this. It's not the same."

"Why?"

"Because… Well, I actually don't have an answer for that right now, but one will come to me," she muttered and Liam couldn't help but laugh at her indignant expression.

"Jasmine, darling, the things we do mean more when we do them with the people who care about us. When you're a hundred years old, being an absolute menace in a nursing home, do you think you're going to give a shit about what you achieved alone? No. You're going to cling to the memories of the people who loved you so much they wanted to help you. Unlike your parents, we're not all just sitting around waiting for you to fail."

"I know that you believe that. And I believe that you believe that. I just don't know how to make myself believe it," she replied, throwing her hands up in frustration. "It's easier not to fail if I just don't try. That's what makes sense in my brain. How am I supposed to change three decades of thinking?"

"Ruff-ruff."

They both turned to look at Bray, who was trying to reach his little paws up to the tub, as if trying to join the conversation.

"Thank you. That's a very helpful suggestion, baby boy." Jasmine laughed softly, the frustration melting from her voice. She turned back to Liam, and her eyes were dull.

"I don't regret any of this, but I also wasn't expecting to be questioning my own brain so much. It was just supposed to be sex. I'm exhausted, Liam. I'm so fucking tired."

"Come here." He held out his arms, and she slid into them. "I know it's exhausting right now, but it's not forever. One day, you're going to wake up and everything's going to feel a little easier. And the next day, and the next day. And you're not doing this on your own."

"Rule number three," she droned.

"Fuck the rules. You, Jasmine Cannon, are my favorite person in the entire world. As far as I'm concerned, you're never going to have to do anything on your own again. I'm here, and I'm not going anywhere, if that's okay with you."

"It is," she said after a moment of silence, and Liam knew that it would take more than one conversation for her to believe him. He knew it would take time after time of him reassuring her, and it would take work, on Jasmine's part, to relearn how to exist in a world that she'd spent so long hiding her true self from. But when she was ready, he would be there. Forever, if she let him.

CHAPTER THIRTY

Jazz

Had bars always been this loud, or was she just not drunk enough? Sierra had suggested the Greek-themed bar, claiming they had the best garlic fries and cherry old fashioneds in the city. The fries were mediocre at best, but the old fashioneds were delicious.

When Sierra had mentioned the theme, Jazz had been expecting something like a semi-clean frat house, but it was more like a dark academia Pinterest board had thrown up all over the place. There was entirely too much fragile shit dotted around, considering the smell of liquor permeating the air.

Floating shelves were lined with busts and books, globes and typewriters, candlesticks that she was pretty sure had been burned only for decoration. Comfy armchairs were scattered around the room, and the walls were covered in prints, schematics, and pages that looked like they'd been ripped out of old textbooks. There were even tall marble-esque Greek statues, one by the door and another on a dark wood plinth in front of a window.

She really had to bring Liam here. He would love it.

Jazz swallowed the dregs of her cocktail and slammed the glass down on the table a little harder than she intended, the room tilting a little. Maggie raised a brow.

"Damn. Apparently those orgasms you're getting now aren't doing anything to chill you the fuck out."

"Maggie."

"What?"

"We're sitting in a bar on a Saturday night and we're the oldest people here by at least five years. And we're talking about work! Doesn't that bother you?"

"Should it?" Maggie asked, looking confused. Jazz sighed. So much for *just like old times*.

"Yes! We used to be fun. We used to go on three-day benders and fuck strangers in airplane bathrooms and stay up all night watching shitty Rom-Coms instead of sleeping. What the hell happened to us?"

"We grew up, Jazz," Maggie answered softly, looking at her with concern. "We were in college when we did all that shit, and I wouldn't want to go back even if I could. Even if I didn't have Cal, I have no interest in being that hungover ever again."

She laughed like it was all some big joke, like the panic spreading through Jazz was all in her head. But it wasn't. It couldn't be. She was the fun one—why did it suddenly feel like she didn't even know how to be *fun*?

"But don't you miss it? Don't you miss dancing on tables and not giving a fuck about anything?"

 320

"I've never not given a fuck about anything in my life," Maggie pointed out, which was true, but completely beside the point. "And no, I don't miss it. I don't miss any of that. I'm happier now than I've ever been. What is there to miss?"

Jazz pushed away from the table, running her hands through her hair. Maggie didn't get it, and she couldn't explain it, so where the fuck did that leave them? "I need another drink," she muttered, ignoring Maggie's sigh of her name as she walked away.

She leaned against the bar, watching the group of early twenty-somethings beside her toasting a birthday and downing neon yellow shots.

"What can I get you?"

Jazz turned to the bartender. "Whatever they're having."

"One, three, or six?"

God, she hadn't done shots since Maggie's bachelorette party, and even then, only one or two. "Three," she said, and the bartender poured the shots, sliding them across the sticky bar top.

Jazz took a deep breath and threw one back, sour pineapple flooding her tongue. She shuddered, slamming the shot glass down and picking up the second. It was no better, but at least she knew what to expect this time. She picked up the third.

"What the hell are you doing?"

She turned toward Maggie's concerned voice to find her best friend staring at the shot in alarm.

"Shots," Jazz said, wrinkling her nose and swallowing the last shot. "You want some?"

"No?" Maggie was staring at her like she'd grown another head. Jazz rolled her eyes and turned back to the bartender.

"Can I get a Long Island with no ice, please?"

"Sure thing."

Maggie tugged her back from the bar as the bartender started throwing her drinking together. "Don't you think you've had enough to drink?"

"I'm not a child. And what happened to a night *just like old times*?"

Maggie leaned back with an exasperated sigh. "I meant a night without Cal and Liam. Not a night where we tried to test the alcohol tolerance we had in college, for fuck's sake. We're too old for that."

Too old for that. Jazz threw her head back and groaned. "Lighten up, Maggie. What's the worst that could happen?"

She swiped her drink from the bar and took a big gulp.

Jazz twirled around in time to the music, the beat pulsing through her. What had she been so worried about again? She loved this bar! Everyone was so friendly, the drinks were delicious, the vibes were top tier. Even Maggie was having fun.

As night had fallen, and the dinner crowd had cleared out, the music volume had risen and several of the people still hanging around drinking had started dancing. A group of grad school students on a girl's night had absorbed them into their midst and Jazz couldn't remember a single one of their names. They were celebrating something—a birthday? A graduation? She didn't know, but she clinked her glass and cheered whenever everyone else did.

It was easy to ignore the fact that the girls they were dancing with were closer to Rose's age than her own when she had multiple kinds of liquor flowing through her veins. Maggie had stopped counting her drinks and protesting eventually. She'd even done a shot herself, then forced herself not to throw up and ordered another old fashioned instead.

But she was up, she was dancing, she was holding Jazz's hand as they twirled around each other singing along to songs they hadn't heard since middle school.

"I haven't heard this song in so long," Maggie squealed when one of their old favorites came on, jumping up and down and shaking her hair.

"We spent hours making up a dance for this one, remember?"

"Doing it? Yes. The dance? No chance." Maggie laughed. "Jesus, that was almost twenty years ago. Remember how Hallie used to copy the dances we did?" From the age of eleven, Maggie had been stuck at home most nights, babysitting her younger siblings, which meant Jazz had been there too. Maggie had three siblings and the youngest, Hallie, had trailed them around like a puppy, copying everything they did and swearing she wanted to be just like her big sister when she grew up. And now, like the rest of Maggie's family, Hallie wanted nothing to do with her sister.

"How old would she be now?" Jazz asked.

"Hallie?" Maggie frowned when Jazz nodded, as if struggling to do the math through her drunken haze. "God, she'll be twenty-three in September."

"Fucking hell. How did that happen?"

"She grew up," Maggie replied with a laugh that sounded more pained than anything else. "We all did. Then my parents got their claws in her, and now my baby sister doesn't give a shit about me."

"Maggie—"

"I'm fine, don't worry. I just got in my head a little." Maggie waved her away, sipping from the glass clenched in her hand. It was mostly water from the melted ice. Though she claimed to be okay, Jazz could see the hurt in her eyes. She couldn't fix things with Maggie's family—she couldn't even fix things with her own—but she could distract her.

"Come on," Jazz said, grabbing Maggie's hand and tugging her toward an empty table by the window. She kicked her heels off and climbed up onto a chair, putting one foot on the table before Maggie clocked what she was doing.

"Jazz! What are you doing? You've had way too much to drink for that."

"Live a little, Maggie!"

Maggie pulled her hand. "Get down. You're going to hurt yourself."

But Jazz wasn't paying any attention as she danced on top of the table. The song faded into another one of their teenage favorites and she cheered. "I love this song!"

She jumped, clapping her hands, but when her feet

touched down on the wooden tabletop, her foot slid out from underneath her and she toppled from the table, falling to the floor as Maggie cried her name.

Her ass cushioned her fall, but her legs kicked out and she cursed as her foot connected with something hard, blinking in the hope that the room might stop spinning for a second. The fall had knocked the wind from her and her blood was rushing in her ears, which was probably why she didn't hear Maggie screaming until her voice faded in, "… OUT OF THE WAY!"

Jazz looked up as soon as the words registered, with enough time to see the five-foot statue of a Greek goddess teetering on the edge of the plinth, but not enough time to get out of the way. The statue tilted toward her and Maggie rushed forward, pushing it in the other direction.

It was like it happened in slow motion: the statue smashed through the window and Maggie landed on Jazz, covering her head as glass shattered everywhere. Maggie pulled back just in time for them both to watch the statue hit the sidewalk and break into a dozen pieces, scattering all over the concrete.

For a moment, everything but the head of the statue was still. Jazz followed it with her gaze as it rolled along the pavement and halted inches from two on-duty police officers.

Fuck.

Never in a million years could Liam have imagined hanging out with his dad while the two women they were head over heels for had a girls' night at a college bar. Nor could he have imagined his dad, fifty-eight-years-old, sitting on the floor with a catnip mouse in one hand and a mini tennis ball in the other, playing fetch with an overexcited puppy and a cat who wanted nothing to do with him. Peach wasn't happy about her new family member—her nephew, Liam supposed.

Anytime Bray got too close, she hissed at him. Bray, having never met a cat, had no idea what that meant. But his dad had found a way to occupy both of them and keep the peace. He was a professional negotiator, after all, but Liam thought it had more to do with the treats he had stashed in his t-shirt pocket.

Liam snapped a picture of his dad. Peach had two paws on his left knee, and Bray was copying her on the right. His dad leaned down, kissing them both on the nose. Liam took another picture and send them both off to the family group chat. His moms replied almost immediately:

MOM E

Always knew he'd been a good grandpa!
(hint hint, Liam)

Liam laughed and locked his phone, smiling at the picture of Jasmine snuggling Bray in bed that he'd taken the day before, and immediately set as his lock screen. She was grinning, ear to ear, her nose pressed to Bray's with the covers crumpled around her. She had sheet marks on her face, and the nightstand on her side of the bed was cluttered with chapstick, her tumbler, *his* Kindle because she'd stolen it to read the steamy scenes in the book he'd just finished, a handful of loose bills, and a tiny lopsided cactus she'd bought at the grocery store and immediately dropped in the parking lot.

If someone who didn't know them looked at the picture, Liam knew they would think she looked right at home. At his place, with him, and their puppy (that was technically his puppy, yes, but the details weren't important).

They hadn't heard from Jasmine and Maggie, beyond a few pictures when they'd arrived at the bar: a selfie of the two of them, and then almost identical pictures of the dark academia decor with two very different messages:

JASMINE 🤍

This place makes me think of you. I love it
:)

As much as he appreciated Maggie complimenting his eye for detail, it was Jasmine's message that had made his heart damn near stop in his chest. He couldn't wait to fall into bed with her later.

His dad's phone lit up on the table, ringing loudly. Liam peered at it. "It's an unknown number."

"Can you put it on loudspeaker? It's probably just a spam call, but it could be work."

Liam answered the phone on loudspeaker. "Hello?"

"Liam?"

His dad was on his feet faster than Liam would've thought possible, considering his age, the second Maggie said his name, her voice shaking. Why was she calling from an unknown number, and why the hell did she sound so weary?

"Yeah," Liam replied as his dad sat beside him. "You're on loudspeaker. My dad's here."

"Are you alright, love? What's going on?"

Maggie took a trembling breath down the phone. "I need you to come pick us up. We've been arrested."

CHAPTER THIRTY-ONE

Liam

They were silent on the drive to the police station. Liam assumed, like him, his dad was torn between panic, not knowing what to say, not wanting to make assumptions, and just desperate to get his person back in his arms.

Was Liam surprised that Jasmine had been arrested? Probably not as surprised as he should've been. Was he surprised that Maggie had been? Absolutely. She hadn't explained much on the phone, but he was sure it was over something small, and he didn't care what it took to fix it as long as they were both okay.

He'd never been more grateful for his dad's air of authority as he followed him into the Seattle North Precinct.

"Can I help you?" the smiling woman at the front desk asked, beaming at his dad.

Liam tuned his dad out as he relayed why they were there to the woman. He was too on edge, peering around the bright, sterile lobby. He tuned back in as the woman told his dad that the arresting officers would be with them to explain everything in a moment.

He couldn't sit, pacing back and forth in front of the metal chairs, while his dad sat still as a statue. To someone who didn't know him, he would appear completely calm and collected, but Liam knew he was just as stressed as he was. He just had more experience hiding it.

"Mr. Michaelson?"

They both looked up to see two officers striding across the lobby toward them. His dad stood to greet the officers, one of whom had a tablet in her hands, presumably with Jasmine and Maggie's arrest file, if that was a thing. Liam had no idea how any of this worked.

"Hi. Yes. Are Maggie and Jazz okay?"

"They're fine, sir. Thank you for coming out for them. We weren't comfortable letting them go, given how inebriated they are," the taller of the two officers explained, and Liam frowned.

"They were arrested for being drunk? Just how drunk were they?"

"Very drunk," the officer with the tablet confirmed. "But that's not actually why they were arrested. There was an incident at the bar. I guess one of them was dancing on a table and they fell and knocked over a very expensive statue, breaking a window, the statue, and a table."

Shit. Liam didn't need to ask who was dancing on the table. "Is Jazz okay? Was it a bad fall?"

"We offered to get her checked out by a paramedic, but she declined and said she felt fine," the officer assured him. "We were outside when the window broke and we became quite concerned about them when they got into an argument —well, it was mostly one sided, actually. Maggie has quite a temper, if you don't mind me saying."

"That sounds like Maggie," his dad replied.

"Your daughter?" The officer gave him a look that Liam thought was supposed to be in commiseration, but it quickly morphed into shock and embarrassment when his dad pinched his brow and replied:

"My wife."

"Oh god, I shouldn't have assumed. I'm so sor—"

"Don't worry. We're used to it." His dad's shoulders were less tense now that he knew Maggie and Jasmine were okay. "Do you know if the owner of the bar is pressing charges?"

"They don't want to press charges. As long as the damage is paid for, they're happy to draw a line under it. We can pass your details along to sort that out between your-selves, if that works."

"That's perfect, thank you."

"Great. They'll be out with you shortly," the woman said. "They've sobered up, probably because of the shock of everything, but they've still had a lot to drink tonight. Although neither of them hit their heads, they still fell, so I would recommend you keep a close eye on them for the next twenty-four hours—especially Jazz."

He had no intention of taking his eye off Jasmine for the next twenty-four hours—longer if he could manage.

Liam started as his dad clapped him on the shoulder. "At least they're okay."

"Yeah. At least they're okay."

Except it became abundantly clear that *okay* was relative when Jasmine and Maggie stepped into the lobby. Maggie's jaw was set, her blue eyes like thunder. Jasmine eyed her best friend warily, smudges of black eyeliner and glittery gold eyeshadow all over her face.

"Hey, love." His dad wrapped Maggie up in his arms, but she barely hugged him back. Liam could see the explosion building in her.

"Thank you for coming to get us." Maggie swallowed. "I need to be outside."

She pulled out of his dad's hold and walked toward the door, her shoulders set.

Jasmine brushed a hand over her face, grimacing as she watched Maggie walking away. "Shit," she said under her breath, running after Maggie. "Maggie, wait up. Can we talk about this, please?"

Liam and his dad exchanged a worried expression before following them.

Thin rain misted the air, unseasonably cool for Seattle in August. Jasmine had her arms tucked around herself, rubbing her skin as if trying to stay warm.

Maggie was heading straight for his dad's car, her fists clenched into balls.

"Please talk to me," Jasmine begged her as they all caught up and Maggie spun, her dark hair flying behind her.

"I don't even want to look at you right now, let alone talk to you. What the fuck were you thinking? Oh wait, you *weren't* thinking, because you had so much to drink you couldn't fucking see straight."

Jasmine reared back, as if Maggie had physically

slapped her with her words. "I fucked up, okay? I'm sorry. But it's really not that big of a deal. They're not pressing charges and I'll pay for the damages and—"

"YOU WORK FOR A FUCKING LAWYER, JAZZ." Maggie sucked in a breath, angry tears springing to her eyes. "At any point, did you stop and consider how this might look for Cal if people found out his assistant *and* his wife were arrested for getting so drunk they caused property damage?"

"Maggie, love—"

But Maggie was on a roll, and Liam didn't think she even heard his dad saying her name. "Or did you think about how this might look for me and my business if people found out *I'd* been arrested? I'm barely established. I can't afford bad publicity right now. I have employees fucking depending on me. This is my livelihood, Jazz."

"I said I was sorry!" Jasmine shouted at her, throwing her hands up. "What else do you want from me? It's not like I can turn back time and drink less."

"I want you to grow up," Maggie said through gritted teeth, and Liam winced. "You're thirty years old. I want you to act like it. We're not twenty-one anymore. There are actual real life consequences to the shit you do now. It's time to grow the fuck up."

Shit. Liam couldn't blame Maggie for being angry. He couldn't even blame her for saying what she'd said, but it was, arguably, the worst possible thing to say, given everything that Jasmine was struggling with. And Liam knew, no matter how angry she was, Maggie would never have said it if she'd known. Which meant Jasmine hadn't told Maggie she was struggling.

And he saw in Jasmine's face the second she decided she'd made the right call in keeping shit from her best friend. Fuck.

"You know what, Maggie? Get off your fucking high horse. Just because *you* decided to settle down, get married, and start a business so you could do the same old shit of taking on too much responsibility and lashing out when you can't handle it, doesn't mean the rest of us want such a boring fucking life."

"*Jasmine.*" Liam stared open-mouthed at her, but she refused to look at him. She didn't mean it. Fuck, they all knew she didn't mean it. She didn't even sound angry, just tired and sad. But even though Liam knew that Maggie knew that, she still looked absolutely gutted by her best friend's words.

She looked down, staring at her shoes. "Can you open the car, please? I want to go home."

His dad fished his keycard out of his pocket and held it up to the car door until the lights flashed. Maggie wasted no time pulling the door open and disappearing inside. His dad rounded the car and jumped into the driver's side. Though the windows were tinted, Liam was close enough to see him immediately reaching across the center console for her.

Jasmine loosed a long, watery breath.

"Darling…" He stepped toward her, but she held up a hand, looking up at him with tears streaking down her cheeks.

"Please don't touch me. If you touch me, I'm going to fall apart and I can't. I just… I can't."

"Okay. It's all going to be okay. Let's just get you home and into bed, and everything is going to be better in the morning."

She nodded, and he reached for the back passenger's side door handle. "Liam?" she whispered, and his hand stilled.

"Yeah?"

"I don't know why I said all of that. I didn't mean it. Any of it." Her voice was barely audible, cracking as more tears spilled down her face.

It took everything in him not to just pull her into his arms and wipe her tears away.

"I know, darling. And Maggie knows too. She'll cool off and you can talk things through when you're both feeling better."

He opened the door and closed it gently behind her once she was settled, then rounded the car and got in the other side. Bray, who they'd had to bring along because they couldn't trust him not to piss Peach off too much, was standing on Jasmine's lap. He was wagging his tail, clearly happy to see her, but staring up at her with his head tilted, as if he couldn't quite understand why her cheeks were wet. Jasmine's hands shook as she scratched behind his ears.

His dad cleared his throat and turned back to look at him. "You're staying at our place tonight."

Both Maggie and Jasmine piped up in protest, but his dad interrupted them both. "I don't want to hear it. You've both had a lot to drink and the officers we spoke to said you fell. Liam and I have been worried shitless since you called us and we're both going to sleep better knowing we're all under one roof."

Jasmine nodded, staring at her lap, and Maggie just stared out of the window, her mouth in a thin line.

It would be fine. They would talk in the morning and make up and everything would be fine. It had to be.

Jazz

The amount of alcohol in her blood should have knocked her out the second her head hit the pillow, but Jazz didn't sleep a wink. Though they didn't talk, Liam stayed awake, clutching her hand, until his grip loosened and his breathing evened out around four.

Jazz watched him sleep, memorizing the lines on his face, each individual hair on his mustache, the errant freckles dotted around his nose. He was perfect in heart, and soul, and body, and mind, and she was a fuck up who said shitty things she didn't mean to the one person who had been on her side forever.

How the hell had everything gotten so messed up?

Jazz carefully untangled herself from Liam, trying not to wake him or the puppy sleeping in the crook of his neck. She threw on shorts and the sweatshirt Liam had been wearing the night before, then padded quietly down the stairs, needing to feel daylight on her skin.

Sun streamed through Maggie and Cal's window, the clock on the microwave showing just past six. She squinted at the light, poured herself a glass of water, and sat at the dining table to chug it. She didn't feel nearly as rough as she'd expected. It was fucking ironic that the one time she deserved a hangover from hell, she felt more or less fine. What a joke.

She wasn't alone for long. Tiny feet tapped on the hardwood floor, followed by louder footsteps.

"Morning," Cal said, squeezing her shoulder as he passed, Peach leading him across the kitchen to her food bowl.

"Morning."

Peach didn't spare a passing glance at Jazz—she was singularly focused on her food bowl. And Cal, it seemed, wasn't moving fast enough. Peach stood at his feet and meowed continuously while her dad opened the can of food and meticulously scooped the supplements Maggie had curated for Peach.

Jazz knew Maggie was usually the one to wake up for Peach's breakfast, because she often woke up to a text from her time-stamped 6:30, that was entirely too chirpy for so early in the morning. But Maggie was a morning person. Cal wasn't. Which meant Maggie had probably chosen to stay in bed to avoid bumping into her. Jazz squeezed her water glass so hard she was surprised it didn't shatter.

"Christ, you'd think we starved you," Cal muttered sleepily as he placed Peach's bowl on the floor and she dove in whisker first.

He busied himself making coffee and Jazz stared down

at the table. How was she supposed to look at him? She'd basically implied Maggie was boring for marrying him. Nothing could be further from the truth. Cal had brought Maggie out of her shell, and Jazz loved seeing the change in Maggie after she finally found someone who valued her. So why the fuck had she said it?

She looked up as Cal slid a glass across the table toward her. "Iced lavender latte with oat milk."

Her favorite. Jazz wrapped her hands around the glass and thanked him, her eyes burning.

"Are you okay?"

Jazz forced herself to look up and there wasn't a shred of judgment in his green eyes, the mirror of his son's. Only concern shone on his face. A tear slipped down her face before she could stop it, and she wiped it away with Liam's sleeve. "No. I don't think I am. I'm sorry," she said, her voice cracking and tears falling faster than she could wipe them away. "I didn't mean what I said last night. I don't know why I said it. And the arrest… Fuck, I'm sorry. For all of it."

She buried her face in her hands and then, suddenly, Cal's arms were around her, pulling her into a hug.

"It's okay, Jazz. I promise it's okay. You made a mistake. That doesn't mean we love you any less."

Jazz had never had a *fatherly* dad, but she could only assume this was what it felt like. What must it feel like to grow up with someone who held you when you cried and reassured you, even when you fucked up? Who would she be if she'd grown up without a fear of trying, just in case she made mistakes? Probably not the kind of person who said such shitty things to her best friend.

"Maggie…" she began, with no idea how to finish her sentence. What could she even say?

"Maggie loves you," Cal said, sitting back so he could peer down into her face. "She knows you, and she knows you were just lashing out. This is Maggie we're talking about, so maybe give her a couple of days to stew, but she will forgive you."

Jazz nodded and tried to make herself believe it. She and Maggie had fought over the years, but she'd never made it so personal. And Jazz had almost always been the one behind their fights. This was just another in a long, long line. Everyone had a breaking point—what if this was Maggie's? It wasn't just the shit she said, but the complete and utter disregard she'd shown for Maggie's business. And Cal's.

"About work," she said, wringing her hands. "I'm so sorry, Cal. You know I love my job, and I care about the firm. I would never want to do anything to cause problems for you or the team. I wasn't thinking. Clearly."

"Do you really think you're the first person on the team to get arrested? I've had to help more than a few people out of trouble over the years, which Maggie knows, for the record. I promise, drunken property damage is minor."

Well, shit. Apparently Jazz didn't know her colleagues as well as she thought she did.

"No one at the office needs to find out about this if you don't want them to," Cal promised. "And speaking of property damage, I know you said you'd pay for it, but it's a lot of money, and—"

"I have savings," she interrupted. "I can pay for it. I *need* to pay for it. It was my mistake."

Cal, who was familiar with Maggie fighting him on offering to pay for shit, even though they were married, didn't look happy, but at least he didn't argue. Jazz was used to being around people with money, thanks to her parents and their business, and she'd never met a more generous millionaire than Cal Michaelson. Or a more frustrated millionaire, because everyone around him refused to let him spend money on them.

But Jazz had to prove to herself that she could pay for her own mistakes. She had to feel the consequences.

"Okay," Cal reluctantly. "But if you need help, you let me know."

"Thank you." She swallowed, her voice thick with emotion.

"I mean it, Jazz. You're family, and even if you just need to talk or rant to someone who isn't Liam right now. You know where I am."

Jazz nodded, grateful when Peach finished her breakfast and started yowling for more food, distracting Cal. She didn't deserve him. She didn't deserve any of them. And just like her parents, eventually, they were all going to figure out she wasn't worth it.

CHAPTER THIRTY-TWO

Liam

"What if—and this is just a suggestion—you didn't keep stealing my socks?"

"Ruff." Bray tilted his tiny little head like he had no idea what Liam was talking about. In his defense, he probably didn't, considering he was a puppy and didn't speak English.

"Good chat, buddy. Our son is a tyrant," he told Jasmine, who was perched on the edge of the couch, fidgeting with a lavender scrunchie. Bray stood on his back legs and waved until Liam picked him up. "You're cute, though," he muttered to the dog, who just wagged his tail, happy to be there.

Jasmine said nothing, and Liam wasn't sure if she'd even heard him. She just stared at the scrunchie, passing it between her hands, purple smudges below her hazel eyes.

She hadn't spoken about the night before since they'd

left his dad and Maggie's house. Jasmine had been ready to run out of there the second he'd come downstairs, even though he was hoping Maggie would come down and the two of them would talk.

When 10 a.m. passed, it had become abundantly clear that Maggie wasn't coming down. She rarely stayed in bed past eight, and her missing presence had been deafening. He and his dad did their best to act like everything was normal, but Jasmine sat in an armchair, staring into space until he'd given up on any kind of conversation between her and Maggie and driven home. To his place, because, although he was giving her the space to process as she needed, he wasn't willing to let her out of his sight.

"Are you alright, darling?" he asked, and she looked up, blinking, as if she'd forgotten he was there. She offered a jerky and unnatural nod. "You sure?"

Jasmine drew her lip between her teeth. "We need to talk, Liam."

Liam's stomach dropped. He could see it in the resignation in her eyes, in her lips, bitten raw. In the way her body kept slipping forward until she wrapped her arms around herself, trying to hold herself up. Even in the spot she'd chosen on the couch, as far away from him as she possibly could. She didn't have to say anymore for him to know where she was going with this.

"No," he said, simply, firmly, not letting his panic show on his face.

Confusion contorted Jasmine's features. "No we can't talk?"

"No we're not breaking up."

 342

It was a risk. He couldn't actually do anything if she really wanted to end things between them, but he was confident that she didn't. He hoped, anyway.

Jasmine's nostrils flared, her eyes blazing, and Liam could have cried with relief. It was a sign of life. It was something.

"What are you talking about? We're not actually in a relationship—how could we break up?" Jasmine asked, her voice stronger, steadier.

And just like that, the time for taking it slow was over. "Of course we're in a relationship. What else would you call this?"

"We're casually seeing each other!" Jasmine spluttered.

Liam exchanged a weighted look with Bray before looking back at her. "And what's the casual part, exactly? The way we spend all our free time together? The dates we've been going on every few days? Or maybe the way we're co-parenting a dog together?" Bray barked. "That's a great point, buddy. Maybe it *is* the way you're literally all I think about—and have been for months, years even. Or the way you told me you loved me that one time—"

"I was sick and it was an accident!" Jasmine stood up, her brows drawn together. He knew her well enough by now to know that she was pissed—he just had to hope it was because he'd derailed her, and not *how* he'd derailed her. And pissed was better than broken. Flames had replaced the emptiness in her hazel eyes.

"No take backs, I'm afraid."

"Liam." Jasmine raked a hand through her hair, gaping at him. "You can't just decide we're in a relationship.

You're supposed to ask me if I *want* to be in a relationship."

"Okay." He set Bray down on the couch and stood so he was facing her. "Do you want to be in a relationship?"

"Oh my god. I'm trying to end things here."

"Right, and like I said: no. That doesn't work for me."

"Jesus Christ, I've stepped into a parallel universe." She spun around and stomped all the way to the bedroom.

Liam winced and looked at Bray. "Too much? Never mind, you're a dog. Fuck. What am I doing?"

He trailed after Jasmine and paused in the doorway. She was sitting on the edge of the bed, her head in her hands, but she looked up as he shuffled closer and her eyes were blurry with tears.

"Darling…"

"This wasn't supposed to happen like this. You were supposed to just let me walk away. It was supposed to be easier this way."

He sat down beside her, and though his fingers itched to reach for her, he resisted. "Easier for who?"

"For you. Because you're too nice to actually end things with me when you realize what a fucking mess I am, and I'd rather break my own heart than ask you to do it when I know what that would do to you."

Oh. "Jasmine, let me make one thing very clear: I know how much of a mess you are, and I'm going nowhere. Not now, not tomorrow, not six months from now."

"But eventually—"

"No. Never. I'm not going anywhere. And you don't get to burn this thing we've built to the ground because you

made a mistake and you're scared. This is just fight-or-flight mode, and we're going to fight through it."

Jasmine huffed out a breath, standing up and taking several steps back is if she needed to put some space between them or her resolve would crumble. But Liam didn't want her resolve to crumble; he wanted her to fight; he wanted her to shout and scream, throw shit around. Anything was better than her being broken down, feeling like she had no option but to leave. If that took antagonizing the shit out of her for now… Luckily for Liam, he'd learned from the best: her.

So he stood up too and stepped forward. Jasmine glared at his feet like she couldn't quite believe he had the gall.

"Why do *you* get to decide we're fighting? First you decide that I'm your girlfriend without asking me and now you get to decide that I'm not allowed to end things?"

Liam raised a brow. "I don't recall using the word girlfriend…"

"For fuck's sake."

"But hey, if the shoe fits, *girlfriend*." It really wasn't the time, but Jesus, that felt good. "And I get to decide we're fighting because right now, I'm the only one of us who cares about your wellbeing. You want to take some time, consider everything fully, and then break up with me?" He narrowed his eyes. "Honestly, I'd still probably say no, but I'd be more inclined to listen."

Jasmine stepped closer. "You are fucking infuriating," she said, punctuating each word with a prod to his chest.

Liam cupped her chin, tilted her head up so she was

facing him, and winked. "Maybe, but no take backs, remember?"

Jasmine growled, pushed him back on the bed with her finger, and tackled him. Liam grunted as he fell back on the bed, the mattress bouncing beneath his body. He barely had time to blink before Jasmine's lips were on his, fierce and unrelenting. Her thighs pinned him to the bed, squeezing his legs and setting him alight as she rolled her hips, brushing against his cock. She wasn't wearing pants, just one of his old sweatshirts, underwear, and mismatched fuzzy socks.

He ran his hands up the back of her sweatshirt—*his* sweatshirt—and she cursed into his mouth as his cool fingers connected with her blazing skin. She tore at his t-shirt, pulling it over his head and tossing it on the bed, before sitting up on her knees. She pushed his sweatpants down just enough to free his cock, wrapping her fist around him and drinking down the whimper that fell from Liam's lips. Jasmine didn't bother to undress, she just pulled her underwear to the side and sank down on his cock until he was deep inside her. She gasped, squeezing his cock with her pussy, and Liam grabbed her hips, fighting the urge to take control.

He could let her run this show, if that's what she needed, despite how badly he wanted to fuck her. Jasmine moved slowly over his cock. Her fingers were bone white where she gripped the fabric, her body tense, as if she couldn't quite decide whether to keep fighting, or fuck him.

"Are you mad at me?" he murmured, brushing his nose over the edge of her jaw.

"Yes. No. Fuck, maybe. I don't know. I'm mad, I just

don't know if it's at you or me or everything." She pressed her forehead against his chest, her voice dripping with frustration.

"You want to work it all out on me? Use me. I can take it. I'm not going anywhere."

Like she'd been waiting for permission, a flip switched in Jasmine. She growled, gripping his shoulders hard enough to leave bruises in her wake and caught his bottom lip between her teeth as she fucked him, riding him hard and ruthless. She slammed down on his cock, over and over again, and Liam's lungs strained as he held his breath, trying not to come in a single fucking second.

Liam cupped her breasts, toying with the gold bars in her nipples

"Harder," she gasped, and he obliged, bending his head so he could capture her nipple in his mouth. He tugged it with his teeth, pinching the other, and Jasmine threw her head back, her nails digging into his shoulders.

She cried out his name, her voice cracking on the second syllable, and Liam looked up, drawing his eye along the line of her body. Flushed splotches of red dotted her skin, her hair was in knots, and the sight of her knocked the wind out of him. The pressure in him reached a boiling point, and he cursed, balling his hands into fists and slamming them on the mattress.

Jasmine's movements didn't slow, but she looked down at him with a hazy smile that bordered on a smirk. She released his shoulder and ran two fingers over his mustache before pushing them into his mouth. He closed his lips, moaning around her fingers.

"Do you want me to let you come? *Boyfriend*," she added in a semi-mocking tone, but Liam didn't miss the way her eyes lit up when the word passed her lips.

Jesus.

He nodded, unable to speak with her fingers in his mouth. But he was sure his eyes were begging her to have mercy on him.

"Make me come, and come with me," she groaned, and Liam realized she was holding off as much as he was. She was fucking close, her pussy clenching around him. All it took was a light brush of his finger over her clit and she let go, tumbling down into the depths of pleasure and dragging him along with her. Liam held onto her for dear life as he came, pretty sure he was biting down on her fingers but not totally conscious of his actions. Jasmine sobbed his name, her hips slowing as her own orgasm faded.

She pulled her fingers out of his mouth and dipped her hand between her legs, dragging her fingers over the spot they were joined, where his cum spilled out of her. Licking her lips, she brought her fingers to her mouth and groaned.

"You look good coming for me," she quipped, and Liam chuckled, leaning his forehead over her chest, feeling her heart race.

"It's always for you, Jasmine. Every single time."

He felt her swallow, and she sat back, both of them gasping when he slipped out of her. Liam grabbed a box of tissues from the nightstand and wiped his lap off. It wasn't perfect, but it was enough for him to climb into bed, beckoning Jasmine with him. She followed, tucking the covers up to her chin.

"I'm still mad at you," she said, but there was no bite to her words. She snuggled into him and sighed contentedly when he kissed her forehead.

"So mad that it's a *no* on us being in an actual relationship?" Liam asked, his tone more confident than he felt.

"Not that mad."

"I can take that. *Girlfriend.*"

"Shut up."

Liam laughed and turned out the lamp, plunging the bedroom into darkness. Jasmine turned around, and he looped his arms around her, spooning her.

"Liam?"

He said nothing, just waited until she cursed.

"For fuck's sake. *Boyfriend?*" Jesus, he had no right getting hard again.

"Yes, darling?"

"I want to fall asleep with you inside me again," she said, sleepily, angling herself toward him. Liam's heart raced. He was still half-hard, but her words turned him on to a torturous degree. What the hell had she done to him? "But, just to reiterate," Jasmine continued, "I'm still pissed."

"So I've heard," he replied, rubbing his cock over her pussy and pressing into her, savoring her happy little whimper. "Goodnight, darling."

CHAPTER THIRTY-THREE

Jazz

Cal was sitting on the couch outside his office, reading a worn and bent paperback with a cup of coffee in his hand. She dropped onto the couch beside him with a heavy sigh, and he looked up with a bemused smile.

"Hello to you too."

"Hey. Remember when you said if I needed someone to do girl talk with while Maggie and I aren't speaking, I could come to you?"

Cal dogeared his page and set his book down, squinting at her. "I'm absolutely certain I didn't phrase it like that."

Perhaps not, but he *had* told her to come to him if she needed to talk or rant, and oh boy, did she need to rant. "I considered forcing Sierra to listen to me, but that seemed like a breach of boss-assistant boundaries, you know?"

"Probably not the best person to comment on those," Cal offered with a wry smile. "But I am on board with the girl talk. What's up?"

"It's about Liam," she warned.

"I figured that's what *girl talk* would entail. Shoot."

If her mind wasn't so muddled, she would laugh out loud at Cal's eager expression. The man was such a gossip, but she trusted him to keep whatever *she* told him to himself. She knew he wouldn't even tell Maggie, unless she asked directly, and why would she?

Jazz took a deep breath and considered her phrasing. This was Cal's son she was talking about, after all. "Okay. Liam won't let me break up with him."

Cal opened and closed his mouth no less than three times, confusion on his face. "I didn't even realize you were officially together," he said finally, and Jazz groaned.

"Me either! But Liam says we're in a relationship and I don't seem to get a say in the matter."

"Huh. That's pretty bold. I didn't realize we were allowed to do that." Cal raised his brows and ran a hand over his jaw, clearly impressed with his son.

"Cal!"

"Sorry." He gave her a sheepish, dimply smile that was exactly like Liam's. Fucking Michaelsons. "Okay, so you don't want to be together? Officially, I mean."

Jazz crossed her arms and scowled. "I didn't say that."

"But you're trying to break up with him."

"Exactly, he just won't let me."

Cal had a slight deer in headlights expression as he nodded. "Mmm. So just to clarify, you don't *not* want to be together, but you also want to break up with him?"

"Right."

He pinched the spot between his brow and closed his eyes for a moment. "Okay. I can do this. So you want—Um no. It's not that—Fuck. Right, scratch that. Why do you want to break up with him?"

"What?"

"You want to break up with him, so I assume you have a reason for that. What is it?"

Jazz leaned back. "Well, he's… you know."

"I think it's safe to assume that I don't."

She sighed, staring down at her shoes. "Maggie would know," she grumbled.

"Of course she would. She's Maggie. Maybe you could talk to her about this? Not that I'm not happy to girl talk. But I also don't have a fucking clue what you're saying."

Her heart sank into her stomach. "I want to talk to Maggie. I miss her. I just… I don't know." She'd wanted to call Maggie the second Liam had sprung the relationship they were apparently in on her. Though, knowing Maggie, she'd probably figured it out long before Liam had had to spell it out for Jazz. Her brain was confused; her heart was fucking thrilled. She had no idea what to make of any of it.

"She cried for three hours last night," Cal said gently. "She misses you like crazy. You're both just so stubborn, and if you keep waiting around for the other one to reach out, it could be weeks, for Christ's sake." He wasn't wrong.

"I'll think about it."

"And when it comes to you and Liam, I don't really know what's going on, but I know I love you both and want you to be happy. Maggie and I wasted months refusing to let ourselves be in love. We'll never get that time back. Don't make the same mistake that we made."

Jazz had become entirely too comfortable wasting time

in the name of fear, she knew that. But knowing that didn't make it easier.

"Thank you. I'll try my best not to mentally discount everything you said," she added begrudgingly, and Cal laughed.

"That's all I can ask for. C'mere." He stood and held his arms out, folding Jazz into a warm hug. "You're going to figure it all out, Jazz. And you have lots of people on your side. We're not all like your parents." Cal patted her on the back.

"Thank god."

The elevator dinged and Sierra shouted, "Knock knock," as she stepped out. "Ooh, I'm so getting in on this hug." She barreled into them both, closing her arms around Jazz and squeezing. "Is this just a *fuck Mondays* hug, or is there a special occasion?"

"It's an *I'm doing a great job ruining my life and also Cal is probably going to be my father-in-law someday* kind of hug," Jazz offered, disentangling herself from her boss and her assistant. She would never survive in a totally professional setting. "Daddy-in-law?" she suggested, and Cal winced and shook his head. "No, you're right. That would be weird. Anyway, what's up, Sierra?"

"Your sister's here to see you. She's downstairs."

And there went the tiny shred of comfort she'd taken from the hug. "Wonderful. Lead on," she said, mouthing *thank you* to Cal as she followed Sierra to the elevator. "Did Rose say what she was here for?"

Sierra shook her head. "Nope. You know, she's pretty hot." She wiggled her eyebrows and Jazz shot her a warning glare as the elevator doors slid open, spitting them out into the din of the first floor.

"That is my baby sister. Don't even think about it."

"This place is nice."

Jazz watched her sister glance around Ethel's diner with zero interest, her hazel eyes dull.

"It's pretty good. We come here a lot," Jazz replied, cupping her mug of tea. She'd always been a coffee person through and through, but, these days, something about tea was oddly comforting. Fucking Liam.

She'd taken one look at her sister, waiting for her in the lobby, and her heart had sunk. Whatever Rose had to talk to her about, it wasn't good. Her face was drawn, nails bitten to the quick.

"So what's going on, Rosie?"

Rose wrapped her arms around herself, chewing her lip. "I know we don't really talk often, so I definitely have no right to do this, but I need to ask a favor."

Jazz had never heard her sister so dejected. She reached across the table and took her hand. "You're my sister. Even if we don't talk, I'm here for you. Whatever you need."

"Thank you. I was hoping I might be able to crash on your couch for a few weeks? I can't afford to rent a place on my own, so I just need time to find a roommate who won't murder me in my sleep."

"Is that all? Of course you can stay at my place. Shit,

you can take my room and I'll sleep at Liam's." It wasn't like she and Liam were spending nights apart these days.

"Thank you. Seriously. I owe you big time." Rose breathed a sigh of relief.

Jazz narrowed her eyes, Rose's request sinking in. She still lived at home with their parents, the drive to school less than an hour. "Why are you moving out so suddenly? Do you want to be closer to school for the new semester or something?"

Rose sipped her flat white before answering, her voice shaky. "I got kicked out."

"Of med school?"

She shook her head. "No. But I did *drop out* of school. Mom and Dad found out and kicked me out. I'm not allowed to step foot in their house until I re-enroll, which I couldn't do even if I wanted to."

Holy shit. Of all the things she'd expected, Rose dropping out of school hadn't crossed her mind. "How did they find out?"

"You know Kami's terrible mother-in-law?"

"Unfortunately." Xander's best friend, Kami, had more of a monster-in-law than a mother-in-law. She despised Xan, and she didn't seem to be a particular fan of Kami either.

"She saw me on a date and overheard me talking about dropping out. Not only did she tell Mom and Dad about school, but she also outed me as a lesbian, so that's great."

Jazz was significantly less surprised to learn her sister was a lesbian than to find out she'd dropped out of med school. "Jesus. Tell me they didn't give you shit for that," she said. Her parents had rolled their eyes when she'd come out as pansexual in high school, but they never seemed to have a problem with it. Nor had they had a problem with Xan being bi—in fact, her parents had both been devastated when he'd broken up with his high school boyfriend, because he was a baker and always brought dessert when he came over for dinner.

"They didn't care about that," Rose confirmed. "I mean, they're pretty shitty parents, but at least they're not homophobic, I suppose."

"It's something. God, Rosie, I'm so sorry. Why did you drop out?"

"I've never wanted to be a doctor." Rose shrugged, and she looked lighter just talking about it. "I only went to med school because they wanted me to. Remember last summer when I got a job in that lab?"

"Sure. Infectious disease research or something, right?"

Rose huffed a laugh. "Something like that. Well, I loved it. Like really, really loved it. And they loved me. They offered me a full-time job at the end of the summer, but I couldn't take it because of school. So they said they'd call in a few months to see if I changed my mind, and they did, in March. I was in the middle of studying for finals and just completely miserable. So I withdrew from all my classes and I took the job. I started in May."

"Shit, good for you. Are you happy?"

A smile spread over Rose's face. "So happy. I love it. The pay isn't great right now, but it'll go up a lot once I pass the two-year mark, and the benefits are decent. And they're willing to pay for me to get my masters in a couple of years. But mostly, I just really love the work."

"I assume Mom and Dad didn't care about that when you told them?"

"No." Her smile fell away. "Even if I do get my masters, they're not interested unless I have *Dr.* in front of my name."

"Assholes."

Rose laughed, but it sounded more pained than anything else. "Yeah, well, they've always been assholes. They pushed and pushed me and now they're surprised that I might want a little control over my own life. I've always been so jealous of you, you know."

"Jealous of *me*?" Jazz asked, gaping at her? "Why on earth would you be jealous of me?" Rose was the prettier sister, the skinnier sister, the smarter sister, the more successful sister. The easier, better, less disappointing sister.

But Rose looked just as confused as Jazz felt. "Are you kidding? Xan and I are both so jealous of you, Jazz. You're your own person, you're fun, and you have a life outside of this family. You've never given a shit about Mom and Dad's expectations. I wish I could be like you."

God, she'd done a good job of faking it, hadn't she?

"It's not real," she said, running her finger over the handle of her cup. "I give a shit. Like a *lot*. Sure, I don't try with them anymore, but it's kind of really fucked me up, actually, how much I give a shit."

"Oh." Surprise flashed over Rose's face, but she quickly schooled her expression into something fierce. "Maybe that part's not real, but the rest is. You are your own person, and no one can take that away from you. Not even them." She took a deep breath, shaking her head. "I thought it was better to just give in to them. To just try to be good enough. I thought that one day, I would finally be good enough."

She looked away and Jazz's stomach twisted as she realized Rose was wiping her face. "You had the right idea not to try. I don't know what the hell they want, but it's not us. It was never us."

Jazz loved her parents. For a long time, she'd resented them, she'd begrudged them, but she'd never hated them. Not until she watched her sister wiping away tears, thinking she wasn't enough.

"Promise me something, Rosie. Promise me you won't stop trying. Not for them, but for you. Because once you stop, fuck, it's hard to start again."

Rose's eyes widened, but she nodded. "Yeah. I promise. I'm looking forward to figuring out how to live for myself, and not for them."

"I'll be here for you," Jazz promised. "Whatever you need."

Rose gave her a grateful smile. "Thank you. And I promise not to be in your hair for too long. I don't suppose you know anyone looking for a roommate?"

Jazz remembered a hazy conversation she'd half paid attention to a couple of days ago before her first coffee of the day had sunk its claws into her. "I think I do, actually. You know Sierra, my assistant? Her roommate is moving to Florida. I could give her your number?"

"That would be amazing. Thank you, Jazz. For everything."

Jazz felt some of the tension she'd been holding for days, months even, slip away. "Thank you for coming to me. And you're more than welcome at my place for as long as you want." She rummaged around in her purse and pulled out her keys, unclipping the apartment keys from her car keys. Rose eyed the paddle-shaped *brat* keychain Liam had surprised Jazz with after her first orgasm with a touch of judgment, but said nothing. "Did you get your stuff out of Mom and Dad's?"

"I packed everything, but I couldn't fit it all in my car. I was going to ask Xan to pick it up once I knew where I was staying."

Resolve straightened Jazz's spine. "I've got it. Leave it with me."

CHAPTER THIRTY-FOUR

Jazz

She made two calls from the road: one to let Cal know she wouldn't be making it back to the office for the last couple hours of the workday, and one to Liam, to let him know she would be staying with him for a while until Rose found a place. Her apartment might have been big enough for the two of them if she didn't have so much stuff, but she couldn't fix all her problems at once. That would come later.

Thankfully, Liam's phone went to voicemail, so she didn't have to hear him smugly call her *girlfriend*. God, she loved him so fucking much.

She pulled up outside the house and took a deep breath. She could do this. Gravel crunched beneath her shoes, the August sun beating down on her neck like she needed something else to sweat about. She stopped outside the door, raised her fist, and knocked.

Footsteps sounded beyond and Jazz steeled herself as the door opened. Surprised eyes blinked at her.

"Liam's not here. He's working on site today," Maggie

said, eyeing her warily. Her expression alone made Jazz want to get to her knees and beg for her forgiveness.

"I know," she replied, her voice steadier than she felt. "I'm here to see you. If that's okay."

"Of course it's okay," Maggie said, her voice warm. "Did you think it wouldn't be okay?"

Jazz lifted a shoulder in a half-hearted shrug. "I didn't know what to think, to be honest."

Maggie opened the door further and stepped back. "Get in here. We've said worse shit to each other over the years, Jazz. You're my person. It's all good."

Jazz flinched. *It's all good.* Just like that.

That was the old Maggie speaking—the people-pleasing, put everyone else first, scared to disappoint the people she cared about, Maggie. The Maggie she shouldn't have to be anymore.

Jazz crossed the threshold and closed the door, taking a shaky breath as Maggie reached for her, folding her into a tight hug. "Thank you. But it's not all good. It wasn't okay. I have to start holding myself accountable for the shit I do and say."

Maggie pulled back, an impressed expression on her face. "Okay then. Yeah, let's talk."

Jazz followed her through the townhouse, to the big living room the team usually used as their office base. It was quiet, and Jazz assumed Maggie must be the only person working in the office. She'd spread notecards out all over the table, her version of a physical spreadsheet.

They both took a seat on the couch, Maggie waiting patiently, giving Jazz space to open the conversation.

"I love you," she said, after a moment. "I love you more than anything in the whole world, Maggie. How I acted the other day—how I've been acting in general lately… I've been so shitty. I'm so fucking sorry. I didn't mean any of what I said. I don't think you're boring, and I don't think you're overworking yourself. Well, you are, sometimes, but not for the reasons you used to. I'm sorry."

"Thank you for apologizing," Maggie said, reaching for her hand. "You really don't have to, but I appreciate it."

"I do have to apologize. You don't deserve to be treated the way I've been treating you lately."

Maggie frowned, her brow pinched. "I've noticed you've not been yourself for a few months. What's going on?"

"Honestly?" Maggie nodded and Jazz blew out a long breath before continuing. "You got married, and I think that made me panic a little. I couldn't be happier for you, for the record, but it just made me feel… I don't know, like you were leaving me behind. You were growing up, and I didn't think I was ready for that, and then you've been making other friends who are all incredible, amazing women who are achieving so much and I'm just… me."

"Oh. Jazz, I could never leave you behind," Maggie promised. "I've been trying to push myself out of my comfort zone a little this year and meet people, because my therapist told me I should, but honestly? I wanted you with me. But after inviting you so many times, I guess I just assumed you didn't want to hang out as much anymore."

"I convinced myself you were just asking me to hang out because you felt sorry for me," Jazz admitted. "I didn't want to be a third wheel for you and Cal, or tag along with your new friends, just because you felt obligated to invite me. But I should've talked to you."

"Probably," Maggie agreed. "But I should've asked. Just so you know, Nadia and her friends intimidate the hell out of me too. They're amazing, but I feel like I've accomplished nothing next to them."

"Are you kidding? You're amazing. You've made all your dreams come true."

"Most of them, yeah. And you can see that, just how I can see how amazing you are and you can't," Maggie pointed out. "We weren't raised to be proud of ourselves. It doesn't come naturally to us. But you know what does?"

"Being proud of each other?" Jazz asked, and Maggie wrinkled her nose.

"Shit, I was going to say self-sabotage, but that's so much nicer. Listen, it doesn't matter how old we are, or how married I am, you'll always be my number one."

Jazz drew in such a big breath that her lungs burned. "I know," she said, after a moment. "But I think… Shit. I think maybe it's okay if I'm not anymore." Her voice cracked, tears springing to her eyes.

Maggie's face fell. "Jazz—"

"No, Maggie, it's okay. Really, this isn't a bad thing." Jazz wiped at her face. "I love Cal so much, and I love him for you. I couldn't have dreamed up anyone better for you than him. And I know you loving him doesn't mean you love me any less, so it's okay if he's your number one now. He should be. If you'd asked me a few years ago, I would have confidently said that there was no one in this world good enough for you. But Cal… He really is."

"He is." Maggie sniffed, silver lining her eyes. "He really, really is. I wouldn't have him without you. You know that, right?"

"Yeah." She could take a little credit for helping Maggie and Cal get where they were, and it might just be her favorite thing she'd ever done. "You deserve that kind of love, Maggie."

"You do too, you know."

Jazz rubbed her face, chuckling. "Yeah, well, Liam seems to be taking that choice out of my hands anyway, so."

Shock and anger crossed Maggie's face. "He ended things? You have to be fucking kidding me."

"Whoa, no, no, the opposite actually," Jazz clarified, and Maggie's expression turned to confusion. "*I* tried to end things, and he said no and told me we're actually in a relationship, and there's nothing I can do about it."

"Oh. Damn," Maggie said, looking as impressed with Liam as Cal had. It *had* been pretty impressive. Jazz could begrudgingly admit that (but not to him—where was the fun in that?) "Clearly, you have a lot to catch me up on. Tell me everything."

So Jazz did. She gave Maggie a rundown of the night before, stumbling through her feelings just as she had with Cal. But unlike her husband, Maggie understood right away. Because Maggie had been there.

"You don't want to end things," she said with complete certainty. "That's not the problem here."

"It's me. I'm the problem. He's perfect and I'm… This."

She gestured to herself, and Maggie's face fell. "I'm chaotic and messy, selfish and difficult, and I fail anytime I try something, so I just don't try because I'm scared. I'm so scared."

"You're human, Jazz. You're made up of thousands of things, millions of things, and I promise there is more to you than the things other people have deemed unworthy. There's more to you than your parents have deemed unworthy." Maggie's words hit her like a punch in the gut.

"I'm so scared," Jazz whispered, her nails digging into her palms. "I love him, Maggie. I really, *really* love him. I mean, how could I not? He's perfect. How can *I* possibly be enough for him?"

"No one's perfect. Not even Michaelsons," Maggie pointed out. "They just seem that way to us because of how we grew up. They're pretty close to perfect, but let's not forget it took Liam two years to do anything about the fact he had the world's biggest crush on you. And he didn't tell you about said crush before you made your orgasm pact, then he decided you were dating and in a relationship without asking you. Not to mention the mustache."

"I kind of love the mustache," Jazz begrudgingly admitted. "Actually, I kind of love all of it—all of him."

Maybe she'd been pissed at Liam for keeping shit to himself in the moment, but she also understood why he did it. Because he understood her, and he knew she'd bolt if he came on too strong. It wasn't like the signs hadn't been there. Jazz could have protested until the day was done that they weren't dating, but what the hell else could it have been? He hadn't hidden what they were doing from her, he just hadn't explicitly labeled it. Maybe that was wrong, but Jazz found it hard to care. She said as much as Maggie laughed.

"Of course you do. Because when you love someone, you love their imperfections too, right?"

"I guess."

"So it stands to reason that Liam loves all of *your* imperfections too," Maggie said gently, like the mere idea of it would scare the shit out of her. Which it did. "You're not the first person to freak out because you fell in love. Are you forgetting that Cal pushed me into agreeing to a date with Liam? Or that I literally quit my job and fell off the grid for months?"

"But I'm not you or Cal," Jazz protested. Why could no one seem to understand that? "You always land on your feet, both of you, no matter what life throws your way. If you want something, you just make it happen. Everything I touch fails."

"That's not true, Jazz. Cal and I wouldn't be together without you. And I've known Liam for eight years and I've never seen him as happy as he is now. You did that."

"Maybe I did that, but then I do shit like Saturday night and ruin it." It was impossible to reconcile the version of her that held Liam's hand, keeping him calm at the wedding, and the version of her who tried to break both of their hearts because she was scared to try. The version of her who hyped Maggie up when she and Cal broke up, and the version of her who called Maggie boring for marrying him.

"You haven't ruined anything. But you have to forgive yourself. Give yourself a little grace and try."

Jazz sniffed, her brain a swirling mess of emotions. "What if I mess things up? What if I try and I fuck it all up?"

"Well, luckily for you, you fell in love with a Michaelson man. And they have a weird amount of patience for emotionally stunted women who escaped Marysville with a boatload of trauma."

Her words drew a watery chuckle from Jazz. "Shit, our parents really did screw us all up, didn't they? Actually, speaking of them, I have even more to tell you. Is there any chance you can ditch work for the rest of the day and I can catch you up from the road?"

"That depends—are we running away from Liam?"

Jazz shook her head. "No." Never. Well, perhaps in a sexy way, but... Not the time to be thinking about that. "You're right. I need to try. I'm going to try." And she would trust herself, and Liam, that they'd work through things if they started to crumble. Together.

"Excellent. So where are we going?"

"We're going to Marysville," Jazz said with determination. "To stop my parents from fucking up my siblings any further."

CHAPTER THIRTY-FIVE

Jazz

Jazz's parents still lived in the house she'd grown up in: a six bedroom, picture perfect house on the outskirts of the suburbs of North Marysville. It was modest by her parents' standards, and Jazz had spent a long time trying to understand why they'd chosen to live somewhere where they believed themselves above everyone else. Until she realized, one day, that they enjoyed feeling like they were above everyone else.

It was the biggest house in the area, where most had two or three bedrooms. Maggie had grown up in one of those houses, squeezed into a two bedroom with her parents and three siblings. Most of the time, she'd slept on the couch since she was up so late and didn't want to wake her younger siblings up by climbing into her bunk bed. Meanwhile, Jazz's parents had more bedrooms than kids.

She'd kept a close eye on Maggie as she'd driven past the *Welcome to Marysville!* sign, but, if Maggie was fazed by their unexpected homecoming, she didn't show it. Still,

Jazz intentionally took the long route to her parents' house so she could avoid driving past Maggie's parents' cafe.

Jazz spent the drive telling Maggie about her conversation with Rose, and by the time they pulled up outside the Cannon family home, Maggie was more than ready to confront Jazz's parents.

"We're going to be civil, remember?" Jazz warned Maggie as she followed her up the path.

"Civil. Right."

She hadn't forgotten how quickly Maggie had jumped to her defense when she'd thought Liam had ended things. "Maggie. I mean it. Civil."

Maggie sighed, but nodded as Jazz raised her fist to knock on the front door.

Her mom answered, her eyes as wide as the Botox allowed. Lilia Cannon was, unmistakably, gorgeous. She looked exactly as she had when she was Jazz's age, and she'd put in a lot of work to make that happen.

"Jazz, Maggie. What a surprise."

"Hey, Mom. Sorry to drop by without calling, but I was hoping we could talk."

"Oh no. What did you do, Jazz?" She ushered them in and Jazz tried not to let her mom's instant suspicion sting. "Alexander! Jazz and Maggie are here," her mom called up the stairs, before turning back to them. "Did that boy get you pregnant? Or is it not his baby? Because he never needs to know if you don't tell him. But he seems like a good man —the kind of man who would do the right thing by you and raise the baby anyway." She looked entirely too happy about the idea.

Jazz counted to three inside her head. "I'm not pregnant, Mom."

She pouted. "Oh. Well, that's disappointing." She turned on her heel and walked toward the kitchen, leaving them to chase after her. "Any babies in the future for you, Maggie?"

Maggie rolled her eyes, only because Jazz's mom couldn't see her. "I already have so much on my plate being a new stepmom. It's a big adjustment for Liam." Jazz almost choked on her own tongue, trying not to laugh.

"I'm sure," Jazz's mom replied, completely missing Maggie's sarcasm. They sat around the kitchen island and Jazz's mom poured iced coffee from a glass pitcher in the fridge without asking. "It's cold brew," she explained. "Your dad's going through a phase. It's really not bad."

"Thanks, Lilia," Maggie said, sipping the cold brew. Her mom beamed at Maggie as Jazz's dad stepped into the kitchen. For all their faults, Jazz's parents had always treated Maggie like family. As much as they treated anyone like family, anyway.

"Hi, girls. What brings you all this way?"

"Hi, Dad."

"They're here to talk to us, Alexander."

Jazz's dad sighed, rubbing his forehead. "What have you done, Jazz?"

Jesus. "I've done plenty, but that's not why I'm here." Maggie snorted. "I'm here to talk about Rose."

"Oh, what a headache that's been," her mom said, taking the barstool beside Maggie.

"And to find out from Lynda Sims, of all people," her dad chimed in.

"Ugh, she's awful. I don't know what Kami was thinking marrying into that family. Between us, I think Lynda was more concerned with Rose being a lesbian, which is a little ironic considering she claims to be an ally on Facebook every June. Really it's a—"

"We're not here to talk about Lynda Sims, Mom," Jazz interrupted. Once her mom started gossiping, she'd never stop. "Rose."

"Rose, yes. Do you think you can talk some sense into her? She's throwing her life away, Jazz, and we don't want her to end up like you."

Maggie put her coffee glass down hard on the island. "And what exactly is that supposed to mean?"

"Maggie—"

"No, I'm really interested to hear what you mean by that, Alexander." Maggie had known Jazz's parents for twenty years, but it was the first time she'd ever made her feelings about them clear to their faces. Gone was the people pleaser who treated keeping the peace like an art form. Jazz's heart swelled with pride.

Shit, maybe therapy did work. But she could circle back to that when she wasn't having the longest Monday of her life.

Jazz's dad pursed his lips, his eyes flashing with surprise. "All I mean is that Rose is supposed to be a doctor. That doesn't mean Jazz's job isn't… good."

Maggie opened her mouth but closed it when Jazz shot her a *leave it* look. "That's not important right now. What's important is that Rose is happy, and she wasn't happy in med school."

"No one's happy in med school," her mom said with a laugh. "But she would've been happy with the title and the paycheck once she got there."

"Maybe. In a decade," Jazz reasoned. "But she has a job she loves and she's happy *now*. Why can't that be enough for you?"

"Well, it's not exactly what we expected for—"

"That's the problem!" Jazz interrupted her dad, pushing back from the island. "Look, I don't want to fight with you about this. I brought Maggie here so you could see what's going to happen if you don't apologize to Rose and do everything you can to fix this with her."

Her parents frowned at her and Maggie. "What are you talking about? Maggie's doing great."

Maggie cleared her throat. "I've barely spoken to my family in two years, and we've been completely no contact since February."

Jazz's parents stared at Maggie in wide-eyed surprise. Her dad recovered first. "Good for you, Maggie. I hope you don't mind me saying, but your parents were terrible to you."

"I don't mind. It's true," Maggie said with a shrug. "But also, pot kettle." She gestured to Jazz's mom and dad. Really, it was as civil as she could expect her to be.

"I think what Maggie means is that you're going to be in the same situation with Rose if you don't undo this."

Her parents exchanged a concerned look. "You really think Rose would go no contact with us?"

"Yeah, I do. Is her not having a stupid title in front of her name worth you losing her?"

"Of course not," her mom said instantly. "We just want the best for her."

Maggie raised a brow. "And kicking her out is what's best for her?"

"We didn't think she'd actually go. We just thought it would be enough to make her see sense." Her mom's cheeks turned pink, something akin to shame flickering in her hazel eyes. Jazz blinked, and it was gone.

"I can't tell you what to do here, but you are going to lose her if you're not careful. And do you think Xan will be okay with you treating his baby sister like this" Jazz sighed, balling her hands into fists and releasing them.

"I figured out a long time ago that I don't fit into this family, and I'm working on making my peace with the fact that I'm not the daughter you wanted, but Rose is only twenty-five. You have a chance to fix this before you really mess her up. That's all I wanted to say. Let's get Rose's stuff and go, Maggie."

She turned away and heard Maggie's footsteps following behind her, heading up the stairs. Rose's room was mostly empty, and Jazz and Maggie grabbed the left-over bags and boxes with ease. She breathed a sigh of relief when they made it outside, filling the trunk with Rose's stuff—she was so ready to get out of there.

Jazz had done what she'd come to do. It was up to her parents now. Either way, Rose wouldn't have to deal with it alone. They'd wasted enough time letting their parents pit them against each other, and Jazz knew Xan would feel the same once he knew what had happened. Enough was en—

"Jazz, wait a second."

Jazz exchanged a wary look with Maggie, who was seconds from climbing into the driver's side. "Yes?"

Her parents wore matching stunned expressions, like she'd knocked them over the head. And she supposed she had, with a hard truth that had been a long time coming.

"What do you mean you're not the daughter we wanted?" her dad asked, stepping closer to her. "Of course we want you. You're our daughter and we love you."

Jazz took an involuntary step back. She couldn't remember the last time her parents had told her they loved her. Shit, had they ever? She'd never heard them say it to her siblings either, nor to each other. They weren't that kind of family. Her brain didn't even know how to process it, let alone believe it.

"Every conversation we've ever had has suggested otherwise," she said, and she sounded more tired than angry. Thirty years she'd been dealing with her parents' expectations. Thirty. Fucking. Years. The exhaustion was bone deep.

"Nothing I've ever done has made you happy. I've always known I don't measure up to Xan and Rose. In fact, I'm pretty sure you saying my boyfriend is a good man earlier is the closest thing to praise you've ever given me, and it wasn't even about me. I've built my entire life around the fact that nothing I ever do is good enough, so I might as well not bother, because you've never shown me any differently."

"Jazz." Tears swam in her mom's hazel eyes. "You're our baby. You're all our babies and we love you exactly as much as we love your brother and sister. I promise we really have only ever wanted the best for all three of you."

"Clearly," her dad added, clearing his throat, "we've gone around that the wrong way and we haven't shown you how much we love you. For that, we're very sorry." He frowned at his shoes. "And I assume that also applies to Xan and Rose. But we do love you, Jazz. And we are proud of who you are, even if we've never told you."

White noise rushed through Jazz's brain, rattling the foundation she'd spent thirty years building. It felt a little too convenient for her parents to see the light in one conversation, and Jazz was in no rush to forgive them until they proved they weren't just saying what they thought she wanted to hear. "I… I don't know what to say to that. I'm sorry, I just… I need time."

"You have nothing to apologize for," her mom said, her voice soft and thick with tears. "I can imagine this is a lot for you to process. So take all the time you need. When you want to talk, we'll be here. Or maybe we can make the drive out to you next time."

Jazz sucked in a shaky breath. "I'll think about it. I don't know when, or if, I'm going to be ready to believe you, but I'll think about it. And I love you too, for the record."

She opened the door, and all but collapsed into the passenger's seat of her car, staring resolutely out of the windshield and not at her parents. Maggie got in a moment later.

"Hey," she said, wrapping her arms around her from the driver's seat in a hug that Jazz desperately needed. "You did amazing in there."

Jazz wiped her face. "Thank you. I—Shit, I'm so sorry." She would never have asked Maggie to come with her if she'd known her parents would apologize. That was all Maggie had wanted for so long.

"Sorry for what?"

"That you had to see that after everything with your parents. I—"

"Are you kidding? I'm happy for you. Really. Do I wish my parents had been able to apologize? Absolutely, but no more than I've wished your parents would. This is a good thing."

"You think so? I don't know if I believe them." Could she really let herself hope they were being honest and risk being let down again?

"They seemed genuine, but you made the right call asking for time. And if you are going to forgive them, you should definitely make them grovel a little more."

"Probably," Jazz agreed with a laugh that slowly turned into a long, drawn out breath. "It all seems too good to be true. My parents apologizing, you forgiving me, Liam loving me. Real life doesn't work that way." It was like she'd stepped right into the happy ending of one of Liam's books.

"Maybe it is all good to be true. But maybe it's not. You're never going to know unless you see it through."

"I guess so. What now?" she asked, and Maggie turned the car on, smiling at her best friend.

"Now you go put Liam out of his misery and stop trying to break both of your hearts."

CHAPTER THIRTY-SIX

Jazz

Exhaustion weighed heavily on her shoulders by the time she made it to Liam's place. She'd offered to stay with Rose, but her sister looked as worn out as she felt, and Jazz knew she needed space. So she'd dropped off her stuff, made sure she had enough for dinner, and left her in peace. She hadn't told her about what their parents had said. It was up to them to make good with Rose themselves.

Jazz unlocked the front door and was greeted by a tiny bark and a wagging tail. "Hey, baby boy." She dropped her purse on the floor in favor of picking Bray up and holding him to her chest. He was growing so fast. "Where's your papa?"

She knew he was here—she could smell garlic and basil and tomato. "Liam?"

He stepped into the living room, his hair wet from the shower. Jesus, how could he possibly look *that* good when she was this tired? His t-shirt fit snuggly to his body, and Jazz wished it was her wrapped around him instead. It was a print of a painting she hadn't seen before, but she knew it was Matisse. She had no idea when she'd started recognizing the art styles—perhaps somewhere in the hours they lay awake at night, when she just listened to him talk about his favorite pieces and fell harder and harder for him.

"You're home," he said, a smile covering his face as he crossed the room toward her. "Still mad at me?"

"I suppose not."

Liam chuckled, plucking Bray from her arms and setting him down so he could pull her in for a kiss. "Good," he murmured against her lips, and Jazz's heart calmed as she breathed him in.

"I'm pretty sure this has been the longest day of my entire life, and I've missed you like crazy," she admitted, and Liam squeezed her tighter.

"I've missed you too. But you're home now." There was that word again. *Home*. "Come on. You can tell me all about your day over ravioli, and then I have a surprise for you."

"What kind of surprise?"

"The kind that's only a surprise if you don't know what it is," he said, grabbing her bag from the floor and swatting her on the ass before pulling her to the kitchen.

They ate at the table, and Jazz told Liam all about her conversations with Rose and her parents. Liam listened with rapt attention, his expression morphing from furious on Rose's behalf, to shock at how things had ended with her parents.

"They told me they were proud of me," Jazz said quietly, their plates clear and glasses drained. Liam reached across the table and grabbed her hand, bringing it to his lips and pressing a soft kiss on her palm. "I didn't realize how much I needed to hear it until they said it."

"It's about time. I'm happy for you, darling. Does that mean *I'm* allowed to say it now?" Liam asked, his eyes twinkling. "I'd really love to be allowed to praise my girlfriend every now and then."

"Fine," she relented. "But still no praise in bed."

"I can handle that. And hey, no complaints about me calling you my girlfriend this time? It really has been a day."

"While I'm still not thrilled with how you just decided for us, I *am* happy to be your girlfriend. Your partner," she said, remembering how nice it had felt when he'd called her his partner at India and Bart's wedding. Liam's entire face lit up.

"Partners. I like that. We're a team. And I promise not to make any more decisions without you. Unless you try to break up with me again in the name of self-sabotage. Or at all, actually. Rule number six: we are never ever breaking up. Like ever."

"Deal. Write it on the board," Jazz said, rolling her eyes and taking the hand he held out for her to shake. "But that goes both ways, baby. If you get sick of my chaos   too bad. You made the rule."

"I could never get sick of your chaos. It's my favorite. *You* are my favorite," Liam promised, and Jazz weighed up the fastest way of crossing the table and pouncing on him. Crawling over the tabletop was a little extreme, but he'd probably like—

"Don't look at me like that," Liam warned, pushing

back from the table. "We still have your surprise. Go get into something comfy while I get set up."

She grumbled, but did as she was told. This *was* Liam after all, so whatever he had in store, she was sure she was going to enjoy it. She changed into a pair of cycling shorts and one of Liam's t-shirts—the Cézanne one, which was definitely her favorite of his ridiculously giant collection. At least she'd never struggle to find a Christmas present for him. She balled her work clothes up in the corner of the room.

"Can I come out yet?" she called through the door, stepping back into the living room when Liam confirmed she could.

She stopped just short of the table, her jaw dropping at the spread before her. "What is this?"

"This is me understanding why you have so much crafting stuff," Liam replied, a little sheepishly. "Those little old ladies at the craft store are very persuasive. On a related note, we're scheduled for a screen printing class in a couple of weeks."

"They really do get to you." She nodded in understanding. Liam had hundreds of dollars' worth of stuff on the table—beads in every color, gold and silver charms, at least six trays of alphabet beads, a literal pile of elastic, string, and fastenings. "But why exactly did you go to the craft store and spend a small fortune?"

Liam pulled out a chair for her and she sat down. He rounded the table and sat opposite her, handing her a glass of red wine. "I know you probably have all this at your place—" She had no idea. She'd long since lost control of her stash. "—but I didn't want to disturb Rose while she was settling in, and I just thought… Bracelets." He gestured to the beads. "You said you've never finished a bracelet, so let's change that. I'll make one for you, you make one for me, and we can cross it off your list."

If she didn't already love him, that would've done it. It wasn't about the bracelets, not really. He'd listened to her, he'd heard her, and he hadn't given up on her.

Jazz reached across the table for a spool of clear elastic. "Okay. Let's do this."

It took them close to two hours. Two hours of cursing, chasing beads as they rolled across the hardwood, and wincing when the elastic snapped in their faces. Multiple. Times.

They had to shut Bray away in the guest room with a bunch of toys and the dancing fruit show he loved to watch on YouTube, just so he'd stop barking and distracting them. Jazz seriously considered giving up after the third time she dropped her bracelet and the beads fell off the string, but she pushed through.

She held the bracelet in her hand and stared at her, pride blooming in her chest. How could something so little mean so much? She'd chosen colors that made her think of Liam —warm and cozy and safe. Deep oranges, emerald green to match his eyes, warm dark browns, and gold. She'd kept it pretty simple, considering how fucking long it had taken to make, since she wanted the text to stand out. And even though it had been a complete nightmare to make, it was perfect.

"Close your eyes and put your hand out. We can look at the same time," Liam said, doing just that. He'd been just as frustrated by the fiddly beads as she had—enough so that Jazz would actually consider doing this again. Riled up Liam was her favorite.

She closed her eyes and held out her palm, and they both sat in silence for a moment before she said, "How are we supposed to swap bracelets if neither of us can see?"

"Shit. I'm coming around."

She hid the bracelet she'd made as he rounded the table and took a seat beside her. This close, it was easy to hand their bracelets over with their eyes closed. And Jazz was just happy to be closer to him. He dropped a bracelet on her waiting palm, and she did the same, butterflies fluttering in her stomach.

"On the count of three," he said, counting down.

Jazz took a deep breath. She was doing the right thing. He already knew. The bracelet was just a formality, really. It wasn't a surprise.

"Three."

Jazz opened her eyes and took in the bracelet, tears immediately springing to her eyes. She knew without asking that he'd done the same thing she had, picking the colors that reminded him of her. It was bright—turquoise and bright orange, spring green and sunshine yellow. And like her bracelet, he'd kept the focus on the letters:

I love you.

She traced the white letters with a finger, a perfect match to those she'd used for his bracelet, and a tear slipped down her cheek. Liam cupped her face, catching the tear with his thumb. She looked up, meeting his gaze. For the first time since she'd met him, Liam looked entirely at peace. And for the first time that she could remember, she *felt* at peace.

"I love you, Liam," she said, because it wasn't enough to string some beads on a bracelet. She had to say it out loud too. "I meant it the first time I said it, and I mean it now. I love you."

He cupped the other side of her face, the bracelet in his hand pressing against her cheek. "I love you so much, darling. So much. And this is so much better—*you're* so much better—than all the books say."

Jazz sighed happily when he leaned in and caught her mouth with his, tasting the truth of his words on his tongue. It was a slow kiss, a deep, sweet, languid kiss full of promises and peace. When they broke apart, Liam pressed his forehead to hers, his emerald eyes so fucking *happy* she thought she might burst.

She snagged the bracelet clenched in his hand and slipped it over his wrist, surprised by how much she liked seeing something she'd made on him. Liam did the same with the bracelet he'd made her, running his thumb over the beads and drawing in a shaky breath.

"You know, between this, the t-shirt, and the Snoopy tattoo, I think I might have a thing for seeing me all over you."

"I wouldn't mind seeing a little more of you all over me,

if you kn—Liam!" Jazz squealed, laughing as Liam stood up so quickly his chair toppled. He tugged her to her feet and pulled her to the bedroom at lightning speed. He pushed her against the dresser, grabbing the hem of her t-shirt—his t-shirt.

"I need you in nothing but that bracelet, darling," he groaned, and Jazz helped him out, wriggling out of her cycling shorts while he pulled the shirt off. She hadn't bothered with underwear—she'd had a pretty good idea of where the night was going when she'd gotten changed. Despite how helpful she'd been to him, Liam was uninterested in returning the favor, running his hands all over her and making it damn near impossible to undress him. She whined his name, and he took pity on her, shedding his clothes and walking her back toward the bed, his teeth and tongue lavishing her neck.

"Liam?"

"Yeah?"

"Now that we're disgustingly in love, you're not going to start being all gentle with me, are you?"

Liam pulled back from her neck, clasping her cheek. "First, I've been disgustingly in love with you for years. You just took your time catching up."

She prodded him in the ribs. That stupid, perfect, dimply smirk would be the death of her. "Shut up."

"Second, are you going to stop being a brat?"

"Fuck no."

His eyes dilated, her favorite wicked glint taking over his face. "Then I guess I'm going to have to keep punishing you. What a damn *shame*." On the last word, he spun her around until her back was pressed against his front, then bent her over the bed, pushing her face against the blankets.

She gasped as he brushed the head of his cock over her, pushing her hips back against him. If she didn't get him inside her, she was going to fucking lose it.

"*Please*." It slipped out before she could catch it and Liam stilled, gripping her hips so she couldn't move. *Fuck*.

"Begging already? You must be pretty desperate for me." He sounded damn cocky, but Jazz really was too desperate for him to even pretend to fight.

"Quit talking and fuck me," she groaned and Liam stepped back. She tried to turn around in protest, but he brought his hand down on her ass unexpectedly and her knees buckled, forcing her further into the bed. Her legs spread, her arms lying useless above her head, her pussy practically dripping with desperation... Liam didn't need restraints to have her entirely at his mercy. And he knew that.

He cupped her pussy, putting pressure on her but not directly touching her clit. It was fucking torture. "You done talking back?"

"Yes," she whimpered.

"Then ask nicely, darling." She could hear him fighting a laugh. He was infuriating. And she loved him.

Jazz took a deep breath. "Please will you fuck me, boyfriend whom I love more than anything in the whole wide wor—*fuck*." He slammed into her and Jazz blinked away the stars that crossed her vision.

"Since you asked so nicely..."

There was nothing nice about the way he fucked her,

and Jazz loved every messy second of it. He was ruthless and unforgiving, spanking her between thrusts until she was sobbing all over the bed, begging for more.

Liam leaned over her, offering her two fingers. "Get them wet for me," was all he said before pushing them into her mouth. Jazz groaned around them, sucking and swirling her tongue. When Liam pulled them out, they were dripping. He barely gave her a second to tense before he circled the rim of her ass and pressed them inside her.

"*Fuck, fuck, fuck...*"

Liam curled his fingers, moving them in time with his cock, and Jazz fell apart, screaming his name as she came, her pussy and ass clenching tightly around him. Kaleidoscope colors flashed behind her eyelids, shockwaves of pleasure rolling over her body. Liam groaned, pulling his fingers out of her, then his body folded over hers. He reached above her head, clasping her hand and coming inside her with a whispered, "I love you, Jasmine."

"I love you," she murmured back, hoarse and depleted, but so fucking happy.

They cleaned up in the shower, retrieved their sleepy four-legged baby from the guest bedroom, and climbed into bed, clinging to each other.

There was so much to talk about, so much to worry about, to be scared about, but, for once, she was trusting herself. She was trusting him.

The big conversations would come. She would keep exploring the facets of herself that she wanted to work on, she would go to the doctor and figure shit out with her periods so she could have the family she'd always dreamed of, the family they both wanted. She would grow up a little and be okay with it, because she wasn't doing it on her own.

And Liam would be proud of her. Maggie and Cal, and Eliza and Danisha, would be proud of her. Maybe her parents would be proud of her, or maybe they wouldn't, but it didn't matter, not really. Because most importantly, Jazz would be proud of herself.

"I love you," Liam told her with a sleepy smile, his green eyes glassy. Jazz pressed her forehead to his, wondering how in the hell she'd gotten so lucky to be loved by such an incredible man.

But even in love, Jazz was who she was, and she couldn't stop her lips from lifting in a smirk. "Rule number seven: I love you more."

"You can't do that!" Liam protested.

"Rules are rules, baby."

Liam's eyes twinkled with a warning that made her toes curl. "You're going to pay for that, darling."

And she was going to enjoy paying for it—for the rest of their lives, if she got her way.

"Bring it on."

EPILOGUE

Jazz

"**I**t's perfect."

"Exactly how I pictured it," Liam agreed, squeezing her hand.

She turned and smiled at Liam's side profile. In an unsurprising turn of events, the slicked back hair, ruffled white shirt, and sweeping black cloak were *really* doing it for her. But it was the black leather-style gloves and white plastic mask covering half his face that really brought Liam's Phantom of the Opera costume to life—and it was those she'd be asking him to keep on when they got home later. She wasn't a big fan of the musical, but Liam was, and she couldn't resist the chance to see him in the mask. Even she could admit that the mustache only added to the look.

Jazz had curled her hair in tight ringlets, adding long extensions that fell down her back. She'd pinned the front away from her face, and painted her cheeks and lips scarlet red. The Christine to Liam's Phantom. Her dress was white lace, falling off her shoulders, and showing off plenty of cleavage that Liam was struggling to keep his eyes from. It was almost bridal. Which was, of course, the point.

Jazz stared out at the party—cobwebs, bats, LED candles, and twinkling lights hung from the ceiling. Black lace tablecloths covered every table, and bloody hand and footprints had been stuck to the floor. Servers milled around, dressed in intricate clown costumes, serving shots with gummy eyeballs in them and strawberries dipped in white chocolate, decorated to look like ghosts. It was exactly as she'd imagined, when she'd dared to let herself dream of her and Liam's Hallowedding.

"Look at you two," Maggie said, approaching them with a grin. Cal had chosen their costumes—Shrek and Fiona—and Maggie looked good painted green. "You look amazing. Is this why you were forty minutes late to your own party?"

"Oh, no. We were late because—"

"Maggie doesn't need to know what we were doing, darling," Liam interjected, and Maggie just rolled her eyes, smiling.

"That's answer enough. Now that you're here," she raised a brow at Jazz. "Did you seriously hire clowns to serve food at your Halloween party even though your brother is terrified of them?"

"Maybe."

"They're following him around. Wait, did you tell them to do that?"

Jazz almost felt guilty. Almost. She shrugged. "I'm just saying he should've thought twice before hiding in my closet and jumping out at us after we watched The Blair Witch Project when we were twelve."

"We'll call off the clowns," Liam said, but his mustache twitched like he was trying not to laugh.

"Thank you," Maggie said. "I don't see why you need clowns any…" She trailed off, her eyes pausing on Jazz's dress and widening as it clicked into place. They *had* promised to have clowns at their wedding. "Oh my god. Am I—is this—are you—"

Jazz grabbed her hand and pulled her back through the crowd. "We'll be back," she called to Liam—her fiancé, she supposed, even if they had skipped the engagement. They'd known they'd have to factor in time for Maggie to freak out. It's how she worked through things. Jazz had even pre-planned a quiet spot for them to hide away.

They'd chosen the venue Cal used every year for the firm's New Year's Eve party, and even the lobby outside the function room was gorgeous. Marble floors, with high arched ceilings and swooping faux-cobwebs over the doors.

She dragged Maggie into the storage room she'd heard about from Sierra, who had seen two paralegals sneaking off together last New Year. It was pitch black, but she felt around the wall for the light pull and tugged, illuminating them both in harsh fluorescent light.

"Okay. Let's talk," Jazz said, dusting the wall with her hand before leaning back against it.

Maggie took a deep breath. "You're getting married."

"Yep."

"This is your wedding."

"It is."

"I'm dressed as an ogre at your wedding."

"I bet the green really brings out Cal's eyes," Jazz

offered, and Maggie palmed her forehead. "I know you probably need to freak out and ask a million questions. Go for it."

"I say this with all the love in the world, but you've only been together for two months, Jazz. This is unhinged, even by your standards."

"Liam's been on board for longer than that," Jazz pointed out. "And when you know, you know."

"Sure. But why the rush?"

"Why wait? We already know we're going to be together forever." She wasn't trying to convince Maggie. Jazz and Liam both knew everyone would think they were rushing things, but they loved each other and that's all they cared about.

They didn't want to wait the expected two to three years before starting the next stage of their life together. They wanted marriage, and babies, and a house with a backyard for Bray to sunbathe in because he was too lazy to run around. Jazz had found a new OBGYN to get to the bottom of her inconsistent cycle so they could start trying for a baby, they'd hired Nadia—who she actually liked a lot, now that she'd stopped being a jealous asshole—to help them find a house, and they would be walking out of their party as husband and wife.

She saw the moment her best friend recognized the resolve in her expression—Maggie's panicked eyes softened into a smile, her shoulders relaxing.

"You're sure? You're really ready for this?"

Jazz nodded. The coiling panic that she shouldn't bother with anything, because she'd only fail, was nowhere to be seen. This was Liam. As far as she was concerned, they were a guaranteed success. "Yeah. I'm sure."

Jazz and Maggie stared at each other, Maggie's eyes glistening. "Holy shit," Maggie said, with a watery laugh, a tear slipping down her green cheek. And like cascading dominoes, Jazz followed suit. "You're getting married."

"You're going to be my mother-in-law."

Maggie groaned. "Great, but let's not make that a thing."

"I'll think about it," she lied. She absolutely was going to make it a thing. Maggie was getting Mother's Day presents for the rest of their lives, as far as she was concerned.

"I'm so happy for you. For both of you. This is how it was always meant to be," Maggie said, squeezing her in a tight hug. "I love you so much, Jazz. You deserve this."

Jazz didn't think she could ever, in a million years, truly deserve Liam. But that didn't mean she wasn't going to hold on to him for dear life and treasure every single second they had together.

There was a soft knock at the door, and Maggie opened it to find Liam. She threw her arms around his neck, wrapping him in a hug. "I'm so happy for you. If you hurt her, I'll kill you."

"I'd expect nothing less," Liam replied with a chuckle, hugging her back. They broke apart and Maggie grabbed a paper towel from a shelf and dabbed at her cheeks, wincing when it came away green.

"Do you need anything? What can I do?"

And that was reason number one they hadn't told her.

They wanted Maggie to actually enjoy the night, not exhaust herself worrying about what needed done.

"Everything is taken care of. Are you ready, darling?" Liam held a hand out to Jazz and she threaded her fingers with his.

"I'm ready."

The three of them headed back into the party, the light from the mirrorball dancing across the floor. Everyone they loved was there: Liam's moms, Sierra and most of the Michaelson and Hicks team, Nadia, Rose, Xan and his best friend Kami. Kami's brother Leon, and his business partner, were catering the party and were the only people they'd told about the wedding ahead of time.

They'd gotten lucky that Halloween fell on the same week the Michaelson family had planned a reunion, making the trip to Seattle from Ireland to celebrate Liam's grandma's birthday. They were loud and chaotic and Jazz loved them.

And then there were Jazz's parents. As promised, they'd given her space and been patient while she thought through their apology, while she talked things out with Maggie, Liam, and her siblings. Xan and Rose had been as surprised as she was by her parents admitting they'd fucked up. Rose had been more distrustful of their apology, but the three of them had met their parents for dinner and started clearing the air. They had a long way to go to be like the kind of family Liam had grown up with, if they ever could be, but they were trying. Jazz no longer hated being a Cannon, but that didn't mean she wasn't excited to officially become a Michaelson.

Every single person in attendance had taken their *dress to possess* instruction seriously. There were ghosts and vampires, princesses and witches, a menagerie of creatures, and no less than three Han Solos. It was chaotic and beautiful and exactly what they'd hoped for.

They stopped in front of Cal and Liam's moms, Cal's gaze falling to Maggie's face. His eyes widened.

"Have you been crying, love? Is everything okay?"

"Everything's fine," Maggie assured him, clinging to his arm. "Happy tears."

"About what?"

Liam grinned at his parents. "Don't freak out."

To give Cal and Danisha their credit, they held it together when Liam told them why they were there. Eliza, on the other hand… Her blue eyes immediately filled with tears, a smile stretching over her face. She bounced up and down on her heels. Apparently, they needn't have worried about Liam's parents' reactions.

"I'm so happy. My babies," she blubbered, pulling both Liam and Jazz into her arms.

"Don't cry on the bride, honey," Danisha said gently, but, when they all pulled back, Jazz noticed her dark chestnut eyes were lined with silver too. She grasped Liam's shoulder. "Happy for you, kiddo. I can't imagine a better partner for you. We love you both so much."

Jazz swallowed, her throat thick with emotion. She held her tears at bay until she met Cal's eye. He was looking between her and Liam with nothing but love and pride on his face.

He said nothing, just folded them both into crushing hugs.

"We'd like you and Maggie to be our witnesses," Liam said, and Cal nodded, wrapping an arm around Maggie's waist as she took her place beside him.

"We'd be honored."

Liam helped Jazz up to the small stage. He smiled down at her and squeezed her hand, accepting a microphone from the DJ, and nodding. The DJ cut the music and Liam took a deep breath.

"Hi everyone. Thank you for coming out tonight. You all look incredible." Every eye in the room was trained on the stage as he spoke, their guests listening with rapt attention.

"A couple years ago," Liam continued, turning his gaze on Jazz, "at my dad and Maggie's wedding, Jasmine told me she was going to force me to marry her so she could be a Michaelson, too." Jasmine, not Jazz. He always called her Jazz when he was talking to other people, but this wasn't for everyone else in the room. This was for them. "Little did she know, I've been absolutely obsessed with her since the first time we met. We spent the next few months joking about our hypothetical wedding, and, along the way, it all started to feel a little real. And you see, because this is Jasmine we're talking about, our hypothetical wedding was always going to be complete chaos. A Hallowedding, we called it. So with that in mind," Liam turned back to face the room. "We're so excited to welcome you all to our wedding."

The room erupted, but Jazz hardly heard it. All she

could focus on was Liam, on the love and joy in his eyes. He handed the mic over to the officiant—another clown—and, with their arms wrapped around each other, they said their vows.

She could barely take it all in. It was… chaos. But the good kind. The kind that was full of love and joy and pride. The kind that made her heart race and her palms sweaty, and her jaw hurt from smiling so much.

Life with Liam, she'd learned, was made of many things, but mostly it was a mix of the fiery chaos she'd had inside her for thirty years, and the steady, warm peace that Liam personified. It was a give and take, meeting in the middle and finding the sweet spot they'd both been searching for long before they'd met at the office. Chaos and peace were not the natural enemies she'd once thought they were. And the life she and Liam were building promised both.

As the clown declared them husband and wife, and Liam captured her lips in the kind of kiss that was half kiss half smile, Jazz thought about Liam's favorite painting: *Nothing Lasts Forever*.

But they would. And Jazz couldn't wait to spend the rest of their lives proving that painting wrong.

Thank you for reading False Confidence!

I hope you enjoyed Jazz and Liam's chaotic love story. If you did, please consider leaving a review and sharing False Confidence wherever you like to talk about books!

False Confidence is the second book in the Spicy in Seattle Series. If you haven't already, you can check out book one, Legally Binding, for Maggie and Cal's story. Rose and Sierra's book, Dearly Unbeloved, is up next!

You can find a bonus deleted scene, of Jazz and Liam's first meeting, by visiting *www.sophiesnowbooks.com/bonus-scenes,* or scanning this QR code:

Author's Note

False Confidence is a work of fiction and is not intended to be used as an educational tool.

As much as we all love reading spicy romance, the sexual acts described in False Confidence are not intended to be used as a guide. Please always do plenty of research and have clear discussions of consent before trying anything new.

There is an incident in this book in which two characters are arrested for drunken property damage. They're treated well by the police and released with minor consequences. It's important to recognize that this may not have been their experience if they weren't straight-passing, able-bodied, white women.

Discriminatory and biased practices by police are entirely too common across the world, and pose a major threat to many communities. I encourage you to research these practices within your community and use your voices and votes to advocate for everyone affected by biased policing.

The Spicy Stuff

If you should, for whatever reason, wish to revisit *just* the spicy moments… you'll find no judgment here! But you will find the spicy scenes here:

- Prologue
- Chapter Six
- Chapter Ten
- Chapter Eleven
- Chapter Thirteen
- Chapter Eighteen
- Chapter Twenty-one
- Chapter Twenty-four
- Chapter Twenty-nine
- Chapter Thirty-two
- Chapter Thirty-six

Enjoy!

Acknowledgments

When I started writing Legally Binding, I assumed it would be a standalone. Until the moment where Maggie shows Jazz Liam's Instagram profile and Jazz completely took over in my head. She is, hands down, the most difficult character I've ever written and every single page of thing book felt like a fight just trying to get her to let me tell her and Liam's story. But I would do it all over again in a heartbeat to give them their happy ending.

I was truly insufferable while writing False Confidence and I wouldn't have made it to the end without my wonderful friend Claire, who's always there when I need to brain dump and bounce ideas off someone. Thank you for everything.

Thank you to my husband, Kyle, for helping and supporting me through every day of this new author journey I've embarked on, and our sweet baby, Pumpkin, for being the best boy.

Thank you to my author besties, Alaina Rose and Emily Shacklette, for your unwavering love, support, and matching my Taylor obsession.

Thank you to my wonderful beta readers for helping to make False Confidence the book it is—Cara Dion and Emily Shacklette, Claire, and Bancy. I know you all hate the mustache and I appreciate you trying your best to ignore it.

Thank you to Ellie from Love Notes PR for helping me get False Confidence out in the world.

Thank you to my amazing Street Team. Abigail, Aimee, Alaina, Allie, Ashley, Caitlin, Charley, Claire, Danie, Demi, Hayley, Jenna, Jess, Jessica, Kai, Karina, Kate P, Kate R, Kayleigh, Lil, Molly, Rebecca, Robyn, Sam, Sarah, Shannen, Sophie D, and Sophie R—I appreciate all the support and hype you've shown my books so much.

Thank you to Noah Kahan, who has inspired so much of my writing, for the title of this book, which comes from the song False Confidence on his incredible album, Busyhead. I'm incredibly grateful for all the artists whose music helped me turn a little spark of an idea into a whole book.

Thank you to Taylor Swift, who told us to make the friendship bracelets—which we did, even though it was actually super stressful, and I think we can all understand why Jazz procrastinated that one.

Thank you to the readers who allow me the space to share my stories. Words can't describe how much I appreciate every read, every comment, every message, every review.

And to everyone with a chaotic, unhinged heart, searching for a little bit of peace in the world, I hope you find it—but the chaos is pretty great too.

Love,

Sophie

Sophie Snow lives in Scotland with her husband and cat, Pumpkin (who she loves dearly, even if he does bite.)

She writes spicy romance books with messy, queer characters and too many Taylor Swift references to count. She has been in love with love stories for as long as she can remember, and writing them as songs and novels since she was twelve.

A forest fairy in a past life, Sophie loves spending time in nature, drinking too much coffee, and trying out more hobbies than she can keep up with.

You can find more from Sophie by visiting her website at www.sophiesnowbooks.com, or scanning this QR code: